MARS

CROSSING

MARS
CROSSING

GEOFFREY A. LANDIS

A TOM DOHERTY ASSOCIATES BOOK
NEW YORK

MARS CROSSING

Copyright © 2000 by Geoffrey A. Landis

Edited by Patrick Nielsen Hayden

Design by Lisa Pifher

                    Library of Congress Cataloging-in-Publication Data

Landis, Geoffrey.
    Mars crossing / Geoffrey A. Landis.—1st ed.
       p.   cm.
    "A Tom Doherty Associates book."
    ISBN 0-312-87201-1
      I. Title.
   PS3562.A4766 M3 2000
   813'.54—dc21   00-056764

A Tor Book
Published by Tom Doherty Associates, LLC
175 Fifth Avenue
New York, NY 10010

www.tor.com

Tor® is a registered trademark of Tom Doherty Associates, LLC.

First Edition: December 2000

Printed in the United States of America

0 9 8 7 6 5 4 3 2 1

FOR THE CAJUN SUSHI HAMSTERS

THANKS

ACKNOWLEDGMENTS

This book owes a clear debt to Robert Zubrin and David Baker, from whose Mars mission concepts I have liberally borrowed. Thanks.

Thanks are also due to Mary, Levin, Toby, Julie, Malcolm, Ben, Becky, John, Bonnie, Astrid, Charlie, Steve, Marta, and Paula, for reading, comments, and general support.

All great and honourable actions are accomplished with great difficulties, and must be both enterprised and overcome with answerable courages.

—William Bradford, *Of Plymouth Plantation* (1621)

Mars tugs at the human imagination like no other planet. With a force mightier than gravity, it attracts the eye to its shimmering red presence in the clear night sky. It is like a glowing ember in a field of ethereal lights, projecting energy and promise.

John Noble Wilford, *Mars Beckons* (1990)

MARS
CROSSING

PROLOGUE

LANDING

Don Quijote approached Mars in perfect silence.

At one end of the spacecraft was the habitat, a squat, rounded cylinder sitting on a heat shield. It was separated from the main rocket engine and now-empty fuel tanks by two kilometers of tightly stretched rope, a super-fiber tether so thin as to be nearly invisible. The spacecraft and the fuel tanks slowly rotated around the center of the tether.

"Arm tether separation."

"Tether separation armed."

"Navigation?"

"Nav is go."

"System status?"

"Systems are go."

Mars loomed, crescent in the sky, a mottled brick of craters and wispy shreds of cloud.

"Check terminal descent engine preheat."

"TDE preheat on."

"Check parachute deploy preheaters."

"PD preheat on."

"Fire pyros for tether sep on my mark. Three, two, one, now."

The spacecraft jerked, and the tether, suddenly cut free, recoiled away from the spacecraft, writhing and twisting like an angry snake. The engines, solar arrays, and fuel tanks sailed slowly off into the distance. They would miss Mars and sail outbound on an endless trajectory into interplanetary space.

"Tether separation confirmed. We're committed."

"How's the trajectory?"

"We're on the numbers. Looking good."

"Instrument check."

"Instruments green."

"Nav?"

"Everything green. We're sliding right down the groove."

"Then buckle up, everybody. We're going in."

The spacecraft burned through the Martian atmosphere, leaving a trail of fire across a pink sky.

A parachute bloomed, another, and a third; bright yellow flowers blossoming in a lifeless sky. A moment before it hit the ground, the heat shield fell away from the back of the vehicle, and a landing cushion mushroomed out of the bottom. At the instant of contact, a cloud of orange dust billowed up into the air, painting the bottom part of the spacecraft with yellow-brown dirt. The spacecraft tilted, swayed at the edge of falling over, and then rocked back toward vertical as the airbag deflated.

"Engines off, tank pressurization off, APU status green, all systems looking good. We're down. Navigation, you got a position?"

"Working on it . . . Looks like we hit the kewpie. Should we say something for the history books?"

"Nah. I don't think anybody is going to write down what gets said by the third expedition to Mars."

"Tell me it ain't so. You saying that we're *not* going to get a parade when we get back?"

"You got it. Welcome to Mars."

PART ONE

JOHN RADKOWSKI

Having an adventure shows that someone is incompetent, that something has gone wrong. An adventure is interesting enough—in retrospect. Especially to the person who didn't have it.

—Vilhjalmur Stefansson,
My Life with the Eskimo

There is no easy way into another world.

—James Salter, *Solo Faces*

WELCOME TO MARS

Through the viewport there was nothing but a yellow-pink fog. Then, slowly, the fog faded, and the ridged plains of Felis Dorsa emerged out of the haze, at first misty and colorless, and then, as the dust raised by the landing thinned out, sharply delineated.

John Radkowski looked across the landscape at plains of sand gently undulating beneath a pale butterscotch sky.

Mars.

It was hard for him to contain his fierce joy. Mars!

He wanted simultaneously to cry, to laugh, and to shout out a loud cry of exaltation. He did none of these. As mission commander, it was his duty to keep the mission businesslike. Decades in the astronaut corps had taught him that showing his emotions, even for such an event as landing on Mars, was a move that would, down the line, give him a reputation for being emotional, and hence unreliable. He stayed silent.

At fifty, John Radkowski was the oldest member of the crew, and the one most experienced in space. He was short, wiry rather than overtly muscular, with gray hair cropped closely to his head. His eyes had the slow, restless motion of long years of training; he focused on the task at hand, but always part of his attention was glancing around the cabin, looking up, down, checking for that small forgotten out-of-place something that might spell trouble for the mission. One hand, his left, was missing three fingers. His crew knew better than to offer him help.

Mars! After all the decades of work, he had finally made it!

There was work to do. As commander, the other five crewmembers depended on him to get the mission done safely and bring them back home. He had better get working.

The crew was occupied with their landing tasks, shutting the flight systems down and bringing the surface operation systems up, then verifying that they were running according to spec. He knew that all of them wanted to stop their work and crowd to the viewport, but for the moment they were all too busy, even Trevor, and so he had the viewport to himself.

Off to the southeast, close enough to be easily visible through the residual pink haze, was the squat form of *Dulcinea*.

The field glasses consisted of a flat rectangle, about the size of a paperback book. They had been designed to function equally well with or without a space-suit helmet. He raised them to his eyes. The computer adjusted the focus to match his eyesight, and the result was as if he were looking through a window at a magnified view of the landscape.

Like Chamlong said, they had hit their landing site right on the nail, with *Dulcinea* no more than half a mile away. That was of critical importance to them: *Dulcinea* was their way home, a fully fueled return vehicle that had landed on Mars six and a half years earlier. He examined her minutely, then examined the ground between the landing site of *Quijote* and the return vehicle. It was sand, sculpted by a million years of intermittent wind into hillocks and waves. There was an assortment of randomly scattered rocks, some boulder-sized, half-buried beneath the sand, but he saw no obstacles to their easy travel. Good.

The viewport forgotten, he turned to the copilot's console. The floor was tilted at an odd angle; the lander must have set down on a slope, and he had to move carefully to avoid falling. He studied the sequence of images taken during landing. Both visual and radar images had been taken, and he plotted them as a topographical map of the terrain. Again, he saw no obstacles. Good.

When he got up, he saw that Trevor, Estrela, and Chamlong were all crowded around the viewport, pushing each other out of the way to jockey for a view of Mars. He smiled. They must have been watching for the very instant he had vacated the position.

"Why look out the window when we can go out and see for ourselves?" he said. "Get your suits ready, gang, it's time to go outside and play. Get a move on; in six weeks we'll have to go home, and we've got a full schedule before we go."

With the lander resting at a pronounced tilt, the ladder splayed out at a cockeyed angle. Climbing down was not really difficult, but it was a challenge to descend gracefully. To hell with it, Radkowski thought, and jumped, landing off balance in a puff of dust.

As mission commander, it was his task to say some immortal words for the watching cameras. He had his lines memorized, extemporaneous words to be remembered forever, written for him by a team of public relations experts: *I take this step for all humankind. In the name of all the peoples of Earth, we return to Mars in the spirit of scientific endeavor, with the eternal courage of human adventure and bringing with us the voice of peace among all men.*

Stumbling up onto his feet to stand on the red sands of Mars, with Ryan Martin shooting him on high-definition television out the window of the lander, John Radkowski uttered the immortal words of the third expedition to Mars. He said, "Holy shit, I just can't believe I'm really here."

The sand had a hard, crunchy surface, and crackled underfoot as if he were walking on a thin crust of frost. Beneath the crust, the surface under his feet had the consistency of packed flour. Tiny puffs of rusty dust billowed away from his feet every time he raised a foot, and within a minute, his boots and the bottom half of his suit had been lightly spraypainted in ochre. He felt light. They had maintained half of Earth's gravity by the tether during the seven-month journey on the *Quijote*; the Mars gravity was noticeably lighter, and despite the eighteen months of training in Mars-simulation tanks on Earth, he felt as if he were buoyed up by invisible floats.

As he'd figured, *Don Quijote* had landed on the slope of one of the small ridges, and sat at a precarious tilt. Fortunately the ship had never been intended to take off from Mars, and in a day they would move their living quarters out of the cramped *Quijote* and into the inflatable habitat that had been landed on Mars with *Dulcinea*.

Behind him, his Brazilian colleague Estrela Conselheiro hopped down the ladder. She bounced on the ground, bounded into the air, and stretched her arms overhead as if worshiping the sun. "Oh, it is magnificent, is it not? Magnificent!"

Much better words than his own, Radkowski reluctantly admitted to himself.

Behind Estrela, Tana Jackson came down. "Yikes!" she said. "That's one bodacious step." She looked around, and caught her breath. "My god, it's magnificent," she said.

Finally Chamlong Limpigomolchai jumped down, negotiating the jump without any comment. Once on the surface, he pivoted slowly around to look in all directions in silence. The other two crew members, Ryan Martin and Trevor Whitman, stayed behind in the lander; they would only leave *Quijote* and come down to the surface when Estrela, Tana, and Chamlong rotated back to the ship.

It was everything he had wanted, what he had struggled and worked and lived for. The rust-encrusted, ridged terrain, the distant buttes barely visible through the cinnamon haze on the horizon, and *Dulcinea*, their ticket back to Earth, sitting ready for them, no more than a fifteen-minute walk away—he had seen it a hundred times in his dreams.

So why was he suddenly depressed?

John Radkowski had no tools for analyzing his mood. Self-inspection had never been encouraged in the astronaut corps; the main purpose of the many counselors and psychologists, according to the gossip, was to weed out the weak sisters from the active duty roster. Focus on the task, get the job done, don't complain; that had been the motto of the people that

Radkowski had worked and trained with for years. Now, suddenly, his entire future seemed to be an anticlimax; even the remainder of the six-week stay on Mars and the flight back to Earth, featuring a swingby and gravity boost from the planet Venus, seemed to him like nothing but tedium. He had been focused on reaching Mars for so long, he had never set personal goals for beyond the moment. His life, as he knew it, was over, and he had not even the faintest inkling of what would lie beyond.

A man's reach should exceed his grasp, he thought. I've grasped my dreams. What do I do now?

2

T he kid who called himself Trevor Whitman stood pressed to the view-port, looking eagerly out at the surface of Mars. With half of his attention he was scanning the landscape for signs of . . . He had no idea, really: an alien artifact, maybe, or footprints of dinosaurs or the imprint of fossilized ferns in an overlooked rock. None of these, of course, were things they had any expectation of finding on Mars, but if nobody looked for such things, they could be right on top of them, and nobody would notice.

But with most of his attention he was not looking at anything in par-ticular, just drinking in the sight of Mars. After seven months crammed into the tiny crew cabin, it felt good to focus his eyes on something in the distance. In the background he could hear the radio communications from the astronauts on the surface. *The surface fines are more cohesive than we'd expected.* Sounded like Captain Radkowski's voice. *Looks like there is some amount of salt cementing the particles together. It is clogging up the treads on my boots, but so far no problems with traction.* Definitely Radkowski; nobody else would be so concerned with the picky details like that. He tuned it out. Ryan Martin was communications officer, if anything happened—not that anything was likely to—Ryan could cope with it.

Mars, finally Mars. He watched Estrela bound across the surface, leap-ing and pirouetting with the grace of a dancer, and he felt a gnawing jeal-ousy. He itched to get out on the surface, and it seemed unfair that he had to wait before it would be his turn down.

At eighteen, Trevor had yet to learn patience.

It was simply not fair.

After what had to be an hour, Chamlong Limpigomolchai came back up the hatch, and Trevor waited impatiently as the airlock cycled with the painstaking chug, chug, gurgle of the roughing pumps. The lock opened, and Chamlong's helmeted face appeared. His suit was dusted with a light powder of ochre dust. The dust tickled Trevor's nose like bursting bubbles of some metallic champagne.

Chamlong pulled off his helmet. He had a grin the size of Texas. He had brought with him a half dozen rocks.

"I figured you'd be in a hurry to get outside, not so?" Chamlong said. "So I came back in to let you get a chance to go."

"Thanks, Cham," Trevor said. "I really appreciate it. How was it?" For the whole journey, the Thai astronaut had been his favorite friend among the adults, and his simple friendliness counted for a big reason why. The rest of the adults too often just ignored him, or gave him orders.

"Oh, kid, you will not believe how much excellent it is to get outside again, and just stretch," Chamlong said. "I tell you, get out there, see for yourself."

"You got it," Trevor said. "Give me a suit inspection, okay?" The suit inspection had been drilled into them by Captain Radkowski in every one of the hundreds of practice runs for surface operations during the mission. Never leave the spacecraft until you have had somebody else go through the checklist on your suit. Never. It had seemed like overcaution to Trevor—nobody would skip a vital step on a suit. That would not just be stupid, it would be suicide. But when he'd said that, Radkowski had only given him a look like he was a child, and started out with another of his rambling astronaut stories, this one about some buddy of his who had skipped the checklist, went through a hatch with a purge valve that had been clipped open for an inspection and almost got himself killed. Actually, Trevor liked to hear Radkowski's astronaut stories—and he made himself a mental note never to clip open a purge valve—but when they were just a way to pound home some simpleminded moral like "always take care," they sometimes got a bit tiring. While Chamlong gave him his inspection, he thought only, Mars, I'm finally going out. Mars, I'm finally going out. Mars, I'm finally . . .

He hesitated on the ladder, looking across the surface. He'd seen Mars a thousand times in virtual reality simulations, of course, but this was different. The sunlight was brighter than he'd expected. This far from the sun, he'd expected the surface of Mars to be dim, but the light was as bright as any afternoon on Earth. The helmet had a visor, and he slid it around to give him some shade.

He had to do something. He jumped, a six-foot drop to the ground, and almost lost his balance when he landed. Then he tried a handstand. It was a little awkward in the suit, but after one false try he managed to balance. After thirty seconds he started to lose his balance, tucked in and rolled in a cloud of dust, then stood up.

Everybody was looking at him. It wasn't as if he had done something actually dangerous; the transparent silicon carbide of the helmets was for all practical purposes unbreakable.

"Shit, kid," was the voice on his radio. "You sprain an ankle, we're not going to carry you sightseeing, you know." It was Tana's voice. She didn't sound like she was mad, so he decided he could ignore her. Everybody else went back to what they were doing; examining the soil, chipping at rocks with hammers, digging little trenches. Boring.

"Mars, I love you," he shouted, ran up the the top of the nearest dune, and then slid down to the bottom on his butt.

Mars was great.

3

M E M O R I A L

Tana Jackson wanted to run, to skip over the surface, to hop like a bunny. Adrenaline sang in her blood: *I'm here, I'm here.*

The Mars landscape was just uncanny. It looked hyperreal, the horizons too close, the mountains too small, the sky looking like dirty paint. She could run to the horizon in a few minutes.

She sat down on the surface and tried to scoop up a handful of the sand. It was surprisingly hard to scoop. There was a crusty layer on the surface, and when she scraped through that, the soil underneath was fine powder, like rouge, sticking together into clods that broke apart into nothing in her fingers.

Commander Radkowski stood watching them all patiently. When he had given them all time to stretch out their legs and adapt to the surface, he went back to the lander and retrieved a small chest. Then he called them to gather around a boulder. The rock he had chosen was about chest high, dark in color, carved by the wind into almost a cubical shape. "Ryan, are you getting this?"

From inside the lander, Ryan's voice said, "I'm taping, Captain. Go ahead."

Radkowski opened the chest and removed a plaque. The plaque was a small rectangle of black-anodized aluminum, inscribed with seven names in gold. He turned to Estrela Conselheiro.

She reached into the chest and took out a second plaque, identical in size and color to the first, but with only two names on it.

Together they bent over and laid the plaques against the rock. This time Radkowski did not hesitate over his lines. "In honor and in memory of the explorers from the first and second expeditions to Mars, we place these memorials on the surface of Mars. As long as humankind dream of exploration, you will never be forgotten."

Estrela repeated the words in Portuguese, and then added, in English. "Mars is for heroes."

Commander Radkowski took a step back. "A moment of silence, please."

Tana bowed her head and looked at the ground.

"All right. As you were," Captain Radkowski said.

Mars was just as beautiful, the colors still as intense, but after the memorial it seemed a little more sinister. If anything went wrong, they were a hundred million miles away from any help.

Two expeditions had been to Mars before them. Neither one had returned to Earth.

Tana suddenly shivered, although there was nothing wrong with her suit heater. She had known for a year that, if there was a failure on this mission, there would be no rescue.

Mars was for heroes. But she was suddenly not so certain that she liked being a hero.

4

Commander Radkowski returned to the ship with the cloud of aimless disappointment still hanging over him.

Ryan Martin and Chamlong Limpigomolchai were in the cabin. Out of habit, the first thing he did was to check the viewport, to see how his outside crew was doing. Tana and Estrela were working together on rock studies, Estrela chipping the outer surfaces off of rocks and Tana pressing the portable X-ray crystallography unit onto the freshly exposed surface to map the microcrystalline structure. He was glad to see them collaborating; during the voyage they had been at each other with their claws bared almost every week, and he had worried that they would be unable to work together. Chalk it up to confinement syndrome; now that there was some space to breathe, they were apparently getting along fine.

Tana Jackson was a biologist, not a geologist, but they had all cross-trained at each other's specialties. Radkowski could see that they had taken the SIMS unit—the secondary ion mass spectroscope—out of its storage bin, but they had not yet set it up. He tuned to the general frequency, but they were apparently communicating on a private band. As commander, he could listen in, of course, but from long experience he had learned that it was best to give a crew its illusion of privacy unless there was a definite emergency.

Trevor Martin was somewhere out of sight, possibly behind the dune-form. Radkowski worried about the kid; sometimes he acted as if he were younger than his twenty-one years. Still, the enthusiasm and sheer joy of living that the kid exuded—when he was caught unguarded and forgot to be sullen and uncommunicative—was almost contagious, a drug that lifted the spirits of the whole crew. Radkowski had opposed the whole idea of bringing a crew member as young as Trevor along, but he seemed to be working out, and his presence definitely gave the crew a lift in morale. Although they pretended not to, and possibly didn't even realize it themselves, everybody liked the kid and wanted the best for him. As long as he didn't manage to kill himself by being impatient, impetuous, ignorant, aggravating, and generally clumsy—in short, acting like an adolescent instead of an adult—he'd be fine.

John Radkowski could hardly blame the kid for acting like a kid. When he was young, he had been a lot worse. It was only by a miracle of God that he had straightened out. Certainly none of his acquaintances, not even his own mother, would ever have guessed he would one day be the commander of the third expedition to Mars.

There are good neighborhoods in Queens, but the one John Radkowski grew up in was not one of them. The Harry S. Truman public-assistance housing unit was an incubator for raising junior criminals, not young scientists. By the time he had reached age six, Johnny had already learned that you never show weakness, and you stay alive by being just as mean as the other guy.

One time, when he was fourteen, he had been hanging around the apartment with his gang. It wasn't a real gang with colors, just the bunch of kids he hung around the neighborhood with. They kind of watched out for each other. Stinky and Fishface had been there, he remembered. His mother was gone, probably at work at one of a series of interchangeable jobs she held at fast-food restaurants. They were bored. They were usually bored.

John and his older brother, Karl, shared a small bedroom. Karl was gone, probably hanging out with his gang—he was a member of the Skins, a real gang, the local white-boys' gang. Karl was way cool, but he never wanted Johnny to meet his gang buddies; said he wanted Johnny to have something better out of life.

Stinky was smoking a cigarette he'd found in Johnny's mother's cupboard, and Fishface was sitting on Karl's bunk bed. Karl would have gone ballistic if he'd seen one of Johnny's friends on his bed, but Karl wasn't there, so fuck him. Fishface was picking at the wall, the cheap plasterboard coming loose from the studs. One end was already free, and Fishface, bored, wiggled and pried at it until he worked it loose enough to pull out and look at the ragged insulation underneath.

"Shit, boy," Stinky said, "what the fuck you got there?"

Fishface didn't bother to look up. "Nothing."

"Nothing? Shit." Stinky dropped the cigarette on the floor, walked over, and reached down inside the hole. "You dogfucker, you call this nothing?"

Stinky held up what he had found: a nine-millimeter automatic, gleaming dull gray and malignant in the feeble sunlight filtering through the dirty window.

Johnny hadn't realized that his brother had it. "Hey, Stinky, I think you'd better put that back," he said, nervous.

"What, are you a pussy? Afraid your badass brother gonna see?" Stinky held out the pistol, pointed it at Johnny's head, and squeezed the trigger.

"Bang," he said.

Johnny had flinched when he saw Stinky's finger whiten on the trigger. The trigger hadn't moved. "You faggot," he said.

Stinky laughed and popped the safety. "Thought you bought it there, didn't you?" He turned the gun over, ejected the magazine, and looked at it. "Full load, too. Man, your brother is *packing*." His voice held a tone of envy.

"Look, this isn't funny," Johnny said. "You'd better—"

Stinky held the magazine in one hand and the automatic in the other. He pointed it at the window. "Bang," he said, and pulled the trigger again.

The gun firing in the tiny room was louder than anything Johnny had heard in his entire life. It jumped in Stinky's hand, and all four of the boys jumped.

"Holy shit! You asshole!"

There was a huge hole in the ceiling above the window. Plaster dust and gunpowder smoke swirled in the air.

"Hey, how the fuck was I to know it was loaded?" Stinky shouted. "I took the clip out." As if to show it, he rammed the magazine back into the gun. "It was empty."

"Put the safety back on, you asshole," Johnny said.

The door kicked open, slamming against the wall. Johnny's brother was silhouetted in the doorway. "The hell you assholes are doing?"

"Oh, shit," Johnny said. He stood up. "Hey, Karl, we was—"

"Shut up," Karl said. He was looking at Stinky. "Asshole, give me my gun."

Stinky pointed it at him. "Hey, man, be cool. We were—"

Karl slapped the gun out of Stinky's hand with a move almost too fast for Johnny to see, and in the next instant he had Stinky by the throat. "You point that gun at me again, fat boy, and after I rip your balls off I'm going to shove them up your ass. Got it?" He didn't give Stinky a chance to answer, but reached down with the other hand, grabbed the crotch of Stinky's pants and picked him up and tossed him toward the door. Stinky staggered, bounced off the doorframe, and then caught his balance and ran.

"I ever see you around here, they won't scrape up enough of you to fill a jockstrap," Karl shouted after him. Then he turned around and looked at Fishface. "You got some business here?"

"No, sir," Fishface said.

"Then get the fuck out."

"Yes, sir!" Fishface said, and ran out of there so fast that Johnny wondered whether his feet even touched the ground.

Karl didn't bother to look at Johnny, just reached down, picked up his gun, put the safety on and jammed it into his pants. Then he walked over and looked down on Johnny.

"Hey, Karl," Johnny said, tentatively. He knew that he was going to get a pounding, but it was best to see if he could defuse his brother as much as he could. The sharp smell of powder and the dust from the ceiling seemed to choke all of the atmosphere out of the room. His ears were still ringing. "We didn't mean nothing."

"I know that, kid." Karl sighed. "What are we doing to you, kiddo? Just what are we doing?"

"It was an accident," Johnny said. "We just sort of found it by accident—"

Karl slapped him. Johnny saw it coming and tried to dodge, but he wasn't near fast enough.

"What was that for?" Karl said.

Johnny's ears were ringing from the blow. He tried to frame his words. "For taking your gun—"

Karl slapped him again, this time with no warning. "Asshole. I don't care about the gun." Karl raised his hand again, and Johnny cringed.

"That's for having stupid friends," Karl said. "Your friends are stupid, and you're stupid, for having stupid friends. What the hell were you morons thinking about?"

"I dunno. We weren't thinking about anything."

"That's right, you weren't thinking. You've got a brain, but nobody would ever know, since you never bother to use it." Karl sat down on the bed, hard, and put his head in his hands. "Oh, shit, kid, what the hell are we doing to you? We've got to get you out of here."

That had been a long time ago. John hardly ever thought about his brother Karl anymore, except sometimes when he got drunk, and he almost never got drunk. By the time he had gotten into high school, Karl had dropped out of school and had spent time in jail twice.

Nobody else in the projects seemed to have noticed the shot, or if they had, they paid attention to their own business. The hole Stinky blew in the ceiling had seemed huge to Johnny, but nobody from the housing authority had ever noticed it, even when they came around once a year to do the inspection.

Yeah, John Radkowski thought, Trevor can get a little annoying sometimes. But on the whole, he was okay. Not half the trouble that I'd been.

Now that both he and Chamlong were back in the cabin, it was Ryan Martin's turn to go out on the surface. Ryan was deeply engrossed with the computer. Radkowski walked over and put his hand on Ryan's shoulder. "Hey, how's it going?" he said. "You ready to take a look around outside?"

"I've been checking out the *Dulcinea*'s systems," Ryan said.

"So?" Radkowski said. "We checked her systems a dozen times during cruise. I can't think that anything's likely to have changed in the last four hours."

"Well, sure, but now that we're on the surface, I have a higher band-width connection," Ryan said. "I can command sensors in real time now, get more than just the health check signal."

"And?"

"These readings are screwy." Ryan shook his head. "Take a look at this," he said. "Here. I'm looking at the fuel temperature. The tanks ought to be holding steady at about 90K, but they're up over 200K, both of them. Tank pressures are fine, both tanks are full, but I can't understand these thermal readings."

Radkowski looked at the display. "Looks like a broken thermistor to me."

"Both sensors on both tanks? Seems unlikely."

"Shit," Radkowski said. "According to the mission plan, we're not sup-posed to check her out until the morning. Look, why don't you go on out-side and take a walk around. If you think we need to check her out today, that's your call, but think about it for a while first, okay? We're all running a little bit on overload." The commander clapped him on the shoulder. "Anyway, it's clear to me—you need a break. Go on. You deserve it."

"You got it, captain," Ryan said, and stood up. "I'm out of here."

5

RYAN

To Ryan Martin, the *Don Quijote* looked like nothing so much as a mushroom pulled from the ground and sitting on its half-wilted cap. Getting to Mars was a great accomplishment, and cramped and smelly as the *Don Quijote* had been, Ryan Martin would regret abandoning the *Don* on Mars. Ugly it was, yeah, stinky and cramped, but it had done the job, a dependable workhorse.

Getting back, though—getting back would be the real triumph. *Dulcinea* was their ride home, and if there was a problem, the sooner they found out what it was, the sooner they would be able to start fixing it.

The screwy readings from *Dulcinea* continued to worry Ryan. Even when he was on the surface, while he was thrilled by the beauty of the landscape and enjoyed the freedom of walking on a planetary surface after being cooped up in a soup can for seven months, with a corner of his mind he could not leave *Dulcinea* alone.

Anomalous readings are always a worry; they indicated something malfunctioning. There were other readings that looked wrong to him as well, readings that weren't obviously wrong, like the temperature reading, but still they had a wrong feeling. He hoped that the commander was right and it was a sensor failure. God knew that those happened often enough; sensors sometimes seemed like the practical jokers of space, always choosing the middle of the night or some equally inconvenient time to wake up a crew for what would invariably turn out to be a false alarm—but he would be more comfortable if he knew for sure.

The timeline called for them to check out the return ship on the second day on Mars, when the crew was refreshed by a day's sleep after the long day spent in landing and surface preparations. The commander didn't want to alter the plan, and he respected that, but if it had been up to him, he would have gone to *Dulcinea* immediately.

He couldn't help but glance over at the return ship, temptingly waiting for him just a kilometer away. *Dulcinea* looked not at all the way Ryan thought a rocket should look, a squat bullet shape aimed skyward. Instead, *Dulcinea* was a lumpy potato, with just the faintest wisp of white vapor trailing away from the oval tanks at the bottom of the first stage.

At various times, the *Dulcinea* had been nicknamed by the engineers at the launch complex the pig, the turd, and the flying cow. It was low and fat. With only the near-vacuum of the Martian atmosphere to penetrate, streamlining had been sacrificed for efficiency, and *Dulcinea* had all of the aerodynamics of a fire hydrant. One of the launch technicians had accidentally referred to it as the "incredible flying turd" in the presence of a reporter. He had been reassigned to launch sounding rockets from Kodiak Island, and the nickname had been hastily changed to "the amazing flying toad" for damage control. That nickname stuck, although in the presence of management or the press it was always, carefully, the Mars Return Launch Module.

Ryan worried about *Dulcinea*. If there was something wrong, he wanted to know *now*.

6

THE FIRST
EXPEDITION TO MARS

Don Quijote had landed on the edge of a region of Mars known as Felis Dorsa—in Latin, "the cat's back," or, less literally the cat mountains, since dorsae was the term Mars geologists had given to flat plains broken by long, low ridges. The site had been chosen with great care. The sand between the ridges was smooth and level enough to make a safe landing, but it was an easy traverse by Mars buggy to the Valles Marineris, the feature that the geologists had picked as the highest priority exploration target. The dorsae themselves—low, rounded ridges a hundred miles or more long—made for an additional target for investigation, as geologists continued to argue over the geophysical origin of the ridges. In the Martian tropics south of the equator, the Felis Dorsa featured a relatively mild climate—or at least mild for Mars, where temperatures of a hundred below at night were normal.

And, as a bonus, the two previous expeditions to Mars had both landed in the northern hemisphere, so while the crew of *Don Quijote* could not claim to be the first humans to the red planet, as a consolation, they could claim a new hemisphere.

The crew, however, had a goal of achieving a different first. They planned to be the first crew to return from Mars alive.

The American expedition to Mars had been planned for decades.

Going to Mars is easy. The difficult part is getting back. If you want to come back, you have to send to Mars an interplanetary ship capable, and with enough fuel, to launch from Mars to Earth. Getting that ship to Mars, fully fueled, is a herculean task.

It is far simpler to land a vehicle unfueled.

The expedition was planned to launch nearly a decade ago, in 2018. The first ship of the expedition, *Ulysses,* would have no crew. *Ulysses* would carry with her a robotic fuel manufacturing plant and a payload of liquid hydrogen. While the hydrogen was bulky, over the course of a Martian year it could be used to manufacture twenty times its weight in rocket fuel from the thin Martian atmosphere. When, two years later, the *Agamemnon* came with the exploration crew, seven astronauts handpicked for their scientific training, *Ulysses* would be fully fueled for its return, and waiting for them.

It was a plan that had been invented in the 1990s by two Mars enthusiasts, Robert Zubrin and David Baker, and refined over decades to distill out the maximum possible amount of exploration for the smallest investment from Earth.

As a backup, a second return vehicle, with its own fuel-manufacturing plant, was launched to follow behind them on a slower trajectory to Mars. It would be ready if the *Ulysses* should fail. If the *Ulysses* worked as planned, the second ship, *Dulcinea*, would be targeted to a second spot, to wait for a future expedition.

That was the plan. Painstakingly, piece by piece, the building blocks of the expedition were put together by the exigencies of politics and engineering.

Nobody paid attention to the Brazilians.

With the new millennium, chaos had come to the nation once known as the Soviet Union. During the height of the ferocious Russian civil war, rather than let their factories be destroyed and their knowledge lost, a team of rocket engineers had come up with a plan. They had stolen an entire factory, the main Khrunichev engine manufacturing plant, from the digitally controlled milling machines right down to the paper clips in the supervisors' desks. They got out just days ahead of the tanks of the retreating Russian People's National Liberation Front, pounding across the steppe toward Moscow under orders to leave no building, no tree, no bridge or lamp post or telephone pole standing.

They had fled to Brazil.

Brazil welcomed the refugees, and, in turn, the refugees had absorbed the Brazilian spirit. Over the decades, Brazil had gradually grown into the economic giant of South America. It was, as ever, a nation of contrasts, where abysmal poverty shared the same street with ostentatious wealth and corporations combined businesslike cool with wild Latin exuberance. Over the first decades of the millennium, Brazil built up its space program. At first, Brazil was no more than a junior partner in the American-led space station. Partly with its own growing engineering force, and partly with the engineering skills of the Brazilo-Russians, they developed an offshore launch platform at Alcântara, just south of the equator, to launch commercial satellites on Brazilian-designed and Brazilian-built launch vehicles.

But nobody—or, nobody outside of Brazil—expected that they would go to Mars. And nobody in the world would have guessed that they would get there first.

The Brazilian expedition was audacious. Rather than choosing a conservative landing site on sandy plains near the Martian equator, they chose to land at the north pole of Mars. This was a calculated move. The northern polar cap of Mars consists of a two-mile-thick glacier of ice, covered in the winter with a blanket of carbon-dioxide snow. To the engineers of the Brazilian space program, ice was more valuable than gold. Ice—ordinary water ice, hydrogen and oxygen—is rocket-fuel ore. During the Martian summer, when the pole received twenty-four hours and forty minutes of sunshine each day, they would mine ice out of the polar cap, electrolyze it into hydrogen and oxygen, and then chemically convert that into methane and hydrogen peroxide, fuels that could be stored at the polar cap without the use of refrigeration.

By their bold choice of landing site, they had simplified the mission, eliminating the requirement to haul hydrogen from Earth and the need to use cryogenic coolers for the propellant they manufactured. They simplified their mission in another way as well. Instead of having a separate vehicle land first to manufacture the propellant, they used a single landing. One vehicle with a two-man crew would land on Mars, manufacture their return fuel, and take off. They bet the mission on the ability to make fuel, with no mistakes, the first time. There was no margin for error.

They launched in 2020. Two years before the American expedition.

Even if they had wanted to, there was no way to hurry the *Agamemnon*; it had to wait for the *Ulysses* to make its fuel and for the planets to return to the alignment needed for the launch. The American expedition watched, envious and impotent, as two astronauts planted the Brazilian flag on the snows of Mars. They watched, by video broadcast, as the Brazilian astronauts filled their fuel tanks for their return and used hydrogen peroxide–fueled snowmobiles to explore the polar regions surrounding their spacecraft's landing site.

As the world watched on live television from Mars, the two Brazilian astronauts played in the polar snows, drilled core samples, and analyzed the embedded soil and dust for information about the climate and biology of Mars. The worldwide audience cheered. They had no hint that anything was going wrong.

One moment, João Conselheiro, the expedition leader, said calmly, "Puxa, estou muito cansado." *I am very tired.* He sat down on the snow.

The second astronaut walked toward him. "Acho que tem alguma coisa errada com o João." *I think something's wrong with João.* Then, a moment later, he fell over.

Neither astronaut moved again.

After two months—the camera broadcasting all that time—the Martian winter blanketed their bodies with snow.

The Brazilian commander João Conselheiro had left behind a young and beautiful wife who was also a pilot, a geologist, and a mountain climber. Her name was Estrela Carolina Conselheiro.

7

T A N A

"The way I figure it," Radkowski had once told Tanisha Jackson, "I'm the one who's actually black. You're just another nice white girl from the 'burbs." Between the two of them it had been a joke, how he had grown up in a ghetto, raised by a welfare mother with a brother in jail and a father he'd never met, while she had been raised in Pennsylvania suburbs, with both parents doctors, and gone to an expensive private school.

Tana never complained, but nevertheless it stung her when people called her white. Just because she hadn't been raised in a ghetto and didn't talk like a gangsta, that didn't mean she wasn't black. She still had to deal with all of the crap that people brought her because of her skin color.

Nevertheless, she got along fine with Radkowski. She'd even slept with him a few times. Once had been in the space station, but that hardly counted, since sex was one of the very first things that everybody did when they got into space, once they got over throwing up. It was a rite of passage, and Radkowski, who had been a veteran, was a good person to initiate her. But she'd done it a few times afterward, too, and although she was by no means in love with him, it had meant more to her than just a pleasant way to kill an hour or two.

She'd thought about it a few times on the voyage out, but even when they were alone together—something that didn't happen very often in the crowded ship—he had given no indication of interest. It would be bad for the crew morale if they had paired off, Tana had realized, and Radkowski knew it, and was keeping it cool for the sake of crew unity. Although that didn't seem to be any barrier to Estrela.

There was, as far as Tana could see, no actual written requirement that a female astronaut from Brazil had to be a sultry spitfire who flirted with every single male she met—but Estrela was, and did.

Tana was compact and muscular and wore her hair in a practical style, barely longer than a crewcut. Estrela, on the other hand, was tall, slender, and curved in all the places that Tana wasn't. And to top it off, she had kept her thick hair. Tana advised her that it was impractical, possibly even dangerous, for her to wear it long, but Estrela had ignored her, and in freefall, when her hair floated around her face like a dark halo, even Tana had to admit—if only to herself—that it looked glorious.

The rest of the crew—even Trevor—had gone back inside. Only Tana and Estrela stayed on the surface to watch the sunset.

Even in training, back on Earth, they had often watched the sunset together. "When I can, I always watch the sunset," Estrela had told her. "It is so romantic." Sometimes Estrela brought her boyfriend of the moment. Sometimes she was alone.

The Brazilian Mars expedition had taken no video of the sunset; at their landing site, the sun had never set. By now she knew it would be unwise to remind Estrela of that. The first international expedition had taken videos of the sunset, plenty of them, and she had seen them, of course, but the real thing was surprisingly different. The colors were subtler. The sky was a luminous hue closer to a golden bronze than the washed-out pink of the videos, and shaded imperceptibly to almost pale blue as she looked toward the sunset, a ball of light hovering above the yellow sun. The sun was smaller than the sunsets she was used to, and in the deep shadows the ridges of Felis Dorsa were a dark brick, almost brown.

They watched the sunset in a companionable silence.

It was cold. Through the day Tana's suit cooler had been rejecting heat nearly at full capacity, as her body produced more waste heat than she lost by conduction through the well-insulated material. Now, though, in the cool of the Martian evening, even at their landing site near the equator the temperature dropped to forty degrees below zero, and the microcontroller monitoring the suit's environment was sending electrical currents through thin-film heaters pressed against the thin inner lining of the suit. The soles of her feet, in thermal contact with the cold Martian soil, were cold; so were her hands.

The sun had set. Behind them, the external lights of *Don Quijote* beckoned. Tana checked the time. "Yikes!" she said. "I think it's time to come in now."

In the dark, she couldn't see Estrela's face behind her visor, only the reflection of the afterglow. It could have been anybody with her. For a moment Tana allowed herself the indulgence of imagining it was John. She reached out and impulsively touched Estrela's hand.

She wondered what Estrela was seeing.

THE SECOND
EXPEDITION TO MARS

When the news came that the two astronauts of the Brazilian expedition to Mars had died, John Radkowski should have already been on the way to Mars. He had been picked to be the copilot of the *Agamemnon*.

Eleven days before launch, Jason, the nine-year-old son of the woman who lived in the duplex next door to Radkowski, had been doing his house chores. Radkowski had a lot of sympathy for Jason; he knew how hard it was to grow up without a father. When Jason went outside to empty the garbage, he had found a skunk in the garbage can. Apparently the skunk was foraging through the garbage, slipped into the can, and had been unable to get out.

The skunk had been sleeping on top of the garbage. Little Jason was old enough to have known that he should leave a wild animal strictly alone—let alone never to mess with a skunk—but the skunk had been so cute, and seemed so harmless, so pettable.

So he petted it.

Jason's shrieks from next door fetched John immediately from his study, and with his first whiff, it was obvious that he had encountered a skunk. John told him to take all his clothes off, right there in the backyard, and when Jason had done that, he sprayed the screaming child with the hose. He followed that up with two gallons of tomato juice. It was only after he washed the tomato juice off with another spray of the hose that John discovered that not all of the color was juice; a part of it was blood. The boy had been bitten as well as sprayed.

John cleaned the wound as well as he could with soap and water and taped gauze over it, telling Jason over and over that everything would be okay. Then he doused him one more time with more tomato juice, and, ignoring the stink, took him to the hospital to have the bite sutured. Meanwhile, another neighbor called the animal control. The skunk that had bitten Jason had scrambled away when Jason knocked over the can after being sprayed. The animal-control officers shot three skunks in the area, and it was impossible to tell which one had bitten him.

One of the three had been rabid.

Even though it had been the child next door that had been bitten, not him, John Radkowski was taken off the crew roster for *Agamemnon* because of possible secondary exposure. The three-year trip to Mars was too long to take even the slightest chance, and there wasn't enough time before the launch window to wait to see if he had actually been exposed to the disease.

Agamemnon, the ship that John Radkowski should have been on, had launched perfectly. It had flown the interplanetary traverse to Mars with no problems, except for one event so trivial and embarrassing that it wasn't even mentioned in any of the videocasts with the Earth, but only on the private medical channels.

Shortly after launch, one of the crewmen complained of athlete's foot.

It spread among the crew, and by the time *Agamemnon* was approaching Mars, everybody had it. Normally, natural skin bacteria keep fungus in check, but zealous biological contamination protocols had killed the natural bacteria, leaving the fungus to multiply unchecked.

A spacecraft provides an ideal environment for fungus to grow: crowded with people in close contact, and warm, and with the crew able to take only sponge baths.

Once they found that the fungus was beginning to eat their clothes, they took to placing their clothing in the airlocks to expose them to vacuum for an hour every day.

Agamemnon made a flawless landing on Mars, only a few hundred feet from the return ship *Ulysses*, waiting for them on the eastern edge of the Martian plain known as Acidalia. By this time, the fungus had spread to the air filters. One of the crewmen opened up a panel behind one of the navigation computers and found rot growing on the circuit boards. A quick inspection showed the entire electronic system of the ship cultivating slime.

On some of the crewmen, the fungus infection moved to the sinuses. They were treated with antihistamines to dry out the sinuses and make the nasal environment less hospitable, but it was almost impossible to combat the infection.

It was never declared on the public channels, but the *Agamemnon* expedition was rapidly turning from a triumph into a disaster.

They launched from the surface of Mars early, using up their safety margin of extra fuel to fly *Ulysses* on a faster trajectory that swung by Venus on its way back to Earth. The revised trajectory would shorten their return time by nearly a year but required an additional rocket burn at Venus to correct the orbital inclination. But by this time they were beginning to be desperate.

As *Ulysses* passed Venus, telemetry relayed to Earth from *Ulysses* sent down the data that the fuel valves were opening in preparation for the burn, and then *Ulysses* fell silent. After an hour, telescopes from Earth revealed an expanding cloud of lightly ionized gas, primarily oxygen, in the position where the spacecraft should have been.

A faint, miniature comet glowing in the sunlight marked all that was left of the *Ulysses* and her crew.

Much later, the accident investigation board determined that the fungus must have entered the fuel-controller electronics. Nothing had happened until the command was given for the engines to fire, and then far too much had happened. Instead of a smooth, controlled burn, the short circuit in the electronics had resulted in both fuel lines opening, but no ignition. The computer should have sensed this and shut down the engines, but the same short circuit had rebooted the computer, and fuel and oxidizer continued to pour into the combustion chamber. When the mixture of fuel and oxidizer finally did ignite, the result was not a rocket, but a bomb. *Ulysses* had been doomed.

John Radkowski should have been on that expedition. A rabid skunk had saved his life.

And now he was on the third expedition to Mars.

TRANSMISSION

"This is station Trevor Whitman, broadcasting live, live, live to Earth from the red planet. Hello, Earth! I want to tell you, Mars is great! I really love it here, and I have to say that, you know all those months of training that I was complaining about, you know, well, just the thrill of being here has made it all worthwhile. It's so great! Did I say that already? I think I said that. Anyway, it's great.

"Today we landed, I guess you saw the descent pictures? From the lander camera? Okay, after we got down, we went outside, and I went out bouncing around. The colors, I guess you know that Mars is red, you know? But it's really more than that. I can't describe it, it's more like a, well, yellowish reddish brown kind of color, sort of a caramel color, but there are so many shades, and it seems like the longer I look, you know, the more colors I can see, more shades of yellow and orange than you could ever name, and pinks and yellows and even some kinda purple colors, too.

"These space suits are great; you hardly know you're wearing them, and the gravity's so light it feels like you could jump up forever. I climbed up one of the sand dunes today. We haven't seen any dust storms or anything yet, I mean, we just got here, you know? But it's great. I think I said that. I can't think of what else to tell you. There are mountains in the distance, sort of ridges. They aren't really that far away, and doesn't look like they will be so hard to climb, so maybe we'll go climbing them after we check out the return spaceship tomorrow. I can't wait.

"And to all of Trevor's friends, I mean, to all my friends on Earth, this is Trevor Whitman, saying, see ya!

"Station Trevor Whitman, signing off. Talk to you again tomorrow! Goodbye, Earth!"

10

THE BOREDOM OF
INFINITE SPACE

Space exploration conjures up in the imagination an image of endless horizons, infinite vistas of space. The reality, however, is quite different: The main enemy for a space crew to combat is the unrelieved boredom of confinement. The cabin of the *Don Quijote* could best be described as a prison cell, but with less of a view.

In the seven months it took to fly to Mars, there was plenty of make-work, but little in the way of actual useful tasks to do. They had measured cosmic-ray exposure, made measurements of the solar wind, and used the long baseline of the *Quijote* from the Earth to make precise timing measurements of gamma-ray bursters. But these experiments could be done just as well from an unmanned probe; their main justification had been to give the crew something to do.

By the time the *Quijote* had been in space for a month, the crew's unofficial motto had been, "Mommy! Are we there yet?"

A month before the landing, when Mars was little more than a small yellow smudge on the velvet sky, Ryan Martin had complained, "I'm going out of my mind. I don't care what happens on Mars, just so long as it's not fucking *boring*."

"And I don't care if I never see the inside of this damn cabin again," Trevor Whitman added.

As circumstances would have it, they both had their wishes granted.

DULCINEA DOWN

As the systems engineer, the task of checking out *Dulcinea* and certifying her ready for launch was Ryan Martin's responsibility. Chamlong Limpi-gomolchai, the Thai geologist, had cross-trained on the propellant manu-facturing plant, and probably was more familiar with its workings than Ryan was. He was Ryan's assistant and backup on the EVA.

EVA—what an awkward term. Extravehicular activity. They had agreed before the mission that they would root out and destroy all of the confusing acronyms that space missions were prone to use, but somehow the use of the term "EVA" for any venture through the airlock of the *Quijote*'s cabin had slipped out of their net. They needed a new word. Marswalk, maybe.

Okay. He walked over and touched Cham on the shoulder. "Ready for a Marswalk over to the *Dulcinea*?" he asked.

"I'm go," Chamlong said.

"Then let's suit up."

Ryan's suit was a light blue and sported a Canadian maple leaf painted on the chest. Each suit was color coded, to avoid possible confusion as to which astronaut was out on the surface at any given time. Chamlong's was the one with yellow-and-black stripes, and had the icon of an elephant neatly painted on the front.

The Martian EVA suits—Marswalking suits—were a marvel of engi-neering. They had a hard shell for the torso with armadillo joints at the abdomen, shoulders, and crotch. The chest carapace was made from a light-weight composite, coated on the outside with an inch of foam thermal insulation. The sleeves, gloves, and leggings were piezoelectric fabric, as light and flexible as ordinary cloth, but woven out of a fiber that contracted with an electrical signal to a perfectly contoured pressure fit around the limbs. It was a compromise design: The chest carapace allowed easy breathing, and the contractile fiber allowed free arm and leg motion. The only bad part was that you couldn't scratch your nose. It seemed to Ryan that his nose always started to itch just the instant he put the bubble helmet over his shoulders. He had discovered that if he twisted his head to the side and stretched his neck, he could rub his nose against the radio speaker mounted just above his shoulders.

Each suit had a thermophotovoltaic isotope generator mounted in the middle of the back, which provided electrical power for the oxygen production machinery. Heat from the radioactive isotope's decay was pumped through capillary-sized tubes in an undergarment to keep the chest and abdomen warm; the arms and legs were electrically heated to keep the astronauts from frostbite in the subzero Mars temperatures.

The tough silicon-carbide bubble helmets absorbed ultraviolet and had a visor like a baseball cap that could be turned to keep the sun-glare out of your eyes, as well as a second dark visor that could be pulled down like sunglasses.

All in all, they were practical suits, providing a self-contained Earthlike environment for traveling on Mars. On longer Marswalks, like all space suits, the suits would collect feces and urine for recycling. Ryan had long ago learned that when an astronaut stops in the middle of a task with an abstracted look on his face, it is proper to look the other direction and not bother them for a moment.

Once they had suited up, checked each other's suits, and descended to the surface, it was only a short trek over to the *Dulcinea*. The upper stage and the four huge booster tanks sat on the sand like a slightly battered beer can surrounded by ostrich eggs. The whole assembly rested on four mantis legs.

Ryan circled her, doing an external inspection. Both of the oxygen tanks were venting a thin, wispy trail of white vapor. That was okay: it indicated that the tanks were full. The zinc white of the thermal paint on the booster tanks was shaded lightly pink at the bottom with dust; that was expected, though, and the thermal modeling allowed for it. Other than that, there was no external damage visible.

"So far she looks okay," he said slowly. There still seemed something just a little bit odd about the condition of the ship, as if there was something he should have been seeing but wasn't, but he couldn't put a finger on what it might be. "Anything look out of place to you?"

"Negative here," Cham replied.

"Pretty good condition for an old lady who's been sitting out in the cold for six and a half years," he concluded. Maybe that was all it was; he had expected the ship to look more worn, dirty, and wind-battered from half a decade of exposure on the surface.

Between the number two and number three booster tanks was an access ladder that led to a small circular hatch. He climbed up while Chamlong waited on the sand below. The hatch release rotated freely, and he unsealed the hatch and wriggled through the opening, which was just barely big enough to take a Mars suit. An awkward design, but for the return ship every kilogram counted, and there was no need for a hatch that would allow a more dignified entrance. Inside, he flipped the circuit breakers on, and lights illuminated the cabin.

It was a near duplicate of the cabin on *Quijote*, except for the presence of an additional set of indicator panels for the chemical machinery that had manufactured the fuel. The computer system was already running. He powered up the CRT to read out the internal displays, and while it was coming to life, looked over the mechanical gauges.

They had checked the fuel a hundred times by radio link, both before launch from Earth and during flight. But from the gauges inside the cabin, the indicators didn't make any sense. What they showed should have been impossible. The computer came up, and he turned his attention to it. It didn't make any sense, either.

Chamlong poked through the hatch and took a look at him. "What is it?"

"Wait one," he said. He sat down at the system engineer's station, staring at the readings but not really seeing them. What was different?

Dulcinea had been designed to sit on Mars for two years, making propellant for the return mission. It had instead been sitting on Mars for nearly seven, waiting for her crew. But it still had propellant; the almost invisible plume of white vapor from the tanks proved that. So why were the sensors wrong? The mechanical gauges for the two oxygen tanks read zero; the two pressure gauges read screwy—one tank impossibly high, two other tanks way too low.

Ice, he thought. Mars is cold and dry, and the Martian atmosphere contains very little water vapor. But over the course of seven years, the tiny bit of humidity the air did hold would condense onto the cryogenic lines and freeze. Some ice could be clogging the sensors. That shouldn't be a failure mode, but building up over seven years? He called up a schematic for the mechanical gauge and studied it.

Maybe. He showed the drawing to Chamlong. "Right there," he said. "The heat exchanger pipe for the intake manifold. Suppose it built up a layer of ice?"

"You think that could really happen?"

Ryan shrugged. "Got any other ideas?"

Chamlong looked at the drawing. His doctorate was in planetary science, but he also had a mechanical engineering degree and a good understanding of the mechanism. "If I were to go down and tap on the manifold, if there's ice on it, it might break it free."

Ryan was dubious. "I suppose it's possible. Might adhere too tightly, though."

"I'll try it." Chamlong stood up. "If I knock some of the ice free, the reading will change, and at least then we'll know what the problem is. If not—well, if not, we'll have to think of something else."

Ryan nodded. "Okay, sounds good. At least it's a plan, anyway."

He would remember that phrase, later. "Sounds good."

Ryan toggled over to an exterior camera—still working fine, after sitting useless for almost seven years—and watched Chamlong bend over and select a rough volcanic stone about the size of a brick. He picked it up, walked to the first of the booster tanks, and then moved around behind the tank to where the heat exchanger was.

"It's hard to get in close enough to see very much, but I think I see some ice," Cham's voice said over the radio link. "You ready in there?"

"I've got my eye on the gauge."

Steadying himself with one hand against the tank, Chamlong gave it a light tap with the rock.

The gauge hadn't moved. "Nothing," he reported.

"Okay. I'm going to try a little harder."

Chamlong drew back the rock and gave the side of the aluminum manifold a solid thump. A snowstorm of white burst out of the interior, settled on the ground, and then quickly evaporated in the dry air.

The gauge jumped, overshot, and settled down. 22.8 tons. Perfect!

"You did it," Ryan said.

"All right! Okay, let's try the other one." Chamlong went to the second tank.

There was a thump, and ice broke free. The needle jumped and pinned itself against the high end of the gauge. A moment later there was a shuddering that he could feel from inside the spacecraft, and then Ryan heard Cham saying "Oh, shit!" over the radio. He looked at the view from the external camera but could see nothing—the entire outside view was blanked out in billowing white. Red warning lights started to come on in the cabin—overpressure, flow-rate monitor, temperature alert.

"Shit!" he said. "Cham! Are you all right?" There was no answer. He jumped out of the chair and out the hatch. He ignored the ladder and jumped down into the sand, raising a plume of dust that momentarily obscured his vision. "Chamlong! Report!"

Through the haze of cloud and dust, a torrent of liquid oxygen was jetting out of a broken pipe. It was insanely beautiful, a foaming fountain that glistened in the most delicate shade of pale blue. The pipe was waving back and forth, spraying the precious liquid over the spacecraft, and he could see the panels bowing as they encountered the sudden shock of liquid oxygen at a temperature of a hundred and eighty degrees below zero. He heard a bang—it must have been incredibly loud to be audible in the near vacuum of the Martian ambient—and on the other side of the ship, he could see that the second oxygen feed pipe had also burst. Both tanks were venting now, liquid oxygen foaming and bubbling like a torrent of blue champagne flowing across the sand, freezing and boiling at the same time.

There had been ice in the valves, oh yes. But the ice had masked a worse problem.

"Chamlong!" Ryan waded into the cloud of mist, and the faceplate of his helmet frosted over instantly. Blinded, he hit his emergency locator beacon and staggered back. "Chamlong, where are you!" He fumbled with his suit controls, overriding all of the thermal regulation to push the heat up to maximum, and then he waded back into the mist. Flakes of white, flash-frozen liquid oxygen, swirled around him, sparkling like fireflies in the sun. The yellow-and-black striped spacesuit had been deliberately designed to be easy to spot. It couldn't possibly be hard to find him.

It was already far too late.

12

AFRICAN INTERLUDE

John Radkowski's personal trainer, a woman named Alicia, loped beside him at an effortless jog as he sweated and clumped. She made it look so easy, but then, he figured that this was her job. "Concentrate on your breathing," she said. "Let your arms swing freely. Deep breaths. In, out. Loosen up. That's better."

The dusty grass felt like rubber under his feet. It always did.

Alicia never sweated, never even breathed hard. She was running backward in front of him now, doing stretching exercises with her arms as she ran, and having no difficulty keeping the pace. Her breasts bobbed tantalizingly, the two breasts out of phase, but he figured that keeping him excited was part of her job as well. It was probably why she was running backward like that in front of him. If he didn't like it, there were plenty of other trainers he could have chosen.

"Looks like you're about warmed up," she said. "Ready to do some running?"

"Ready," he said. Actually, he felt fat, clumsy, and out of breath, but there was little point in saying that.

"Great. Here's the trail. See you after your run."

"Sure thing, beautiful."

Alicia curved around and headed back, and he went on into the savanna.

It was low grass, yellow in the sunlight. In the distance a huge, solitary acacia tree stretched fractal fingers into the sky. He could see a series of gentle uphills terraced ahead of him. Not too bad. The African sun was bright but gave no warmth on his body, and the air was breezeless. He looked around and behind him.

Emerging out of the forest from a break just a few feet away from the spot he had started from, the lioness stretched, yawned, and then stretched again. The yawn revealed enormous teeth. She roared, a deep rumbling cough that tingled deep in his belly. Then she looked up, eyeing him speculatively, and began to pad after him.

The appearance of the lioness sent a thrill of adrenaline through him that nearly erased his tiredness. There was, of course, nowhere to hide. The hills ahead of him looked impossibly far away. It would be an endurance contest. He wouldn't want to sprint too early. He kept up his pace, remembering to breath regularly. Uphill, slightly, but there was a level spot at the top of the rise.

Behind him, the lioness started into an easy lope. Her eyes glowed yellow-gold with an interior light. She wasn't sweating, either.

No point in looking behind him. He concentrated on his breathing, on his rhythm, on staying loose. He felt good.

On the patch of level ground the lioness broke into a run, and he picked up his pace to keep her from gaining too much. He could hear her footsteps, hear her beginning to pant from exertion. This was what running was for, he thought. Man against beast, the original, pure competition. Uphill again, now, and the lioness behind him slowed to a walk. He couldn't maintain the pace, either, and slowed down as well. Then another stretch of level ground, and they both began to run.

Then the lioness roared, and he knew that the final lap was on him. Sprint like nothing you've ever done, or you'll be caught. He pushed himself, trying for new records. A minute of this, two, and he thought he was going to burst. Surely he couldn't take any more. A hundred more feet. Fifty.

A distant bell rang in his ears, and he slowed down to a stop. Behind him, the lioness slowed as well. When he looked back, Alicia had come up beside him.

"Don't stop, you need a cool-down. Keep moving, keep moving."

"Right."

"That's better," she said. "Pretty good time. You sustained an average of 320 watts for almost ten minutes there. Watch your form on the sprints, you're going to turn an ankle if you're sloppy."

"Got it," he said. "Turn an ankle. Bad."

"Okay, then," she said. "Good workout. See you in two days?"

He doubted he would see her in two days—now that they were on Mars, he would probably be too busy to keep up his exercise routine—but there was no point in saying that, either. "It's a date, beautiful."

He raised his hands to his head. He couldn't see anything—it looked for all the world as though he was in Africa—but he could feel the helmet, and grabbed it and pulled it up. Africa shrank to two dimensions and pulled away.

He put the virtual reality helmet back on its stand by the treadmill, grabbed for his water bottle and took a long pull, then pulled back the curtain on the exercise booth. The exercise sessions were tiring, but he always felt refreshed and fully energized after. He wished that *Don Quijote* had a better exercise facility, one with a full sensory reality. In Houston, he would have been able to smell the lion, would have felt a breeze, and the texture of the ground under his feet would have varied as the terrain changed. He would have been able to climb the rocks, swing from trees.

More than that, though, he wished he could shower after exercising, but in the cramped cabin of *Don Quijote* that was clearly impossible, and, as always, a sponge bath was the best he could do.

With Ryan and Chamlong out checking the *Dulcinea*, and Tana and Estrela out on EVA samples, the cabin seemed almost spacious. Trevor should have been monitoring the radio, but as Radkowski grabbed his sponge, he saw with some disgust that Trevor's eyes were masked and his attention distant, involved with some sort of simulation or video game. So nobody was paying attention to Ryan and Chamlong checking out the *Dulcinea*.

Well, if there had been a problem, Ryan or Tana would have contacted him by an emergency page, which would get to him wherever he was. Still, it was a breach of discipline.

While he started his sponge bath, he reached toward the radio to listen to what the rest of the crew was doing. And, as if in response—he hadn't even yet turned on the radio—the emergency page lit up. Somebody had hit the panic button.

He hoped that it was nothing, but John Radkowski's instinct for trouble was already giving him warning signals. He had the sudden sinking feeling that they were in deep trouble.

13

CHAMLONG

When Chamlong Limpigomolchai had been a small child, perhaps five or six, his parents took him to a temple. The golden Buddha had seemed uninteresting to him, but he vividly remembered the Nagas, the huge, brightly painted, seven-headed serpentine monsters who guarded the stairs. After the temple, his mother had taken him to have his fortune told. The fortune-telling woman had seemed more like a clerk than a wizard; she had taken his mother's money, barely glancing at the number written on the lucky stick he had shaken from the fortune tube, and pulled a sheet of tightly rolled paper out of a pigeonhole and handed it to her without a word of comment.

YOU WILL TRAVEL FAR, the fortune said, BUT WILL ALWAYS RETURN HOME.

Later, when he went to Japan for schooling, he thought, yes, I am traveling far, but I will always return home. The thought gave him comfort; he knew that he would not die while abroad. And later, when he went to study for a doctorate in an American university by the name of Stanford, he thought, yes, this is it, this is what the old woman meant when she said I will travel far. But I will return home.

And he traveled further yet. His fellow astronauts had always marveled at the calm way that he faced danger. He had been on extravehicular activity once—a spacewalk—and an incorrectly programmed robotic arm had moved unexpectedly, severed his tether, and tossed him spinning into space. He had turned on his emergency locator beacon—his radio had been smashed in the same accident, so he had no idea if his beacon was being heard, or even if anybody had seen the accident. He turned down his oxygen partial pressure to the minimum to extend his breathing time and calmly closed his eyes to meditate. Two hours later, when he was picked up, he opened his eyes, nodded once, and said, "Ah, there you are."

And now he was on Mars. But I will return home to die. As it had been all his life, he knew that, no matter how bad things might get, he would make it home.

The fortune-teller had been right about his traveling, far more right than she could possibly have known.

But she was wrong about his returning home. Chamlong Limpigomol-chai, the farthest-traveling Thai in the history of his country, would never leave Mars.

14

A FUNERAL ON MARS

Chamlong Limpigomolchai had been a quiet man. John Radkowski had always respected Chamlong—he had thought that of them all, he had been the best among the crew—but he had never really understood his motivations. He did his job, never complained, never did less than his best, and never talked about his personal life. Now he would never know him better.

Radkowski had seen people die before; death was an old familiar feeling. First was the shocked feeling. Why? Then, following hard on after the first shock, was the awful feeling of relief. He had known that the mission was going to be dangerous, and that there was a good chance that one or all of them would die. And now it had happened—and he was still alive. He damned himself for what he felt, but he couldn't help feeling it.

And, following the relief, the guilt.

The Mars soil was harder to dig in than he had expected. There was a slight breeze, which helped carry the dust of digging away, but by the time they had dug a grave for him, all of their suits were painted a dull yellowish orange. Tana and Estrela carried his body. After Tana had done the autopsy, they had put him back in his suit for burial. Radkowski had looked over Chamlong's meager personal effects, trying to find something that would have meaning for him. He had no photos, no letters from home. He knew that Chamlong hadn't been married—that had been one of the criteria for crew selection—but surely he had some person at home to share his life with. But if so, he left no trace of it. The only personal item Radkowski found was a tiny yellow and red dollhouse, something that seemed almost ridiculous among his other utilitarian possessions. Radkowski carefully placed it in with the body.

"Ashes to ashes," he intoned. "Dust to dust." Back in the Air Force, they had their own second verse to this reading: "And if the Lord won't take you, why, the devil, he must." But it was one thing to say that when getting drunk over a dead friend, and quite another to say it aloud at a funeral, so instead he said, "A moment of silence, please."

And Estrela, Ryan, Trevor, and then Tana, one at a time, put a shovel-ful of Martian dirt into the grave, and then silently piled a cairn of rocks over it.

John Radkowski stood watching, silent with his thoughts. It's not a dis-aster, he told himself. One dead, a stupid accident, we can deal with it. Thank the Lord the rest of us are okay. If this is as bad as it gets, we're lucky.

He could never admit it to his crew, but John Radkowski was scared.

The expedition is fine, John Radkowski told himself. The expedition is fine.

15

MAPPING THE DISASTER

The expedition was not fine. Ryan consulted by video-link with support engineers on Earth until the Earth had set below the horizon. It was annoying that the communications relay satellite that *Agamemnon* had left in orbit had failed; after working perfectly for seven years, it was just bad luck for it to fail when it did. Without a communications relay, they could consult Earth only during the Martian day, when the Earth was visible in the sky.

Without mission support, Ryan worked alone, late into the night.

He answered questions from the other crew members in monosyllables or not at all.

Fiber-optic probes lowered through the piping and into each of the tanks confirmed what Ryan knew: The *Dulcinea*'s fuel tanks were dry.

While Ryan Martin and John Radkowski worked, Tana and Estrela cooperated in leveling a patch of ground with shovels and then anchoring and inflating the habitat bubble. There was no way they could help with *Dulcinea*, and, regardless of the decisions made regarding their future, the habitat was needed. Once it had been inflated and the interior fittings checked out, they had a comfortable living area with, for the first time in seven months, actual privacy for sleeping and other bodily functions.

There were no firm conclusions from Earth by the time Earth had set the next day and they went to sleep. Between Ryan's testing and that of the engineers on Earth, though, they had the beginnings of an understanding of what had happened.

Mars is a sulfur-rich planet. Without an ozone layer, far-ultraviolet radiation from the sun reaches all the way to the surface. A consequence of this is the presence of a small amount—less than a few parts per million—of highly reactive, UV-energized sulfur radicals near the surface. Over the seven years that the *Dulcinea* had been making rocket fuel on Mars, contamination by sulfur radicals had crept into all of the parts of the system, including the microelectromechanical sensors that measured the fuel capacity and the pipes and seals of the propellant manufacturing. The pressure sensors on the tanks had been fooled by the contamination, and the microprocessor control system, following the readings unquestioningly, had allowed the fuel manufacturing to proceed until all of the tanks held a far higher pressure than they had ever been designed for. The backup mechanical gauges, frozen by ice buildup, had failed to report any problems.

Worse, though, the energetic sulfur radicals had slowly hardened and embrittled the polymer of the seals that had isolated the liquid oxygen tanks from the propellant production system. When Chamlong had tapped on the manifold, the fragile seal ruptured, and the consequent spray of liquid oxygen had caused the seal on the next tank to burst, and in short order all the tanks had ruptured and drained their contents to the sand.

The first American expedition to Mars, the *Agamemnon* expedition, had had an entire second ship ready for a backup in 2022. Contingency planning, they called it. That backup ship had been the *Dulcinea*.

After *Dulcinea*, there was no spare return ship.

The crew of *Don Quijote* were stranded on Mars.

16

THE CAPTAIN AND THE KID

While Ryan Martin worked on the problems with *Dulcinea*, Commander Radkowski instructed the rest of the crew to continue with their science activities on the Mars surface. Whatever had gone wrong, he knew, it would only be made worse if the crew was left idle to brood it over. That included his own activities—which at the particular point in the schedule were listed as aiding the other crew members as he saw fit. None of the crew members, at the moment, seemed to need assistance.

He was getting used to the surface. At first Mars had seemed odd, the horizon too close, the rocks unexpectedly rough, the color of the light too yellow. A speckling of dark rocks gave the ridge face in the distance an oddly dappled appearance, always changing slightly as the shadows moved with the sun. Now it was beginning to seem familiar.

Trevor came up and walked next to him. Trevor's suit was a bright lime green, so strongly contrasting against the yellowish-orange Martian terrain that it nearly made his eyes hurt. Trevor had his own list of science activities—a whole schedule of things to observe and look for, from a list contributed by the brightest students at fifty elementary school classes across America. But at the moment, he seemed more interested in Radkowski.

"Did you ever have a brother?" Trevor asked.

Commander Radkowski was startled. How could Trevor have known he had just been thinking about his brother? Just making conversation, he expected. Trevor didn't seem to be very good at making friends and small talk, but give him some credit, at least he was trying. "Sure," he said cautiously. "Sure, I had a brother."

"Just one?"

"Just one. Karl. Two years older than me." He paused. "How about you?"

"The same, an older brother." Trevor stumbled, and then said, "No, no, younger. Why did I say older?" He laughed. "Younger. A kid brother. Brandon."

Radkowski had known that already; he'd read the kid's dossier. But if the kid was going to ask about his family, he would carry his half of the conversation. It was funny, on all of the seven-month voyage out, they had been bored as hell, but he didn't recall talking about his family at all. None of the crew had asked him.

They walked on in silence, and then Trevor asked, "What was he like?"

"Karl? He was okay, I guess." Radkowski thought about it. "Kinda bossy, I suppose, now that I think about it." He paused, and then said, "I guess older brothers are like that."

"You said it," Trevor said.

"How about your brother?"

Trevor shrugged. "He's okay." He paused for a moment, gathering his breath. The kid was trembling, Radkowski noticed. What was going on? And then he asked, "Did you ever do anything really awful to your brother?"

Radkowski's heart stopped for a moment, and then life went on. "Like what?"

"You ever betray him? Did you ever make him lie for you? That sort of thing—you know."

He didn't want to think about it. Why was the kid asking these questions? He looked around. Estrela was out of sight behind the ship. Tana Jackson was working on a rock, levering it up in order to sample the soil beneath for signs of organic material that might have been protected by the rock from the harsh ultraviolet. "One moment," he said. "I think Dr. Jackson could use my assistance. Would you excuse me, please?"

Trevor looked disappointed, but he nodded.

Radkowski brooded over it. The kid knows, he thought. Somehow he sensed something. God, he's a lot like I was. Was I really like that? There's an aura of guilt over me. I wonder if the others can see it?

17

RADKOWSKI

John Radkowski had grown up without ever meeting his father. His mother and an aunt had tried to raise the two boys as best they could, but they had been wild, and paid little attention to adults, or to any authority figures. More than anyone else, it had been his brother Karl that had raised him.

Karl's gang was the Skins. The Skins were every bit as tough as the black gangs and the Hispanic gangs and the Vietnamese gangs, and they made sure that everybody knew it. When they moved into an area, resplendent in their purple Dacron jackets, with their skull tattoos and pierced eyebrows and buzz-cut hair, everybody with any sense quietly found another place to go. Even the other gangs mostly steered clear of Skins turf.

Johnny had done a little boosting, some drugs, but wasn't in any of the gangs yet. He didn't really like what drugs did to his head, but it kept him cool with the other high-school kids, and his school was one where it was not wise to stand out.

Karl disapproved: He wanted Johnny to fly straight and grow up to be somebody, not some punk-ass low-life criminal like him. He was constantly telling Johnny to stay out of trouble. You've got some brains, he said. You've got something on the ball. You don't want to end up as just another one of the dead-enders and burned-out crackheads in the projects. But Karl was a hotshot gangbanger himself, and, although he did everything he could to discourage Johnny, he was the only role model that Johnny had.

Johnny was a sophomore in high school, not flunking out, exactly, but he was careful not to get grades that would get him noticed.

Weasel was a year older than the rest of Johnny's buddies; he'd been held back in school. He had a driver's license already, and a car. On that Thursday night, they had driven into Brooklyn, into a neighborhood where they wouldn't be recognized. They'd cruised by the storefront three times, checking it out. It closed up at midnight, and the car was idling at the end of the block, the four of them sitting inside smoking and talking, waiting for the cash register to get full.

"I don't know," Johnny said. "I tell you what, you wanna just go back, pick up some girls, maybe get high?"

"You crazy? No way," Weasel said. "You gotta do it, man. You ain't chickening 'cause you're a fag, are you?"

Fishface gave him the gun.

Johnny shoved it in his waistband. He didn't feel very good. The smoke was beginning to make him light-headed. He didn't have to use the gun; he could just show it, and the guy would open the register right up. He definitely wasn't going to use it.

A simple transaction: Johnny would show him the gun, and the cashier would give him the money in the register. Easy. Anybody could do it.

"So what'cha waiting for, pussy?" Fishface said.

He opened the door, took a deep breath, and pulled his T-shirt out over the gun to keep it from being quite so noticeable. The air was a relief from the stale, smoky air in the car, but he barely noticed. He walked the quarter block to the store.

The store on the corner had bars over the dirty glass window. A glowing orange worm in the window flickered UDWEISER. He stopped at the counter by the cash register. It sold Lotto tickets, cigarette lighters in the shape of buxom women, gum, condoms, and cigarettes.

After a moment, the cashier—who was also the owner—looked up and said, "You want to buy cigarettes, you better show some ID."

He pushed the shirt over the handle of the gun, exposing it. "I don't—"

I don't want anybody to get hurt, is what he'd started to say, but he didn't get that far.

The man said, "Shit!" He reached under the counter and pulled out a shotgun.

Johnny had to shoot, there wasn't any choice. He didn't even have time to think, but only to grab the gun and fire. At the same time the shotgun went off with an incredible concussion, and Johnny thought, I'm dead. A rack of Stolichniya behind him blew apart, spraying him with shards of glass and vodka. Johnny's shot hit the owner and jerked him backward. A small bubble of blood appeared in his chest and popped. He dropped the shotgun, a surprised expression on his face.

Johnny dropped his gun and ran.

It wasn't supposed to be this way. A simple transaction. His buddies were waiting with the car, but even in the confusion of the moment, Johnny realized that going to the car would be stupid; the sounds of the shots had certainly drawn attention, and they could track down Weasel easily enough from the license plate.

He ran down the street and into an alley, jumped up and caught the lower rung of a fire escape, then across two roofs and then down into a subway and over the turnstile. No train on the platform, so he ran up again and outside. Three blocks away, and the Pitkin Avenue A train was waiting at the elevated platform. He ran onto it, panting, and changed to the F train at Jay Street. Only when the train had pulled out, when he could see he wasn't being followed, did his heart stop racing.

His efforts to avoid being tracked had been useless. A bystander had noticed the car full of a gang of teenage delinquents loitering in front of the convenience store when the shots were heard, and written down the plate number when it had sped off.

And there had been a security camera.

When Weasel had returned, police had already been waiting for him. Half of the neighborhood watched as they took him to the station for questioning.

"You moron," Karl said. "What the hell kind of trouble are you in this time? Spill it, asshole."

Johnny didn't have any real choice. He'd never been able to keep anything from his older brother anyway. He told him the whole story.

"Shit," Karl said. "You sure do know how to pick friends, you. That asshole Weasel's no friend of yours. The cops push on him, threaten him with a little time if he doesn't talk, you know he'll roll over so fast you won't even see him move."

"Shit, Karl. What am I going to do?"

"You're gonna do nothing. You're going to shut up and sit tight. If the cops come here, tell 'em you know nothing, got it? You've been home all day. I'm going to talk to the police."

"What are you going to tell them?"

"Shut up and trust me."

It was two days before he saw his brother again.

Karl had gone directly to the station, asked to see a detective, and told them he did it. The detective called an attorney and two more cops as witnesses, told Karl his rights, and asked him if he wanted to say that over again. Karl did.

The police were overloaded with crimes to solve, and had no compulsion to put any extra time into investigating one that had already been solved. The loose ends didn't matter; with a confession from Karl, the case was closed, and the police had no reason to go after Johnny.

It was Karl's third offense, and he got twenty-five years, no parole. The convenience store owner had gotten shot in the lung. He was in intensive care, but would probably pull through.

"I'm doing this for you, asshole," Karl told him. "I'm inside, but I got contacts. If you stray off the straight and narrow, I'm sending somebody after you to break your teeth. You dump those rotten friends of yours and fly straight. I want you to keep your nose so clean that when you pick it, it squeaks. You gonna be the teacher's pet. I'm taking the fall for you to give you a chance, you asshole, and you better use it right or I'm going to be pissed. Don't think I can't pound your ass just because I'm inside. I got friends."

Johnny nodded. He was crying. It was the last time in his life that he would ever cry.

"I got some money saved up," Karl said. "Guess I can't use it now. It's enough to put you in a boarding school upstate. We gotta get you out of this shithole we call a 'hood. Get you a scholarship, maybe one of those ROTC things, whatever it takes, just get yourself into a college, and never come back here, you got that? Never come back."

18

MEETING

"It's chickenshit," Trevor Whitman said. "Chickenshit! How the hell can the tanks be empty?"

They sat or stood around the tiny fold-out tray that served the *Quijote* as a conference table. "Does it matter?" Ryan said. He was sitting on the arm of the pilot's station, leaning back with his eyes closed. He hadn't been sleeping, and his face showed it.

"They were full when we took off, they were full when we came in for a landing. How the hell could you have screwed them up so that they're empty?"

"I explained that," Ryan Martin said. "I'm not going to explain it again."

"Why is irrelevant," Commander Radkowski said curtly. "What I'm looking for right now is suggestions as to what we do about it."

"Perhaps Mars is cursed," Estrela said. "The first expedition, the American expedition—they all died. Everybody who comes here dies. Now we're going to die."

"What does the mission contingency plan say?" Tana asked. "Is this covered?"

"The contingency plan," Radkowski said, "says that we restart the propellant manufacturing plant on *Dulcinea* and make new propellant."

"So what's the problem?" Tana asked. "We replace the corroded seals, we weld the broken lines, and we run. Yeah, maybe, we miss the original launch window, but we're okay. Right?"

"The problem," Ryan said, still with his eyes shut, "is that we can't do that."

"Why not?"

"What a propellant manufacturing plant does is to convert the reactor heat into rocket fuel," Ryan said. "You need energy."

"Yeah?"

"The energy came from a little Brayton-cycle nuker that was landed with the *Dulcinea*. The nuke uses a turbine to convert the reactor heat into electrical energy. That means moving parts. The degradation mechanism is for dust to get into the bearings."

"The bearings are shot?" Tana said.

"Bearings corrode, then they freeze up. The engine seizes, welds the parts together."

"So then you're saying that we have to replace—"

Ryan raised a finger. "No coolant flow, thermal overpressure bursts the pipes. When the coolant's gone, the reactant core overheats. The fuel rods expand and break out of their sleeves. End result, the reactor is a useless chunk of hot metal. Repair it? We can't even get near it."

"Chernobyl?" Trevor asked. "You're saying we're sitting next to a meltdown?"

"Not so extreme." Ryan raised both hands, palm up. "We're not getting sprayed with radioactive smoke, if that's what you're asking. But the bottom line is, propellant manufacture is majorly dorked. It's out of commission. For good."

"So, you're saying that the contingency plan is fucked."

"Nobody really thought we'd still need the nuke." Ryan shrugged. "I guess nobody really thought at all."

Everybody was silent.

"So what do we do?" Trevor said. "Are we stuck here? How long will it take for the rescue expedition to get here?"

John Radkowski shook his head. "There won't be a rescue expedition," he said.

"But there has to be one," Trevor said. "When Earth finds out, they'll—"

"We've already reported the situation to Earth," Radkowski said. "We're on our own. You know the political situation back in America. Hell, the only reason the expedition was approved at all was that the politicians thought it might take attention away from the worldwide economic depression. Two pairs of ships for the original Mars expedition. Two. That's all that they ever built. What are they going to rescue us with? *Quijote* was the last ship we had. You were at the preflight briefing, you know that."

"The Brazilians?"

Estrela shook her head. "We are a poor country, you know, not like you rich North Americans. We could only build one ship. We couldn't even afford to send a ship to bury our own astronauts. We have nothing."

"So what do we do?" Trevor said.

Radkowski nodded his head. "That's the question, isn't it. That's the question."

Nobody had anything more to say.

After a while, Radkowski said, "Okay, I can see we're not getting anything done here. Back to your duties, everybody. Ryan, Tana, think it over and come up with some options."

"You're saying that we're dead, aren't you?" Trevor said. "We're dead. We just haven't fallen over yet."

Nobody replied.

19

THE SACRAMENT OF CONFESSION

His mother was Catholic, but John Radkowski could barely remember going to church. He had not gone since he had been what, in second grade? Before they'd moved to the projects, anyway. The church had seemed huge to him, and the people inside solemn and stiff. The voice of the priest had echoed across the vast interior like a huge cave.

It had been years since he had been back to New York. The neighborhood was like an alien landscape, dirtier and more broken down and, yes, even a little frightening. There was nothing for him here now anyway. The only person he had really cared about was his brother, and Karl had died in prison. His mother was still here, still living in the same dingy little apartment in the housing project, but she had refused to see him. A neighbor told him to go away, that she didn't want to ever talk to him again.

The church was gray stone, and looked as if it was built to last for millennia—it probably had been. He was slightly ashamed for visiting a Catholic church. Catholicism was for immigrants, Italians, and Mexicans. It's lower class, he thought. Not something for a college graduate.

Friday afternoon. The confessional was at the back of the church, and the dim indicator light above the carved wooden door showed that it was in use. Outside, a few older women were waiting quietly, kneeling. When they left the confessional, they went directly to the altar rail. He loitered inconspicuously until he saw nobody else waiting.

Stained glass saints looked down. Their faces were glowing, but their expressions were cold and unforgiving.

He entered quickly, knelt, and crossed himself. He was surprised to realize that he still knew how to do it. The booth was dark and smelled of velvet and of the perfume of the previous occupant. He felt grateful for the dark, and the anonymity.

When he heard the dry whisper of the window sliding open, he said, "Bless me, Father, for I have sinned." When there was no response, he remembered the rest, and added, "It has been, ah, twelve years since I have been to confession."

"Your voice is unfamiliar," the priest said. The priest's voice was ordinary, conversational. "I don't think I've heard you before." The priest sounded young, perhaps not much older than Radkowski. It wasn't something that Radkowski had expected. He wondered if the priest was new.

"No, Father."

"That's okay. Welcome to our church. You are Catholic?"

"Yes, Father."

"How have you sinned?"

"I—" Radkowski had never told anyone his secret, and suddenly he realized that he couldn't. His tongue was paralyzed. "I can't say it, Father."

"Ah. More than just not going to Mass, I take it?" The priest chuckled, as if sharing a joke, but at Radkowski's silence, he added in a more serious voice, "Well, then, can you be a little more specific? One of the ten commandments?"

"A mortal sin, Father."

"Can you tell me about it? Don't be afraid, nothing you say will shock me. I am here to listen, not to judge you."

Radkowski shook his head without saying anything.

"It would be best if you told me, my son. Do you need advice? Do you need to talk to the police?" After a moment of silence, the priest asked softly, "What did you come here for?"

"I don't know, Father."

"Are you seeking absolution?"

"Yes."

After a moment, the priest said, "I cannot absolve you if you do not confess."

"I'm sorry, Father." He paused, and when there was no reply, he said, "Am I damned?"

"That is not for me to judge, my son. But you must remember this, that there is one above us who loves you unconditionally, no matter how far you have fallen or what your sins are. If you cannot tell me how you have sinned, at least tell me, can you make reparations to the one you wronged?"

"It is too late for that, Father."

"Ah." A soft sigh. "It is God who will be your judge, not I. I will pray for you, and I have faith in His mercy. Go forth and do your best to sin no more. That is as much as any mortal human can ever ask."

The next day, ROTC cadet John Radkowski was commissioned into the Air Force as a second lieutenant. Six months later, he was sent to Africa.

"I need to talk with you," Ryan said.

Estrela was lying face down in her bunk. "Go away," she said.

"This is serious. I need to talk with you before I go to the Captain."

Without looking, she grabbed a sheaf of papers—technical manuals for the mass spectrometer—from the reading ledge and clasped them over her head. "I'm not listening."

"Look, I think there might be a way back. For some of us. But I have to talk to you."

Estrela rolled over, scattering the papers, and looked at him. "I'm listening."

In the darkness, it seemed to Ryan that her eyes were glistening. He wondered if she had been crying. Estrela? No, not her. She was cool and beautiful and played with hearts like children played with marbles. She would no more cry than a statue.

"Here's the way I see it," Ryan said. "We need a return ship. *Dulcinea* is dorked big time. Forget her. There was the *Ulysses,* but she's gone. But there is a third return ship on Mars, and it's still there."

"*Jesus do Sul,*" Estrela said.

"I'm serious here."

"*Jesus do Sul,*" she repeated. "Our return ship. Santa Luzia, you're right—it's still there." She sat up suddenly. "Martin, it's at the north pole. That's half the planet away. How could we possibly get to it?"

"I don't know. If it's still there, we'll think of something. What I need to know is, is it still good? After seven years on the surface, will it still fly? Can we use it?"

"I don't know," she said. "I don't know."

21

D R I V I N G   L E S S O N S

Ryan spent two days examining maps and orbital photographs, trying and failing to plot a workable way to get them north. It would not be an easy journey. They had over six thousand kilometers to travel—four thousand miles—over territory that had never been viewed from the surface. The territory was rough, and it was unlikely that they could maintain a very high speed. His plan was that he and Estrela would set out first, at the dawn of their seventh day on Mars. They would drive north and east on the two dirt-rovers, checking the terrain and plotting courses around any major obstacles. The others would follow in the rockhopper.

The dirt-rovers were technically called single-person extravehicular mobility units, or SPEMUs. In the crew's campaign to eliminate acronyms, the nickname "dirt-rover" had stuck, since they had oversized balloon tires designed for travel on a variety of hypothetical types of Martian soil.

They were two-wheeled vehicles, looking like a comic-book exaggeration of a steroid-enhanced motorcycle. They featured enormous tires with knobby protruding treads like polyps growing on a bagel, and a light aluminum-lithium alloy frame that allowed the Mars-suited rider to recline against the spherical tanks that held oxygen and consumables. Each was as brightly colored as a molded plastic toy, with colors carefully chosen to make them stand out against the landscape: Day-Glo shades of turquoise and green that fluoresced almost painfully bright in the ultraviolet-rich Martian sunlight.

No one had ever ridden one on Mars.

Ryan found it both easier and harder than his rides in the simulator on Earth had led him to expect. The traction on Mars was worse than he'd expected. The oversized tires bit into the surface, but tended to spin uselessly in the soil, digging down rather than giving traction. After some experimenting, he found that if he was very gentle on the throttle, careful not to accelerate faster than the wheels could bite, he could slowly build up speed. Stopping and turning was a similarly gentle process—he made a note to make sure to leave plenty of stopping room in front of obstacles.

Ryan was meticulous and cautious in learning how the dirt-rover handled on Mars, checking each maneuver point by point. He found that it was far easier to keep the dirt-rover upright than it had been in the simulator. He could heel the dirt-rover way over, and in the lighter gravity, he would have several seconds before it would fall over.

After gaining a cautious familiarity with how the dirt-rover handled on Mars, he looked up and caught a glimpse of Estrela, practicing on the second dirt-rover.

"What the hell are you doing!?"

"Hey, Ryan! This is a blast!"

"Stop!"

Estrela stood up in the seat, leaned back, and popped the front wheel up off the dirt. The bike pivoted on its rear tire in a neat turn. Ryan noticed with dismay that, for all the apparent danger of the maneuver, she managed to do a turn in about a tenth of the radius of one of his carefully calculated, gently banked curves. The front tire came back down, and she leaned forward and throttled up, firing a roostertail of dirt behind her. She sped up to him. Just before he thought he would have to dive out of danger, she yawed the bike around ninety degrees and skidded to a stop, plowing up a hill of soil in front of her. Like the turn, he noted, it was a far faster way to stop than any he had managed.

Where had she learned to drive a dirt-rover like that? It certainly wasn't in the manual.

"Loosen up," she said. "You handle that bike like it's made out of glass. My grandmother drives faster than that. Come on, I'll give you some lessons."

While they were practicing on the dirt-rovers, Radkowski and Tana were unloading the rockhopper from its stowage bin on *Dulcinea*.

The dirt-rovers had been designed to give extra mobility to astronauts on the surface of Mars, but had not been intended for long distances. They had no redundancy in the drive system, and the mission regulations forbid the crew from taking a SPEMU any farther from the habitat than the astronaut could walk back in case of a failure.

The rockhopper, the pressurized Mars buggy, was far larger and could carry more equipment. The official name was pressurized vehicle for extended extravehicular traverse—a PVEET—but nobody could even agree on how to pronounce that one, and people giggled every time the acronym was used. Unlike the SPEMU, the PVEET was designed with articulated wheels that could actually step over any rocks that might be in its path, so "rockhopper" became its name. It featured a pressurized cabin, so that the astronauts could remove their suits, although the manual noted that the cabin pressurization was not a redundant system, and they should always wear a pressure suit when the vehicle was in motion. It was built for a crew of two.

The rockhopper was an odd-looking vehicle. The crew pressure vessel was a decahedron of green-anodized aluminum-lithium alloy, with pentagonal viewports of transparent silicon carbide that gave the crew windows that looked ahead, ahead and down, and downward to the left and right. Mounted in front of the crew cabin was a jointed robotic arm that could be used to pick up samples, tip rocks out of the way, or even lift up one of the dirt-rovers and carry it over an obstacle. Behind the crew cabin was the drivetrain and the power plant, thermal radiator wings, pressure tanks for consumables, and a small omnidirectional antenna that could transmit either to the orbital relay satellite or back to the habitat module. Every spot of bare metal was either blanketed by layers of flimsy gold multilayer insulation, or else anodized in the distinctly un-Martian color of lime green.

After Tana and Commander Radkowski unloaded it from its storage bin, it unfolded like a spider. The whole vehicle sat on six wheeled legs, each leg a short triangular truss with an independently powered, wire mesh wheel at the end. The legs were articulated, and could be lifted or dropped to clear obstacles. It seemed surrealistically complicated. The effect was rather that of a mad Victorian metalwright's mechanical octopus.

With Radkowski in the cabin, the legs straightened under it and it stood up to its fullest extent, stiff-legged, the cabin at the top of a tower almost twenty feet in the air. Then it squatted down, and stood up again, and then lifted up one leg at a time, doing mechanical calisthenics as Radkowski checked the mechanical systems.

"Checks out," Radkowski's voice said. "I'm ready to take it out for a checkout cruise. Ryan, you there?"

"Right here," he said.

"Okay. Stay listening on this channel and ready to fetch me in case I have mechanical difficulties."

"Copy," Ryan said. "You expecting problems?"

"Just going by the book."

The rockhopper set out, the legs rolling up and down with the terrain with a weirdly organic floating motion. Ryan watched it climb up the nearby dune, vanish into the valley, and then reappear on the face of the next dune.

Then it was out of sight.

"Come on," Estrela said. "You're supposed to keep listening, the boss said, he didn't tell you to just sit there. Now, come on. You drive like a baby. First, you have to learn how to get traction. Watch me. When you start up, you lean over like *this* . . ."

22

Once again, Trevor thought, the commander has told him to stay inside while the others—the *adults* of the expedition—went outside and were doing the *fun* things. He was afraid, he said, that Trevor would slow them down or get in the way.

Trevor was beginning to hate the commander. It seemed to him that Ryan and Estrela were having the time of their lives riding the dirt bikes, and piloting the enormous rockhopper vehicle looked like it would be a blast. He had practiced it enough times in the virtual reality simulation; he bet he could pilot it a whole lot better than the commander could. But, no, he had to stay inside while the adults played.

Tana was inside with him, but that hardly made it any more fun. She was wearing a set of headphones to monitor the conversation from the outside, and meanwhile was calling up Mars maps from the computer, seated at the copilot's station with her back to him. Quite pointedly ignoring him.

So screw her.

Yeah, if only he could do just that. Tana was, in fact, a bit reticent about showing off her body to the men on the crew. Quote unlike Estrela, who sometimes seemed to be deliberately showing off her curves. Nevertheless, in the months together on the ship, when he thought she wasn't looking, he had seen plenty of Tana's body while she was exercising or changing. Lean and muscular, with dark brown skin that was—when she was exercising, anyway—shiny with sweat, he could just imagine her legs wrapped around him, his hands caressing the slippery chocolate skin—

Yeah, sure. As if she had ever looked at him twice. Not likely. Time to think about something else, guy. Think about music, how about.

Trevor sang stomp songs inside his head. The stomp lyrics were as if they were spoken directly to him, only to him. Negative Ions was his favorite band, and no one else could ever understand how their songs were beamed directly to him:

Abbas abd'el Sami, he's the sultan of the sands
He's the prince over the desert, he's a prophet in his land
His only home's a silken tent, he wanders with the wind
With the sighing of the lonely desert wind

That's me, Trevor thought. I'm Abbas abd'el Sami; wandering with the wind.

"Stop it," Tana said without turning around.

Was she talking to him? "Stop what?"

"Stop your bouncing around. You're shaking the whole spacecraft."

He had been tapping his toes to the music in his head. Well, he'd been dancing, just a little. *Yeah? So, suffer,* he thought, but he knew better than to say it. Tana outranked him on the crew—everybody here seemed to outrank him—and it would be unwise to cross her openly. If he did, he might *never* get a chance to ride one of the dirtbikes.

Trevor knew that he was, in fact, the celebrity on board. Estrela had her half-hour recording session every day to send her messages to her fans in Brazil back on Earth, and Chamlong had recorded his messages in Thai and in Cantonese to send back to his supporters, but as for the rest of the crew, whenever there was an interview, Trevor got more questions than the rest of the crew put together. Even the potatoes born in the last century knew who he was, not to mention the fame he had among the stompers and the bubblerazz generation. If things got really bad, he might be able to use his popularity back on Earth as a tool to get what he wanted. But he wasn't ready to try that quite yet.

The others had gotten onto the expedition due to hard work, exhaustive training, and study. Trevor's place on the *Don Quijote* was the result of luck.

After the catastrophe of the *Agamemnon* expedition, there had been a series of investigations and a sharp backlash against space. The public pressure to shut down the program meant that there was no possibility of paying for a launch with public funds.

But the ships for a second Mars expedition—the ships that would later be named *Don Quijote* and *Dulcinea*—had already been built. *Dulcinea* was already waiting, already on Mars; it had been launched to Mars at the same time as the *Ulysses*, a backup in case of a failure. And *Don Quijote* was all but finished and ready for launch.

The result had been a compromise. The ship could be completed and outfitted for a second expedition, as long as no government money was used.

As a result, the *Don Quijote* expedition was an unusual mixture of high and low technology. The expensive one-of-a-kind payload of the *Agamemnon* expedition had not been duplicated. There would be no billion-dollar

Mars airplane such as the fragile *Butterfly* that the *Agamemnon* had taken to Mars but never used. Instead, the rockhopper and dirt-rover vehicles had been designed and donated by Mitsubishi America and by Mercedes-Ford. But even with such donations from around the world, the expedition needed almost four billion dollars in hard currency to launch.

Thailand, the economic giant of Asia ever since the collapse of the Chinese government in 2011, had contributed a billion dollars in exchange for their participation. Brazil, poorer but still ambitious, had contributed an equal amount. The remaining money had come from a lottery.

One crew slot on the expedition was allocated for the winner of the lottery. Anybody could enter. If they were over twenty-one and under sixty, could pass the Class IV pilot's physical, and could make it all the way through the training process, the grand prize winner would get to be picked to go on the mission.

A ticket in the lottery cost one thousand dollars. Nearly two million tickets had been sold. Trevor Whitman and his little brother Brandon had each bought thirty.

The winner of the lottery had been a fifty-seven-year-old woman from Long Island. She had been given a ticket as an anniversary gift by her grandchildren. When she was told that the prize was not transferable, and she couldn't let her son take her place on the expedition, she chose to take the ten-million-dollar second-place prize instead. "Goodness," she had said. "It's quite an honor, and I'm sure that it would be a lot of fun, but two years away from my home and my family? I couldn't possibly."

The second drawing picked a personal-injury lawyer in Cincinnati. He failed to pass the physical: He was overweight and had a minor heart arrhythmia, either of which factors would have precluded him from flying. He was given another ten-million-dollar consolation prize, and a third drawing was held.

The winner of the third drawing was an adolescent from Scottsdale, Arizona, named Trevor Whitman. Over the course of an hour, he went from being an obscure rich kid to being the most famous boy in the world.

If there was any person who seemed born for the expedition, it was Trevor Whitman. He was an Eagle scout, an adept horseman, skilled in rock climbing, and an amateur musician. More important, he was in perfect health. Despite this, though, through the whole training sequence he had felt that the rest of the crew viewed him as not really qualified for the mission—an impostor. None of the other crew members said anything of the sort, of course, but he knew what they must be thinking it. Every time he screwed up a suit check, or crashed the ship in one of the emergency scenarios that they practiced continuously (not that they would ever let him fly the ship, even in an emergency)—whenever he failed a task, he could

imagine them watching him, judging. He was an impostor. They were waiting for—even expecting—him to fail.

It made him nervous, and being nervous made him screw up even more.
There was nothing he could do about it.

23

IN TRAINING

"**W**hy are we so interested in going to Mars?" the lecturer had asked. He was a tall man with a potbelly and a huge black beard who waved his hands around as if he were washing invisible windows with his thumbs. He talked as if he were trying to keep up with thoughts that raced faster than he could speak; sometimes he tried to go too fast, and his words jumbled and stuck like cars in a traffic jam.

"Because it's stomping cool," Trevor answered.

"Right!" the lecturer said. "Right, right right! It's way cool. But just *why* is it way cool?"

"Giant volcanoes," Angie Kovalcik said. Angie was Trevor's backup. She had won the second-place drawing. If Trevor screwed up, got sick, or for some reason was washed out of the mission, she would take his place. She was a forty-year-old housewife from New Jersey, the wife of a dentist, and in Trevor's opinion had no right to even be considered for the mission. But when she had been told—on international television—that the second-place winner in the lottery could chose to train as a backup for the mission instead of taking the two-million-dollar second-place consolation prize, she'd said yes without even a heartbeat's worth of hesitation.

She worked out in the gym for an hour and a half each day, and her dedication and physical shape made Trevor look like a slacker. Worse, everybody liked her. She had a knack for getting along with people, a skill that Trevor had never quite learned, and her two teenaged boys—cheering, "Go, mom, go!"—played well on television, getting almost as much air time as Trevor himself did.

Trevor hated her.

She was a constant threat at his back, seeming to whisper to him that if there's anything wrong, if they find out that you're not qualified, if you screw up . . . He knew that if they ever found out his secret, they would boot him off the team, and it was eating him away to be constantly reminded that he had a rival who would slide into his place in an instant.

Even worse, she honestly seemed to like him. She was constantly smiling, giving him advice and asking him for his, even baking cookies and acting as though she were his mom. Didn't she realize that they were worst enemies?

They were in Houston, training, taking a crash course that was meant to bring them up to date on everything known about Mars. The instructor who was drilling them right now, Alexander Volynskji, was a biologist or a geologist or something. They were in a large lecture hall at the Lunar and Planetary Institute, although Trevor and Angie were his only two students.

"Volcanoes, sure," he said, waving his hands dismissively. "Sure, everybody loves volcanoes. But we're not going to Mars to look for volcanoes. Why are we going? One word: life!"

"But there is no life on Mars," Trevor said.

"No life on Mars?" The lecturer looked at Trevor as if he were a second grader who had just confidently stated that the sun revolved around the Earth. Then he seemed to change his mind, bobbing his head and then shrugging. "Well, okay. Certainly that's what most scientists think. I guess I'm just a heretic, an old-fashioned Percival Lowell who just refuses to see the evidence.

"But answer me this, young man. We know that life started on Earth damn near just as soon as the crust had cooled down enough to allow liquid water to pool. Now, we know that Mars was once a warmer and wetter planet. Sure, it's a cold dry desert now, but it once had liquid water, maybe even oceans. So why shouldn't we think that it once had life?"

"So you're saying that we will be looking for fossils?" Angie said.

I will be looking for fossils, Trevor corrected, not *we*. But he kept that to himself.

"Well, sure," Volynskji said. "Absolutely, no question, certainly. Look for fossils, yes indeed. But that's not all you should keep your eyes out for. Look, what do we know about life on Earth? We know it's tenacious. It lives in hot springs, at bottoms of glaciers, even on the insides of rocks. Every possible niche, what do you find? You find life.

"If there was ever life on Mars—and I tell you there was, there had to have been!—If there was life, I say it is still there. Life is tenacious. Once it got a toehold, it's going to survive, it is going to adapt and evolve and find a way to hold on.

"Mars is dead? Sure, sure, that's the conventional wisdom. But I, Alexander Volynskji, tell you, don't be so sure. Maybe the robot probes couldn't find life. But don't close your eyes.

"Somewhere, maybe in hot springs hidden away deep inside caverns, maybe inside some volcanic crevice, maybe buried beneath the surface— somewhere, there will be life.

"Now, let me tell you about a rock from Antarctica . . ."

24

PROBLEMS

There were too many problems with his plan. Ryan started to write them down on a sheet of paper.

One, he wrote. *We don't know if* Jesus do Sul *even still works.*

Two. It could save only three of the crew.

The Brazilian expedition had only sent two astronauts, and their return ship had not been designed with any thought of carrying a five-person crew. If they left out the Martian rocks and ice samples that the Brazilian expedition would have carried back, Ryan calculated, they would be able to easily get three of them onto the ship. But not, by any calculation, five.

He thought for a moment, then scratched it off his list. The others hadn't been forced to face it yet, but Ryan knew that every one of them would die if they tried to stay here. Saving three of them was a step forward, not a drawback. He looked up to make sure that nobody was watching him, then went over it and obliterated the note he had written with heavy black lines until it was completely illegible. The *Jesus do Sul* was their only chance, and if they could only save three, it would be best to just not mention that fact until they actually made it to the pole. If they got to the pole.

Two, he wrote. *Valles Marineris.*

The enormous Valles Marineris stretched like a huge barrier across their path. They would have to cross it to get to the northern hemisphere. But the key to the expedition would be the rockhopper, the six-wheeled, pressurized Mars rover, and how would they carry the rockhopper up and down a vertical cliff two miles high?

They'd have to deal with it somehow.

Three, he wrote. *Can we carry enough consumables?*

Oxygen would come from the zirconia cells in their suits and the larger zirconia electrolyzer built into the rockhopper; as long as they had power, they would be able to break down carbon dioxide for oxygen to breathe.

But what if they malfed? Could they carry enough spare parts? Could they carry enough food?

Four, he wrote. *Breakdowns*. The rockhopper would eventually break down; it had an expected time before failure of only one thousand kilometers. When it failed—

Five, he wrote. *Not enough range.*

That was the killer problem: simple distance. Ryan Martin plotted it, and came up short. They didn't have enough range. He replotted, and even with more optimistic assumptions, there was simply no way that they could make it to the north pole. They just didn't have the range. It was just impossible.

He leaned back and rubbed his eyes to think. There was only one other place on Mars that humans had been. Acidalia.

The landing site of the ill-fated second expedition to Mars.

Painstakingly, Ryan began to plot the path to Acidalia.

25

INDECISIVE
DECISIONS

It was a wild idea, and John Radkowski distrusted wild ideas. A desperate journey to the pole, on an unlikely chance that they could salvage the Brazilian ship? Ryan Martin was a danger. He was too young, and had too strong a tendency to go off on a wild idea without paying attention to caution.

The cautious thing to do would be to stay right where they were.

But they would die.

They would probably die if they headed to the pole.

It was an impossible dilemma. John Radkowski didn't like dilemmas. For every problem, he had always believed, there was one right solution. But this problem didn't seem to have a right solution.

Radkowski still wondered if it had been some error of Ryan's that had killed Chamlong. He would have to hold Ryan Martin back. It might be tough; Ryan had a great feel for machines but no common sense.

With his right hand, John Radkowski rubbed the place where three fingers were missing on his left hand. He often did this when he was uncertain or worried; he didn't even notice that he was doing it. Caressing the rough scar tissue gave him a sort of tactile comfort: Whatever came, he could survive it.

The crew was looking to him for guidance, but he didn't have any better solutions to offer. He knew that of all the things that a commander could do, the decision that was always wrong was to be indecisive. Better to be wrong, and boldly wrong, than to dither over the right solution.

But that didn't mean to act without learning the facts. "Check the maps and orbital photographs, and give me a briefing in two days," he'd told Martin.

But now the two days were over, and he was no closer to an idea of what to do than when he'd started.

They would die if they stayed.

There really wasn't a choice. Desperate and stupid as the idea was, it was their only chance. They had to go.

He let nothing of his feelings show when he called the crew together.

"Engineer Martin has explained his plan to you," he said. "I'm not going to lie to you and say that it's going to be easy; it's not. It's a tough haul, and it's not clear whether it's even possible at all.

"You have discussed it among yourselves. Ryan has come up with some refinements of his plan, but before we go any further, I want to hear from you. All I want from you is one single word. Do we accept his plan or not? Yes or no.

"Martin, we know your opinion. Doctor Jackson?"

Tana nodded.

"Say it," Radkowski said.

"It's our only chance."

"I take that for yes. Ms. Conselheiro?"

Her eyes were shadowed. "We die here. I don't like that choice."

"Your vote?"

"I vote to live."

"Mr. Whitman?"

"I haven't heard any better of a choice, have you? Hell, let's stomp."

Radkowski nodded. The decision was made, and they had bought into it. He didn't even have to vote himself.

Under the circumstances, that was the best he could hope for.

"Then it's decided," he said. "Get yourselves ready. We leave tomorrow at first light."

26

There is a visceral feeling to piloting a jet fighter that can never quite be described. It is a feeling of power and of control, of riding a bestial strength tamed just barely enough to respond with fury to your least suggestion of stick pressure. John Radkowski would never admit it, but if there had ever been a choice between the two, he would rather fly than have sex. In its way, piloting the F-22 fighter was better than sex.

Two years at the Eastthorpe Military Academy, paid for by his brother's drug dealing, and four years of ROTC at New York University had changed Johnny Radkowski. He was no longer the rebellious punk from the projects. He had learned caution and discipline. His classmates admired him, but none of them were particularly close to him.

He's got the killer instinct, his Air Force flight instructor wrote in his recommendation for him to move on to train on fighters. He was not, in actual point of fact, a spectacularly good pilot; he was more than competent, but he would never reach that mystic fusion of the machine with his own nervous system, the unity with the machine that marks the very best pilots. But what he lacked in finesse, he made up for in sheer determination. *The kid has guts*, his flight instructor wrote.

So John Radkowski, bad boy from the bad side of Queens, became a fighter pilot. A year later he was flying fighter escort for the relief missions in Africa.

It was a stupid, dirty little war, or rather, a tangled matrix of wars, all linked together in hard-to-understand ways. Nobody in the fighter corps really knew what they were fighting for, or why.

"We're talking a mix of colonialism, neocolonialism, tribalism, religious conflicts, foreign troops, modern weapons, economic decline, political aspirations, international debts, racism, nationalism and pan-nationalism," the briefing officer had told them, before they had first shipped out for Africa.

He was reading from a list that had been prepared in a book. "Don't even try to understand it. We've got a job to do, and we're going to do the best we can."

That evening he had been flying escort for a bomber. Columns of greasy black smoke rose from burning rebel camps like signal fires to reticulate the African sky. However many camps, or purported camps, they had bombed, there were always more.

The African unification wars were going badly for all sides.

He had been enjoying the flying, coming back from a run over territory that had been cleared as friendly. He was not paying any attention to anything in particular when an antique Russian heatseeking SAM leaped away from a crag below and homed in on his wingman. He cued his mike. "Bravo, Alpha, looks like you've picked up a hitchhiker."

A laconic reply. "I got him." The jet next to him hit afterburners and rocketed upward, trailing flame. The missile, outclassed, fell away and then curved off to crash somewhere distant in the African twilight.

By luck, Radkowski had been looking in the right direction and had gotten a good fix on the hilltop the missile had come from. He made a wide turn and came back around and down, holding close to the treetops and then pulling up into position to rake the mountaintop with cannon fire. He cued his mike. "I'm gonna teach the bastards a brief lesson," he said.

"Teach 'em good, Radko," his wingman replied.

Only at the last minute did he see the face in his sights, a boy who could not have been any older than nine, frightened and alone, the empty missile launcher discarded at his feet. And then his cannon fire blew apart the hilltop, and the face disappeared into smoke and rock dust.

The face continued to haunt his nights for years.

After that night, he put in a transfer to fly evacuation transports. It was a lower prestige job, and the word that spread in the fighter squadron was that he'd lost his nerve. Nobody said that to his face, though.

Flying evacuation was better. He could at least pretend that he was helping people, ferrying endless planeloads of refugees, pencil-thin and nearly naked, each one carrying all of their belongings held wrapped up in a cloth or in a molded plastic basket balanced precariously on his head. The refugee camps outside Bangalore were not paradise, but they were better than the war zone. He could tell himself that he was saving lives.

It was no safer than flying fighters, and already he had been hit twice. The first one was a lucky rifle shot from the ground that had penetrated the transport's sheet-metal skin right between his feet and ricocheted around the cabin. It had shattered the glass on his instruments, but done no actual damage. The second hit was from a surface-to-air missile that had detonated close enough to rip his right aileron to shreds. Despite the loss of control, he had babied the transport down to a flawless landing right on the numbers at the Diego Garcia airfield. After that, with no injuries from either hit, his ground crew started called him by a new nickname: Lucky Radkowski.

The third time he was not so lucky. Taking advantage of heavy cloud cover to hide from watching satellites, the Splinter faction of the Unification Army had set up an antiaircraft battery on the coast, in the mistaken belief that the evacuation transports were French bombers supporting the rebel Ugandan Liberation Front. The evacuation fleet flew right over it. Stoddart, on his left, took a hit dead center. Ritchmann, on his right, took fire that ripped off his left wing, and fell, in pieces, to the beach. Radkowski's luck still held. The first SAM hit took out his outboard left engine and half his fuel. The second took out both his right engines.

Leaking oil and fuel, there was no way he could make the base at Diego Garcia on his one remaining engine. He broke radio silence—little point in it, now. "November seven two niner to base, two niner to base. Mayday, Mayday, Mayday. I'm hit."

"Copy, November seven two niner. Can you make it as far as Mahajanga?"

"Will try." He checked the charts, although he had memorized them long ago. Madagascar, if not friendly territory, at least was noncombatant.

He coaxed the damaged bird as far as he could, but even Madagascar turned out to be too much to hope. He ditched over open ocean.

The last thing he remembered, as the dark water came up like a fist to meet the airplane, was a fierce joy. It is over, he thought. My debt is paid. And then, immediately after, he remembered the refugees he was carrying, and thought, no! They have nobody. *For he shall give his angels charge over thee*, he thought, *to keep thee in all thy ways.*

And then the water hit, and the airplane broke apart and sank.

Later, they said he was a hero. They said that he saved half the refugees.

He had been clinging to a shred of floating wreckage for over five hours when the rescue helicopter pulled him out of the water, in shock, bleeding, and semiconscious from blood loss and exposure. A shark had bitten off half his hand, and then apparently found other food in the wreckage. He didn't even remember it.

Post-traumatic amnesia, the medical examiners told him. Don't worry about it. Maybe the memories would surface later.

Maybe they wouldn't.

He had already been accepted into the astronaut corps. The evacuation had been his last mission in Africa.

27

"Hello, Earth! Hello, stompers and rats and all the hominid life-forms on that big fuzzy ball we call home. This is Trevor Whitman, station T-R-E-V, your intrepid reporter, calling in from the pink planet, Mars.

"This is taped, but Commander Radkowski assures me that he'll put it up to play to Earth over the low-gain antenna overnight, so you'll be hearing this tomorrow, I guess. Anyway, tomorrow our time, that is!

"I'm sure you're all watching our epic trek across the red desert back there. Mars is after us big time, but we're not dead yet. I'm reporting in that we've got a tough goal of a hundred and fifty miles to cover on day one of our epic adventure, and we're raring to get going.

"Uh, I guess Commander Radkowski has told you that we're not going to be receiving your broadcasts once we start moving, so I won't be answering mail this time. Something to do with the high-gain antenna back at the *Don Quijote*. I don't know the technical stuff; I guess the commander told you all that stuff anyway, right? I have to admit here that I guess I sort of slept through some of the lectures about communications links and bandwidth and all that techno stuff. Anyway, I'm not receiving right now, but just keep those questions coming, right, and I guess they'll forward them on to me when we get the communications from Earth back up.

"Uh, it's been a great trip so far—I can tell you that for certain, once we get moving we are going to be seeing more of Mars than any other humans in history. I mean, that's going to be some kind of record. It's real big, there's a lot of Mars to see, and they tell me just wait, it gets better.

"So stay tuned, okay? Don't forget about us up here.

"So this is Trevor Whitman, your main man on Mars, signing off.

"Bye, Earth!

"Okay, that's it. Okay, Earth? Mission control? Is there a mission control out there? Okay, don't broadcast this part, okay? Look, things out here aren't real good. I don't know, but I think we're in trouble. We need a rescue ship here, okay? Look, the commander tells me that it's impossible, there isn't enough time, but don't listen to him, okay? Just send a rescue ship. We need a rescue ship. I don't believe it when he says you won't do it. Look, we're going to die up here, and that's going to be, like, major bad publicity, and you can count on that. Big-time bad publicity. So send help.

"Send help.

"Help.

"Please?"

PART TWO

ESTRELA CONSELHERIO

The destruction and abandonment of the ship was no sudden shock. The disaster had been looming ahead for many months, and I had studied my plans for all contingencies a hundred times . . . The task now was to secure the safety of the party, and to that I must bend my energies and mental powers and apply every bit of knowledge that experience of the Antarctic had given me. The task was likely to be long and strenuous, and an ordered mind and a clear program were essential if we were to come through without loss of life . . .

—Ernest Shackelton, *South* (1919)

Our nature lies in movement. Complete calm is death.

—Blaise Pascal

1

N I G H T

Estrela would never tell it to other members of the crew, but the nightmares were coming again. In the middle of the night she would be alone, huddling in the dark, terror squeezing her ribs, afraid to breathe or move or make a sound. The purple afterimage of rifle fire faded away from her eyes and the urine stink of fear clogged her nostrils, far more real and more vivid than the smells of the ship or the sounds of the sleeping crew or the whir of the air circulation fans. Her ears straining at the darkness for sounds that she hoped she would never again hear.

She didn't know why she was alive.

João had been the only one who could take the nightmares away, and João was dead. She clung to his memory, the one real thing she knew, and refused to cry.

They were going to die.

2

J O U R N E Y

The journey started before dawn.

Estrela and Ryan set out first to scout the terrain ahead of them on the two dirt-rovers, heading north and east from the landing site. The dirt-rovers were laden down with supplies: spare zirconia cells, bubble tents, fuel cells and solar arrays, repair tools and extra parts for the dirt-rovers along with a spare thermophotovoltaic isotope generator, superfiber cable and a winch and pitons, water, and fifty days' supply of the highly condensed and nearly tasteless bricks of food that the astronauts referred to as Purina Human Chow. The main supplies for the expedition would be carried on the rockhopper, of course, but they had loaded up the dirt-rovers to the limits of their carrying capacity in order to haul the maximum amount of support equipment on the expedition north. Their survival, they all knew, would depend on their forethought in bringing with them the equipment that they needed.

Northward and eastward.

The ground was smooth, easy traveling even for the overloaded little dirt-rovers, and as they moved the dust hung in the still air behind them like a pale yellow fog. They were traveling in a flat-floored valley between parallel ridges on either side.

The predawn light was orangish red. Ryan had intended to take the point position, with Estrela following, but she had quickly grown annoyed with his pace and took the lead without asking.

"Don't get too far ahead," he radioed to her.

"Relax," she said. "No problem."

A few kilometers down the trail, Ryan stopped his dirt-rover atop a small rise and got off. He had told himself that he would not look back, but after five minutes, he couldn't help himself. *Don Quijote* stood on the side of a small dune, surrounded by the deflated airbags and tilted at a drunken angle, looking as if it would topple over at any moment. Behind her in the distance was *Dulcinea*. From here, it was impossible to guess that anything was wrong.

It looked so forlorn. He knew that he would never see them again. He had a sudden urge to turn back, that there must be some way to fix the problem, but he knew it was impossible.

Ryan got back on his dirt-rover and started the engine. The next time he looked back he was ten kilometers away, and the *Don Quijote* had disappeared over the horizon. There was nothing but gentle undulations of sand stretching as far as he could see.

Estrela's dirt-rover had vanished ahead of him, but he could tell where she was by the plume of dust hanging in the air. He concentrated on following the tracks of her rover, distinct enough in the sand to follow easily. From time to time her voice would come in over the radio to remark on a possible obstacle or an interesting landmark, but for the most part they rode in silence.

The flatness of the terrain was broken by the occasional crater. At first he detoured around them, but after a while he saw that Estrela's tracks didn't deviate at all, and he started following. Up, teeter at the crest, and then down like a roller coaster to the flat, sand-covered bottom, then again at the other side.

During the drive, he mulled over their situation. Slowly, he began to convince himself that it might not be as bad as he'd thought. The Brazilians had surely put some margins of safety into their return ship. Engineers always plan for a worst case. If they would shave every single ounce of excess weight and rely on using up all of the safety margin, it was quite likely that they would be able to fly five back on the *Jesus do Sul*. He would work the numbers again as soon as he got a chance. He had been right, he told himself, not to alarm the crew by bringing up the problem of who should return. Hell, it would be a jinx to dwell on the possibility, but it was not out of the question that one of them might die on the trip north. It would be a tragedy, but surely the *Jesus do Sul* would be able to launch four. Four might be no problem at all.

"Rover one, Radkowski," Commander Radkowski's voice came over the radio. "Anything to report?"

Ryan slowed down and cued his radio. "The way has been fine," he said. "Mostly compacted sand. A few rocky outcroppings and some boulders, but nothing we haven't been able to go around."

"Got it. Okay, we've packed up here and we're setting out. Stay in touch."

Behind them, the rockhopper set out.

3

RIDING THE
ROCKHOPPER

At first Trevor found it exciting. All through the morning, there were constantly new vistas, every mile a new planet, fresh and exciting. The occasional dry voice of Ryan or, less often, Estrela, broke in on the radio to apprise them of landmarks ahead. The six-wheel suspension kept the rockhopper level, and it moved over the sand with a motion more like a boat than a wheeled vehicle.

For Trevor, the drive was disconcerting. It continually seemed to him that they had made a mistake, that they had circled around and were heading south, instead of north. He would look at the inertial guidance readout on the rockhopper's console, and think, That's wrong. We're going the wrong way. But then he would look at the sun, and realize, no we're going the right way. And then the entire planet would seem to spin around him for a moment until he was reoriented.

Mars confused his sense of direction.

Three of them in the cabin of a Mars rover designed for two was one too many. They were crammed together so tight that Trevor could barely move without hitting one of the others with his elbow.

After a while watching Mars was almost hypnotic. It didn't really change. One ridge of yellowish stone would dwindle down to a wall no higher than his waist and then disappear, and be replaced by another just like it. When they got closer to a ridge, he saw that the surfaces were smooth, blasted by millennia of sand to a soft, pillowed surface.

The sky was a sheet of hammered bronze.

"That one looks like a bear," he said.

No one answered him. It was a boulder the size of a small house, half-buried in the sand, with a rough, dark gray surface, almost black. A chunk of lava that had been thrown out by one of the enormous volcanoes? Trevor wished that he had paid more attention in training to the geologists. When they had gone out on the training field trip to El Paso, the geologists had been ecstatic to point out minute details of the shapes and textures of the rocks they saw, but Trevor had forgotten most of it.

It did look like a bear, crouching with its head turned away.

Trevor hummed, softly so as not to attract unwelcome attention from the others. It was too cramped to tap his feet, but he cracked the joints in his toes to the beat of the music in his head. The rockhopper's wheels bumping over Martian rocks set up a syncopated percussion line, and inside his head, Negative Ions accompanied it with a stomp soundtrack:

> *—though no voyage has an ending,*
> *though the winds forbid returning,*
> *still our path is ever onward,*
> *even yet we're on our journey.*

4

COMPARISONS

It was all his fault.

John Radkowski thought about his brother like a dog worrying at a wound, knowing that it hurts, but unable to keep from chewing at it.

Karl had been a hero, not him. In the moment of truth, he had failed to speak up. He had run.

And now, he had not run far enough. The expedition was failing; his leadership was failing, and it was all his fault.

It was his fault.

His fault.

To the others in the crew, the expedition to Mars was the fulfillment of a dream. From childhood they had wanted to see the small blue planet dwindle to no more than one bright star among a million others, and know that they were on their way, part of something larger than themselves, the expansion of humanity into the cosmos.

John Radkowski had not looked at the stars. His brother Karl had told him what to do: Get out of the projects, get away from the gangs, go as far away from here as you can get and don't ever look back.

To John Radkowski, leading the expedition to Mars was nothing more than following his brother's instructions. And, driving across the desolation, he had only one thought:

What would Karl do?

5

THE CALCULUS OF
SACRIFICE

Estrela drove her dirt-rover as far and as fast as she could. She barely paid any attention to the scenery, and she had turned her radio to the "emergency only" setting, where only a priority-one page would beep through to her.

Estrela had some thinking to do.

When Ryan Martin had proposed his plan, she had instantly noticed the huge and disturbing fact that Ryan failed to present to the rest of the crew. She knew the *Jesus do Sul* very well. She, more than anybody else, knew that at its heart Brazil was still a poor country, and that the mission had no luxuries, nothing extra—not even the capability to return more than few grams of Martian dust.

The margin that Ryan Martin had been counting on did not exist.

The Brazilian Mars mission hadn't been designed to carry samples back. Perhaps once, in the optimistic days when first the mission had been designed, the sample return had been real. But by the time that *Jesus do Sul* was being built, Brazil was in the slow process of national bankruptcy. There was no money for extras. *Jesus do Sul* was, first and foremost, a public-relations mission, designed to show off the expertise of an insolvent nation in a desperate attempt to attract investors from outside, richer nations. The well-publicized two hundred kilograms of rocks to be returned, the weight that Ryan had counted on leaving behind, was a carefully crafted fiction.

The Brazilian ship had not been designed to carry back even one kilogram of rocks. João had explained it all to her one evening, slowly and patiently. With any extra payload it would fail to get into orbit. The Brazilians had sent an expedition of two; they could return an expedition of two. Two astronauts, and not a kilogram more, was what their return ship was capable of launching home.

She had remained silent. If Ryan Martin did not mention to the crew that his plan could, at best, only save two of them, why should she?

The fact that he had left it out frightened her as much as anything else. It showed that he knew that their situation was desperate, and that in his opinion sacrificing some members of the crew would be an improvement on their current situation. He was afraid that the crew would panic if they knew. At that moment, she knew that they must be very close to death.

Could it possibly be that he didn't know? The specifications of the *Jesus do Sul* were not public knowledge. Could he possibly believe that they could cram five people into a ship that had been designed for two? It seemed unlikely.

Estrela turned her head to take a sip from the nipple of the drinking bottle. The suits had not been designed for long-term use; until she took her helmet off, the electrolyte-replacement drink would be the only nourishment she'd get. She reminded herself not to suck too much; it would have to last. But the thought only made her thirstier.

The alternative was slightly more sinister. Suppose that Ryan Martin did know that only two of them could return to Earth. Could he have a reason to keep this fact secret?

Clearly, he intended to be one of those persons.

A trek to the north pole would be an ambitious traverse even for a fully functional, well-planned mission. It would take the skills of the full team of five to make it. Once they got to the north pole, though, three of the five must somehow be persuaded to remain on Mars. The easiest way to do that would be to make sure that three of them were already dead.

She knew what it was like to have to kill for her life. When it comes to a matter of life or death, anybody would learn to lie and to kill.

Any way she looked at it, Ryan Martin looked to her like a killer.

6

A CHILDHOOD IN RIO

Whenever anybody would ask her where she came from, Estrela Carolina Conselheiro would tell them she was from Ipanema. "I'm the girl from Ipanema," she said, tossing her head and smiling. "Just like in the song."

It was a lie. She was from Rio, yes, but although the mother she could barely remember had given birth to her no more than ten kilometers from the chic restaurants and boutiques of the Visconde de Piraja, Ipanema might as well have been farther away than the moon.

Most of her history was a lie. She had not grown up sheltered, staying out of public schools with a private tutor. Her parents, she said, had been an artist and a successful businesswoman who had been killed in the earthquake and fire of 2009, the same fire that destroyed her birth records. It was quite plausible. Earthquakes are so uncommon in Brazil that the 2009 earthquake, catching Rio completely unprepared, had devastated a large portion of the city, including many records. It was also completely untrue.

She had grown up on the streets. She had her virginity taken away by age seven, and seen her first man killed with a knife at age nine. All she knew about the beaches of Ipanema was that, if you were caught shoplifting there, after they shot you they would take your body up to Madureira to dump it, so as not to frighten the tourists away.

Her brother Gilberto had taught her how to read. He had been all the family she ever had. "You have to learn to read, Estrela," he had told her. "Then, one day, when you've become rich, we'll kill them all." His smile gleamed in the dim light. He had been completely serious.

But there was no way they would ever become rich.

They survived by stealing, begging, selling drugs for the gangs when they could, and going through garbage when there was nothing to steal and nothing to beg and no European tourists to sell drugs to. When there was no garbage, they ate nothing. Gilberto would offer to sell her body when he thought he could find a taker who would pay for the thrill of sex with a girl not yet even close to puberty, but most of the customers he offered her to would only curl up their lips in disdain. There was little market for a whore that was starved and dirty and probably diseased.

That life ended when she was eleven.

It had been a warm night, and a full moon shone down on the alleys. She slept huddled up against Gilberto, for the little comfort it gave her rather than for warmth.

Gilberto was flatlined. He had stolen a quarter of a liter of gasoline and had spent the evening with his head in a bag, inhaling the fumes. Once he passed it over to her, and she had tried it as well, sticking her head into the bag and taking a big inhalation from the gas-soaked rag, but she had gone reeling back, her head singing from the fumes, her nose suddenly feeling as if cockroaches had crawled inside her nostrils and were clawing around somewhere above her mouth. Gilberto watched her and laughed, his eyes red and swollen from the fumes.

Now he was asleep, fallen over on his back with his mouth wide open, not even hidden away in a doorway. His instincts, his secret antennae that sensed trouble before it showed itself, his secret sense that had kept them both alive, had failed him, blotted away by gasoline fumes.

The policemen were not quiet. They came down the alley with flash-lights so bright that they hurt her eyes, swinging their rifles like clubs. She tugged at Gilberto's arm frantically, and at last he moved. He looked up, his eyes out of focus and leaking a gummy fluid, said "Huh," and then threw up a thin stream of watery yellow.

It would not have mattered even if they had run. The police had block-aded both ends of the alley. She couldn't see the faces of the policemen; they were wearing riot helmets with darkened bulletproof visors lowered down over their eyes. One grabbed her arm and pulled her to her feet, than shoved her down the alley. She staggered and ran, and another policeman hit her with a rifle-butt and knocked her down again. Guided by blows from the butts of guns, she and Gilberto were herded down the alley until they were crowded together with a dozen other street urchins, ranging in age from four to almost fifteen.

She knew almost all of them, the children who lived on the streets. When they had extra, they would share it with her, and she with them. The had no loyalty and no love, but they were as close a thing to friends as she had ever known.

No one talked to her, no one ventured a reason for the roundup, nor did she expect to hear one. Perhaps a policeman had been killed up in one of the favelas, and they were exacting revenge. Perhaps a merchant had complained of shoplifting, or of shit bespoiling the street, and the police had decided to clean out the human vermin. Maybe there was no reason. Street children in Rio did not expect to live very long.

She was kicked, and then picked up and tossed against the brick wall. She looked up, stunned and bleeding. She knew this place. It was an empty lot where a building had been torn down two years earlier. They had slept there for several weeks, until the people who owned it has seen fit to send guards around to kick them out. Was that it? Were they still mad that they had had squatters? Where was Gilberto? She couldn't see him.

Somewhere in the darkness, one of the policemen shoved a cassette of the Rolling Stones into a portable stereo tape player and turned up the volume. It was cheap stereo, and the distortion turned the lyrics of "Under My Thumb" into an angry, shouted manifesto.

The flash of the first rifle was like a brief strobe light; the report punctuating the distorted base line of the music.

The policemen had moved back. They formed a line, dark silhouettes with rifles raised, laughing and smoking American cigarettes and shooting children. One at a time the rifles flashed, and at each shot, another of the children jerked and died.

She would be next. She huddled over, whimpering. The humidity of the night was suddenly oppressive, like a weight pressing down on her chest. She wished Gilberto was next to her.

And then suddenly there was bright light, not just flashlights, but the burning glare of searchlights. Someone kicked the tape player, and in the sudden silence the cut-off guitar chord echoed off the buildings. Then there was the amplified booming of voices too loud to comprehend. "DROP YOUR WEAPONS. YOU ARE SURROUNDED. DROP YOUR WEAPONS AND RAISE YOUR HANDS."

"Gilberto!" she shouted. In the harsh blue illumination of the searchlights, the bodies of the street children looked like no more than piles of empty clothes, heaped helter-skelter in a puddle of blackness that slowly seeped away toward the gutter. She ran to it; frantic, searching the faces.

Gilberto was not there. No, there. There was the dark red shirt, torn at the sleeves, the shirt he had worn, and those were his pants, but where was Gilberto? Surely that could not be him. She ran to the body inside Gilberto's clothes, but it was too small. Surely Gilberto couldn't have been this small, barely more than a mannequin made out of sticks. The body couldn't have weighed more than twenty kilos. She looked into its face, and Gilberto's eyes, bloodshot from gasoline fumes, stared back at her out of a lifeless body. But it couldn't be Gilberto, Gilberto was too clever, Gilberto had escaped, he always escaped.

Then they dragged her away.

She didn't cry; long ago Gilberto had told her never to cry, never to show emotion, never show weakness. No one looked at her, no one comforted her, no one even treated her as a human being. She didn't expect it.

"Thieves," one of the policemen said. "Beggars, drug dealers, and whores. Who cares about them?"

"The death squads make us look bad, you know that," his companion told him. "It's the foreign journalists."

"Yeah, but why couldn't we have waited until they finished shooting before coming in to arrest them? Or we should sell 'em for their organs. I hear that the North Americans pay a thousand dollars per kidney." He looked down at Estrela, a look like a hawk examining a mouse in its claws. "You figure that's right?"

"How should I know? But you better not try to sell this one; the lieutenant saw her rounded up alive."

The first policeman snorted. "What, you think I'd dirty my hands?" He spat on the ground in front of Estrela's feet. "So what do we do with her?"

"What do you think? She goes to Father Tomé." The second one shrugged. "He takes in all the filth of the city. One more, to him, it's nothing."

And so, in one night, her life on the streets of Rio ended. Estrela the street urchin of Rio vanished silently away, and a new Estrela, a person she had never imagined that it was possible to become, was born.

7

RIDING THE ROCKHOPPER

T ana was excited.

The desire to explore is a disease, and for all that Tanisha Jackson had been struck by it later than most, she had been still been hit hard. Driving the rockhopper across the sands of Mars was, to her, the fulfillment of her wildest imaginings. Everything about it was exciting. The color of the shadows, the patina of cementation on the soil, the very shapes of the rocks told her she was not on Earth. Every mile they drove she saw something new.

After two hours of driving, Radkowski called for a stop to give them a chance to stretch. Two hours was long enough inside a tiny pressurized cabin meant for a crew of only two, and they all needed some relief, a chance to stretch, to walk around a little, to give their stiff muscles a chance to relax.

Ryan Martin, on one of the dirt-rovers, pulled in next to them and dismounted. His suit was filthy, spattered from head to foot with a coating of dust. "All yours, Commander," he said. "I'd hand you the keys, but I seem to have misplaced them. Guess you'll have to hotwire it."

He turned the dirt-rover over to Radkowski, who would take the next shift on forward scouting, and Radkowski in turn gave him command of the rockhopper and wobbled away slowly on the dirt-rover for a test drive.

"How is it out there?" Tana asked.

"Wild and desolate," he said. "But in its own way, beautiful." Through his visor, she could see him shaking his head. "No place to raise children, though."

That was an odd thing to say, she thought. Ryan had never expressed any interest in children. He was widely known as a confirmed bachelor. The girls had privately tagged him the heartbreaker of Houston; he was interested enough in the opposite sex, sure, but just for the night. He just didn't seem to have intentions of settling down with one woman.

Tana was scheduled to take over from Estrela on the second dirt-rover, but Estrela was nowhere around. Ryan said that she had called in, saying that she was twenty kilometers ahead and didn't see any point in backtracking to meet them; she would wait for them, and they could change drivers when they caught up.

So she would have to get back in the rockhopper. Fine. That was just like Estrela, thoughtless and self-centered. But she didn't have to get in just yet.

"I'm going to look around," she told Ryan.

"Fine, as long as you don't go far away from the rover," he said. "It's a fifteen-minute stop, no more."

"Got it, boss," she said.

They weren't far from the ridge. Although it was covered with loose rocks, it looked like it would be easy enough to climb, but she knew she wouldn't have time. It was basic basin-and-range territory; she knew that from the geology field trips in Nevada and Texas that had prepared them for what they would see on Mars. Not a good place to look for signs of fossil life. Still, she examined three rocks that looked like they had signs of carbonate globules, and cracked one open to inspect the cross section. The call to return to the cabin came all too soon.

She looked at the tiny pressurized cabin. Shit. She couldn't go back in there. It was just too crowded. Now that she had stretched, she just couldn't force herself to go back inside.

She climbed up on the rockhopper and continued up, until she found a place to sit on the very top, her legs straddling around the crew cabin, one leg on either side. There was even a tie-down eyelet that could be used as a handhold.

"Ryan? I'm staying out here."

"Negative. We're ready to go." There was a pause, and then he said, "Where are you?"

She could see him standing below her, looking around in all directions. "Look up," she said.

"What?" He looked up at the mountain range, his back to her, rotating his whole body from side to side to scan the slope.

"No, here," she called. "Up here on the rockhopper."

He swiveled around to look at the rockhopper. "You can't ride up there!"

She smiled. "Want to bet I can't? Think you can get me down? And, anyway, I'm just riding with you for fifteen more miles. If I ride up here, I can just hop off and switch with Estrela; you don't even have open the hatch. Well, except to let her in."

Trevor was already inside, waiting. Ryan stared up at her in silence for a few moments, started to say something, and then stopped. "Well, don't think we're going to stop to pick you up if you fall off," he said at last, and swung around and up into the hatch to the pressurized cabin.

She knew that he would, in fact, stop for her if he had to; Ryan was not about to lose one of the crew. But she had no intention of falling off. She had won. "Got it, commandant," she said. "Falling off not allowed."

"Damn kid's gonna want to ride up there next, I know it," he muttered.

As the rockhopper started up, it lurched, and then swayed from one side to the other. "Yikes!" she said.

The rockhopper stopped abruptly, and she had to grab suddenly to stay seated.

"You okay up there?"

"No problem," she said. "I'm fine. Go ahead." She kept a solid grip on the handhold this time. Once she got used to the side-to-side swaying and found her balance, it really wasn't bad. No worse than balancing on skis or a skateboard, and far easier than the time she had tried riding on a camel.

Now, *this* is more like it, she thought. Riding across Mars in style. Plenty of room, and the greatest view on the planet. Best seat on the bus.

"Yahoo!" she shouted. She had made sure to turn her voice-activated microphone off before she shouted, and there was no reply, not even an echo. There should have been an echo, it would have completed the effect.

"Yahoo!"

8

FATHER TOMÉ

Nobody had told Estrela where she was being taken or tried to explain what was happening, nor did she ask any questions. Estrela already knew that her comfort, health, or opinions were of no interest to those who had her in their custody. She kept alert for a chance to dart away, to disappear into the shadows of the city. But she had been handcuffed—although she'd not been accused of a crime—and there were no clear opportunities. After the brief reprieve, she thought, she would be taken farther away and shot.

Instead, they put her on an ancient bus, and without explanation she was driven what had seemed like hundreds of kilometers inland. She had huddled in the corner, hissing and baring her teeth when anybody got near her. She had never been inside a motor vehicle before; the experience made her queasy, and if she had not been fairly faint with hunger, she thought that she would certainly have thrown up

The School of the Beneficent Jesus of the South was a rude collection of tin-roofed cinder block huts and dirt pathways. She didn't have any clear image in her mind of what a Father Tomé would look like, but the bald, smiling, roly-poly Anglo man in a faded Ipanema Beach Club T-shirt did not fit any of her expectations.

"Oh, my," he said. He looked at the driver, shook his head, and then looked pointedly at the plastic handcuffs.

The driver's hands were unexpectedly gentle as he cut the handcuff away from her. "She's all yours now," the man said, and went back to his bus.

She was ready to bolt now, but the wide-open spaces and the mountains disoriented her. She had no idea where the city was, if it was near or far. She had no idea of what was safe, or where she could hide, or what she could eat, or who she could trust.

Father Tomé smiled at her and held out his hand. In it was something, a little fur-covered purple object that, after she'd stared at it for a minute, she recognized as some sort of an animal, a stuffed animal. A lizard, no, a dinosaur. A purple stuffed dinosaur.

"Here, my frightened little avocado, this is for you," he said. "Take it. It's yours."

It looked forlorn in his huge hand.

She wanted it. She snatched it out of his hand, hugged it to her breast and began to cry.

"Poor little avocado," he said. "Welcome to Jesus do Sul. You are safe here."

She was turned over to the ministrations of three laughing girls, who were not really much older than she was, although in their self-confidence they seemed to be much older and more experienced. "I am Maria Bonita," the first one told her. "I am Maria da Glória," the second girl said. "I am Maria Araujo," the third one said. "The Father calls us the three Marias," they said, all three together, and they exchanged glances and nodded solemnly at each other, secure in their identities.

They stripped her—she fought—and plunged her into hot water—she shrieked and flailed. Then they held her and scrubbed her firmly with huge wooden brushes, and she fought again. Finally they soaked her hair with kerosene. She screwed her eyes shut and held her breath, terrified, waiting for the flare of a match, and when they rubbed the kerosene briskly into her scalp, it felt as if her head was on fire, but a cold fire, chilling and burning at the same time. But the fire did not spread, and all they did was to wash it away again, covering the sharp odor with some bubbly soap that smelled like exotic flowers. Finally they dried her with huge fluffy towels. They gave her back the little stuffed dinosaur, which she clutched to her chest, and then dressed her in pajamas that were two sizes too large. It was the cleanest clothing she'd ever worn.

She didn't even know who she was. Not the starved street child. Not anybody she knew. She didn't know who she was, and there was no point in fighting any more.

"Why, she's beautiful," a voice said. "Father Tomé, your little waif is no avocado at all. She is an orchid, precious and beautiful."

She had been called many things in her life, but never beautiful. She peeked out from between her fingers to see who had said it.

A young man stood next to Father Tomé, a *mestico*, tall and slender with dark skin and dark eyes and a lion's mane of dark hair. He was smiling at her with a smile that lit up the very air and set her heart to glowing with an ache like a hunger she could never name. She ventured a smile of her own, tentative and small, and he raised his hand and took a half step backward as if her smile had the force of a sudden gale.

"I am João," he said, his voice rich and deep with the familiar street accent of the *cariocas*. "Ah, my beautiful little orchid, I can see that you will break many, many hearts, but you will never break mine."

Wherever he goes, she told herself, I will follow in his shadow.

Following in João's footsteps, she discovered, would not be easy. He had himself been a student of the Jesus do Sul. He had excelled in his education and, at age fifteen, had already been accepted at the College of Saint Adelbert, far away in North America, to study for a degree in geology. The Holy Order of Saint Anselm, Father Tomé's order, was paying his tuition; the School of Jesus do Sul was itself assisting him with the expenses of travel. "The best of my children ever to leave Jesus do Sul," Father Tomé said. "How could we do otherwise than to help him?" In return, João would return to Brazil every summer and assist with the teaching.

Father Tomé, she discovered, called all of his wards avocado; she never learned why. He was a communist who talked fiercely of overthrowing the government of Brazil and redistributing the country's wealth to the poor. What she knew of economics was that the rich people had huge houses and servants and drove around in chauffeured limousines with darkened windows and ate ice cream whenever they felt like it. The poor people had nothing and were invisible.

She was going to be a rich person, and one day eat ice cream in her own automobile.

No, Father Tomé told her, that's wrong, my clever little avocado. You should learn to share.

No, she told him. She would be rich.

Father Tomé smiled. "Then you will have to learn. You will have to learn manners, and how to dress, and how to behave nicely, and how to have a nice mouth that does not swear. Sister Isabel will teach you."

I will, she promised herself. I will. I will!

In later days, she rarely saw Father Tomé. There were always too many children in the *escola*, for Father Tomé could never turn one away, and the escola was as crowded with tossed-together shacks as any *favela* shantytown. The teacher who assisted most with the street children, the new ones who needed instruction in even the most simple matters of grammar and etiquette, was Sister Isabel. She was four feet tall and at least as wide, quite simply the ugliest woman Estrela had ever seen. Sister Isabel had a boundless patience and a deep love for her charges. "You shall be a little lady," she told Estrela. "Don't you want to be beautiful? Don't you want people to love you? Then you must learn to talk properly." She had a heart as big as Brazil. Estrela felt safe with sister Isabel.

And so she found, for a while, a home, and learned to be a lady. She never forgot her brother Gilberto, although much later she would think back on her life before the school and wonder whether, after all, he really had been her brother.

All things change. In time, Father Tomé was reprimanded for his support of radical politics and left the Catholic church. Sister Isabel left to be married, a fact which astonished Estrela, who had not believed it possible that she could have had any life outside of the school. And Estrela herself, driven by forces that she herself could not name, excelled in her studies and did exactly as she had promised the very first day she met him: followed in the footsteps of João Fernando Conselheiro, north to the United States of America to study geology.

9

ROVING ON MARS

The surface beneath Estrela's wheels turned from sand to a pea-sized gravel, and then from the gravel to a dark rock. Desert pavement, it was called, a bare rock surface swept clean of the sand overlayer. From time to time the rock was fractured with jagged cracks filled with smaller rubble. None of the fractures were deep enough to be a danger to the rover, but the ride was jarring, and the dirt-rover's traction on the bare rock was poor.

The fracture lines ran east and west, making them parallel to the Valles Marineris, invisible over the horizon to the north. Another sign of tectonic stress, she guessed.

Estrela parked her dirt-rover on a rise and settled back to wait for the others. She looked out across the rocky plain, but didn't really see it.

Radkowski was the commander of the mission; he would be the one to make the final decision on who would return. Could she argue that, as a Brazilian, it was her right to return on the *Jesus do Sul*? It was, after all, a Brazilian ship; would he accept for that argument? Maybe. It would be worth a try.

It might help him see it her way if she seduced him.

She saw the dust long before the rockhopper came into view. The trail of disturbed dust hung in the air, winding like a fuzzy yellow worm across the landscape, the rockhopper an iridescent green insect ahead of it.

Tana, she saw, was perched precariously on top of the rockhopper like a mahout riding an elephant. She jumped down when the rover stopped.

"The territory's getting a bit more interesting as we get closer to the Valles," she said. "Not just the craters and boulders—was that a butte I saw back there? Did you get a chance to take a closer look at it?"

"Wasn't doing any sightseeing," Estrela said. Was Tana blind or stupid? she wondered. Then she thought, no, she just hadn't figured it out yet. Well, that might be all for the good. If Tana didn't yet realize that somebody

was going to get left behind, Tana wouldn't be competition when she tried
to seduce the commander.

That was going to be tough. The members of the expedition were
crowded together like bugs, and she couldn't see where they would find any
privacy. And the commander had good cock, but kept his pants zipped.
She'd seen him eyeing her when she was changing, but he was prudish
sometimes, didn't like to diverge from the rule book. That struck her as
odd: He talked like he grew up on the streets, and you'd think that he
would know that you had to grab what you can get when you can get it.
But he acted like God was watching him at every moment and he'd get
blasted by a lightning bolt if he bent the rules a little. But that was the way
commanders were, she knew. The ones who bent the rules didn't get picked
to command missions.

Not like Ryan Martin. Ryan would bend rules. Of course, Ryan
wouldn't ever get promoted to captain.

But then, the majority of them weren't going to get promoted to anything but two meters of Martian soil and maybe a cairn of rocks.

Hell, maybe she should be thinking about seducing *Ryan*.

"So, you want the spot on top?" Tana said, breaking in to her thoughts.
"Great view."

It did look like fun, but Estrela wanted to be inside with the commander. She shook her head, and then, realizing that with all the dust on
her visor it was hard for Tana to see her, said, "No." Then, to justify herself,
she said, "Let the kid take it—he'll enjoy the hell out of it."

Tana nodded. "You got that right."

10

J O Ã O

The College of Saint Adelbert was a small but well-regarded college located in a city named Cleveland, in Ohio, in the United States of America—ten thousand kilometers distant from her home. In return for her tuition, Estrela was expected to tutor in the department of languages.

She found the Americans almost incomprehensible. They spoke too fast, seemed interested in nothing except loud music and expensive clothes, and their slang was bizarre—the first time one of her students said to her, "I'm pooped," she translated it in her mind and broke out into uncontrolled laughter. The student had been baffled; apparently in American dialect the phrase wasn't even slightly naughty.

The study required by the college was almost too easy. She was bright, and the mission school had been strict and rigorous and had punished errors with a firm rap on the knuckles with a stick of bamboo. It was the freedom of the university that was hard for her to adapt to; it was like the blast of some illicit drug. She struggled to keep her goals firmly in mind, to avoid distractions.

And the college had boys as well, boys who would strut and preen for her, fighting over the chance to sit next to her and simply talk. The college made a token attempt to keep the girls under control, but the rules, she discovered, were openly ignored by the students. She was in a dormitory with two other girls, and they were surprised to find that she had no skill at flirting. Her roommates had to teach her how to enjoy teasing the boys with her presence, or by giving them a carefully casual glimpse of her bare shoulder. When that became boring, they taught her how to take them into her bedroom. It was not long before she had strings of lovers. The sex, to her, was not really the point; what she craved was the attention of their hands, their lips, their eyes on her body.

It helped, sometimes, to take away the nightmares.

When she caught up with João, she found him already a graduate instructor. He had filled out into a handsome boy. He was dressed in a silk shirt covered over with a black leather vest gleaming with chrome studs and chains.

She waited until he was leaving a class, and then walked up behind him. "One time," she said, "you took me up the mountain to see the stars. The sky over the school, it was very dark. You pointed out to me the glowing clouds, like a distant fire in the sky, and told me that it was a baby galaxy, the Magellanic Clouds, and it was so far away that we were seeing it as it had been thousands of years ago, and that if every star there had burned out, we would not know for a thousand years. Do you remember?"

João did not turn around. "Yes," he said. "I remember."

I thought you were going to kiss me, she thought. But you didn't. She didn't say it.

"And the mountains," she said. "You took me into the mountains. You had a hammer, and we looked at rocks. Do you remember that?"

"Yes," he said. "I remember that, too."

Without warning, she punched him on the upper arm, as hard as she could hit, hard enough to spin him halfway around.

This time he looked at her.

She smiled at him, with a smile that she knew had broken the hearts of a hundred other boys. "So," she said. "How the hell have you been?"

11

Commander Radkowski didn't want to push the machines too hard on the first day out, while they were still getting used to the equipment, and so they quit for the night well before the sunset. Commander Radkowski and Estrela inflated the bubble habitat for them to sleep in, while Ryan downloaded the electronic navigation logs of the vehicles.

"Perfect agreement," Ryan announced. Each of the vehicles had a separate inertial navigation system, and comparing the three readings was a way to check that all of them were working, even over an extended traverse. "Two hundred ninety kilometers. Not bad for the first day."

Tana translated in her head; a hundred seventy-five miles. No, not bad. If they could keep up that rate it would take them twenty days to reach the pole. And they should go faster, once they got used to the feel of driving real equipment, instead of the virtuals they had trained on.

This territory had a different feel, Tana thought. Rougher. The ground was a dark volcanic rock, riddled with grooves and pockmarks and cracks and crevices. The indentations were filled in with light-colored dust, making odd patterns that looked like a weird, alien writing. She ran her hand over the rock. Even through the glove, she could feel its texture, probe her fingers into the shallow depressions and cracks.

After inflating the bubble, Estrela had disappeared back into the rockhopper with John Radkowski. Tana wondered why.

She wondered what motivated Estrela. Estrela seemed open and uninhibited, all of her virtues and vices superficial, but Tana had come to suspect that she had a core of opacity, a secret level of self that she never allowed to show.

Since her own disastrous marriage, Tana had been discreet with men— quite willing enough to take an enjoyable interlude when the opportunity presented itself, but not promiscuous. Her job was tough enough; she didn't need complications in her life. Estrela, though—she flirted with every man she met. How could she?

Tana suddenly thought, what business could *she* have with John in the rockhopper that could be taking so long? She had a sudden pang of jealousy. But surely not—it was ridiculous to even think it.

Still—there had been that briefing.

"Six astronauts, four male, two females," the psychologist had told them, in a preflight briefing to the female crew. There had been dozens of such briefings, role-playing lessons in conflict resolution, mandatory courses on cultural awareness. This briefing had been her and Estrela only; the men had been lucky enough to be sent on a training run, Radkowski and Ryan Martin flying a jet fighter across the skies of Nevada, Trevor and Chamlong identifying rocks in a classroom in Houston. "An odd split. Why do you think we chose it that way?"

"No problem," Estrela said. "A woman can take more than one man."

"Wrong," the psychologist had said. The psychologist was an older woman, with a dumpy figure and gray hair. "It's because if we split it up evenly, the crew would pair off into couples. That will be disastrous. Disastrous for the crew function, and disastrous for the people involved—since there will be a strong social pressure to pair off whether you like to or not."

"So this way two of the men stay horny?" Estrela said.

"No. I suggest that *all* of the men should stay horny. I would strongly suggest that you do not engage in sexual relations with any of them. You fall in lust with one of them, that's fine, but save the bump and grind for until you get back." She paused. "It doesn't actually harm men to be horny, you know," the psychologist said. "In fact, in some ways it even increases male task-related performance ratings."

"I think maybe I take three of them," Estrela said. "That skinny girl can keep one for herself. In fact, maybe I just take all four, leave nothing for her." She smiled a wide innocent smile, and looked at Tana. Tana kept her face impassive.

"Now, I can't tell you how to behave," the psychologist said, "but I strongly suggest that is not a good idea."

Estrela had been just twigging the psychologist, Tana had thought. She had been quite vocal in telling Tana that she was none too fond of shrinks, and liked to rattle their cages.

Or so Tana had thought at the time. Now she wished that she wasn't wearing gloves. If she could, she would be biting her fingers.

What *did* Estrela want with John in the rockhopper?

And then the emergency band of the radio turned itself on. It was Ryan Martin's voice, and for a moment she couldn't figure out what he was saying. Then she suddenly realized.

He was singing.

12

J O Ã O

Estrela sometimes swore by Santa Luzia. She said that her mother always swore by this.

In actual fact, her mother had been a prostitute. While she was alive, she had used a strong and colorful language that liberally mixed blasphemy, obscenity, and scatology.

João had, slowly and patiently, broken her of her language. It doesn't matter how sophisticated you look, he said, the moment you lose your temper and swear, everybody will know you were born in a gutter.

It was João who had taught her to swear by Santa Luzia. "Everyone has to swear by something," he said. "Learn something that's not crude."

It had been hard to practice. She had held out her hand, and closed her eyes, and when she relaxed and didn't expect it, João hit her on the hand with a broomstick. "Santa Luzia!" she was supposed to shout. "Santa Luzia!"

"Yes, but as if you mean it," João would say, and suddenly hit her with the broomstick again.

"Santa Luzia!"

"If you could blush after you say it, that would be even better," he told her, but she could never manage that trick. For a long time she was hard pressed to avoid giggling when she said it—it was such a silly, harmless thing to swear by, who could possibly take it seriously?—but after a while it became second nature to her, so much that she now even said it without thinking when she was actually startled.

When she was among Americans, she was silently amused by the poverty of what they thought was swearing. "Fuck!" the Americans would curse. "Fuck you!"—as if *that* were a curse. They were like children, pleased with a petty daring.

João lived in an enormous ugly concrete building that was a kilometer or so away from the college. He shared a cramped apartment with two other boys from the college; none of them ever bothered to clean, and the apartment was so cluttered that it was hard to find the floor.

Estrela would come to João's apartment in the afternoon, after class, and they would talk. João would buy coffee—only little amounts, his teaching assistantship paid very little—and he would make two small cups on the single working burner of the tiny kitchen stove. João told her about his dreams and his plans for the future. None of their other classmates at the college could actually know what we lived through, he would tell her, only you. You are my only true friend, the only one who knows me for who I really am.

He told her how he had decided to study geology. Even from the worst slums, he had stared from the city up at the mountains in the distance, the mountains that were ever changing and always the same. He had decided that people were untrue, but the mountains were a solid thing that he could always rely on, and if he ever understood them, really understood, that he would have something—he could never quite explain what, but something.

Everyone needs something to hold on to, Estrela knew. A mountain was as good a choice as any.

Estrela loved to hear João talk about his dreams and plans, but she secretly marveled that a ragged street boy could hold such elaborate dreams. She, herself, had far simpler hopes. Her dreams at night were broken by images of being alone, huddled against a terrible darkness, with the stench of fear and rifle smoke assaulting her nostrils, and the night punctuated by the beautiful and awful flares of rifle shots. Her hopes and her plans were the same. She had, by her luck and her dogged study, managed to leave Brazil. Her only plans were to never go back.

João helped her learn geology. Her growing up on the streets meant that she had preternatural senses, he told her. You have situational awareness; you observe with a detail that verges on suspicion, detecting every small detail is second nature to you. Turn that to your study and make it work for you.

She didn't try to hide from João the fact that she had boyfriends. She hoped that perhaps he would become jealous, but he never did. Sometimes he gave her advice. Stay away from this one; when you're not around he talks like you're a piece of shit. That one's violent when he's drunk.

It is like he said when we met, she thought. I will never break his heart.

And then she thought, he has armored his heart so I won't break it.

And then she thought, if he has armored his heart, there must be a reason; he is afraid of me.

Someday, I will capture his heart.

13

WALKING ON MARS

In the Martian evening, in the little amount of free time they had after the bubble habitat was inflated and before the sun had yet set, Trevor went out walking. Ryan Martin followed along with him. Trevor was pretty sure that the commander had instructed Ryan to keep an eye on him. It annoyed him—he was not a child and shouldn't have needed a baby-sitter—but there was little point in complaining, so he made the best of it.

Besides, Ryan was one of the nicer ones. Ryan usually treated him like an adult, like a full member of the team, and not like a spoiled rich kid.

"Take a look at this," Ryan said. He was standing of the lip of a depression, looking down.

Trevor walked over and looked down with him. It was an irregular pit, with a jumble of dark rocks, nearly black, inside it. "What is it?"

"Collapsed lava cave, I think." Ryan bent over and picked up one of the pieces of rock. It was flat and curved like a shard of pottery. He looked at it, then handed it to Trevor. The outside was smooth, but the concave side was rough, almost sharp. "Doesn't look two billion years old to me," he said. "I'd bet there's been recent volcanism here."

That was interesting. "Recent?" Trevor asked.

"Less than a billion years ago, I'd say," Ryan said. "Maybe even within the last million years."

"Oh," Trevor said.

"What, you were thinking yesterday? Get real, kid."

Ryan turned and wandered off. That was odd, Trevor thought, if he was watching me. But he took his freedom as a chance to climb on some of the rocks and look around.

Desolate. This place was worse than Arizona; absolutely nothing green at all. If there were even one single cactus, or even a clump of grass—but there were only rocks and sand.

Ryan was saying something that he couldn't catch, and he suddenly realized that Ryan was singing.

"—had a hammer," he sang. "I'd hammer on Ma-ars—"

Not real music, not stomp or even bubblerazz, but old stuff, some folk song from the previous century. It certainly was an odd thing to do.

"And if I had a rock—" he sang.

Trevor turned his receiver volume down.

And then suddenly the singing stopped. Trevor waited for a moment, then cautiously toggled the volume back up.

Ryan was just standing there, staring at the rock. Trevor walked over to see what he was looking at, but nothing was there, just a wall of rock.

"What is it?"

"Did you see that?"

"What?"

"It moved. That rock, did you see it? It flowed, just like water." Ryan knelt down to put his hand on the rock. "It's moving. I can feel it."

"Where?" Trevor put his hand against the rock, but felt nothing.

"Hey, feel the heartbeat? This rock is alive. It's not a rock at all, it's an animal. I can feel it. Here." He took Trevor's hand and pressed it against the rock. "Can you feel it?"

It felt like rock. Rough, pitted, volcanic rock.

Abruptly Ryan got up and walked away. He was swaying, unsteady on his feet. Could he possibly be drunk? Now he was listing to one side as if he was about to fall over.

The rocks couldn't possibly be alive. Trevor pressed his hand against the boulder again, and closed his eyes and held his breath to better feel the surface. When he concentrated he could feel his own pulse in the tips of his fingers, but the rock was still just a rock.

"Maybe a dinosaur," Ryan said. "It's sleeping, though. Say, kid, you know something? I've figured it out. We're not on Mars. It's all a hoax. We're somewhere in Nevada, not on Mars. Look, I bet that's Vegas right there over the horizon." He put his hand up to his visor to shield his eyes from the sun.

"Stupid suit. Why the hell do we have to wear these things, anyway?" He put his hand up to the helmet ring-fitting, but then dropped it. "Kid, they tricked us. It's a training mission. Look, take a look at the gravity." He picked up a rock and dropped it. It fell, taking a second or so to hit the ground. "Look, was that slow, or not? Was that Mars gravity? I couldn't tell." He picked up another rock and dropped it. "Maybe it is. How do they fake that, I wonder?" He picked up another rock, but then seemed to forget what do with it.

"Hey, this rock is carved," he said. "Carved, I tell you." He dropped it and tried to pick up another. "Look, it's a bowling ball." He tried to pick it up, and couldn't.

Trevor was seriously frightened now. Was Ryan psychotic? Was he going to go off on a killing spree, like a psycho killer in the movies? He looked around, but they were out of sight of the rest of the party. In fact, he wasn't quite sure exactly where they were in relationship to the habitat.

Ryan sat down with a thump that Trevor thought he could hear even through the thin atmosphere, and picked up a handful of dust. "If I had a bowling ball," he sang, "I'd go bowling—"

Trevor walked up to him. Just under Ryan's collar, in the control section of his suit, was the switch that turned on the emergency broadcast frequency. Trevor reached over, flipped up the protective cover, and tapped it. When it didn't light, he hit it again, this time hard.

"Hey, what are you doing?"

"Brushing off some dirt."

"Yeah?" Ryan looked down at his suit. "Say, the suit is dusty, isn't it. You think I should take it off?"

"Uh, no, I don't think that's a good idea."

"Okay." Ryan went back to his singing, changing tunes. "I was lost, and now I'm found—"

From over the ridge across from them, a figure in a bright purple spacesuit came racing up the hill toward them.

Ryan looked up. "Tana! Hey, Tana, join the party! Where's the beer?" He started to get up.

"Stay right there!" Tana commanded. "Shit! Kid, how long has he been like this?"

Ryan staggered to his feet, but seemed to have trouble staying upright. His voice was puzzled. "I think I'm drunk. That's funny, I haven't had any beer yet."

"Hold still, hold still, damn it!" She had a cylinder of compressed oxygen out, and was fumbling with the pressure fitting on Ryan's backpack. "Trevor, hold him steady."

Trevor held onto Ryan with both hands. He had never been so glad to see anybody.

"Say, Tana," said Ryan conversationally, "have I ever told you how cute you are? I'd really like to—" He cut himself off. "But you don't want to. No, you'd probably die."

"Hold still. You'll be okay. Hold still, I've gotta purge you."

"Of course," Ryan continued, "you'll probably die anyway. Did I tell you that only three of us can fit on the ship? Little teeny ship. Those Brazilians were little teeny guys, too. Maybe just two."

Then the oxygen purge got into his life support system, and his voice trailed off. "Kid," he said. "Kid, I've been really really dumb."

"You said it," Tana replied.

During the training exercises, Ryan had tagged the bubble habitat the "hobbit habit," since it was so small that ordinary humans had to hunch over when standing inside. "Damn thing is built for hobbits, not humans," he'd said. From the outside, the bubble habitat looked like three golden brown biscuits baked together into a single mass, with a smaller biscuit, an airlock, stuck to one side. The yellow was the natural color of Kapton, a puncture-resistant polyimide, reinforced with invisible strands of high-strength carbon superfiber. The walls were just translucent enough that, from the outside, the hobbit habit shone with a deep, almost incandescent glow.

All five of them were inside now. Tana had seated Ryan on one of the supply cases and had strapped an oxygen mask on him. She drew a sample of his blood to analyze later. "Who's president?" She hit him on one knee and watched his reflexes critically.

"Yamaguchi." From under the oxygen mask, it sounded something like "Yohmoosh." "Unless he's been impeached. Or better yet, hanged."

"Dream on." Yamaguchi was not well liked among the Mars crew. As a senator, he had sponsored the legislation that killed the NASA Mars program after the *Agamemnon* disaster; as president, he had tried—unsuccessfully—to stop the *Quijote* expedition by demanding a billion-dollar payment as usage fee for the government equipment.

She tapped his other knee and watched the reflex. "What's your mother's maiden name?"

"Sagan, just like the astronomer. No relation."

"Stick your hand out straight and hold it steady." She watched it critically, looking for tremors. "Good. Touch your nose with your index finger, please. Good, now again with your left index finger. Excellent. Tell me, where are we right now?"

"Inside a teeny little hobbit room that smells like plastic and"—he sniffed—"something else, maybe peroxide."

"And where is that?"

He grinned. "On Mars."

"Good," Tana said. She peeled one eyelid up and shone a flashlight in his eye, watching the pupil contract, then did the same in the other. "I'd say that you're oriented times three. You had a bad case of anoxia there, and I'm not real happy about it, but it looks like there's no permanent damage. You can take the oxygen mask off now if you want. Do you have a headache?"

Ryan pulled the mask off. "I'm okay."

"Roll it up neatly and put it away. Any idea what happened?"

Ryan shook his head, wincing slightly as he did so. Tana thought that he probably did have a headache. She would have liked to do a full PET scan workup to make sure she hadn't missed anything, but without equipment, that was obviously impossible. "I'd say that something went wrong with the zirconia cell, but I don't know what," he said. "It wasn't feeding me oxygen. I'll take it apart tomorrow."

"Do it tonight. None of us are going anywhere until we know what's happened and can be sure it won't happen again."

Ryan winced slightly again, but nodded his head. "You're right. Okay, tonight."

Tana called through the opening, "I'm done here. Come on in."

Commander Radkowski came into the bubble-segment, then Trevor, and finally Estrela, Estrela managing to be graceful even when she was hunched over like a caveman. With five in the segment, it was extremely crowded.

Now Ryan was the center of attention, and he fidgeted.

"Something you said," Tana remarked casually. "Right at the end. Do you remember it?"

"It's kind of hazy," Ryan said, but when Tana gave him a sharp glance, he added, "Yes, I think so."

Tana looked over to Commander Radkowski, hoping he would help, but he didn't seem ready to take over the questioning. "Only three of us can fit on the ship, was that what you said?"

Ryan nodded, and when everybody was silent, looking at him, he cleared his throat. "Well, it's a small ship." Nobody said anything. "I did tell the commander."

Tana turned and looked at Commander Radkowski. "You knew this, and you kept it from us?"

"I—well, it seemed a good idea at the time."

"You're saying, if we do make it all the way to the pole, only three of us can go home? And you didn't tell us?" She turned to Estrela. "And you?"

Estrela looked away. "It is our ship. I know the specifications."

Tana looked at Trevor. He shook his head mutely. "So, the only ones who didn't know that two of us have to die were the nigger and the kid, is that right?"

She'd used the word hoping for some shock value, and it seemed to work. Radkowski spread his hands out, and turned them palms up. "It's not like that—"

"Really." She crossed her arms. "Okay, explain it to me."

"All I was thinking was, we get to the ship, anything can happen. We need to work as a team. We can't have everybody worrying. And, besides, who knows? It's a tough trek anyway, I can't be sure everybody is going to make it. If two of us die—"

Tana widened her eyes dramatically. "You're saying that you were actually *planning* for two of us to die on the road?"

"No! Not that at all! I just meant—" Radkowski lowered his head. "I just thought that if we went, at least three of us could be saved."

"Or maybe we could fix the ship so it could launch four," Ryan added. "I don't know for sure that it can't."

"Okay," Tana said, and looked back at Commander Radkowski. "Now, tell me another thing. What were you and Estrela doing in the rockhopper an hour ago?"

Tana didn't think that Radkowski could blush, but he did. He looked down at his feet. "Nothing."

"Nothing?" She looked at Estrela as she said it. Estrela looked back imperturbably, her head cocked slightly to the side. "You must have been doing something."

"She wanted to talk to me."

"Really? In private? About what?" She was still looking at Estrela, and Estrela's slight hint of a smile told her more than she wanted to know.

Radkowski said, almost mumbling, "I should have realized she would know how big the ship was." He looked up at her. "Nothing happened. She just wanted to talk to me."

When Trevor's broadcast had gone out, it had taken almost ten minutes for Radkowski to get to Ryan. It shouldn't have taken him two.

They must have been doing something. Tana had a very good guess as to what.

T he mood the next morning was subdued. Commander Radkowski told Trevor Whitman that it was time for him to practice driving the dirt-rovers, and sent Estrela to supervise him. Apparently Trevor's reaction to the episode of anoxia had met some threshold of the commander's approval. Or perhaps Ryan's encounter with anoxia had impressed the commander with the fact that a crew member could be incapacitated at any time, and he might need the help of any of the crew, even Trevor.

Ryan, meanwhile, had finished analyzing the failure of the zirconia electrolysis unit in his suit. It was a replication, in miniature, of the same problem that had attacked the *Dulcinea*. The oxygen partial-pressure sensors had been suffused by sulfur radicals, and both the primary and backup sensor gave a false reading of oxygen overpressure. As a result, the feedback mechanism in the suit had turned down the oxygen production rate, until the gas mixture that Ryan had been breathing was nearly depleted of oxygen.

An overnight thermal bake-out of each of the sensors should be sufficient to clear away the accumulation before it reached a dangerous threshold. It would be best to do it every night. To be safe, Ryan changed the parameters in the oxygen control software so that if an apparent excess of oxygen occurred, the suit's computer would keep oxygen production going, rather than cut it to zero. Finally, he suggested that when they were on the surface, everybody should run a manual oxygen level check on their suits twice a day—the manual system used a different sensor that should be immune from the problem—and they should swap out sensor elements if they saw any sign of trouble.

That would give them three layers of fail-safe against a recurrence of the failure. Nobody was happy about trusting their lives to a sensor that they knew could be faulty, but with the changes Ryan suggested, it should be as safe as anyone could make it. And he could see no alternative.

"What do we do now?" Tana asked.

"We continue north." Commander Radkowski looked at her steadily. "We still have no other choice."

Estrela and Trevor took the dirt-rovers ahead on pathfinder duty.

Ryan had worked most of the night on the problem, and Commander Radkowski assigned him to the first shift riding as passenger in the rockhopper. Radkowski piloted the rockhopper himself, and Tana once again took up her position perched on top of the vehicle. The commander gave her a disapproving look. If he had been the pilot of the rockhopper on the previous day, he would have forbidden her to ride outside in the first place, but now that it was established, he didn't bother to try to stop her. And, besides, it did make the rockhopper's tiny cabin a little less crowded.

The morning sky was the color of adobe, streaked with feathery clouds, tiny crystals of carbon dioxide ice in the Martian stratosphere. The terrain was rockier, and Tana's ride was quite a bit bumpier. Still, once she fit herself into the rhythm of it, it wasn't a problem to keep her balance.

"Hey, Estrela, wait up!" Tana could hear everything that Trevor said over the communications link. "Hey, you're going too fast! Slow up, okay? Wait for me!"

Estrela didn't answer, but Tana could see that she was staying ahead much less than she had the previous day, probably in deference to Trevor's inexperience.

16

JOÃO'S SECRET

One day, for no reason that Estrela could say, she realized what had been really quite obvious all along.

João had his crowd, and despite the fact that he had almost no money, he was every evening at bars. He spent the nights drinking in the company of boys dressed in elaborately casual attire, bright primary colors adorned with sporting logos like Nike and Polo. They seemed an odd crowd for the João she knew, a João who was moody and studious and intently focused. But he hid this side of him well when he was with his American friends, assuming a mask of frivolity. Estrela assumed that he was social climbing.

She was herself climbing as high and as fast as she could, erasing her past and inventing a new one, studying the dress and the mannerisms of the North American girls and imitating everything, or at least as much as she could copy without thousands of cruzados to spend on clothes. Her origins in the street were a secret she never talked about, and most of the other girls, who knew only that she was from Brazil and had her tuition and living expenses paid from the charity of the order, assumed that she must be the daughter of a maid or a shop worker, poor but unexceptional.

But one day she was waiting in João's dingy apartment, and João came by with one of his impeccably high-class friends. The boy gave her a look that dismissed her utterly, as if she was of less interest than the furniture. And when he bid farewell to João, his fingers lingered a little too long on João's arm, and his glance lingered a little too long on João's eyes, and she thought, Why, he is looking at João just like a lover would. And then, never even having articulated it to herself until that moment, she thought, But of course, why shouldn't he? He must be João's lover.

Until then it had never struck her as odd that João had no girlfriends. He was handsome enough; he could have had any of Estrela's friends if he had but once called their name in his gentle, commanding voice, but she had only thought that he was too good for them.

Why, João is a *veador*, she thought, and suddenly all that had been opaque to her became clear.

João, when she mentioned it, shrugged. "I can't believe that you didn't know," he said.

"Aren't you afraid of diseases?"

João looked at her.

"You know. The homosexual disease. The—*you* know!"

"Say it."

"You know! AIDS!"

"I am far more cautious than you are, my little orchid," João said. "You have, what, a dozen male friends who skewer you like a barbecued goat on a spit? Are you not yourself afraid?"

"I take precautions," she said, indignantly tossing her hair.

"What precautions?"

"I make them all wear—" She made a gesture with her hand, like unrolling a tiny inner tube. "You know. The tiny shirt. *Camisinhas.*"

"Ah, so you do make your knights wear their rubber armor," João said. "As well you should. I am glad to hear it. And so do I." He lowered his eyes. "Am I afraid?" He raised his eyes and looked directly at her, his dark eyes penetrating through her like fire. "Yes, of course I am afraid. It is a horrible thing, when love is death and death is love. It is my worst fear, and each time I love, I think, is this it? Is this one to be my death? But what can I do? Can I change the stars in their course, or keep the ocean from surrounding the world? No more can I change the way I am. If it is fated that I must die, well, then, every man must die. And I will have lived a little, and have known the love of a few men. I am careful, my love, I am as careful as I can possibly be, but death comes for all men. And for women too, little orchid."

Oddly, once she knew his secret, it brought her closer to João. He would now bring her out with his drinking buddies, and after a while they accepted her as just a rather odd friend of João's. She saw them, at first, as shallow poseurs pretending at an assertive masculinity, unworthy of João's affection; later as confused young men, uncertain of their sexuality or their identity; and finally she didn't see them as anything at all, just friends of João's: Andrew who got drunk and sang, Justin who liked to take her to ancient Hollywood musicals and then discuss the characters and the costumes all night long, Dieter who taught her to ride a dirt bike, Jean-Paul who wrote poetry.

When João broke up with the two others he had shared his apartment with, it was only natural that he took a new apartment with her. João was in a Ph.D. program at Cleveland State University by then, the rising star of the geology department; she had won an assistantship and would be starting the following autumn. Unlike João, who studied rocks with an intensity that sometimes almost frightened her, she had no particular passion for geology. It was as good a subject as any other, no better, no worse.

What does he see in those rocks? she sometimes thought. What does he see in those men?

But it was an excuse to avoid going back to Brazil.

17

TREVOR ON WHEELS

Trevor drove to the theme music of the songs stomping through his head—

riding on that lonesome road, riding riding riding

He was being excruciatingly careful. Driving the dirt-rovers had been easy enough in the virtual reality simulation, but he was acutely aware that this was real reality, and smashing up a dirt-rover would mean that none of the crew would ever trust him again.

hauling down that heavy load, riding riding riding

He stayed well behind Estrela, following in her tracks, watching where she avoided obstacles. Estrela banked it over casually, sometimes weaving lazy S-curves for no reason he could see other than just for the hell of it. The rocky surface had little traction, though, and he was afraid to follow her. If he leaned the rockhopper over very far, he was afraid it would slide out from under him. So he slowly dropped further behind. It was okay. He was practicing being cautious, and there was no real way he could get lost; the dirt-rover had its own laser-gyro-based inertial navigation system that gave him a readout of his position to within a fraction of an inch. In the very worst case, if he lost track of both Estrela ahead of him and the rockhopper behind him, he could radio and ask for a position.

So he didn't mind that he was slowly dropping behind her.

He was almost a mile behind when she drove over the cliff.

18

A MARRIAGE OF CONVENIENCE

In 2014, when Brazil announced its astronaut program, João had studied the application guidelines—both the ones that were written and the ones that were implied. A Mars mission was in the air; everybody knew it. The Americans had already announced their intention to go to Mars, and João studied the Brazilian space program carefully. They were asking for geologists. Why, he considered, with no oil to drill for in space, no mountains, no ores, why would the Brazilians want geologists for astronauts? Why, then, if not for Mars?

João had kept his tastes for young men discreet. In America, to be openly homosexual sometimes would invite an attack, and it certainly meant a dead end for advancement, at least for those not in careers friendly to those who were not straight, such as hairdressing or dancing. No, it was wise to keep his private life silent.

João was already at a disadvantage, being Brazilian in an American-dominated economy. He was working with a petrochemical company now, scouting locations for exploratory wells in the Yucatan. It was work that he enjoyed—of everything, he most liked walking in the field, picking up rocks and examining them and trying to imagine what tectonic conditions had formed them, what their history was, what story they told about the geological conditions deep down under the earth. The rocks of Yucatan were mostly limestone. The core drillings, the seismic tomography, the petrography and magnetometry and analytical chemistry—all of the tools of physical geology he found interesting and was adept at using and interpreting, but at heart what he most liked was just walking in the territory with a hammer and a hand lens, looking at the terrain and picking up rocks.

Did he want to become an astronaut? Yes, he decided.

Estrela had not, in all that time, gone back to Brazil.

Often she stayed with João. His passion was for young men, preferably lean, blond young men with mirrorshades and a taste for suede. But some years lean young blonds were few and far between, and on those evenings when he was between lovers, and bored, Estrela had been available, and so—

Well, it was of no consequence to him, a physical comfort, a small shared intimacy he could enjoy, even though he might have wished that Estrela were a man. She was his friend, and even if she did not share his soul, she was the one he bared his soul to, the only person on earth who really knew him.

He had no idea of what those nights had meant to Estrela. She hid her feelings from him very well. He had casually remarked, long ago, that she would never break his heart. It had been an easy remark to make, since he could easily see her beauty, even admire it, but not feel drawn by it. He had, in fact, long forgotten that he had ever made such a remark. He had no real understanding that if she could never break his heart, he was continuously breaking hers.

So when he decided to apply to be the geologist on the newly formed Brazilian astronaut corps, he asked Estrela to marry him. It was a decision of little consequence to him, a minor masquerade to fool public decency, one that he knew both of them could ignore in their private lives.

Estrela looked at the man that she had loved since she had been eleven years old, held back her tears, and said yes. With a casual voice that made it apparent that the matter was only of minor interest to her, she said, yes, of course she would marry him.

19

FALLING

There was almost no shadow, and little contrast. Estrela saw the edge ahead of her, but she had thought it was just a sharper-than-average crevice. Instead, it was a sheer rock face, almost five meters high. Suddenly the perspective opened out, and there was nothing ahead of her front wheel. She slammed on her brakes, but on the hard rock surface there was no traction, and the only result was that the dirt-rover fishtailed around in a skid. Before she could bring it back under control and slow down, the dirt-rover was over the edge and, for a moment, she was weightless.

She kicked free of the falling dirt-rover, which had started to tumble as it fell, thinking, better to fall clear than to land with a ton of high-energy metal falling with me. In the lower gravity, everything happened more slowly than she expected. She had enough time to watch the dirt-rover hit on its left side and bounce off to the right, and she hit the ground in a sky diver's roll. The ground was loose rubble, and she hit hard, skidding instead of rolling, and threw out an arm to stop her fall.

The pain was startling. She didn't lose consciousness. "Watch out for the cliff, kid!" she said.

"Where did you go?" his voice on the radio said. "You were ahead of me, and you just vanished."

"It's a cliff," she said. "Better slow down."

"Shit! Are you okay?"

"Yeah, sure, kid, I'm okay." She could barely keep her teeth from chattering with the pain. Nothing seemed to be broken, but her left shoulder, where she had thrown her arm out for balance and come down with her full weight on it, felt funny. It felt as if it weren't part of her body at all, but was a dead weight fastened to her shoulder with nails of fire. It would be a good time to go to sleep right now, she thought. I could take a little nap before Trevor gets here. "Say, kid," she said. "Better call up the doctor, okay? Maybe she ought to take a look at me. Just for kicks, you know?"

She was lying on broken rocks and rubble at the base of the embankment. It was surprisingly comfortable. Seems to be entirely igneous rock, she noted. No schist, no slate, no limestone. Some loose fines she couldn't immediately categorize.

Trevor's dirt-rover appeared at the top of the ridge line. He seemed impossibly small and far away. She decided to go to sleep; now that Trevor was here it would be okay to sleep, but when she tried to close her eyes her eyelids hurt, so she decided to go to sleep with her eyes open.

"Shit! Are you okay? Talk to me! Are you okay?"

"Yeah, I'm fine," she said. It was rather hard to talk when she wanted to keep her teeth clenched.

It seemed like hours before the rockhopper showed up—she kept hearing Trevor call to it, although she didn't really pay much attention to what he was saying.

The big robotic arm of the rockhopper wasn't quite long enough to reach down the cliff face and pick her up. It lowered a rope with Ryan and Tana, and the two of them arranged the rope around her. "Not around that arm," she said. "Ouch! You fuckers, not that arm."

With some difficulty, they got a sling around her and lifted her up to the rockhopper. Radkowski was already starting to inflate the bubble habitat.

"Forget the habitat," Tana ordered. "Get her in the rockhopper. Now!"

Inside the pressurized cabin, there was only room for the two of them. It seemed to take forever to get the pressure back up. At last the pressure was high enough for Tana to pull her helmet off. "Stay with me here. Stay awake, stay awake."

"Where would I go?" Estrela said, or maybe she just imagined she said it.

Then Tana started cutting the suit away from her arm, and she was suddenly wide awake again. Her arm was two sizes too large for the suit, and despite the fact that the piezoelectric fabric was fully relaxed, it was as tight around her arm as an athletic bandage. The piezoelectric fibers made the fabric nearly as tough as armor, and Tana had to bring the scalpel up under the fabric and saw at it. The instant that the pressure was released, the arm began to hurt. Estrela bit her lip to keep from whimpering as Tana slowly and carefully sawed it away.

Tana looked up. "I'm afraid you're going to have to tough it out," she said. "I certainly hope we can replace this from the spares we brought. I'm sorry."

"No problem," Estrela whispered, and then she fainted.

"Damn," Tana said.

20

Estrela had intended never to return to Brazil. It was ironic, in its way, that when she did return, it was to become one of the most famous women in the country.

The nightmares had never truly gone away, but she had forgotten how friendly Brazil was. She had forgotten how bright the colors were, how comfortable it was to hear a babble of conversation in the familiar carioca accent again, she had forgotten the scent of the air, humid and polluted and dense with humanity but still tangy with the sea, and the comforting presence of the mountains backing up the city.

She had forgotten what it was like to be home.

And João was selected for the Mars mission.

She had her friends and her lovers. As long as she was discreet, she could find interludes of enjoyment. João was a little more discreet, now that he was in the public eye, but he found that, as long as the public image was pure, in Brazil, few people cared what he did in private. And, even in Brazil, there were lithe blond men for him to share body heat with.

João was on television often, darkly handsome and with a rich, liquid voice; Estrela loved to watch him perform for the cameras. She was surprised when the television wanted her on camera as well, and even more surprised that they loved her. While João was away training, and later when he had launched to Mars, beating the Americans by a full two years, the cameras would follow her around, "the beautiful and mysterious Estrela, our luscious national flower." She has the body of an angel, the tabloids said, and, deeply hidden, a secret core of ice.

"How can you be so calm, with all the women who make eyes at your husband," the commentator for Semana Brasil asked, a bubble-headed blond with a voice like a parakeet. "Aren't you just insanely jealous?"

"No," Estrela said, and laughed. "Let them flirt. No woman could ever take my João away from me." And she had been so calm and certain and beautiful, that everyone in Brazil felt they knew her.

When they asked her opinions of the geology of Mars, she saw no reason to remind them that she had, in the end, never been more than an average student, graduating with a degree to make her respectable but without the passion for the subject that João had. If the reporters wanted to paint her as an expert in the subject, with a mastery somehow absorbed from her closeness with João, that was their affair.

And when the expedition failed, when international television broadcast the terrible images of the bodies of the Brazilian astronauts, lying uncovered in the snow a hundred million miles away from their native soil, she became the symbol of Brazil, beautiful and tragic.

She knew in her heart that João had, in his own way, loved her. Perhaps he had never felt the intense physical ache she had felt for him, but still, he had loved her in a way that none of his silly blond boys could ever know.

She never cried, but she grieved in her own way, and knew for certain that she would never love again.

So when the time came for Brazil to send an astronaut on the third expedition to Mars, there was no real disagreement on the choice of who to send.

PART THREE

THE CANYON

With a surface area of 144 million square kilometers, the Red
Planet has as much terrain to explore as all the continents and
islands of Earth put together. Moreover, the Martian terrain
is incredibly varied . . .

—Robert Zubrin (1996)

Beautiful, beautiful. Magnificent desolation.

—Edwin E. Aldrin, Jr. (1969)

1

LEAVING AFRICA

The glow of sunset lasted far after the sun disappeared. The sky turned a deep, brick red, and the red faded until it was almost invisible. Two stars in the west, a brilliant blue-white one and a smaller one of tarnished silver next to it, were the Earth and the moon.

And then it was dark.

For some reason the hazy darkness reminded Radkowski of his last night in Africa. Sunset fell quickly in Africa, not like here on Mars, and on that night Venus has shone brilliant in the west.

His flying comrades had thrown a going-away party that night. It was partly for him, but more than that, it had been a party for dead comrades who had not returned from the disaster of the last mission.

They had lit torches, and they glowed like votive candles, forlorn hopes against the hot, sullen night. Two of the fliers had guitars, and they had set up amplifiers and played with an almost palpable violence, trying to cover up the badness of their playing by sheer intensity of sound.

They partied desperately. They were in a dead-end war, and they knew it. He walked through the party like a dead man, not talking, not acknowledging anyone, numb, his mangled hand hurting. He was already separate from the group. To them, he was already on his way home.

The party had gone on late into the morning, long after he had left it to collapse in his bunk, too drunk to move, too drunk to care any more.

The Mars night was, really, nothing like that, except that he was alone, and the night was dark.

I'm a hundred million miles away from that now, he thought. I have left it all behind.

But John Radkowski knew that he could never, really, leave it all behind.

Injured or not, tomorrow they would move on.

2

O N W A R D

The dirt-rover that Estrela had been riding had not been badly damaged, and any shop on Earth could have straightened the bent frame, replaced the smashed wheel bearings, and put it back in working condition in a few hours. With neither a machine shop nor parts, though, Ryan said that it was out for the duration.

They loaded it on the rockhopper to use for spare parts to keep the second dirt-rover running.

The Mars suits were form-fitting, and once Tana had cut the suit off of Estrela, her arm and ankle had both started to swell. It looked like she was wearing a balloon around her ankle now.

Estrela's damage turned out to be a fractured left radius, a dislocated left shoulder, and a mildly sprained ankle. Possibly with torn ligaments, Tana said, although it was hard to tell without X rays. In any case, it was lucky that she had not been hurt worse. Tana worked calmly and quickly, without thinking beyond what needed to be done at the moment; it was what she did best. She immobilized the arm with an inflatable, and while the balloon held it in place, mixed up a liquid polymer to set it in a more durable cast. With the broken bone set, she relocated the shoulder and strapped it to Estrela's side to keep her from reinjuring it. She wrapped the ankle and instructed Estrela not to put weight on it, and finally, with the acute problems solved, made a more thorough examination. And only then, when she had verified that none of the other minor bruises masked deeper injuries, did she allow herself to think. An idiot, she thought. What the hell had Estrela thought she was doing?

They had brought along a supply of the piezoelectric fabric, and while they were camped, Ryan spliced a gore of spare material to replace the part of the spacesuit destroyed when Tana had cut it away. It was slow and painstaking work. Each square centimeter of fabric required ten electrical connections to be spliced to the computer that controlled the suit's tension.

He worked on it for several hours. "I think that this will do it," he said at last. He held out the arm of Estrela's Mars suit, flexing it this way and that and watching the seam with a critical eye. "You might have been a little more careful about slicing this thing—you don't want to know what this suit material costs per square centimeter."

"She's not going to put on a suit for a while," Tana said.

"Better to have it ready now for when she needs it later," Ryan said. "But next time, peel it away instead of cutting it, okay?"

It was fortunate, Ryan thought, that Tana had had the presence of mind to insist that Estrela be taken to the rover for treatment, and not put in the bubble habitat. If she had cut away Estrela's suit in the habitat bubble, they would have had to stay where they were until she could put on her suit again; there was no way to get her out of the bubble with no suit. But in the pressurized cabin of the rover, they could resume their journey as soon as they were ready.

Ryan was ready to rig up the block and tackle to take the rockhopper down the cliff the next morning, but that turned out not to be necessary. It was not much of a cliff, a minor upthrust fault, more of a step in the ground level than a real obstacle to their travel. Commander Radkowski walked the territory, and then directed the rockhopper along the edge for a little ways to a place where the height was low enough that the rockhopper was able to simply step down, the articulated struts dropping one wheel down at a time. Once on the bottom, he picked up the remaining dirt-rover with the rockhopper's robotic arm and lifted it down the cliff.

Commander Radkowski directed Ryan to take the dirt-rover ahead to scout, but cautioned him to stay in direct line of sight of the rockhopper. Trevor, now perched in Tana's spot on the top, was given the binoculars, and was told to keep scanning ahead for any additional bad terrain, and to radio warnings ahead to Ryan as he saw fit.

There were several more small cliffs, all of them running east to west, perpendicular to their line of travel. In each case, Trevor was able to spot a place where the wall had slumped, or where a pile of rocks made a natural ramp for the vehicles to continue on. None of these was a significant obstacle.

As it turned out, the next obstacle was more than just a small escarpment. It was a canyon.

3

THE LESSER GRAND CANYON

Ryan parked ten meters or so back from the edge of the canyon and dismounted to look at it. Trevor jumped off the top of the rockhopper and walked over and past him to look over the edge. "Shit," Trevor said. "This is incredible."

"Stand a little further back, kid," Ryan said. "We don't know how stable this edge is."

The canyon was so wide that the opposite wall was misty in the distance. The edges were fluted. Looking down, it was a dizzying drop to an incline of broken rock fragments, the talus slope. Ryan Martin got down on his belly and looked over the edge. It was an absolutely vertical drop, maybe two hundred meters straight, before the rubble at the bottom began to slope outward. The wall looked layered, but it was pretty hard to tell from this angle.

In both directions, the canyon extended out as far as they could see, disappearing in the distance.

"Wow," Trevor said. "I never thought that Valles Marineris would be so spectacular. It's like the Grand Canyon."

Ryan looked at him for a moment, and laughed.

"I don't get it," Trevor said. "What's funny?"

"You think this one is impressive?" Ryan shook his head. "Kid, we've still got a long way yet before we get to the big one. This isn't the Valles Marineris. Just the appetizer."

"Does it have a name?"

Commander Radkowski had exited the rockhopper and was now standing beside them. "Coprates Catena," he said. "We're getting close to the Valles Marineris territory; this is just a groove in the crust that didn't make it to the big time. It runs about five hundred kilometers, and then it ends."

"You want to detour around?" Ryan said.

Radkowski shook his head. "No, that would probably take at least two days, and we don't have extra time to spare. And, besides, we might as well get started rappelling. We're going to be forced to, later, anyway."

Trevor looked into the canyon, and shuddered. "You're joking." He looked at them. "Tell me you're joking."

But neither of the other two were laughing.

Ryan went back to the rockhopper to fetch the block and tackle.

The cable was made of a superfiber material called Spectra 10K. It consisted of a thread of buckminsterfullerine nanotubes woven in a matrix of polyethylene. It was nearly as thin as spiderweb, and despite a coating of fluoropolymer, almost as invisible.

Fifty kilometers of the superfiber was wound up on a silicon-carbide deployment spool barely larger than Ryan's fist. Despite its thinness the cable was plenty strong enough to hold the weight of the entire team, and the rockhopper itself.

Radkowski tested several rock outcroppings at the rim of the canyon, and chose one that was part of the bedrock, or at least something so large that the rockhopper could not move it. The bedrock was a dark, dense basalt, its surface smooth and uncracked. Radkowski drilled an anchor point into the rock, and Ryan fixed a titanium bolt into the hole with an epoxy plug. A second bolt was fixed for redundancy, and then a separate safety line was set with a third and fourth anchor. Radkowski affixed the cables, with Ryan watching over to check his work. When they were done, he called Tana over and made her repeat the checkout as he watched her.

They were ready to go.

Getting Estrela out of the rockhopper was a difficult task. Her sprained ankle, taped firmly, could be forced into the Mars suit's boot, but her arm was still too swollen to slide into the form-fitting sleeve of the Mars suit, even with the piezoelectric fabric fully relaxed. Tana finally solved this problem by taping Estrela's left arm firmly to her chest, as if she were cradling her breasts with her arm. They could then shut the chest carapace with her arm inside the shell. Estrela told her that as long as she did not try to inhale too deeply, it felt okay. A balloon patch sealed the opening where the sleeve should have been.

"That should hold," Ryan said.

"You'd better help me, I think," Estrela said.

By leaning on Tana at one side, and with Ryan supporting her on the other, they got her out of the rockhopper and moved her over to a shelf of rock where she could watch.

Radkowski entered the rockhopper, slaved the controls to a remote unit, and then sealed it up.

"You all know enough not to try to touch the cable with your hands," Radkowski said. That had been covered in their training, but apparently he wanted to make sure. "If you have to handle it, use the deployment spool, or else use a handling tool. But it would be better just to stay clear." He looked at each of them, and waited until they nodded. "Good."

A take-up reel specifically designed for fullerine superfiber was fixed onto the anchor cable. One control on the reel loosened or tightened a friction brake on the deployment reel. A second control allowed them to spool the fiber up onto the take-up reel at a gear ratio of a thousand. A separate attach-point held their safety line.

Using the remote, Commander Radkowski inched the rover to the edge of the cliff. The nose of the vehicle dipped, and for a moment he hesitated. Then, trailing behind him a fiber as thin and as invisible as a spider's thread, he drove the rockhopper off the cliff.

4

THREAD

John Radkowski had had experience with superfiber cable nearly ten years before. On the space station, it had been used to dispose of garbage.

In the twenty-first century, Radkowski discovered, the job of astronaut was a half step down from truck driver.

Expensive, high-tech satellites were delivered by unmanned space boosters: cheap, reusable, and too small to ferry humans, they made fortunes for the farsighted investors who had invested in the low-cost transportation and built the whirling network of satellites that surrounded the Earth like a plague of gnats.

To launch people into space, though, they still used the ancient space shuttle. Refurbishing and upgrading had made the shuttles more efficient, adding all-electronic controls and liquid-propellant fly-back boosters, but they were still recognizably the fragile white elephants that had flown in the previous century. Decades of pampering care had made each shuttle orbiter idiosyncratic, with its own set of operating procedures and engineering work-arounds for misbehaving parts. With never quite enough money to adequately refurbish them, and far too little to engineer a new launch system, the space shuttles were still the best way to reliably launch humans into space.

The job of astronaut meant that Radkowski ferried scientists up and down to the space station and was responsible for shepherding the scientists while they were in space, making sure that they followed safety regulations and didn't do anything that would jeopardize the station or their own lives. This, he discovered, was a tough job. The scientists—pierced and pony-tailed young men with goatees and glasses, earnest-faced young women with irreverent T-shirts and disconcertingly direct gazes that he had trouble meeting—had almost an uncanny instinct for skipping safety rules and getting in trouble.

It was a job.

The first time he had visited the space station he had been impressed with the sheer size of it. The modules had seemed small when he trained in the weightless tanks, but once out there, in orbit, all the modules together with trusses and external experiment modules and solar arrays and appendages, it seemed to be huge.

Inside, the first thing to hit him was how noisy it was. He had expected silence, or perhaps the muted hum of an air circulation fan. Instead it had been full of sounds: clatters and clicking and hums, buzzes of machinery and whirring of fans, computers and lab equipment monitors beeping, voices carrying from modules far away. Then he was impressed with how cluttered it was. Later he amended that: not cluttered, exactly, just crammed. Every wall was filled with things, and in a space station, that meant the "floor" and the "ceiling" walls as well. It was almost impossible to find anything, unless you remembered to make a clear note of where it had been put.

His job was unglamourous, taking care of the routine. His real assignment, he knew, was to be prepared for an emergency, but in the interim there was no end of tasks: vacuuming air filters, calculating garbage dumps, scheduling orbital maintanance burns, and doing preventative upkeep on the ten thousand valves and fans and pumps that kept them alive.

He met Ryan Martin on his fifth ferry trip up to the orbiting laboratory.

Ryan had, at first, seemed to be just another of the scientists: a ponytailed young man with a growth of facial hair just too short to be called an actual beard. He found Ryan buried in the equipment or taking data or talking with the other scientists; John Radkowski had never been good with people, and it took him a long time to even learn his name. Then it surprised him to find out that he was not one of the scientists at all, but actually one of the Canadian astronauts, on his first mission to the space station. It wasn't his job to fix the equipment; it wasn't his job to take data or talk to the scientists. He just liked doing it.

The American space station—it was by name an international space station, but everybody called it American—was not the only space station in orbit.

The Russians had originally been a partner in the American-led space station program, but after the bloody civil war and the war of Kamchatkan independence, they had dropped out. Nobody had ever thought that their space program would ever be resurrected, but, dogged and determined, the Russians had held on. Small, cramped, and perpetually on the verge of breaking down, the *Mirusha* was built and kept operational—barely—as a matter of national pride. Its name, the "little *Mir*," was a tribute to the earlier Mir space station, long since burned up in the Earth's atmosphere. The Russians did not intend for anybody to forget who had had a space station first. It also meant a little world, appropriate for the tiny cylinder of atmosphere in orbit around the Earth; or with a slight change in pronunciation and spelling, it meant "little Mary," which was the pet name the Russian cosmonauts unofficially favored.

As it happened, although the *Mirusha* was at a nearly identical altitude, it had an orbital plane tilted in a different orientation. The laws of orbital mechanics mandated that there is no easy way to change orbital planes. To get to the *Mirusha* from the international space station required so great an orbital plane change that the easiest way to do it would actually be to return to the Earth and take off again into the new orbit.

So when the news came through the grapevine that the two Russian cosmonauts in the *Mirusha* were in trouble, that the station was leaking and the Russians had blown up two launch vehicles trying to rescue them, John Radkowski nearly ignored the news. They would be rescued, or not rescued, but the situation, he figured, had nothing to do with the American space station, or with him.

5

DESCENT

They lowered the rockhopper slowly, with Ryan watching the cables to make sure that they didn't snag or rub. The cliff was smooth and almost vertical. Even in his Mars suit, Ryan Martin was sweating. Lowering the rover was exacting work, and he was terrified that a frayed cable would let the rover slip, or a miscalculation might let it swing into the rock face.

It took them over an hour to lower the rockhopper two hundred meters to the top of the scree. As soon as they had all six wheels resting on the talus slope, to Ryan's relief, Commander Radkowski called a break.

Ryan took a deep breath, and then lay flat back on the ground, face upward. It was a relief to stare into the blank flatness of the sky and not worry about a rope snagging and the rover tumbling down the cliff.

After a brief rest, it was time for the crew to begin descending. The rockhopper was still precariously balanced on the talus slope below, with the taut cable holding it from sliding down the slope. "I can tie off the cable to the rockhopper, to free up the winch to start lowering the crew," Ryan said.

Radkowski shook his head. "Tie it off," he said, "but we can't leave the winch behind up here. We'll rappel down."

Radkowski got into the harness first and clipped the rappelling brake into it. He checked, double-checked, and triple-checked the harness and the connections, then checked the anchors.

"Those anchors held fine when we lowered down a two-ton rockhopper," Ryan said. "I think it will hold you."

"I'm checking it anyway," Radkowski said. He leaned back, pulled at the superfiber with his full weight. The anchor, unsurprisingly, held up. He clipped a second line to his harness. "On belay," he said.

Ryan moved to the deployment spool. "On belay," he replied. He turned and said, "Trevor, watch me on this, you may need to know."

"I have done rappelling before, you know," Trevor said, his voice dripping sarcasm. "I don't think you can teach me anything. It's easy."

"Good," Ryan said. "Have you used bare superfiber?"

Trevor shrugged, a gesture all but invisible under the suit unless you knew what to look for. "I don't see how it makes any difference."

Superfiber ropes were used for rock climbing on Earth, but almost always the superfiber itself was covered in an external woven sheath. The outer coating gave the climbers something to see, and made it less dangerous to handle. "Watch me anyway," Ryan said. "You can let me know if I do anything wrong."

"I'm heading down," Radkowski said. He stood at the edge of the cliff, looked back over his shoulder, and then leaned back over the edge, holding on to the rappel brake with one hand, leaning back farther and farther until he was almost horizontal, and then he matter-of-factly began to walk smoothly backward down the cliff.

6

DUMPING GARBAGE

Each day that he was space station commander, at the end of his shift Radkowski would float through the space station, checking all the seals, verifying that the safety equipment was accessible and that none of the pressure hatches were blocked by cables or equipment. He came across Ryan Martin in the electronics laboratory module. He was working on an electrical breadboard that was connected to a microwave antenna pressed hard against the small external porthole. From the look of it, Ryan had built it himself.

"A C-band transmitter?" Radkowski said. "You have a frequency-control permit for that?"

"Nah," Ryan said. "Nobody uses those old low-frequency microwave bands but the Russians; a permit would be nothing but paperwork. Anyway, it's a low-power rig, not good for much but orbit-to-orbit."

Radkowski liked the young astronaut, but it bothered him when he dismissed management directives so quickly. Who knew what experiments the science crew might be running that could be ruined by unregulated electromagnetic interference? Well, for that matter, Ryan Martin probably did know—he kept up with all the work that the scientists were doing, and seemed to always know what experiment runs were being scheduled when.

Ryan looked at his calculator. "They should be over the horizon any second now." He powered up his homemade transmitter. "*Mirusha*, this is Space Station. *Mirusha*, Space Station. Are you there?"

"Da, *Mirusha* here." A heavily accented voice. "This is Martin?"

"Yes, Martin here. How are you holding out down there, buddies?"

"Holding out not so good."

"Any chance of rescue?"

There was a long pause. "We think not."

"Can you use your return capsule?"

"No."

The *Mirusha* had an ancient Soyuz module attached. The Soyuz space-craft was, according to the design specifications, the lifeboat that the crew was to use to return to Earth in the event of a failure. But the Soyuz had been designed for only one year in orbit.

"We have been using it for junk storage," the Russian said. "We have been removing out the junk and try to power up the systems. No is work-ing." Long pause. "Is designed for one year in orbit. Is now twelfth year. Nothing works. Is junk."

"Better than suffocating."

"No," the Russian replied. The signal was beginning to acquire static. "Cannot undock, my friend. Is welded to *Mirusha*. Not even big hammer can work to undock."

"Signal's breaking up, buddies," Ryan said. "I'd better sign off. Hang in there, buddies."

"Da," the Russian replied. "We will hang here. Where else we hang, no?"

And then there was nothing but static.

"Passed over the horizon," Ryan said. "If we had a joint data-relay agreement, I could relay communications, but as it is, that's it for today."

Radkowski hadn't realized how bad the Russian's situation was. But there was nothing they could do about it, he knew. The Russians would have to solve their own problems. "You talk to them every day?" he asked. It was an odd hobby, talking to the other space station over what was, essentially, an amateur radio link, but there were no regulations against it.

"When there's a line-of-sight window," Ryan said. "I like Russians. They're the friendliest people in the world. And their space station may be small and cramped and low-budget, but it's still a space station, and it's great that they've managed to keep it going, with a budget of old paperclips and broken rubber bands."

He paused for a moment, and then added, "If nobody else is going to do it, I will."

"You will what?" Radkowski asked

"Why, I'll save them."

Radkowski chuckled. "Right," he said. "You do that."

Garbage is a big deal on a space station.

Garbage accumulates. Food containers and byproducts, used and re-used pieces of paper, human waste, broken equipment, worn-out underwear, used chemicals, filled barf-bags, shaving bags, and vacuum-cleaner bags, sanitary napkins, used-up sponges, biological sample containers, dead petri dish cultures, used personal hygiene supplies, wastewater too contaminated to recycle—garbage accumulates. With every docking of a logistics transfer vehicle, more material is brought up to the space station, and all of it, eventually, becomes garbage.

Some of it can be returned to Earth with the shuttles. But more refuse and wastewater is generated on the space station than can be returned to Earth in the empty space in a personnel transfer module.

Garbage can't be just thrown overboard; garbage tossed out a hatch would accumulate in the same orbit as the station, turning into lethal debris at the orbital velocity of 17,000 miles per hour. Not even the wastewater can be vented; one of the benefits of the station is to use the high-vacuum environment of space, and a wastewater dump would contaminate the environment near the station, destroying its usefulness.

Instead, garbage is lowered on a string.

The principle is simple. A month's load of garbage is placed into a plastic disposal bag, which is attached to one end of a spool of thin superfiber. The garbage load is dropped out the nadir hatch and nudged infinitesimally backward in orbit. A satellite in its own right, but tethered to the spacecraft by the superfiber cable, the garbage-satellite drops into a lower, and hence faster orbit. It moves ahead of the station and unwinds the superfiber behind it. A brake on the superfiber reel pulls back on the garbage, and the more the garbage is pulled backward, the lower the orbit it drops into. At its full extension of twenty kilometers, the garbage satellite hangs directly below the space station. Now the superfiber cable is pulling straight outward on the garbage. And then the cable is cut.

When the cable is cut, the garbage satellite drops into an orbit lower yet. The orbit, in fact, has a perigee which is lower than the space station's orbit by exactly seven times the length of the tether. Left to itself, the garbage would diverge from the space station by a hundred and forty kilometers. But an orbit a hundred and forty kilometers below the space station skims through the Earth's atmosphere. Anything in such an orbit will burn up.

And so, in the form of a briefly flaring meteor, the garbage is returned to the Earth it came from. It was a far more efficient way to deorbit garbage than using a rocket; no fuel is needed, and the superfiber tether was a low-technology system no more complicated than a fishing reel.

John Radkowski was in command of the station and had just finished running a garbage dump. It was one of the more interesting duties, actually; if performed incorrectly, the superfiber cable could snag or could go into an oscillation such as the "skip-rope" mode or, in the worst-case scenario, the brakes could fail and the tether deploy too quickly, rubber-band itself back into the station, and hit any of a million possible damage points with a two-ton wrecking ball of garbage.

When he had completed the garbage dump and returned to the lounge area, he found Ryan Martin and several others already there, engaged in an animated discussion.

"Hi, Ryan," he said.

"Radkowski," Ryan said. He was wearing a T-shirt that read: HIGH ENERGY PHYSICISTS HAVE A STRANGE CHARM. He floated with the tip of one foot hooked under a loop to keep him from drifting away. He was oriented sideways to Radkowski's local vertical; it didn't seem to bother him, although Radkowski still had trouble adapting to it. "What do you think?"

"About what?"

"The rescue, of course."

Radkowski blinked. "I'm sorry. I don't know what you're talking about."

"The Russians, man," Ryan said. "The cosmonauts. We're going to rescue them."

Radkowski shrugged. "No, of course not," he said.

Ryan Martin shook his head. His body rotated in counterpoint, and the foot he had hooked under a restraint loop popped loose. He started drifting. "If we don't rescue them, it's damn certain that nobody else will," he said. "They're leaking. They've got five, maybe six days. Who's going to rescue them that fast? Not the Russians—that last blast tore the hell out of their pad; it will take them six months to get back operational. Not the U.S.— we have only four shuttles; two of them are up here with us, and we can't get them down and then back up again that fast. The other two are in for refurbishment; they're going nowhere. Not the Brazilians—they can't hit that orbit from their launch site. So, if we don't save them, then who will?"

"Don't be ignorant," Radkowski said. "Can't get there from here. They're in a completely different orbital plane."

Ryan smiled. "The crew return vehicle can do it."

Radkowski shook his head so vigorously that he had to hold on to a loop to keep from moving. "Not enough delta-vee for a plane change. Not by half."

Ryan Martin nodded. "Nope. So we have to be clever. We have to be very, very clever."

Ryan Martin, as it turned out, was clever.

The crew return vehicle was a tiny, four-person lifting body. It had been designed to be an ambulance, an emergency way to land an injured astronaut fast. It had a rocket engine for the deorbit, but not enough fuel to make the plane change needed to get into the Russian orbit. Plane change maneuvers need a tremendous amount of fuel; even if every drop of rocket fuel in the space station could be used, it would not be enough to get the little vehicle into the right orbital plane.

Ryan's plan was to use the tether. The tether was used to drop garbage downward, but there was no reason it couldn't equally well be used to sling the crew return vehicle outward. He calculated that four hundred kilometers of tether, twenty times the amount used for a garbage dump, would toss the little lifting body into an orbit with an apogee of five thousand kilometers above the Earth. "That's into the Van Allen radiation belts," he said, "but I'll only be there for less than an hour, no big exposure concern there." At the apogee of the orbit, he would fire the crew return vehicle's little rocket perpendicular to the direction of the orbit, as well as two solid propellant STAR booster rockets stolen from the perigee kick motors of satellites being repaired on the station. The trick, as he pointed out, would be to gain altitude before trying to do the plane change. The farther away from the Earth, the easier it is to make a plane change, and the added five thousand kilometers that the tether boost could give him would make an enormous difference.

Radkowski closed his eyes, trying to picture the situation. He wasn't good at doing math in his head. Five thousand kilometers, that was, what, three thousand miles. Slightly less than one Earth radius. "It's still not enough," he said.

"Right," Ryan said. "Not enough. Yet. Okay, here's what happens next. The return vehicle is screaming in from five thousand kilometers, see. It has a lot of excess kinetic energy to dissipate. So what happens? Here's what happens. Highly elliptical orbit. I dip into the atmosphere. But, here's the trick. I don't just use the atmosphere to brake. The return vehicle has lift, right? It's a lifting body. So I point it *sideways*. Roll the beggar over ninety degrees, use the lift as a vector. I can take my excess delta-vee, and I can turn it into plane-change vector. Two passes through the atmosphere, I've got the orbit circularized, and as a free bonus, I get my plane change. Piece of cake."

"Shit," Radkowski said. "Does that really work?"

Ryan had been spinning lazily end over end as he talked. As he finished talking, his head was in the middle of the lounge, his feet next to the computer console. He reached out with one foot and tapped the keyboard. The screen lit up. Ryan smiled. "Believe it," he said. "I've got it all worked out in computer simulation."

Radkowski nodded. What Ryan was looking for, he realized, was not for somebody to check his work—it was obvious that he had complete confidence in that. So what was he asking about? "You're requesting for permission to use the CRV?"

Ryan Martin shook his head. "Radkowski, I'm not asking your permission. I'm going, whether you agree or not."

"You take that CRV without permission," Radkowski said, "and they'll kick your ass so far out of the astronaut corps that you won't need a booster to get into orbit."

"Maybe they will." He shrugged. "Nevertheless, permission or no permission, I'm not going to leave them to die."

"Okay," Radkowski said. "We'll do it."

Ryan reached out a hand to stop his slow spin and looked up at Radkowski in surprise.

"Just one minor detail," Radkowski said.

Ryan smiled. "Name it."

"This mission you're proposing is dangerous as hell, more than likely it's not going to work, and even if it does work, it may already be too late to rescue the Russians. Half-baked, untested, dashed-together schemes like this are a formula for killing pilots. There's no chance I'm going to let *you* do it."

"It's not dangerous," Ryan said. "I know I'm low on pilot-in-command hours, but the computer will be doing the flying. If it looks like I can't make the rendezvous, the computer will tell me, and I will abort to Earth."

"No, you won't. You'd only end up killing yourself, and I'm not about to allow you do that," Radkowski said. "I'm going to fly it myself."

7

D E S C E N D I N G

Rappelling down is the part of a climb that most rock climbers like least. To Trevor, however, rappelling was the best part. It gave all of the giddy thrill of hanging on a rope over immense heights, with far less work than actually climbing. He had rappelled long before he had ever climbed, driving with his older brother to the top of canyons in Arizona and rappelling down the cliffs. So he knew about rappelling.

Nevertheless, he watched Ryan as he fed rope out. The superfiber was different. The fiber itself was coated with a monolayer of fluropolymer that gave it an incredibly low friction; this meant that the fiber was less likely to snag on protrusions or be sawed through by a sharp corner, but also meant that only the specially designed braking mechanisms worked well on it.

The commander was smooth and matter-of-fact about belaying down. Trevor had always descended a cliff in bounces, pushing off and dropping, letting the cable swing him back into the cliff like a pendulum. It was more fun that way. The commander, though, methodically paid out line through the braking fixture, and walked step by step backward, his eyes fixed on the rock at his feet.

Boring.

When the commander got to the rover, he called up "off belay," and Ryan relaxed.

The next step would be harder. With one arm useless, and an ankle that would not take any strain, there was no way that Estrela would be able to rappel down the cliff.

Ryan strapped Estrela tightly into a harness and attached a belay line for safety.

"Santa Luzia," Estrela said. "Be careful, will you?"

Ryan set the fiber into the winch. "I'll do the best I can," he said.

8

THE RESCUE

The tether launch from the space station had been flawless, a high-stakes game of crack-the-whip, with John Radkowski, alone in the crew return vehicle, at the very tip of the whip, flying off on a precisely controlled trajectory at the exact apex of the sling. He had kept his hands off the controls during the descent through the atmosphere. No human could maintain the knife-edge tolerances needed for a hypersonic lifting aeropass, and so the guidance computer, with its crystalline logic and perfect mathematical calculations, had done the flying, comparing the predictions of the computer model with the performance of the actual vehicle a thousand times a second, adjusting in real time for variations in exospheric density and discrepancies between the computer model and the actual vehicle.

Now, floating in the crew return vehicle, there was nothing left to do but wait for the slow pirouette of orbits to bring the *Mirusha* station into range. It seemed as if the vehicle was motionless, and the Earth, endlessly varying, flowing like a sluggish river beneath it. John Radkowski was waiting, alone in space. It was in situations like this, when he had nothing to do but wait, that Radkowski was alone with his inner resources, and found them wanting. He felt lost in an immensity of void stretching off in all directions, and with the realization pounding in from all around him that he was nothing, an insignificant speck in the universe.

The thought both comforted and terrified him.

Focus on the control panel. Check the fuel levels again, for the hundredth time. Check the battery voltages. Check the radios. Focus on the radar. Is that the Russian station? No, it's still too early.

His breath came in short, shallow pants, and he struggled to control his breathing, to avoid hyperventilating.

Focus on the control panel. Breathe evenly. Is that signal acquisition?

Yes. The indicator light glowed with the acquisition of carrier, and then the radio spoke. "CRV-1, here is Nordwijk. We've got you on the screens."

The voice spoke in a crisp, Scandanavian-accented English. "You're looking good."

"Nordwijk, CRV-1," he said. "Thanks for the update. How long before I expect to acquire signal from *Mirusha*?" The mission control at Houston had been cool toward the idea of trying to fly a rescue mission—probably they still remembered the humiliation of the Russians pulling out of the space station project—but they had not actually forbidden it. The European space center in Nordwijk, on the other hand, had been enthusiastic, and guaranteed him as much help as they could give. This was little enough— radar readings from the ground tracking stations to confirm what the interior navigation of the crew return vehicle already told him—but he was glad enough for it.

"CRV-1, you should be getting transponder now," Nordwijk told him.

He frowned. He was getting nothing. No, there it was on his rendezvous radar. But where was the transponder?

He was coming up on it backward; by the strange ballet rules of orbital mechanics, *Mirusha* was coming up from behind him as he rose to meet it. He could see it now, a brilliant, lumpy star blazing in the sunlight. "Roger, I've acquired it visually," he said. He checked the rendezvous radar. Eight kilometers, closing rate one-fifty meters per second. He corrected his vehicle pitch slightly and made a three-second engine burn with the maneuvering engine, raising his perigee to bring his orbit closer to synch with the Russians, and checked the radar again. Five kilometers, closing rate fifty-two. In his window, the *Mirusha* was a fat insect with blue metallic wings. He should be able to raise them on the radio. They knew he was coming.

"*Mirusha*, this is the American ship CRV-1. Do you read? *Mirusha*, CRV-1."

No reply.

The station was dark. He brought the crew return vehicle in cautiously. With the crew on the *Mirusha* not responding to his increasingly insistent signaling, it would be impossible for him to dock to the station as planned. This was a problem. He was wearing a pressure suit, but it was a precaution against a vehicle depressurization only, not a suit rated for an extravehicular activity. There was no help for it, though. He had come this far, it would be pointless for him to stop.

"*Mirusha*, CRV-1. Do you read? Mirusha, do you read?"

He brought the CRV in as close to the *Mirusha* as he dared. He had only one safety line, a twenty-foot line, and he clipped one end of it to the CRV and the other to the hook on his suit. Then he did a final suit check, opened the hatch, and jumped.

The docking hatch was barely six feet. He hit the station's skin, scrambled for a handhold and missed, rebounded away, and as he started spinning away, by flailing wildly he managed to hook the EVA handrail with one hand. He clutched at it and held on, and then, more calmly, pulled himself toward the hatch.

It opened freely.

There was no way for him to stay attached to the CRV when he went into the airlock. He had to unhook. The manual would have instructed him to attach a second safety line to the *Mirusha* before unhooking from the CRV, but there was no second line available. He unclipped the safety line and clipped it on to the EVA handrail, trusting blindly that it would be strong enough to prevent the CRV from drifting away and leaving him stranded.

He entered the airlock and closed the inner door. A light should have illuminated when the inner door closed, but the chamber was pitch black. He flicked on his suit light and by its feeble illumination, found the hand-wheel that opened the inner door.

The wheel spun freely. There was no pressure on the other side.

In the long, slow fight against a steady leak to space, the two Russians on the space station had lost their fight. There would be no heroic rescue. The dark space station and the lack of internal pressure told him that there was no one left to rescue.

Time had run out.

In all his future years, John Radkowski would remember that lesson. You can be clever, you can come up with daring ideas, and sometimes they even work.

But sometimes, all of your work and all of your courage is not enough. Space is cold and empty and unforgiving, it does not care about human tragedy or last-minute heroics or brilliant piloting skills.

Sometimes your time runs out.

9

ON THE SLOPE

The lesson that John Radkowski had learned from the failed *Mirusha* rescue was that Ryan Martin was bright, impulsive, and that he needed to be carefully watched.

And the second lesson he learned was that sometimes, despite the best you can do, missions fail. And then people died.

He had no time to waste in thinking about ancient failures, Radkowski told himself. The footing at the base of the cliff was treacherous. He was standing on a slope of loose rock that had broken free of the cliffs above and sloped down at a forty-five-degree angle to the true bottom of the canyon. He tested the surface cautiously. The angular rock fragments ranged in size from small pieces the size of dinner plates to enormous ones the size of refrigerators and even small automobiles. They seemed to be loosely cemented in place by a coating of some form of desert varnish. It seemed relatively stable. Good. He worked a piece that was roughly the size and shape of a guitar loose with his foot, kicked it down the slope, and watched it bounce and ricochet another five hundred feet down the hill. It knocked a few smaller rocks free, but didn't start an avalanche. Good.

The rock fragments were light yellow, much lighter in color than the dark rocks they had been traversing. The cliff walls were light-colored as well, he noticed, all except for a dark stripe maybe a hundred feet wide at the very top.

He drilled a bolt-anchor into the cliff and tied the rockhopper down to free the winch line. There wasn't much he could do but wait for Ryan Martin to start lowering Estrela. He didn't like not being in control, but there was nothing he could do at this point.

He checked the rockhopper again, to make sure it wasn't about to slide down the slope, and decided it was secure enough that he didn't need to put in another bolt. Right up against the cliff face the loose rock was almost a ledge. John Radkowski sat.

No sense in doing nothing. He was still high enough up to get a good overview of the base of the canyon. He unpacked the binoculars and scanned the terrain.

From here, the base of the catena looked rougher than they had expected from the orbital view. It was a jumble of tilted slabs of rock.

Painstakingly, John Radkowski began to scout out a path.

ON THE SLOPE

"I'm sweating," Estrela said.

"For heaven's sake, turn on your cooling loop, then," Radkowski told her.

"It's already up all the way."

After lowering Estrela, Ryan and Tana disassembled the winch and were lowering it down to Commander Radkowski. This was a slightly tricky operation—they had to lower it by hand—and Radkowski had little time to hold Estrela's hand if she had forgotten how to program her interior climate settings. He ignored her.

Estrela went into the rockhopper, still complaining that she was too warm. She was awkward in climbing in, with only one arm, but she finally got inside and pulled the hatch closed behind her. Radkowski barely noticed.

Trevor, then Tana, and finally Ryan came one by one down the cliff. Ryan had to give Trevor some instruction in rappelling—the kid had a tendency to bounce down, instead of lowering himself down at a smooth walk to minimize the stress on the anchors. But eventually the entire crew was standing on the slope at the base of the cliff.

They abandoned the superfiber cables used to descend the cliff; they had plenty of cable, and it was easier to leave the used cable behind than to retrieve it. Dangling down the cliff face, it was almost invisible against the light rock; in the places where it was in shadow it could not be seen at all. Over a few weeks, the harsh ultraviolet from the unshielded Martian sun would slowly chew away the covering, and once the fluoropolymer sheath was gone, the cable would disintegrate quickly. And all that would be left behind would be a few titanium bolts, anchored in rocks at the top of the cliff, to show that they had passed this way.

They had made it down. It had been a lot harder than he'd expected it would be, but they were all down, and they were all safe.

Maybe they would be able to take the big one after all.

ON THE BOTTOM

The talus slope at the bottom of the canyon was steep, but except for a few minor rockslides when the wheels dislodged loose boulders, the rubble held, and John Radkowski managed to drive the rockhopper down the incline the rest of the way to the bottom of the catena without catastrophe.

As he had expected from his surveying the territory from above, the terrain at the base of the canyon was rugged, cluttered with angular, refrigerator-sized boulders.

At the base of the slope he called a halt for the day, and they found a nearly flat spot and pumped up the habitat bubble. The catena stretched out to either side of them, gently curving cliff faces towering over them, stretching as far as they could see. In the evening sunlight the cliffs turned from yellow to an intense orange.

The habitat had an odd smell, the smell of Mars dust: a sharp, metallic scent, like the smell of a distant thunderstorm, or freshly machined aluminum. It was due to peroxides in the soil. Although they made efforts to keep the suits clean, a little dust had been brought into the habitat with each crew member's return. It wasn't a bad smell; in fact, it was almost refreshing—an improvement over the locker-room odor that the *Don Quijote* picked up, with six people living in it for half a year.

There were the usual evening tasks to accomplish. Each suit had to be checked and refurbished for the next day's action, the filters cleared, the recycling catalysts renewed, the zirconia cells baked out to clear away the sulfur poisoning. The suits had not been designed for as many hours of continuous hard usage as they were getting; twenty hours was an absolute design limit for the suit's oxygen generation capacity, and Radkowski wanted to make sure that they stayed well below that limit. Just keeping the suits in shape took an hour each night.

It was hard to sleep. Radkowski preferred free-fall, where a sleeping bag could be tethered to a wall in any quiet nook of the station and the sleeping accommodations would be softer than any feather bed on Earth. He couldn't stop turning over the events of the day and worrying about how they could rescue the entire crew on a ship that was built for only two crew members. And, if the entire crew could not be returned, how he would choose? Eventually he fell into a restless sleep, but long before he was rested, it was day.

In the morning they set out across the bottom of the catena. The terrain was too rough for the dirt-rover to easily traverse, so Commander Radkowski left the bike strapped to the side of the rockhopper. After a bit of thought he gave piloting responsibility for the rockhopper to Ryan, with Estrela riding as passenger, and ceded Tana her perch on the top. It was a good place for her to scout for obstacles anyway, although he would have never allowed it initially, had he known. He and Trevor went ahead on foot along the route that he had memorized from the ledge above. Since the rockhopper had to pick a slow path over the broken terrain, they were as fast on foot as the rockhopper was.

For the most part, they walked in silence, occasionally making a brief comment over the radio to warn of an obstacle that the rockhopper would do well to avoid. From time to time Radkowski stopped and climbed to the top of one of the larger boulders to make a minute inspection of the terrain with the binoculars. From the far side he had noticed a place on the far rim where it appeared that a runoff channel had been cut into the side of the wall, and he thought that by following the cut upward, they might be able to take the rockhopper to the top with little or even no use of the winch. The bottom of the channel looked rocky, possibly even rockier than the land they were traversing, but nothing he saw made him change his opinion.

"Say, Commander, sir." Trevor touched Radkowski's arm, and then quickly looked away. Up to that point he had been unusually silent during the walk. Radkowski glanced at the radio indicator LEDs mounted on his suit helmet, and noted that Trevor was talking on the private channel.

"Here," Radkowski said.

"I've been thinking," Trevor said.

After a minute or so, Radkowski prompted, "Thinking about what, Trevor?"

"Is it really true, what Ryan Martin said? About the return space ship only being able to carry three of us? It's true, isn't it? Is it true?"

Radkowski didn't say anything. He was tired. It wasn't something he wanted to deal with right now. They were approaching the far wall of the canyon. He pulled out the binoculars and began to inspect the path up the talus slope. From here the route he had chosen didn't look so much like a river channel any more, but it still looked like it might be a good way up.

"It is true," Trevor stated.

"Maybe," Radkowski admitted. But maybe they could do something.

They would have to look over the Brazilian ship, see what could be left behind, calculate fuel capacity and launch trajectories. At this point it was too early to tell.

But Ryan Martin had seemed worried, and Ryan was one hell of a wizard at back-of-the-envelope calculations.

"It is true," Trevor said, more softly this time. "That's like, a real problem, do you know it? Like, how are you going to decide? Have you thought about that yet?"

"No," Radkowski said. He had thought about it over and over, almost obsessively. He had been unable to sleep. "No, I haven't thought about it."

"Oh," Trevor said. "I though maybe you had." He was silent for a while, then said, "But, when you do make the decisions, I'm with the ones going back to Earth, right? I mean, that's not in question, is it? I mean, I'm like a passenger here, not one of the crew. I mean, I'm in the crew, but I'm not one of the professional astronauts."

Radkowski was silent. The footing was a little tricky here; the rock was dusted with dirt and pea-sized loose stone; it would be easy to slip.

"Shit, Commander, you know? It's like, I mean, you guys are old, no offense, right? And I've got my life ahead of me? So if there's only room for three I should be one of them? You can see that, right? Right?"

Radkowski was silent, studying the talus slope and the cliff above it. When the silence got to be oppressive, he said, "I haven't made any decisions one way or the other, Trevor."

"Oh, come *on*," Trevor said. His voice was rising in pitch, almost screeching. "You've got to. I mean, you know it's right, don't you? I'm the passenger here, for the love of God. You couldn't leave me behind."

The rockhopper was coming up behind them. Radkowski stepped aside, waved them around a house-sized boulder that marked the beginning of the upward slope, and pointed up the defile. Ryan, in the cockpit, nodded and waved. It really was a marvel the way the six wheels of the rockhopper rolled up and over the uneven terrain and yet kept the body of the rover nearly level.

"You wouldn't leave me behind," Trevor said. "I mean, it wouldn't be right. You wouldn't do that, would you? Would you?"

"I haven't made any decisions yet," Radkowski said, and deliberately turned his back on Trevor to walk up behind the rockhopper. With luck, he wouldn't have to. With luck, the problem would never come up.

Ascending the cliff on the far side of the canyon turned out to be actually somewhat simpler than descending. The channel Radkowski had found led almost to the canyon rim, close enough that the remaining two hundred feet to the top were easily climbed, and bolts set into the rock to anchor cables to slowly winch the rockhopper up. Once out of the catena, they were able to unstow the dirt-rover.

Dazed, slightly dizzy from the constant pain of her arm, Estrela thought to herself, I've been stupid, I've been stupid, I've been stupid. Every rock that the rockhopper crawled over hurt her.

She wanted to snarl and bite when they treated her like a child. She held back, forced herself to appear calm, because she knew that she needed their help to survive, and more, she needed to get on the captain's good side if she was to be chosen to return.

The crew were beginning to get on each other's nerves. She could see it in the curt language they used with each other, in their short tempers.

Her attempt at seduction in the rockhopper, the night that Ryan had gone haywire, hadn't worked. Even before the radio had broken in, the mood had gone bad. Radkowski hadn't actually told her no, but when she had unzipped his jumpsuit and slid her warm hand inside, he had gently pushed her away. Perhaps if she had a little more time . . .

She was in pretty bad shape for a seduction right now, with a broken arm. The captain wasn't the one she'd really like to seduce, though, not by a long shot. And it sure wasn't Trevor. She saw the way the kid looked at her sometimes, and sometimes she even went out of her way to show him a little skin, to give him a bit of a thrill, but that was just to be nice. She didn't have any real interest in seducing children. He said he was twenty-one, but to her he sure didn't look twenty-one. She doubted if he was a day over eighteen. Maybe seventeen. He was just a kid.

No, the one she'd really like to catch alone was Ryan Martin. His slender, lithe body; his long eyelashes and hazel eyes and the intensity of his gaze when he was talking . . . He was the only one of the crew that she would crawl for. There was something about him, some essential core of sadness . . .

But it was the captain that she had to seduce, she knew. Ryan was candy. The captain was the key to life and death.

The landscape outside the rockhopper's viewports was hypnotic, almost magical. North of the Coprates Catena the land was flatter than it had been. She couldn't name the rocks anymore, but they almost seemed to talk to her. The pain in her arm sang a little song to her, made her head dance. The landscape and the pain, the pain and the landscape; it was all mixed up together in her mind.

13

EDGE OF THE KNIFE

John Radkowski's throat hurt.

The scenery was less varied now, flat, uninteresting. Or perhaps it was he who had lost interest in the scenery.

There was another smaller canyon for them to cross, he knew, a branch of the Valles Marineris, before they even came to the main gorge of the canyon. He debated stopping for a day, trying to acquire Earth with the high-gain antenna and asking for advice, but he knew that their chances of success were best if they could make the dash north as quickly as possible, without stopping anyplace it wasn't absolutely necessary. And, anyway, the advice they had gotten from Earth had been, so far, completely useless. The only useful information he'd received was the part he had gotten on the private channel, the one that the crew—and the population of Earth, following with vicarious attention the unfolding disaster in space—had not heard. The advice had been that they had better come up with a rescue plan to save themselves, because there was no chance of any help whatsoever from Earth.

He didn't need to waste another day for them to tell him that they couldn't give him any help.

His throat hurt. There was a metallic taste in his mouth, as if he had been sucking on a galvanized nail. It must be the Mars dust, he guessed; the dust, finer than talcum powder, got into everything. He took a deep sip of the electrolyte fluid, but it didn't really help.

It was going to be a long day.

Toward midday they reached the next precipice. The canyon was wider here, the far wall barely visible, but he knew that they were south of the main canyon and this was just a spur. Instead of winching the rockhopper down, this time they turned east, following the top of the cliff.

From the satellite photos, it had looked to him that if they navigated right, they could thread a path which crossed over the canyons on a spit of land, a narrow ridge that dropped rapidly on either side.

After about five miles, the cliff edge curved around to the northeast. A few more miles, and they came to a point. To the left, to the right, there was nothing visible but canyon. Radkowski stopped the rockhopper.

Ahead of them, a ridge cut across the canyon, dropping away on both sides. It disappeared into the distance, curving gently downward. It must have been a sharp edge once, carved away from either side by the enormous, unknown knife that had carved the great canyon. But now, millions, probably billions of years later, the sharpness of the ridge had been rounded, and there was, if not actually a level place at the center, at least a wider place, wide enough that perhaps the rockhopper would be able to cross the canyon without descending.

They stowed the dirt-rover on its rack on the rockhopper. He directed Tana, Ryan, and Trevor to walk ahead on foot, roped together for safety. With Estrela in the cabin with him, he took the rockhopper along the narrow trail behind them.

It was like driving on a tightrope. He gave the driving his entire attention; focusing on the tiny ribbon of ridgetop ahead of him as if he could keep the rockhopper balanced by sheer willpower. In a way it was simple; on the narrow cusp of the ridge, there were no obstacles, no boulders, no crevasses. As long as he kept to the ridgeline it was easy.

And at first the ridge was wide enough to be almost a road, sloping slightly downward at a gentle angle. It was wide enough for the three crew members ahead of him to walk side by side, Trevor skipping and running ahead to peer down over the cliff edge on one side, then the other.

"How are you doing there, Commander?" It was Ryan's voice.

He toggled the radio to reply. "Not bad so far."

"If you get tired and want me to take a turn driving, let me know."

"Okay. No problem so far."

But as they went further on, the ridgeline narrowed. Now it was narrow enough that he could no longer keep all six wheels on the ridgeline. He slewed the rover around crabwise, until it was turned completely sideways on the ridge. Each wheel of the rockhopper had independent steering, and he used this feature to turn all six wheels ninety degrees. Now the rockhopper could roll sideways, and he could keep the two middle wheels on the peak of the ridge. The two fore wheels and the two rear wheels he extended downward to the full length of the cantilever struts, conforming to the shape of the ridge, pressing against the ridge on either side to give him balance. The belly of the rover was dangerously close to scraping the ridge, but there was nothing he could do about it.

The pressurized cabin of the rover hung out over the edge of the cliff. Below him he saw nothing but an endless slope downward, downward to a bottom that was invisible in the distance below.

Ahead of him, the three crew members were walking in a single file now, Tana in the lead, Ryan at the back. The trail, narrow for the rock-hopper, was much wider for those on foot, but they had also slowed their pace. It was dangerous for them as well. He knew that Ryan Martin had the worst position. If Trevor ahead of him were to slip and fall off the ridge, Ryan would have to instantly jump off of the ridge on the opposite side, or risk having Trevor's fall pull them all over.

He could feel every bump, every tiny slip of the wheels, and with minute precision, corrected the steering to hold him to the exact top of the ridge. He couldn't tell how long he inched along the crest, eyes glued to the ridgeline under his wheels. Later, when he could spare his attention to look at the time, he was surprised to realize it had been less than half an hour. Below him, the ridge curved to a bottom, and then slowly began to rise. They were halfway across. And then, slowly, the ridgeline began to get wider, inch by inch, and then at last he could get all six wheels on the top.

His throat still hurt. His eyes were dry, and it felt like the inside of his eyelids had been sandpapered with a rough grit.

They had crossed the canyon.

The next one would not be so easy.

14

THE CANOPY OF CREATION

With part of her attention Tana Jackson watched her feet; ropes or not, to stumble here could be a fatal error. But the part of her attention that watched her feet was on autopilot; it was as if somebody else were taking care of the walking. The ridgeline curved ahead of her, and with the main part of her attention, Tana just looked out across the vast sweep of the canyon that stretched to either side of her.

The canyon walls were striped, horizontal bands of deep orange and light yellow, separated by hair-thin lines of black; in the midday sunlight they sparkled as if bits of diamond were embedded in them. Even the sky was colorful, shading gracefully from an almost lemon shade at the horizon to a deeper adobe color higher up. There was no other description for it, Tana thought; it was simply stunningly beautiful.

It was more beautiful, in its own desolate way, than anything else that she had ever seen. Impulsively, she turned on the mike, and said so.

There was no answer. She looked over her shoulder at the two roped behind her. Ryan Martin, she could see, was silently enjoying the view. But Trevor was white-faced, his jaw clenched, his face covered with sweat. He's afraid, she thought.

The rockhopper followed along behind them, going sidewise along the ridge, a mechanical spider. It couldn't be easy to keep it balanced exactly on the top of the ridge, but it was driven so smoothly, it looked as if it belonged nowhere else. A marvel of piloting, she thought. John Radkowski, whatever else he was, was a cool pilot.

She felt a sudden stab of pity for Trevor. He seemed so young, younger than his twenty-one years. Her heart suddenly went out to him. They had lured him away from everything he knew and loved, and now he was going to die with them, die on Mars, his body, dessicating in the dry cold, mummified in the sand. For her, that was okay—she had always known the risks. But for Trevor, it suddenly seemed so unfair. He shouldn't even be here, away from his music and his friends and his virtual realities, she thought. He's not astronaut material, and if it hadn't been for the lottery, that damn silly fund-raising publicity stunt, he would never even have considered becoming one. He'd be safe and having fun with his stomp music and his friends, just at the age when he would be learning to live, learning to love.

No. That was defeatist thinking.

And, despite it all, it was spectacularly beautiful. They were alone under the awesome canopy of God's extravagant creation, this magnificent canyon, never beheld by human eyes since the day of its creation.

Tana Jackson was at peace with the world.

PART FOUR

TANA JACKSON

We know that God is everywhere; but certainly we feel His presence most where His works are on the grandest scale spread before us: and it is in the unclouded night-sky, where His worlds wheel their silent course, that we read clearest His infinitude, His omnipotence, His omnipresence.

Charlotte Brontë, *Jane Eyre*

It was a desert, peopled only with echoes; a place of death, for what little there is to die in it. A wilderness where, to use my companion's phrase, "there is none but Allah."

—Richard Francis Burton,
A Pilgrimage to Mecca and Medina, 1855

1

A PHILADELPHIA CHILDHOOD

anisha Yvonne Jackson's father had wanted her to be the perfect BAP, a black American princess, sweet and rich and virginal.

Tana wanted nothing to do with that. From the time she could walk, Tana was a tomboy, "carrying on and raising hell," as her grandmother put it. She never wanted to wear the frilly, feminine dresses that her father bought for her, played hooky from the lessons in deportment and proper manners, scrubbed off the expensive makeovers and cut short her plaited hair.

All through his life, although her father dutifully attended her graduations, from her valedictorian speech graduating from Drexel to her acceptance of M.D. and Ph.D. diplomas from Case medical school, she knew that deep down her father was disappointed in her. While he would brag to his cronies and the pretentious men in his country club about his daughter the doctor, she always knew that, in his heart, he would rather have had a sweet little girl, perfumed and feminine, a daughter charming and demure who sang in church and broke the boys' hearts, without a single original thought in her head. The kind of girl that she could never be.

She broke her arm falling out of a tree when she was seven; broke the other one playing football with the neighborhood boys when she was ten; collected scrapes and bruises and skinned knees and stubbed toes in the rough and tumble of growing up. She was halfway through high school before it occurred to her that she wasn't pretty, and another two years later before she thought about it again, and decided she didn't care. Men wanted boobs, not muscles, and until she was most of the way through college, all of her boyfriends were companions, not lovers. That was fine with her.

In high school she grew dreadlocks, more to disturb the establishment—and most particularly her family—than to make any statement. She sported a beret in a shade of purple so deep that it was nearly ultraviolet and spent her free time hanging out with the poets and the misfits. Reading science fiction was her one guilty secret; she knew that the aspiring poets and literary snobs she associated with would turn their noses up if they ever knew her reading habits, so she made certain to also have a copy of Proust or Baudelaire to quote. But she loved the heroes in the science fiction books, men who took charge and changed the world. It took her a long time to notice that there were no characters like her, that the books she loved best featured heroes who were mostly white men with Anglo names. But, she decided later with the arrogance of youth, that really didn't matter. They would find out about her soon enough.

She lost her virginity her senior year at Drexel, to a boy who was sweet and serious and believed unquestioningly in all of her hopes and dreams and ambitions. They would talk all through the night, and the next morning go to classes so silly from lack of sleep that their friends wondered if they were drunk. She didn't even realize that they were dating until one day he brought her flowers—a bouquet of pansies and snapdragons and nasturtiums—and she looked at them in puzzlement and asked what they were for, and he told her shyly that it was because they had been seeing each other for six months. She thought back in wonder and realized that, yes, it was true. Shortly after that she admitted him into her bed.

He was a white boy, something that might have mattered to her parents, but was pretty much irrelevant to her. She saw him every single day through her last year of college and the summer afterward, and then she went off to medical school in Cleveland, and he went away to join the Peace Corps and then become a lawyer. They wrote to each other, but the letters came further and further apart, and years later she would remember him with fondness and wonder what ever happened to him.

2

T H E   B I G   C A N Y O N

Another thirty miles across broken terrain—not even an hour's traverse—and they came to the edge of the world.

Or so it seemed.

The commander was being silent. He always tended to be quiet, but now he was like a mime, not talking at all, gesturing with a wave of his hand where he wanted them to go and not answering any questions.

The end of the trail came suddenly. The horizon in front of them seemed funny, too close, and then abruptly there was nothing.

The Valles Marineris spreads east to west across Mars nearly at the equator, stretching from the eastern edge at chaotic terrain of the Chasm of Dawn well over two thousand miles to the western extremity where it separates into a myriad of twisting canyons, the Labyrinth of the Night. Unlike the far smaller canyons of Earth, though, it was carved by no river, but formed when the immense bulge of Tharsis rose on the magma of long-extinct interior fire, cracking open the planet like the split crust of a rising loaf of bread.

Parallel to it were lesser chasms, places where the same tectonic forces that had formed the Valles Marineris had formed additional cracks on a lesser scale through the rocky crust of the planet. It was these that they had crossed before. But this was not one of the lesser canyons. They had reached the real thing, the full-scale Valles Marineris.

Tana Jackson stood on the lip of infinity and looked out, and out, and out. There was no far wall to the canyon; it was well beyond the horizon. The hazy ochre of the sky merged imperceptibly with the haze of the canyon floor.

Before her was a vertical drop of a mile, straight down, and then a slope of broken rock and detritus that extended downward and away for ten miles or more, to a bottom so distant that the features were blurred by the omnipresent atmospheric dust. Tana's voice was almost awed.

"Yikes," she said. "Are we really going down this?"

Radkowski's voice, when it came, was a hoarse whisper. "Yes," he said. "Down and across." He paused, and then in a whisper so soft that it was almost inaudible through the radio noise, added, "We have no choice."

3

TANA IN SCHOOL

Tana's grandmother had told her about affirmative action—that whatever she managed to achieve, white people were going to assume that she got it simply by being black. "Ain't no way you're gonna avoid it," she told Tana. "You just go and pay no attention to them, ignore it and do a good job."

It seemed unfair, Tana told her, but her grandmother disagreed.

"Not a one of them white folks got where they were without help," she said. "Not one. Their parents knew people, they got into the right schools, they got connections, they got a job because their uncle knew somebody. No, they won't admit it. Maybe they don't even know it themselves. But they got help, every single one of 'em."

Tana listened to what she said—her grandmother had always been a sharp cookie and a good judge of character—but she didn't actually believe it. She had every intention of getting where she was going, affirmative action or no.

Her way to medical school was paid by a Hawthorne Foundation scholarship that covered her tuition and expenses and a little bit for her to live on as well. The very first day of med school, before she knew anybody, before she even could find her way around the strange new campus without the map in the med school handbook, one of the boys in her class cornered her in a hall. In a peremptory tone, he demanded to know whether she was paying her own way or if she had a scholarship. When she told him about the Hawthorne fellowship—maybe bragging a little bit, because she knew it was a highly competitive grant—he nodded. Obviously it confirmed what he had already known. And he explained to her that she had only received the grant because she was black. The full scholarships are reserved for minorities regardless of their qualifications, he explained. He, himself, had applied; he had gotten a better score on the MCAT and came from a poor family and needed it more. But it went to her because she was black.

She was up all night, tossing and turning.

The next day she went to the dean and told him that if the scholarship was awarded to her based on her color, they could take it back. She was going to earn her way based on merit or not at all.

The dean pulled a pair of half-glasses with black plastic frames from his desk drawer, and put them on. "Just hold on to your horses, young lady." He turned to his file cabinet. "That name, again?"

"Jackson. Tana Jackson," she said.

"*Your* name, Ms. Jackson, I already know. The name of the young man who is making these peculiar accusations, please?"

Tana hesitated. It hadn't been her intention to be a snitch on the other students, and then she realized that it didn't matter, she had forgotten his name anyway. Or maybe he hadn't bothered to introduce himself.

Before she could gather her thoughts to answer, he picked up a file from his desk. "Ah, never mind, I have it here." Apparently he had known the boy's name from the start and already had the boy's file out. He barely gave the file a glance.

"The Hawthorne scholarship, you said? Odd. According to his record here, he didn't even apply for one. But that is no surprise. He doesn't qualify for a Hawthorne scholarship at all, young woman. It is quite competitive, you know, one must have straight A's to even apply. I can't divulge the young gentleman's grades to you, but let me assure you that this is rather far from being the case. In fact"—the dean flipped a page, reading a handwritten note that had been stapled to the folder—"it looks to me like he flunked out of linear algebra entirely, and some person intervened with the professor to allow him to repeat the final exam. Not that you heard any such thing from me, you understand."

Tana's mouth was wide open. "So he was bullshitting me."

The dean lowered his glasses and looked at her over them. "He was, as they call it, yanking your chain," he said. "The med school here is quite competitive—very competitive indeed, you know. I believe that some students may, on occasion, take it into their heads to try to get an edge over other students with a little bit of creative truth-telling. You shouldn't believe everything you hear." He pulled off his glasses and put them carefully back on his desk. "Now, was there something else you wanted?"

She shook her head.

An instant after she walked away, the dean called out after her.

"One moment, Ms. Jackson."

She turned and looked back through the door. "Yes, sir?"

"Are you aware of the number of medical students needed to replace a lightbulb?"

"No," Tana said, wondering just what he was up to. "I'm afraid I don't."

"It takes four," he said. "One of them to screw it in, and the other three to pull the ladder out from under him."

She wasn't quite sure whether that was funny.

When she confronted the other student, he told her quite indignantly that everybody knew that she had won the scholarship because of her color, and he hadn't applied for the scholarship because he knew they wouldn't give it to him anyway.

As it turned out—she discovered later—the boy wasn't from a poor family, either; that part of his story was another bit of his creative application of truth.

"Bainbridge?" another student told her much later. "Him? He's a dickhead. You don't pay attention to *him*, do you?"

For the rest of her years in medical school and her residency, she chose her friends carefully—and watched her back.

4

A WALK IN THE
TWILIGHT

John Radkowski walked along the edge of the cliff. The bottom was already in darkness, and it was as if he walked along an ocean of blackness, as if he could dive off of the edge and swim into the lapping pool of dark.

Trevor had come to talk to him again, this time not even bothering to disguise the fact that he was pleading for his life, and he had again put Trevor off. Radkowski knew that it was time for him to face up to the decision that was his to make. The return vehicle could not save them all. Who should be saved?

And with this, the thought that he had been avoiding. When they got to the return ship—and he would get them to the return ship, whatever the cost—when it came time for the ship to launch, he would not be one of the ones to return.

He owed a debt.

It was time for the debt to be paid.

5

THE ROAD TO HOUSTON

Tana did her internship and her residency at a hospital in Pittsburgh. She married a bouncer at an East Pittsburgh bar, Derrick; she'd become fed up with doctors in her time at school and at work, and wanted nothing more than to get away from them in her personal life.

Derrick was more than a tough guy; he aspired to be a poet and took her to poetry readings and to gatherings of folksingers and artists. Even in the bar, he would be more likely to deal with a drunken customer by jollying them out the door with a quip than by violence. Nevertheless, her father had not approved of him; he'd still cherished the idea that she might marry the son of one of his banker or lawyer friends, somebody closer to being worthy of her.

Much later, Tana wondered whether, to some extent, her marriage had been an attempt to demonstrate to her father in the most vivid way possible that she had her own independence and was going to live her life her own way.

After a year, she found herself pregnant. She hadn't wanted to have a baby, at least not yet, but Derrick was so pleased by her pregnancy that he almost glowed. They named the child Severna.

When she completed her residency, she applied for a job as a flight surgeon for NASA. She considered it a long shot—she could barely remember her coursework in aerospace medicine after two years stuffing intestines back inside knife slits and sewing up gunshot wounds in the emergency room—but Houston was her best way to get inside, to find herself an inside track to get selected for the astronaut corps. When, to her own surprise, she was accepted, Derrick refused to leave Pittsburgh. "Houston?" he said, his voice incredulous. "Houston? In Texas? Girl, you've got to be joking."

But she never joked about her career. This time, she had never been more serious in her life. Pittsburgh was nothing to her; she'd never even stopped there for gas before she moved there for her residency. But Derrick had roots, cousins and uncles and family back three generations, all living within half a mile.

He was angry when she said she was going anyway, no matter what he thought. She made the paycheck in the family, not him, she told him, and Houston wasn't so bad. Besides, the salary she'd been offered was triple the meager amount she'd been earning. He could learn to live with it.

A woman's place is to follow her man, he told her, and fuck if he's going to leave the city he grew up in to move to fucking Texas. Where was she going to go next, anyway? He had roots in this city. Roots.

"I'm going, Derrick," she said. "With you or without you, I'm going."

He grabbed her blouse and jerked her toward him, almost pulling her off the ground. "The hell you are!" he shouted. The muscles in his jaw, his neck, his shoulders were all bunched up with rage. "You think I'm going to let you just leave me?" His fist was clenched, and she knew that he was about to hit her. They'd had arguments before, but he had never hit her.

She closed her eyes. "Go ahead, Derrick." She could feel his arm trembling with the strength of his anger, the motion of his other arm pulling back to strike. She screwed her eyes shut, clenched her jaw, willed herself not to scream.

He let go.

The release was so unexpected that she almost did scream, suddenly unbalanced. She was afraid to move, afraid to look.

The door slammed, and when she looked up, Derrick was gone.

It was an hour before he came back. He had been walking, he told her, he had to walk it off, or else he would hit her.

Derrick made up to her when he realized what he'd done, how badly he'd frightened her. He was extravagantly affectionate, promised he'd never hit her, never, and they made love. She was still tense, though, still afraid of what he was capable of. He was slow and loving, but she got nothing out of it.

She left with Severna and all the stuff she could cram into the car. She no longer knew Derrick, didn't know what he was, or was not, capable of.

Derrick petitioned for custody. It made sense, he said: He had family in the area—his parents and aunts and brothers and cousins and their multitudinous children. And who did she know in Houston? Nobody.

It was the one time that she broke her self-imposed rule: She went to her father for money. He knew better than to say that he'd told her so. The lawyer that her daddy's money bought told her not to sweat the custody hearing. It would be a slam dunk. The judge had never, he told her, never once awarded custody to the father unless the mother was dead, drunk, or in jail.

The judge was an old, white-haired black man, who looked so old that he might have been on the bench since the Clinton administration. And he seemed sympathetic, cutting off Derrick in midsentence. And it had, indeed, seemed a slam dunk, right up until the judge told Derrick to cut the crap, and just tell him in simple terms, no bullshit, tell him just why he thought he should take the child away from her mother.

"I just don't want my child growing up in the South, judge," Derrick said.

"South," the judge had said. "The South?" He turned to Tana.

Tana looked at her very expensive lawyer, but he seemed at a sudden loss.

"Well?"

"Houston isn't really the South, your honor," Tana replied.

But the case was lost. "I don't think is in the child's best interests," the judge ruled, "to grow up surrounded by rednecks, when she could instead be surrounded by her family. Custody goes to the father." He slammed his gavel on the bench. "Case closed."

Derrick's family bickered constantly—they seemed like they had a constant low-level feud—but they were, all in all, a loving clan. Severna will be okay, Tana told herself, she would never lack for a home to go to. She knew that if she told the court that Derrick had hit her, she could probably win an appeal. He had almost hit her, she told herself. It wouldn't really be a lie. She could say it in court.

She didn't appeal. As a single mother, she would have no chance at becoming an astronaut. It came down to the child or her dreams, and dreams had come late to her; she didn't want to give them up.

She felt guilty sometimes, even now, but she suppressed the feeling.

Derrick had found himself a girlfriend before she had barely even left Pennsylvania, before the divorce was even final. Last she'd been in touch, he'd gone through two more wives, but still didn't have any problem finding women.

6

LETTER HOME

Dearest Severna,

I still don't know when I will be able to send this letter, but I promised to write you, and I will. We are waiting at the edge of a canyon. In the morning we will go down. This will be exciting.

Mars has a stark and terrible beauty, rugged and untamed, more desolate than all the deserts of Earth. They call it the red planet, but when we got here it astonished me to see that it is not red at all, but a rich deep yellow, darker than beach sand, more like peanut butter only a little more yellow. Like buttered toast. The dark rocks look almost magenta, and the shadows are a dark brick red.

I'm sorry that I don't write to you more often. Please know that your momma thinks about you every day and hopes and prays that everything good will be coming to you. I remember when I was your age, and I guess that life isn't always easy, but don't give up. You don't have to be the most popular or the most stylish girl in the class, just be yourself.

I look at your picture every day. I have to say that I think that the shaved head looks funny on a girl to me, but everybody tell me that it's the style and lots of kids look like that, so I guess I'm just an old-fashioned trog.

I'm sorry I can't talk with you every day, but the Earth is disappearing behind the sun and the good communications antenna was left behind at the ship.

I'm sending all my love to you with this letter.

Take good care of yourself and do your best in school and everything will turn out okay, I promise.

all of my love,
your mother

Tana looked over the letter. Did it seem too cold, too trite? She never knew how to write to her daughter. She deleted the "mother" and substituted "mom," and looked through it another time to see what else might look stilted.

What else could she add? Had she told Severna how stunningly beautiful Mars was?

In the evenings, the two little moons come out and play tag across the sky. The larger one, Phobos, moves so fast that you can almost see it move across the sky; it goes all the way from crescent to full and back to crescent in the course of the night.

Surely that was enough. She didn't even know when they might be able to send the message. And in another day they would be descending the canyon. That, certainly, would give her something to write about.

7

THE COLOR OF DIRT

Houston was, in its way, something like medical school. Tana got along pretty well with the others, but she got tired of the rivalry to get on missions. Sometimes Tana was just simply tired of other people's assumptions. That because she was black, she must have grown up in a ghetto with a welfare mother and a drug-dealing father. That she listened to hip-hop music or—what were kids listening to now?—Afro stomp.

Sometimes she went to the mostly black clubs, or to the gospel choir suppers, not because she wanted to hang out with people of her own race, but simply because, once in a while, it was a relief to just be simply taken for herself, not to have to be a representative of her race. She wasn't sure if she even *believed* in the idea of race, at least not the way that white people seemed to.

People—other people—called her skin the color of coffee, or sometimes dark chocolate. She thought that was belittling. Her father had always said that they had skin the color of dirt. Not pale, worn-out soil, like some people, but rich soil, good farming topsoil. They would make things grow.

Her father had never been a farmer—he was an engineer—but his grandfather had been a farmer, proud of it, and had instilled that pride into all of his grandsons.

When she was depressed, when things weren't going well, when people dismissed her without even seeing anything but her color, she sometimes thought about that. We're the color of dirt, girl, don't you forget it. Nothing to hide about it, either. Rich and strong. Organic. Be proud of it.

8

D O W N   T H E   C A N Y O N

They went down the canyon at first light.

Ryan Martin had set the bolts into the rocks for the safety attachments the previous night. The dirt-rover was loaded onto its rack on the rock-hopper and strapped securely in place, along with their supplies. They lowered it first, a kilometer and a half straight down until it touched the talus slope, and then Ryan Martin went down the rope to secure it in place.

As he descended, he gave a running commentary over the radio link.

"Fifty meters," his voice came over the radio. "Seventy. The rock of the canyon wall is black and dense, smooth in texture, maybe a basalt. I'm a hundred meters down now. Oh, that's weird, there's a sharp dividing line, and it turns to reddish stone. It's undercut. The rock has been, it's like it's been eaten away."

"That's not surprising," Estrela said. Her voice was weak, almost a whisper. "The caprock is probably from lava flows, it's going to be harder than the sandstone below it. So the sandstone gets abraded away by sandstorms."

"Maybe," Ryan said. He had stopped descending, and was just hanging in space against the side of the cliff. "It's a lot of overhang. I can't see how far in it goes. It's like a cave, but horizontal, a kind of slot extending the whole width of the cliff face."

"Not exploring," Commander Radkowski interjected. His voice was a rough whisper. "Don't stop long. First priority secure rockhopper."

"Got it, Captain. Just one moment more, let me get a light out. Okay. Wow, it's deep. It's really deep. Hold on, if I go down a little bit more, now if I can just swing a little—there. Okay, I'm standing on the ledge here."

"Don't unhook safety," the captain said.

"Got it. It's high enough to stand up in. Incredible. I still can't see how far back it goes—Hey, up there, the rock you're standing on? Seem solid? Well, underneath you, it's all hollow. It looks like it goes back for miles. The bottom of the cave is quite smooth and level. There are crystals here, they're reflecting my light. Some of them as big as a fingernail. I can't quite tell what they are. They're purple. Some of them are blue."

Purple? Tana thought. Amethyst?

"Wait, further in the crystals are all white, kind of translucent. Doesn't look like quartz, it's not six-sided. Four-sided crystals."

"Hold on," Estrela said. "Four sided-crystals? You said four-sided?"

"Squares and rectangles. It looks familiar."

"I bet it does," Estrela said. "It's halide. Salt."

"Salt?" There was a long pause. "You know, I think that's it. Salt. The cave is covered in salt."

A DESTINY ON MARS

Tana was not extravagant or showy about her religion, but her family had been good Methodists, went to church every week without fail, and she had never questioned her faith. Her faith was just there, something that cradled her and supported her through the hard times, something that made her know for sure that her life had a meaning and a purpose, that even if nobody else loved her, she was loved by God, and that was enough.

It never would have occurred to her to articulate it, but her urge to explore was, for her, inseparable from her unquestioned religious faith. She saw exploration as a way to see the depths of the beauty of God's creation.

Tana had not always been interested in space exploration. She had gone to medical school because it seemed to be something difficult, something that promised hard problems for her to solve, and she felt most alive when she was meeting challenges.

That changed in the spring of her first year of medical school. There was a talk on the campus sponsored by the Mars Society, and she had almost not gone at all. It was certainly far removed from studying medicine. In the end that was why she had gone, because she needed to take a break; she wanted to get away from the medical school and the arrogant pricks who were her fellow students, and the lecture was cheaper than a movie.

They had brought in an astronaut to speak. He was a Canadian, younger than Tana had expected, a boy with long dark hair tied in a ponytail.

Much later, when she spent two years training with him, she would never mention that she had first seen Ryan Martin at a lecture at Case Western Reserve. She doubted that he realized she had met him before; the auditorium was packed, and she was in back, and who was she then, anyway? Just another anonymous face in the crowd. And she would certainly never admit that, once long ago, she'd had an intense puppy crush on him.

But he had spoken with such evangelistic fervor. Mars, he told them, was not an impossible target. With clever planning, it could be done. Should be done. He showed slides and talked about evolution, and about human destiny, and about how, someday, humans would not only have colonies on Mars, but they would terraform the planet. Mars is cold and dry and lifeless, but with coaxing, with engineering, it could be warmed, could be made into an inviting, living planet. And a trip to Mars need not be expensive. It all depends, he told them, on the ability to make rocket fuel on Mars, and he laid out all the elements of the Mars expedition, almost exactly the way that, fifteen years later, it would actually happen. "And you can go," he said. He pointed into the crowd. "You." He pointed a different direction. "You, too." And then he pointed at the back of the crowd, directly at Tana. "And you."

And Tana had been hooked. In college she'd set aside her science fiction as foolish fantasies of childhood. She'd never considered becoming an astronaut before, hadn't even considered the possibility, but now she was ready to go to Mars.

Her infatuation with Ryan Martin didn't last; he left the campus the next day, and she never even spoke with him. Later, when she married Derrick, she had already long forgotten that she'd ever even briefly had a crush on a lecturer. But the dream of going to Mars had been ignited, and it was a flame that would never, quite, go out.

T ana was the next down, and in fifteen minutes she was standing on the smooth floor of the cave and added the beam of her light to Ryan's. The crystals were indeed salt, she realized. Even the purple ones; eons of exposure to cosmic rays had slowly infused color into the crystals nearest the edge of the canyon.

Except for the salt crystals, the cave was almost entirely featureless, with a smooth flat ceiling, and an equally even floor, devoid of stalactites or stalagmites or any other cavelike geology.

The explanation, Tana realized, was that there must once have been immense salt flats here, remnants of some ancient ocean bed that had long since dried up, leaving only the salt behind. And then, over the ages, the salt flats had been buried under ash and lava from the eruptions of the great Tharsis volcanoes. Then, when the Valles Marineris had been carved like a knife-cut into the crust of the planet, exposure to water had dissolved away the salt layer, leaving a wide, horizontal cave in the side of the canyon, ten feet high and hundreds of miles, perhaps thousands of miles long.

How extensive was the salt layer, Tana wondered? Had the entire planet been covered with an ancient ocean? Did the entire planet have a buried layer of salt, hidden under the crust? Or was it just this area near the equator? And, more important, had the ancient ocean ever developed life?

She wanted to stay, to explore the caves, to investigate the rocks with a microscope to search for possible microfossils, but it was impossible. They had to move on or die.

But it wouldn't hurt for her to look just a little bit. In fact, it made sense for the others to rappel down before she moved on.

The crystals—Ryan hadn't mentioned how big they were. Here was a cluster of crystals, each one the size of a milk carton, with edges so rigorously square that they looked as though they had been machined; another one was a perfect octahedron, like some modern sculpture of glass. Were they all salt? The top layer certainly was, but it looked like there was something else underneath, something a whiter color, almost a milky blue. She scraped off the top layer. Yes, it was something softer, definitely different, not just rock salt. There was a mass spec back at the rockhopper; if she took some samples, they could analyze them later.

Was it the same all the way back?

Tana shone her beam into the back of the cave and walked farther to see just how far back it went.

11

INTERVIEW

It was a big conference room, with a faux-mahogany table and upholstered seats that swiveled and tilted. With only two of them in the conference room, it seemed empty. Tana fought the impulse to lean back in the comfortable chair while waiting for the interviewer to speak. She knew she had the credentials; what was important now was not to blow her chances by saying something stupid or giving the wrong impression. She sat up rigidly straight to make it clear she was interested.

At last the interviewer looked up at her. She didn't know him personally. He was one of many anonymous, well-groomed men in impeccably tailored suits. One of a network of interconnecting country-club acquaintances that—regardless of what the organization charts may imply—held the real power in the center. He said, "Do you think you deserve a spot on the expedition because you're black?"

"No, sir," Tana said. "A Mars expedition is no place for deadwood. I deserve a position because I'm the best qualified for the spot."

He looked back down and flipped through her papers again. She could see her application form stapled to the top, then transcripts, then employment files. "Hmmm," he said, without looking at her. "Says here you did your residency in an emergency room . . . Still up to date on your skills?"

"Yes, sir. I volunteer at the free clinic every other week."

"Well, that counts for something. We'll need quick response if we have an emergency. But you're not the only one with ER experience, you know. How's your exobiology?"

"I'm working with Feroz and Papadopoulos," she said. "It's in there."

She suddenly had to pee. She couldn't possibly need to; she knew better than that. Before she went to an interview, especially one as important as this, she always hit the ladies' room. But it sure felt as if she suddenly had a desperate need.

"Yes, Feroz and Papadopoulos . . . good credentials." He looked up at her. "How's the work going?"

They were cataloging stereoisomers found in Antarctic meteorites and in meteoritic dust samples gathered from high-altitude airplanes. The point was to establish whether a chiral asymmetry existed in samples from the primordial nebular material, and, if so, whether it had been modified in the subsequent five billion years of solar system evolution. If they found conclusive evidence that chiral asymmetry predated life on Earth, it would be a landmark achievement in exobiology, since so far the chiral nature of organic compounds on Earth was a sure signature of life. But so far, like the signs of life in Martian meteorites, their evidence remained tantalizingly suggestive, but inconclusive.

She resisted the urge to shrug. "It's going well," she said.

"You like the lab work?"

"I love it," she said. And, to her own surprise, she did. She had started working with Feroz simply as a way to get some exobiology publications on her resume, but she found that she liked being back in a laboratory. It was painstaking, and ten seconds of inattention could ruin ten hours of work, but she found that she liked the challenge.

"Good. I'm sure you do. But all that's not worth a hill of beans, really, is it?"

Obviously, he wanted some response from her here, and she didn't know what it was. Play it cool. "I'm not quite sure what you mean."

"What matters here is just one thing. Can you handle the public?"

"Yes, I think so. In my application, I have listed—"

"I don't care what's in your file. Everybody has a great file." He flipped the file of papers away from him, and it skidded across the table. "I've read two hundred great files. What I care about is, can you handle the public?"

Time to be firm. "Yes, sir, I can."

"Well, good. I hope you can." He looked at his watch and then stood up. Was the interview over? Tana hastily stood up as well.

He walked toward the door at the far end of the conference room, and then turned back to look at her. Perhaps there was a slight smile on his face; if there was, it was the first trace of any emotion she'd seen him express. She wished she could remember his name. He had introduced himself to her when the interview had started, but she hadn't been able to place the name.

"As you may know, on Tuesday afternoons we invite elementary school classes to tour the center. Today we've got a class of fifth graders on a field trip all the way from Tulsa, Oklahoma. We've promised them a special lecture. You're it." He looked at his watch. "You're going to tell them about Mars."

He opened the door. It led to a main lecture hall, with every seat occupied by fidgeting, talking, wrestling, gum-chewing, airplane-throwing, shouting, sleeping, bored children. "They've been waiting about five minutes now, they're probably getting a little restless. There's about two hundred of them, I'd say."

Yikes.

He turned to her, and this time it was quite clear, he was smiling. "You said that you're good with the public, did you now? Well, here you have a chance to demonstrate. Don't let's keep them waiting, shall we?"

Now she really had to pee. She ignored it, took a deep breath, and walked out. Get their attention now, she thought, or else lose it.

She found the microphone and tapped it. For a moment, just a moment, the din of conversation in the room let up. "Hi," she said, and smiled. "I'm Tanisha Jackson. I'm a biologist here at NASA Johnson, and I'm here to tell you all those things about space biology that you haven't quite had the nerve to ask yet. Like, for example, how you go to the bathroom in space."

There was a giggle, first just one, then a bunch all at once, and then outright laughter, and she knew she'd caught their attention.

"But, first, maybe you'd like to hear me tell you a little bit about Mars."

12

PAUSE IN THE
DESCENT

Captain Radkowski stopped briefly at the slot cave—it was, in fact, a convenient ledge to pause on—but did not unhook from the superfiber to join Tana and Ryan at the back wall of the cave marveling over the wonders of salt. From the radio reports, he knew that they had determined that the slot in the side of the canyon wall extended back about a hundred feet and then came to an end.

"It's completely smooth," Ryan's voice said. "Seems almost polished. A blank white wall."

"I wonder how far the salt layer continues?" Tana.

"Don't think we can tell without a drill." Ryan. "A long way, I bet."

"Hundreds of miles?"

It was not of great interest to him. Radkowski was more worried about getting the crew down the cliff to the rockhopper, and making sure it was secure for the long traverse to the bottom of the canyon.

He thought about reprimanding Ryan Martin for slowing down the expedition by stopping to explore the cave, but decided that it was understandable. They had, after all, come to Mars to explore. He would talk to Ryan privately later, caution him that regardless of what they found, getting north as fast as possible had to remain their first priority.

Before descending from the cave level, he checked his rappelling line and safety line attachments again. Both good. He pulled at the superfiber. "On belay," he said.

His anchor points, for both the rappelling line and the safety line, were still up at the top. From his radio, Trevor's voice said, "On belay."

He looked down—it was a long drop, still most of a vertical mile of drop—and then stepped backward off the edge. The superfiber held him, and then, without warning, it gave, and he was in freefall.

Shit. "Falling," he called. "Tension!"

The safety line caught, and he swung out from the cliff, twisted around awkwardly.

And then the safety line broke.

He started to tumble, and instinctively he assumed the skydiver's position, arms spread, legs in a V. "Tension," he shouted, but he knew that it wasn't going to do him any good. The line had snapped, and there was nothing between him and the ground but two thousand feet of thin Martian air.

It took him a long time to fall.

T ana Jackson's selection for the medical position on the Mars mission pushed her to the top of the priority list for assignment to the space station. Her name would not be publicly announced for the Mars billet until after she had been tested in orbit. None of the crew had been announced yet. They wanted to see how she worked out in microgravity, how well she got along with the station crew when she was confined in a tin can, with no new faces to see, with nowhere to go to get away. Her nomination to fly on the Mars mission was a recommendation, not a right; at any time she could be reassigned if they decided she might not work out.

The orders for her to start training for a ninety-day shift on the space station arrived the next day. At the same time, she was directed to take refresher courses in epidemiology, most importantly to memorize the medical details of the reports of the three independent review panels that had evaluated the *Agamemnon* disaster. She was also expected to become an expert on the hypothetical biology of Martian life. And, in addition to all of this, she was to appear cheerful and knowledgeable whenever the press needed a warm body to interview.

She began to train with the microgravity emergency medical kit, until she could unerringly find each piece upside-down and blindfolded: tracheotomy tubes, laryngoscope, oxygen mask, miniature oxygen tank, compresses, syringes, dressings, adhesives, scalpel, stethoscope, blood oximeter.

She had never worked harder in her life. The launch to the space station, when it came, seemed almost like a vacation. She was so excited that she barely noticed the launch, and only when she saw her notepad floating out of her pocket did she realize, I'm really here; I'm in zero gravity. I made it.

Tana's billet was to be the blue-shift medical officer, and in her spare time, a biology research technician and an experimental subject. The bio labs always needed both technicians and subjects.

She liked being on space station. It was crowded and noisy and confusing. It was remarkably easy to get confused, and even—despite its small size—momentarily lost. The familiar route from one module to another that you've memorized as a *left* turn would, if you happen to be flipped, mutate into a *right* turn, or even an *up* or *down* turn. Compartments that she thought she knew completely suddenly became completely unfamiliar when she came in with a different orientation, and the floor had become the ceiling. In a way, it was as if the space station were far larger on the inside than its mere volume, when every floor was also a wall and a ceiling.

On her arrival at the space station, Brittany and Jasmine, two crew members who were already old hands on the station, were detailed to give her the orientation. Brittany was big-boned, tall and square and blonde; Jasmine was small and dark, with a round face. They acted as smoothly as if they had been working with one another since they had been born.

"It's big and ugly and smelly," Brittany said, waving her hand at the station.

"Isn't it just," Jasmine said. "God, don't you love it here?"

"Yeah," Brittany said. She looked at Tana. "Girl, you may not know it, but the moment you get back down, let me warn you, you're going to start scheming how to get back up here."

"Home," Jasmine said. "Come on. I think there's nobody in the number two biology lab." She contorted her body, jackknifed, and with a sudden jerk, was facing the opposite direction. Tana had no idea how she had accomplished it without touching a wall. "Let's go over there, and we can"— she winked at Tana—"give you a briefing in private."

Tana already knew about the zero-gravity rite of passage, or at least the outline of it. The grapevine at the center had been pretty explicit. She didn't bother to try Jasmine's maneuver, but instead pushed off the wall to follow.

As the newcomer, Brittany explained, a tradition as old as the space station itself gave her the *jus primae noctis*, the right to choose who she wanted for the first night, any one of the seasoned crew.

"And it doesn't have to be one of the *men*, either," Jasmine said, and winked. "If you go that way."

Tana wasn't sure if that was a proposition or not. She could feel her ears heating up. "Does it have to be the first night?" she asked.

"Nah, that's just a phrase," Jasmine said.

"There isn't any night up here anyway," Brittany said.

"Sure there is—a new one every ninety-three minutes," Jasmine said. "Great if you like sunsets."

"If you're feeling nauseous, you might want to wait a bit," Brittany said. "Don't want to spoil it."

"Nah, you don't want to wait," Jasmine said. "The first couple of days they still have you on an easy work schedule."

"Yeah, it'll be hard to find some free time," Brittany said.

"Nah," Jasmine said, and laughed. "You can find time. I mean, you don't want to *wait*."

She didn't know why she picked John Radkowski. He was certainly good looking, clean-cut, and athletic, but not much more so than most of the others. He was the commander of the station, but somehow, it seemed to her, he had more depth than the other flying jocks, a core of sadness. She waited until she momentarily brushed against him in a node, and none of the others were close by. She looked at him, and he looked back at her with a long, unwavering gaze, his gray eyes almost disconcertingly direct. And then he said softly, "Would you like to accompany me to the equipment module airlock?"

She nodded, and he pushed off without a word, expecting her to follow.

The airlock, she discovered, was one of the very few places on the space station that had a door that could be firmly and securely shut. Inside it, two space suits were stored. There was a small space, barely larger than a coffin, between the suits. John Radkowski pushed into the space and motioned her to follow.

"You're not claustrophobic, are you?" he asked.

She shook her head.

"Good." He pulled the airlock door shut and twisted the wheel a quarter turn. "Too much room is a problem up here." He smiled. "For some things, anyway. Action and reaction, you know."

There was a dim red illumination, emergency lighting, that was never shut off. The space was close; she was pressing against him slightly, but in the absence of gravity, it was comfortable. She could feel his breath, slow and warm. He had a slight odor of sweat, which she found not unpleasant.

"Nothing is required," he said. He actually seemed slightly embarrassed. "I hope Brittany explained that. You're free to say no."

She answered by pulling him closer to her and kissing him. She had to hold on to keep him from floating away from her. He was more muscular than she'd expected.

"I wouldn't want to break tradition," she said.

He was wearing a T-shirt and shorts; under the T-shirt, she found, his chest was covered with dark hair. Tana unzipped the front of her shirt and freed her breasts. In microgravity, her breasts had no sag, she was as firm as silicone. A side effect of fluid redistribution, she thought. He reached a hand out tentatively, and cupped one of her breasts; she reached up and stroked the back of his hand. She started to slip her arm out of her sleeve to take off her shirt, and he stopped her.

"Leave it on," he said. "One of us has to wear something to hold on to."

He stripped out of his shorts and sent them floating away. He floated nude in front of her. There was nothing tentative about him now. She reached down and touched him.

Sex in microgravity, Tana discovered, was by necessity slow; sudden moves were impossible. She didn't have to worry that his weight would crush her, or if she put an arm around him her arm would be pinned. Even the climax, when it came, seemed almost in slow motion. She had a desperate urgency, but there was a frustrating lack of any leverage for her to take advantage of. She clasped her legs around his body, arched her back, and her whole body shook.

He had one fist tangled in her shirt, keeping them from floating apart, and they floated together, silent. At last, he spoke.

"Welcome to space station," he said. He pulled her to him and kissed her lightly on the nose. "I now declare you officially a member of the microgravity society, with all the rights and privileges that entails."

WAITING FOR ANGELS

John Radkowski lay on his back, on a slope of broken rock and sand, and marveled. He wasn't dead.

That was the surprise. He wasn't dead.

The fall had been slow, so slow. But he had been moving awful fast. He tried to calculate how fast he must have been moving when he'd hit, but he couldn't quite think clearly.

He didn't hurt.

In fact, he couldn't feel anything, just a comfortable warmth about his body.

The helmet hadn't shattered. It really did live up to its marketing, he thought, a technological marvel: light, clear as glass, and damn near unbreakable. He'd have to do a commercial for the company: "I fell off a cliff, half a mile down, hit rocks at the bottom, and the remarkable carbide helmet still held air!"

He wished he could say the same about the rest of the suit. He could hear the shrill whine of escaping air.

He was laying at a crazy angle, half tilted toward the sky. The sky was a most remarkable shade of peach, brushed with delicate yellow clouds like feathers. He wished he could move his head, look around. Out of the corner of his eye he could see blood. It seemed to be pooling in the bottom of the helmet, somewhere around his right ear.

He tried to use the radio to call, but his voice wasn't working anymore. He doubted the radio was, either.

The pool of blood in his helmet was getting deeper.

He felt remarkably peaceful. He owed the universe a death, he knew. One death.

His.

There was no possible way that any of the others could get to him in time. And even if they could reach him, what could they possibly do?

It was getting hard to breathe. The air was getting thin.

Now one of the others would get a chance. Would that satisfy God? Would that, at last, be enough? It was a nice balance. He'd leave the universe with his debts paid.

Around John Radkowski's right ear, the blood in his helmet was a pool six inches deep. It began to softly boil as the suit pressure reached equilibrium with the low atmospheric pressure of Mars.

John Radkowski waited for angels.

15

DEATH IN THE AFTERNOON

By the time they had reached the spot where Commander Radkowski had hit, Ryan Martin knew that it was far too late. The body was on a dangerous slope of loose rock. Ryan made sure that each of the crew members had a safety line firmly anchored to the solid rock of the cliff face before he let Tana go to examine him.

Tana's examination was brief. The impact had killed him instantly, she told them. Even in the light gravity of Mars, nobody could survive a fall like that.

"He looks peaceful," Tana said.

"He looks dead," Estrela said.

Radkowski's body had sealed to the slope by a glue of frozen blood. It took three of them to pry the corpse free, and the moment it came loose, Ryan could not keep his grip on it, and the corpse slid away, spinning slightly as it sledded down the slope in a tiny avalanche.

It came to rest when one foot jammed in the crack between two enormous boulders a few hundred meters down. This time they did not try to move him. The slope was too rocky to dig a grave into. They left him in the notch between the boulders and brought fist-sized rocks to cover him. It was no problem to find rocks; the slope was covered with loose rocks, of every size from gravel to space-shuttle size.

There was no funeral. Ryan made sure that everybody kept their safety lines attached as he got them organized. He wanted to get everybody moving, to get them focused on the task of getting down the slope before the reality of the death had time to sink in. It was too late to turn back, and there was nothing at *Don Quijote* to go back to anyway. There was nothing to do but go on.

The surface they were on tilted downward at an angle of almost forty degrees. It was a treacherous slope. The smallest motion of loose rock set off a tiny landslide; Ryan had to constantly make sure that none of the crew ever stood downslope from another crew member, and worried that a mis-step would result in a twisted ankle, or worse.

Under the circumstances, he decided that the best bet was to put all four of them into the rockhopper, and have the rockhopper work its way down the slope along a superfiber line solidly anchored in rock at the cliff face. He didn't want to trust the superfiber for anything except an emergency, and as a result the progress of the rockhopper was excruciatingly slow. It looked to be a good fifteen, maybe twenty kilometers of downward traverse to reach the level bottom of the canyon. The slope couldn't be this steep all the way to the bottom. Once it flattened out to only thirty degrees or so, they would go off the rope, to keep from depleting their spool of superfiber.

Fitting four of them in the cabin of the rockhopper made for seriously cramped quarters. He had them keep the doors open and their suits on; it was the only way to get enough room for him to pilot it.

And so, hanging out of the doors of the overloaded rockhopper like television hillbillies clinging to a dilapidated Model T pickup, at the head of an avalanche of sliding rocks and dirt and gravel, they drove down into the canyon.

16

IN THE ABYSS

Ahead of them, the avalanches of rock that the rockhopper sent down the slope raised an enormous plume of dust, like a pillar of smoke marking the path to the holy land.

Tana huddled inside her suit, blocking from her consciousness the details of the terrifying descent. Commander Radkowski was dead. She could hardly comprehend it; it was too enormous a concept to get her thoughts around. Commander Radkowski was dead.

He was the one who had kept the team together, who had told them what to do, and where to go. How could they possibly survive now?

Some day, long after they returned from Mars, when it was all just a shared experience they could look back on, John Radkowski would come to her apartment, and they would sit and laugh, reminisce, and maybe drink a little wine. Possibly they would get intimate—her dreams were a little fuzzy on this point—and maybe on that day he would tell her what was inside him, what demons of the past made him soft and sweet and innocent and hard and bitter and cynical.

But that would never happen. John Radkowski would never leave Mars. She would tell herself that, and come to herself again, huddled inside the cramped cabin of the rover, creeping down the endless descent, a slippery incline of loose and shattered rock. Ryan was glued to the wheel, keeping the descent slow and controlled.

When they got back home, all this would be something to remember. Perhaps she could invite John Radkowski over to her apartment, and he would—

But John Radkowski was dead. Jarred free by the wheels of the rockhopper, boulders broke loose and caromed down the slope, pinballing off other boulders toward a bottom that was so distant it was not even visible. It was not an adventure that someday they would laugh about. It was an adventure that would most likely kill them, as it had killed Radkowski, as it had killed Chamlong.

17

R O C K   G L O W

The slope leveled out a bit, and then a bit more, and Ryan cut free of the superfiber cable that served as a safety line for the rockhopper in order to increase their speed. And then the talus slope spilled out onto the canyon bottom. Ryan steered a labyrinthine path through a maze of boulders too large for the rockhopper to climb. And then even the boulder field diminished to scattered boulders, rocks the size of houses, of apartment buildings, but scattered enough that they loomed like alien monuments, no longer a hazard to driving.

Except for the scattered boulders, the canyon bottom was flat. The ground was hard, like fired clay, brushed lightly with a flourlike dust. The canyon was so wide that from the bottom the far wall was invisible. Only the wall behind them was visible, looming dark and foreboding in the evening shadows. Ryan wanted to move as far from the slope, as far from the site of Radkowski's death as they could get. Evening was approaching, and he knew that they could not get across the canyon in the remaining sunlight. But still, he felt that they should move as far as they could, and in the waning sun he pushed the rover to its limits, without offering to stop and unload the dirt-rover.

None of the others asked. They were each silent, each immersed in their own private thoughts.

The shadow of the cliff chased him and caught up with him from behind, and in the sunset twilight he was driving across a landscape of slowly darkening blood. Colors drained away, and then, as the twilight deepened, new colors emerged. Not just the orange and yellow pallet of Mars, but the landscape actually started to seem to have a brightness of its own. Ryan rubbed his visor. The landscape seemed to have a soft glow, so faint that he was unable to tell if it was an illusion, a ghostly glow of neon hues, greens and purples and blues, colors alien to Mars.

No, he was hallucinating, he must be.

Estrela spoke. Her voice was hoarse, and he realized that she had not talked once since she had said goodbye to Radkowski. He had thought that she was asleep. *"Milagroso,"* she said.

"What?"

"Don't you see it too? Look. Just look."

The sky was almost completely dark, but the harder he looked, the more it seemed that speckles of the rocks were luminous, tiny dots of color, glowing so faintly that it must surely be an illusion brought on by exhaustion. After a moment of silence, he whispered, "What is it?"

"Rock fluorescence," she said, and suddenly he understood.

"Oh, of course!" With the sun just below the horizon, no direct sunlight illuminated the surface . . . but the sky scattered sunlight. Rayleigh scattering, he thought: On Earth the scattered sky-light was blue, but with no ozone layer, on Mars the ultraviolet was even stronger, and the sky must be emitting a softly invisible bath of black light. In the near darkness the faint fluorescence of the rocks under the invisible sky-glow was just barely bright enough to see. "Wow," he said.

And even as he spoke, the glow of the rocks began to fade. It must only be visible for a few minutes after sunset, he thought, when it grows dark enough for the faint luminescence to be visible, but before the sky-glow disappeared completely. Maybe it was only visible in the depth of the canyon.

"Unless you are intending to kill us all," Estrela said, "I think it is time to stop now."

18

FALLING STARS

They had inflated the bubble in the twilight, but never before in full darkness.

Tana was too restless to be able to go to sleep; too many thoughts were crowding in her head. She had been crammed inside the rockhopper with the others for hours; she needed to be alone for a while. She hesitated outside the airlock to the bubble.

It was against all safety regulations for her to stay outside unless at least one other was outside to be her suit-buddy. "It's been a long day," Ryan said. His voice was hoarse and sounded weary. "Come inside. We all need the rest."

She shook her head, even though she knew that he couldn't see it inside her helmet. "I'm staying outside," she said. "Just a little while."

"Come on, Tana. You know that you're not supposed to stay outside alone."

"So try and stop me," she said, and she looked at Ryan with a look so haggard and forlorn that Ryan couldn't think of anything to say.

"At least don't get out of sight of the hobbit bubble," he said, and she nodded, then turned and walked into the dark.

The dark. It calmed her to just sit in the dark. She could let her mind go blank. She didn't have to think. She sat on a boulder, her back to the habitat so it didn't intrude on her consciousness. It was like a moonless night in the desert in West Texas, or anywhere. The stars were clear and bright; she was surprised how bright they were, barely dimmed by the dust. They were the same familiar constellations, but oddly tilted: Orion lying on his sword, Leo with his lion nose pointing to the ground. She couldn't find the pole star, and then she suddenly realized that she didn't even know what the pole star for Mars was, or whether it even had one.

A meteor flared overhead, a bright streak of green in the sky, and then darkness again. Then a second meteor crossed the sky, in the same westward direction as the first, and a third followed it, this one bright enough to illuminate the landscape with a faint light. A meteor shower, she thought.

One summer night when she had been six, her grandmother had come into her room and gently shaken her awake. The clock in the kitchen showed two in the morning. They had gone outside, Tana in her pajamas, and her grandmother spread quilts on the grass for them to sit on. Philadelphia spread a ghostly glow on the horizon to the east, and they faced west, toward the darkest part of the sky. "Lie back and watch," her grandmother had told her. The night air was pleasantly cool against her pajamaed skin, but she wasn't at all sleepy. She had always been able to wake up at any time and stay awake. In the speckled darkness above her, she saw a flash of light streak across the sky. And another, and then a pack of three traveling together, and then one that streaked across the sky and exploded in a burst of color.

"It's beautiful," she said. "What are they?

"Folks call them falling stars," her grandmother told her. "They visit us round about this time every year."

"But what *are* they?" she insisted.

Her grandmother was silent for a moment. "When I was a little girl," she said softly, "my grandmother told me that it's the souls of dead folks, rising up to heaven. When they rise, you see, they go and shed all the sin they've been carrying with them, 'cause where they're going, they don't need to carry sins around with them no more." She paused, and another shooting star flashed by, so bright that it lit up the night like fireworks. "Some folks must be carrying around a powerful load of sin, I reckon."

That was long ago. With her rational mind, Tana knew that it was a meteor shower; tiny bits of ice and sand whizzing through space, burning up in the tenuous outer reaches of the atmosphere. But somewhere deep inside, she thought, John Radkowski is making his last flight, and he's leaving behind everything he doesn't need, peeling it away like a soggy overcoat. I wonder what he was carrying round with him, that makes so much of a show when it burns up.

Goodbye, John. Goodbye.

19

METEORS

Ryan Martin had inspected the dome and was hesitating outside when a sudden flash of light attracted his attention. Wow, that was an impressive one, he thought. Looks like it almost hit us. And then there was another, and then a third.

It's a meteor shower, he thought. No, more than just a shower—this was fully a meteor storm. Streaks of light, yellow, blue. One streaked by and seemed barely over his head, as if it were close enough to touch. Jesus, he thought. Could that one really have been as close as it looked?

Are we in danger? Are we going to get hit?

For a moment Ryan was frightened, and then his rational mind whispered, you know better than that. On Earth, meteors burn up in the tenuous fringes of the atmosphere, a hundred kilometers up. A very few of the largest ones may penetrate as low as forty kilometers before being slowed and shattered by the atmosphere. The atmosphere of Mars was thin, but it was not that thin—the meteor shower might look close, but it was still no more than grains of dust burning up tens of kilometers above their heads, a light show of no practical danger to anyone on the surface.

Meteor showers on Mars have different dates, he thought, different radiants from those on Earth. Who knows the dates of Mars meteor showers? This one probably happens every Mars year at this time, and since Mars is closer to the asteroid belt than Earth, the show is correspondingly more impressive.

He watched it for a few more minutes—on Earth he'd always loved meteor showers; he marked them on his calendar so he wouldn't forget to watch—and then went into the habitat.

20

ON THE RIDGE

In the morning the first task was to unpack the dirt-rover from its carrying harness on the rockhopper.

Trevor, as usual, was the first one awake. He stepped outside the dome. He stopped, astounded. The yellow-red of Mars had vanished. The adobe-yellow sky had vanished, and had been replaced with a dome of opalescent white. Not one, but three suns were rising into the sky, and around the central sun was an enormous half-circle of light, a red-rimmed halo that just met the twin suns to either side. Even as he watched, the two second suns stretched out into arcs, and a third luminous arc formed above the sun.

At last Trevor found his voice. "What is it," he said. "What is it?"

Ryan stood beside him. Trevor hadn't noticed him leave the dome. He was silent for a moment, taking in the sight, and then said, "Parhalia."

"What?"

"Ice crystal halos." He looked at Trevor. "It's microscopic crystals of ice, suspended at high altitudes in the atmosphere. They reflect light. I've heard about it."

There were three complete circles in the sky now, and partial arcs of three more. It was geometrically perfect, as if a computer artist had drawn glowing circles across the heavens.

"This must be an ice haze filling up the canyon, because the canyon bottom is so low," Ryan said. "Miles below sea level, if you can say Mars has a sea level."

"Yikes!" Tana said. She had just emerged from the habitat dome. "That's incredible."

The canyon bottom had seemed flat the previous day, but today they realized that, in fact, they had been traveling parallel to a set of ridges. The light, diffusing through the layer of ice crystals, blurred the shadows, gave the rocky plains a softer, more Earthlike look.

The ridge nearest them was a bare hundred meters away. While the others were setting up the rockhopper and deflating and packing away the dome, Trevor climbed up to the top of it and looked out across the landscape. From below it had looked like a sand dune, but the surface under his boots was hard and unyielding, rough, more like concrete than sand. From the top, for as far as he could see in either direction, there were dunes, like an endless sea of frozen waves. The walls of the canyon itself were invisible.

His sense of direction was still acting screwy. He had no idea which way was north, which was south. No matter which way he looked, he could not see the canyon walls. Even from the ridge, the canyon walls were over the horizon.

Trevor was still trying to sort out his feelings about Commander Radkowski's death. Radkowski had never cut him the least bit of slack. It was hard for him to grieve too much at Radkowski's death, but he wondered how bad it had hurt their chances of returning. Ryan had already taken over as mission commander, he guessed—he had been pretty decisive in getting them moved out and away from the canyon wall, when the other two astronauts had been pretty much shocked and useless.

And, with Radkowski gone, his chances of joining the ride home had noticeably improved.

The luminous arcs of light in the sky had slowly faded and vanished, burned away by the heat of the rising sun, and now it was just another clear Martian morning. The sky was a dirty yellow, with only a thin tracery of clouds in the east, a pale shade of translucent blue, like gauze. *When the sun comes up on lonely peaks, he's vanished with the wind,* Trevor hummed. His throat was a little sore, and he didn't feel like singing, but he could still hum. *With the sighing of the lonely desert wind.*

21

THE VIEW FROM THE SPACE STATION

The cupola was the viewing area of the space station, a tiny observation atrium with windows on all sides. When Tana had no other duties, she often drifted there to just look down. It was a place to meditate.

Tana looked out at the everchanging panorama of the Earth. She was beginning to feel comfortable on the space station now. She was fitting in, running the little medical clinic, participating in experiments. Just as planned, she was getting familiar with space. She wondered if the Mars mission would be like this.

Tana felt somebody float up behind her. She shifted to make room—the cupola was barely large enough for two—but didn't turn. "It's so beautiful," she said. "Always changing. Always different."

Out the cupola, the ocean streamed past below. It was a delicate shade of aqua, a color so bright that it looked artificial. The blue was brushed with the crescent shapes of islands outlined in pale yellow sand and deep green vegetation. It looked so fragile, as if it could be made out of blown crystal, eggshell-thin, that might shatter with a touch.

"Yes," the voice came from behind her. "A fractal beauty."

It was Ryan Martin's voice, but she would have known who it was even if she hadn't recognized the voice. Only the Canadian astronaut would see the beauty in terms of the fractal spatter-pattern of large and small islands, the tiniest islets so small as to be no more than specks of yellow in the yellow-green sea.

She didn't recognize any of it. Tana had won an eighth-grade ribbon for her knowledge of geography, but here, where there were no national borders marked, where "north" was not up but could be any direction depending on the space station attitude, she was always lost.

"Where are we?" she asked.

"South Pacific somewhere," Ryan answered. "Want to know exactly? I could find a laptop with STK." He turned to swim down into the station.

"No, no. Pacific—that's fine."

The scenery scrolled past, the aqua of the shallow waters deepening to a rich dark blue, with a wash of thin clouds. She smiled inwardly, knowing that Ryan would probably also be thinking of the cloud patterns as a fractal shape, the graceful pattern of swirls repeated in the smaller bird-feather clouds.

The Mars crew selections wasn't yet official, but she knew that Ryan would be the third member of the Mars team. He had just arrived at the space station for a training mission. She was glad he was on the team.

She had seen him around NASA Johnson, but until they started to train together, she hadn't recognized him as the young astronaut who had given the talk that had given her the incentive to apply to NASA to be a flight surgeon. Why, without a doubt he was the reason she was here, and he didn't even know it. She had a sudden wild urge to turn around, tell him thank you, and kiss him. She wondered what he would do.

She did nothing, of course. It wouldn't be appropriate.

22

The rope shouldn't have broken, Tana explained to Estrela, when they stopped for a moment to rest and swap drivers. It was rated for more than a hundred tons of breaking strength; it could have held a truckload of elephants. "I'm thinking that it might not have been an accident."

"What are you saying?" Estrela asked. "Of course it was an accident. What else?"

"Don't play dumb, you're not blond," Tana said. "You've figured out that only two of us can be on that rocket back, maybe three, no more. Everybody on the whole team knows it. If there are fewer of us, that's more chances to get home."

"Murder," Estrela said. She didn't look at Tana.

"You have another idea?"

Estrela nodded slowly. "So you're saying, we should watch our backs."

"You got it." Tana shook her head. "Trust nobody."

Estrela asked, "Not even me?"

Tana looked at her for a long time, and then shook her head again. "Not even you," she said.

23

Twice they came across dry riverbeds, with dust-covered bottoms of smooth gray stone that looked like slate. "A good place to look for fossils," Estrela whispered, but only Trevor wanted to stop.

And, slowly, the cliffs of the opposite wall grew in the distance, at first no more than a thin ruddy line faintly visible against the horizon, and then a massive presence that came closer and closer, until the stark rocks seemed to be looming over their heads.

Ryan stopped the rockhopper to inspect the embankment with the binoculars. Like the cliff on the south edge of the canyon, eons of undercutting had given the embankment an extensive talus slope of fragmented boulders at the base. He examined it minutely, trying to determine where the slope was least steep, where it came closest to the top of the vertical face. It was a forbidding prospect; the jumbled slope of loose, angular rock would be a dangerous climb, and it rose for miles before it met the face of the cliff.

"Hey, come on," Trevor said at last. "Can't I look too?"

"This isn't a game," Ryan snapped, and then instantly regretted it. "Wait, I'm sorry." He wasn't getting anywhere, might as well let the kid try. He handed him the binoculars "Here. See if *you* can find a good way up."

Trevor put the binoculars to his faceplate, adjusted the electronic focus, and scanned upward. After a few seconds he stopped. "There," he said.

"What?"

"Right there." Trevor lowered the binoculars and pointed. "See?"

Ryan took the binoculars back and looked at where Trevor was pointing. "Where?" He didn't see anything.

"Wait, let me guide you. See the big boulder that looks like a thumb?"

Ryan didn't see anything that looked like a thumb. He scanned left and right, and then suddenly saw a peach-colored boulder that sat alone, sticking straight up out of the ground. It did look like a thumb, now that Trevor had pointed it out. "Got it."

"Okay, go up from there. Up and a little left of that there are two boulders together, almost round? They look like a pair of tits. Okay, now right behind that and a little left you can see a groove. Looks like a stream bed. That's a natural path up the slope."

"Yeah, got it," Ryan said. "But I don't see a path."

"Give me the binoculars for a moment," Trevor said, and Ryan handed them to him before he even had a chance to think, Why the hell am I giving these to him?

Trevor put the binoculars to his faceplate. "Okay, from the two breasts, look upward and left. There's one shaped like a skull, kind of, and one shaped like, um, maybe sort of like an elephant's ass. The path goes between those." He handed the binoculars back to Ryan. "Take a look."

A skull. He found that one, and then the elephant's buttocks. Shit, it was rough, but if you looked at it right, it almost did look like a path.

"See how it goes up toward that notch?" Trevor said. "Okay, now follow it up, keep going. Where it meets the cliff, see that? It's dried up, but looks like it used to be a waterfall. Just to the right there's a big splinter of rock, looks like a knife blade, leaning up against the cliff. You could climb right up that. And then at the top, see the groove in the cliff? That's a natural chimney. Climb up that just as easily as walking down the street, I bet. Easier."

Ryan could see it now. He wasn't sure about the waterfall part, but the rest looked right. He felt foolish. He had been scanning the cliff face for ten minutes, looking for a possible way to get up it, and then in twenty seconds Trevor pointed out a route he hadn't even noticed. "Hey, kid, that's good. How could you find that so fast?"

Trevor shrugged and looked away, but Ryan could tell he was pleased with the praise. "Heck, I live in Arizona. I've been looking at rocks since, I don't know, my big brother used to take me when I was just a kid. Since forever."

Ryan looked around, and saw that the two women were watching him. They'd seen the whole exchange. He cleared his throat, which had been awfully dry and scratchy lately. "Okay. Let's get back on the road. We'll get to the base of the slope and camp. I think that Trevor has just found us a path."

24

INSPECTION DETAIL

Again at sunrise the sky was a luminous white, with a halo surrounding the true sun. Ryan was annoyed to see that Trevor had once again gotten up far earlier than the rest of them—didn't that kid need sleep? By the time the rest of them awoke, he had already donned his suit and was doing the suit check to go out on a morning walk. Radkowski would never have let him get away with it; he'd been quite strict about nobody going out without a buddy. Ryan thought about telling him to forget it, to stick around and help with the deflation of the hobbit hab, but he didn't really feel like being the bad guy first thing in the morning, and really there was little Trevor could do to help until the others had breakfasted. So he let Trevor go out, with the admonition that he was not to get out of view of the hab.

They finished breakfast and deflated and packed away the habitat before Trevor wandered back. Ryan doubted if he had stayed in sight.

"Find anything?" Tana asked, when he came back to the rockhopper.

Trevor shook his head.

"What were you looking for out there, anyway?"

"Anything. Maybe fossils, I don't know." He shrugged. "Or old NASA Mars probes."

"Didn't find anything at all?"

"Rocks." Trevor shrugged again. "Lots of rocks."

"Well, keep looking," Tana said cheerfully. "Maybe you'll get lucky."

In the early morning sunlight Ryan drove the rockhopper as far up the slope as he dared. He gained almost a kilometer and a half of altitude above the canyon floor. When the wheels of the rockhopper started to slide on loose rock, he stopped, backed down to a less slippery spot, and chocked the wheels of the rockhopper with rocks.

He detailed Tana and Trevor to climb the slope on foot.

He still intended to drive the rockhopper up to the base of the cliff under its own power, but the slope was getting dangerous, and a slide would mean the end of the expedition. He wanted a superfiber rope—better, two superfiber ropes—as a safety line.

Ryan wondered if he should do a centimeter by centimeter inspection of each line. He had examined the severed ends of the fibers that had broken to kill commander Radkowski. They had broken cleanly, both the main rope and the safety line the same way, with no sign of wear, friction, or damage. The breaks were so clean that they might have been done with a razor blade. The superfiber wouldn't break like that from simple overload; a clean break like that had to have happened by some preexisting nick or flaw in the rope.

Or a deliberate action. But he wasn't going to think about that. They had to be able to trust each other, they just had to, or else they would all die.

No, it must have been a nick in the fiber. He had discarded the spool that had held the superfiber that had failed, just in case there was a problem with the batch.

An inspection would be a good cautionary step, he decided. Tedious, but safe. As they paid the line out from the reel on the rockhopper, he watched it as it came off the spool, alert for any infinitesimal flaws.

"You're just going to sit there and watch it unreel?" Trevor asked, incredulous. "Every inch of it?"

"Every centimeter."

"Wow," Trevor said. "I don't know if that's dedication or stupidity."

Ryan shrugged. "A flaw killed one of us. I'd just as soon it didn't kill another."

It wasn't easy.

25

ELECTIVE SURGERY

"Overall, I'd say you're in fine shape," Doctor Geroch said to Tana. "I can tell you, I wish I had a heart like yours." She laughed.

Julie Geroch, the NASA flight surgeon assigned to oversee the mission, wasn't in bad shape herself, but she was a little overweight. If Tana had been her physician, she would have suggested exercising more. But there was no point in saying that. The point of the exam was for Tana to get certified as medically fit for the mission, not for her to give advice to others on their personal habits. "Thanks," she said. She slipped off the hospital gown and reached behind the door to fetch her shirt.

"I'll be scheduling you for surgery a week from Thursday," Geroch said. "Is that date okay for you?"

With her brassiere halfway fastened, Tana suddenly froze. "Surgery?"

Dr. Geroch looked at her in surprise. "Sure." She flipped through the stack of papers on her clipboard, and pulled out a color printout, an MRI image of Tana's abdomen. "Your appendectomy."

"Let me see that." Tana's bra dropped on the floor as she grabbed the clipboard away from the doctor. She stared at the image. "Looks fine to me. No swelling—" She checked the legend for the metabolic and physio-chemical data. "Fluids normal, white cell count, nothing special either way, looks good to me. What's the problem here?"

"Oh, no problem," Geroch said. "You've got an excellent appendix; I'd be sorry to see it go, too. But there's no medical evacuation from Mars, and the crew will be leaving their appendices on Earth. Wisdom teeth too, although I see you've already had yours out. Didn't they tell you that?"

It was probably somewhere in the stacks of briefing documents. Tana hadn't read them all.

"Well, forget it," Tana said. "The chances of appendicitis are trivial, and if it comes to it, I can remove an appendix. I've done dozens of emergency appendectomies; you know full well that I was a surgeon on call for the ER. I don't know who called for this procedure, but I don't approve of unnecessary surgery. You can never be one hundred percent sure that there won't be a complication."

"Sure," Geroch said agreeably. "And we'd rather have a complication here on Earth than halfway to Mars."

"I can do an appendectomy," Tana retorted. "And I can deal with complications, thank you."

"That's fine, Doctor Jackson," Geroch replied. "And tell me, can you remove your *own* appendix?"

"Sure. If I had to."

"No problem, then. We won't schedule an appendectomy, then."

Tana smiled, relieved. She had no qualms doing surgery on other people—once you've done it a few times, pulling an appendix was no more challenging, say, than replacing the fuel-cell charge-discharge regulator on her Pontiac—but she didn't like the thought of other people's hands inside her own personal body.

"—as long as you can prove that you can remove your own appendix," Geroch continued smoothly. "Here's the deal. The way you prove that is for you to do it. So, when do you want to schedule the operating room?"

"Let me get this straight," Tana said. "If I show you I can remove my appendix, by removing my appendix, then I don't have to have my appendix removed?"

Dr. Geroch nodded, smiling. "That is correct."

"Either way, the appendix is gone," Tana said.

"That's right."

Tana sighed. "Okay, okay. Let's schedule the damn surgery then."

"Now, you're talking sense. So. A week from Thursday works for you?"

26

UP THE CREEK

T ana and Trevor took the path up, trailing the superfiber from the spool on the rockhopper. Ryan insisted that they rope themselves together, worried that the loose and fragmented rock would give way under one of them, and they would slide down the face along with a few hundred tons of boulders. They carried with them an extra spool of superfiber and a rock drill.

The cliff was farther away than it looked. It took them four hours of hard climbing to reach the face, and at the end of it, even with several breaks for rest, Tana's body was slick with sweat inside the chest-carapace of her suit. Despite the freezing temperature of the Martian air surrounding her, her suit was straining the limits of its thermal control unit to take away her body heat. Trevor unclipped the rope, and they took a well-deserved rest.

"It was a river," Trevor said. "Look at it! Look!"

The spot where they were sitting was a level, sandy area, nearly circular, surrounded by low banks on all sides except the side they had climbed up. A dry pool at the bottom of an ancient, long dead waterfall. Now that Trevor had pointed it out, it was too clear to miss. Tana had suspected that they were climbing an ancient creek bed the whole climb, from seeing the way the stones were rounded, the way the stream had undercut the banks, and the way the path wound around, seeking the lowest level. But the dry pool was clear evidence.

"There was water here," Tana agreed. "No doubt."

Trevor was inspecting the banks. "I wonder if there are fossils?" he said.

After a brief rest, Tana moved to the cliff face and began the process of drilling bolts into the rock to attach anchors for the superfiber. When she had the bolts drilled and the anchors set, she radioed back down to Ryan. "Got the superfiber anchored. Go ahead and reel it in."

"Copy anchored," Ryan's voice came. "I'm ready to reel."

"Take it slow," she advised.

"Copy that," Ryan said. "Slow it is."

Tana noticed that Trevor had disappeared. Exploring, she guessed. The kid couldn't stay put. Typical.

AT THE BASE OF THE CLIFF

This cliff would be easy, Trevor thought, looking up the rock face to the chimney above. A long climb, but not a difficult one. He considered climbing to the top just to show how easy it would be, but decided at last that Ryan would tell him he was violating safety and keep him from exploring any more.

He checked back to verify that he was still in sight of Tana. She was still drilling anchors into the rock. Her bright purple suit, even with a spattered layering of Mars dust over it, was easy to spot. He could still go a little ways without Ryan shouting about safety regulations.

Should he start calling him Commander Martin now? Ryan hadn't said anything. He seemed less interested in formality than Commander Radkowski had been.

He could see, looking up the cliff face, an overhang. He would be willing to bet that it was another cave, a horizontal slot in the rock that was a mirror image of the one on the south rim. The commander's death had cut off his opportunity to explore that one, but if he climbed up the splinter of rock angled against the cliff face, he could get a chance to look at this one. Would that be against safety regulations? Probably would, he concluded with some reluctance.

Anyway, according to Tana and Ryan, who had explored it, it was boring anyway. Nothing but salt. Not even any stalactites.

Instead, he followed the base of the cliff around to the right. It wasn't as if he could get lost here; his sense of direction was still screwy on Mars, but if he just kept his right hand on the wall, he had to come back to the waterfall.

It was a dizzying view down, like the ski slope from hell. It must be miles down; tens of miles, maybe. He couldn't see where the rockhopper was parked on the slope below, it was so far. He tuned in to the radio for a moment to see what Tana and Ryan were doing, but they were just discussing the superfiber cable, so he turned the radio off again.

The cliff face was extremely interesting. It wasn't all uniform sandstone, like he'd first thought, but a whole variety of different layers, even different colors, some of it a smooth, grayish blue stone, other layers made of a mixture of rocks all cemented together. Conglomerate; he remembered that from his geology classes. They had that in Arizona, too. Below the conglomerate was a smooth layer of gray rock that looked like slate. Or shale; he always got those two confused. It jutted out and made a little shelf a few inches thick, strong enough that he could stand on it. He thought about jumping up and down to see how strong it was, but decided that it would be a bad idea.

It must have been a flood or something, he thought. No, more likely a lake bottom, or even the bottom of an ocean. All the mud on the bottom settled in a layer, more rocks and stuff got layered on top, and it squished down on it until the mud got squeezed into rock. All this was once muddy ocean floor. And then the ocean or lake or flood or whatever dried up.

Slate—or shale, whatever—was where you find fossils, he recalled. He followed the ledge along, looking carefully, but it was completely flat and uniformed. Boring.

Sometime you had to break the shale open, and the fossil is inside. He wished he had one of those hammers that geologists use. Estrela would have one, he knew, but she was down at the rockhopper. He looked around. Above the shale layer, he found a piece of the conglomerate about the size of a brick that looked ready to come loose. Trevor pried at it with his fingers, worked it back and forth until all of a sudden it popped loose.

He used the rock as a hammer. The shale broke easily, peeling off in flakes like the pages of a book. He looked at each one carefully, hoping for a fossil, but there was still nothing.

When his arm got tired, he put his hammer rock down on the ledge for a rest. He was so tired that his eyes had been looking at it for minutes before his brain noticed that there was something there to look at.

The piece of conglomerate he had been holding had a smooth, concave surface. It had been molded around something. It was hard to tell just what, but it couldn't be natural. He raced back to the place he had found the rock. The trail of broken shale showed just exactly where he'd been. Yes, there it was, embedded in the rock, the piece that was left behind when he pried out the rock he used as a hammer, like a bas-relief protruding from the wall.

But what was it?

It was maybe six inches long, the diameter of his thumb, a perfect cylinder, but curved slightly, like a piece of macaroni. Looking closer at it, he could see slight pumpkin-ridges on the surface.

He tugged on the rock, but couldn't pull it free. It didn't matter.

A fossil, he had found a fossil. There were fossils on Mars. There had been life on Mars.

And he, Brandon Weber, had found it.

PART FIVE

BRANDON WEBER

But the ethereal and timeless power of the land, that union of what is beautiful with what is terrifying, is insistent . . . The beauty here is a beauty you feel in your flesh. You feel it physically, and that is why it is sometimes terrifying to approach. Other beauty takes only the heart, or the mind.

—Barry Holstun Lopez,
Arctic Dreams (1986)

The horizon was a sea of mirage. Gigantic sand columns whirled over the plain, and on both sides of our road were huge piles of bare rocks standing detached upon the surface of sand and clay. Here they appeared in oval clumps, heaped up with a semblance of symmetry; there a single boulder stood, with its narrow foundation based upon a pedestal of low, dome-shaped rock.

—Richard Francis Burton,
A Pilgrimage to Mecca and Medina (1855)

1

FOSSIL HUNTERS

They all clustered around the base of the cliff, looking at the layer of shale with his fossil embedded in it, examining his find. He felt inordinately proud. He had found it! Everybody else had stopped looking, but he had kept on. He, Brandon, had found fossils of life on Mars.

"It's a great find, Trevor," Ryan said, and he almost couldn't help from dancing at the praise. "You've got sharp eyes."

He ran fingers over it once again, feeling its surface, hoping that from tactile sense alone some message from the distant past would be transmitted through his fingertips. But the gloves were too thick, or perhaps no message was there to be sent.

It looked like nothing more than a six-inch length of some ordinary, dark brown garden hose that had somehow gotten glued into the rock. But that was impossible, of course. There were no garden hoses on Mars.

"Estrela," Ryan said. "You're the rock expert here. What do you think?"

"Me?" Estrela seemed startled to be asked. She seemed worn out, he suddenly thought. He was surprised how haggard Estrela looked. The pain of her arm must be wearing on her, he thought. Perhaps Tana needed to prescribe a stronger painkiller. "Clearly a fossil," Estrela said. "I think."

"What do you mean, you think?" Ryan pressed. "What is it?"

"Let me think." Estrela's voice was distant, a little weary. "This whole stratum was under the ocean," she said. "We're below the salt layer here, right? These are sedimentary layerings from the ocean floor. This one"— she touched the smooth blue rock layer—"is siltstone. Dried and compressed mud. This one here"—she touched another layer—"is a sandstone. This must have been a very shallow layer here. The layer with the fossil is a conglomerate; lots of different sediments pressed together. It's right above the shale layer; more layered mud. Santa Luzia, shales often have a high carbon content. We've got to get the mass-spec here, look for organics."

"But what is it?" Ryan repeated. "Is it a fossil, or not?"

"Truthful? I don't know." Estrela shrugged, and even through the helmet, he could see from her expression that the gesture must have been painful. "The only way to tell would be to see if there are more."

Ryan shook his head. "We can't. Time." He looked at the others and repeated, "Really, we can't. We're spending too long as it is. You know how tight our supplies are; we've been almost ten days on the road so far, and we aren't even a third of the way to the waypoint. Trevor may have found a fossil, but—"

They like me, Brandon thought. It was now or never. He interrupted. "Say," he said, hesitantly. "Commander Ryan? I was, like, wondering. Would you do something? Like, a favor, you know?"

"Of course, Trevor," Tana said, without thinking. "Anything. You name it."

Ryan was slightly slower in replying. "I suppose that depends what, Trevor," he said.

There was a big lump in his throat, he could barely squeak out his name. "Brandon," he said.

"What?"

He took a deep breath. The air was cold, dry, metallic. "Brandon, not Trevor. Call me Brandon, okay?"

"Brandon? But your name's Trevor. Isn't it?"

"Oh, yeah, sure, my name is Trevor. Yeah. But Brandon is, like, a nickname, okay? I like it better. So could you call me Brandon?" He looked down and kicked a rock. It sailed off down the slope, bounced twice, and skidded downward in a tiny avalanche of dust.

Tana looked at Ryan. Ryan gave a minute shrug. "Sure, why not? From now on, you're Brandon." He looked around at them. "But we still have to get everybody up this cliff, anchor some cables, and get the rockhopper winched up. And it's halfway into the afternoon, and we don't have much time.

"So, let's get moving now, shall we?"

2

DIRECTIONS

Brandon Weber had an absolute sense of direction. He never questioned it, never thought about it, but no matter where they were, or how many twisty turns they had made in the wilderness, his built-in compass always knew which way was north.

He never bothered to think how extraordinary this was. After all, his brother Trevor had it too.

One time in high school he, along with a bunch of his high school buddies, had decided to go explore a cave. They weren't organized or anything—Rip, one of his friends, had heard from another friend about a cave that somebody had found over in New Mexico. Kaipo, another one of his friends, had a car, and they drove out to explore it before the authorities found out about it and closed it up.

When he was younger, Brandon had often gone out exploring and rock climbing with his brother Trevor, but Trevor was a junior in high school now, and was busy being too cool to hang around much with his little brother. Brandon didn't even invite him on this one. He'd tell Trevor about it later. This would be an adventure for him.

It was an awesome and claustrophobic experience. The mouth, hidden behind boulders on the side of a cliff, was an irregular hole barely large enough to wriggle through. It opened out into a large chamber. Just enough sunlight came in through the narrow opening to show that the floor held the charred logs of burned-out campfires and the shards of several dozen beer bottles. "Hey, we should have brought some beer," Rip said. Shining their flashlights up, they saw the rock walls were covered with spray-painted names and dates. The oldest, "Dave" and "QT," were written in charcoal. Dave and QT, whoever they were, must have been the first to discoverer the cave. At least their signatures, dated 2015, ten years ago, were the earliest dates on the wall.

Out of five of them, two had refused to venture any further into the cave than the distance that they could see the light from the mouth. The remaining three—Brandon, Rip, and Kaipo—squeezed through a vertical cleft between two boulders at the back and into the real darkness. Only a few names were painted here, in smaller letters. In twenty feet, the passage had turned enough times that, with their flashlights off, it was pitch dark. "A maze of twisty, narrow passages, all alike," Kaipo said.

It would have been smart of them to have brought a GPS, or even a compass, but they had not originally intended to go far into the cave. But none of the three of them wanted to be the one who suggested turning back. Instead, at each branching they marked their path on the walls with a piece of chalk that Rip had had the foresight to bring.

Carlsbad was only a hundred miles or so further on; they had all hoped that the unnamed cave they were exploring might have wonders to rival its vast chambers and arching pillars. But this one seemed to be a labyrinth of rough passages, branching and winding in all directions, only rarely opening into cramped, dome-ceilinged rooms. Sometimes they had to crawl on their bellies, and they never quite dared to stand fully upright. But when one passage came to a blind end, they always found a branch that went on, that might go on to open out into some large chamber just ahead.

After several hours, Kaipo admitted what they had all been thinking: That's enough. Their flashlight beams were growing yellow, and by unspoken agreement they were already beginning to conserve, never shining more than one light at a time. They had better get back while they still had enough light in them to pick out the chalk marks. Rip quickly agreed, and the two of them turned and shone their flashlights back the way they'd come.

"Hey, why are you going that way?" Brandon had asked.

"The chalk marks, you dimwit," Kaipo said.

"But—" He started to point, and then suddenly realized that it was senseless for him to point when none of them were shining their flashlights in his direction. "The entrance is just a little way over here," he concluded.

"No way," Kaipo said. "We're miles away from the entrance by now."

"You're lost, Brandon," Rip said.

"The hell I am."

In the end, he convinced them to follow him a little way farther, probably for no other reason than that they wanted to gloat over him when he failed to get to the entrance. A hundred feet farther, they came into the chamber with the graffiti.

It had seemed no big deal to him. Over several hours, and several miles underground, through twisting passages, Brandon had always known unerringly where he was. On the surface of the Earth, for his entire seventeen years of life, Brandon's sense of direction had never failed him, not even for a moment.

That was why Mars was such a shock.

3

AT THE TOP

In fact, it had taken longer than expected to climb the cliff. Once at the top, it was their task to raise the rockhopper up, but the winching operation was slow and painstaking, and the sun touched the horizon with the rockhopper less than halfway up. Rather than risk damaging it against an unseen protuberance, Ryan called a halt.

"Can we just leave it there, dangling like that?" Brandon asked.

"Sure, it'll be fine," Ryan said.

Brandon was still dubious. "What if the wind picks up over the night?"

"At this atmospheric pressure? Don't worry about it. It would take a hurricane just to get it to budge."

"What about earthquakes?"

Ryan laughed. "It will be fine, Trevor. Don't worry."

"Brandon," he said.

"Oh, yeah. Right. I forgot. It will be fine, Brandon. Just fine. Don't worry."

As usual, in the morning Brandon was the first one up, and started the day by suiting up and walking around the campsite while the others were still getting up. This time Ryan didn't even bother to remind him not to forget the suit checklist, and so Brandon was the first one to look down. The rover was covered by a fine white fuzz. He looked down at it in horror, for a moment too startled to speak. Then he keyed on his radio. "Ryan, come quick," he called. "The rockhopper—it's covered with mold!"

Ryan was checking the winch.

The rockhopper was easy to spot; it gleamed brilliantly white, almost bloody in the red morning sunlight. Fine, fuzzy tendrils seemed to grow out of it and reach up the invisible line of the superfiber cable. Ryan walked cautiously to the cliff edge and looked down. For a moment Ryan seemed disconcerted. Then he laughed. He went back to the winch.

"Well?" Brandon said. "What is it?"

"Frost," Ryan said. "Only frost. No big deal."

"Frost?" Brandon sounded doubtful. "Frost on Mars?"

Ryan spoke as he continued checking the winch. "The rover cooled down more than the rocks. Lower heat capacity. Suspended in the air—I expect it reached minus one-fifty, easy. Water condensed out on it. That's all."

"But I thought Mars was dry."

"Yep, it's pretty dry," Ryan agreed. "But there's still a little water in the atmosphere. More at lower altitudes. No surprise that it would condense on the rover."

By the time they had winched it to the top of the cliff, the frost had sublimed away from the rockhopper. The frost bath had failed to clean it, though; it was still coated with a layer of yellowish dust.

They headed north and west. The ground they drove across was rocky, with a fine soil packing all the cracks and packed into the angles between rocks. Brandon saw Tana, driving the dirt-rover ahead, fighting to keep the dirt-rover under control on the smooth rock.

In the cabin of the rockhopper they still wore the chest-carapaces of their suits, but they all had their helmets and gloves off. It was beginning to smell rank, like the inside of a gym locker; they spent too much time in their suits.

Brandon clutched his fossil, rubbing the tips of his fingers over the smooth stone. Back at the bottom of the cliffs, Estrela had given him her rock hammer. Commander Ryan had complained that they didn't have time to collect specimens, but if Ryan had found it himself, Brandon expected that he would have found the time. So while they had worked on setting up the winch, Brandon had carefully chipped it out of the rock to bring with them.

With his bare fingers, he could feel a lot more. It had fine, almost invisible ripples on the surface, like the pebbly skin of a lizard. It was relaxing to rub it.

Estrela was being quiet. She hadn't been talking much since the accident, Brandon realized. She held her left arm awkwardly, bracing it with her right. He wondered if her arm still hurt.

"Hey, Estrela," Brandon said. "How you doing?"

She turned to him. Her eyes had red rims, he suddenly noticed. His own eyes hurt just looking at her.

"Lousy." Estrela's voice was no louder than a whisper. "Go away. Leave me alone."

In the rover there was no place to go. He wanted to ask Commander Ryan whether he had thought about who he would put on the rocket back to Earth, but decided to wait until he was alone with the commander instead of asking in front of Estrela. He thought about trying to sing a song in his head, but the landscape was too cold, too discordant. There was no way he could reconcile it to music. So instead he just watched the ground disappear under them, mile after mile after mile of endless yellow desert stone.

EXPERIENCING MARS

Yellow stone desert, stretching endlessly away in all directions.

But after your eyes got used to the shades of rust and gold, Tana thought, the subtle differences in shade and the true complexity of the landscape emerged. On the ground they were now traversing, a thin plate of sandstone had been laid down over an immense flow of solidified lava. She could now readily distinguish the dark, almost magenta shades of the underlying lava in the places where the sandstone had been broken away, the lighter yellowish orange of the sandstone, and the lighter yet shade of the wind-deposited dust layer. Boulders were scattered across the landscape like children's toys, spewed out by eruptions of immense volcanoes invisible far over the horizon. In places the sandstone had buckled up to stand in angled walls like the dorsal scales of a buried dragon.

It was tricky to drive the dirt-rover across, but interesting. The landscape was fantastic, always changing, always different. Tana suddenly regretted that she was not a geologist; she had a million questions about the landscape. She passed a column standing vertically in the desert, a black obelisk pointing a hundred feet into the sky. What was it, she wondered? The solidified core of a dead volcano, she guessed. Perhaps it had been buried, and the softer material on the outside eroded away by ten million years of sand-laced winds. She thought about calling back to the rockhopper on the radio and asking Estrela, but Estrela had not been very forthcoming, answering earlier questions only with uninformative monosyllables. Certainly she had spoken with none of the puppyish enthusiasm for rocks and landforms of the geologists that had briefed them.

So Tana stayed silent. It was, in its way, better. She could be moved by what she saw, with no barriers of language between her and the landscape, no need to communicate her feelings with others.

With all its inhuman majesty, its cold distances, its flat and unaccented sky, Tana loved Mars.

THE TWINS

Brandon Weber was nine years old before he discovered that he had an identical twin brother who was three years older than he was.

His parents, back when they had been married, had been unable to have children. In the early 2000s, this had been no big challenge. The fertility specialists they visited had advised in-vitro fertilization; their medical insurance paid the bill. An egg was harvested from his mother, Allison. A sample of sperm had been gathered from his father, examined under a microscope, and a single healthy spermatozoan was selected. By micromanipulation, the sperm cell was injected through the outer cellular wall of the egg to fertilize it.

And then the technician watched. It took the technician three times to get one to successfully fertilize. When the ovum divided, and divided again, it was clear that the fertilization had succeeded. The four cells had been carefully separated, and each one allowed to divide to the blastocyst stage. One of these was sacrificed to microdissection, to verify that the chromosomes held no abnormalities. No Down's syndrome chromosomes, no cystic fibrosis, no less-than-perfect babies would be good enough for Ted and Allison Whitman.

One egg had been implanted back into Allison Whitman's uterus.

And the two others had been perfused and frozen, to serve as backups. If Allison Whitman failed to become pregnant on the first egg, there would be two more tries. As it happened, the backups were unnecessary; Allison got pregnant on the first try.

Ted Whitman, as it turned out, also had a backup plan: He had told his girlfriend Frissa that he had had a vasectomy and that "precautions" would be unnecessary. Now Frissa, too, was pregnant.

In the divorce settlement, Ted held out for custody of the newborn, and in order to get it, he ended up paying off Allison with a good chunk of his accumulated wealth. He had been getting tired of her anyway, and he didn't really need the money. He named the kid Trevor, close enough to his own name of Ted to satisfy his vanity, and got a court order canceling all of Allison's visitation privileges. The last thing that he wanted was some ex hanging around with a claim on his child.

Allison moved back to western Colorado, where her family was from, and took back her maiden name. Unlike Ted—who went through two more wives before eventually giving up on marriage—she never remarried. Once was enough for her. Between the divorce settlement and her job as a private tutor in American history on the Internet, she was pretty well off. But it did occur to her, after a few years on her own, that she would like her own child. An inquiry to the fertility clinic revealed that the remaining fertilized eggs were still there, still waiting in the freezer, and by the peculiarities of Arizona law, were legally her property.

The result was Brandon Weber.

When Ted Whitman died, of a coronary at age fifty-two, his family—a mother and two unmarried sisters—asked to keep custody of Trevor. With Ted's inability to hold onto a wife, they had been doing most of the raising of Trevor anyway. In due course a lawyer visited Allison to ask whether she was planning to sue for her rights. It was then that nine-year-old Brandon unexpectedly discovered that he had an older twin brother. The news to Ted Whitman's family that Ted had a second son, one that they had never heard of, proved to be equally unexpected.

The lawyers turned out to be unnecessary; Allison had always liked Ted's sisters, and they discovered that they had a lot in common, not the least of which was Ted. They got along fine. It was only Ted himself that she had had problems with.

6

ROCKHOPPER

Another day of insanely boring driving over flat, uninteresting territory.

Brandon had to keep on checking the position of the sun to verify that they were driving toward the north. His sense of direction told him that they were driving east, then a moment later that they had doubled back around south, and then that they were driving due west. They were approaching the Martian equator now, and at noon the sun was very near directly overhead. At this time he had to just trust the rockhopper's inertial navigation system on faith. He didn't like it.

Estrela had withdrawn into herself. She said nothing for hours, often not bothering to reply when spoken to. Tana had gone weird. She was talking about the Mars landscape as if it were still exciting, just as if the scenery that they saw today was any different from what they saw yesterday or, for that matter, at the landing site. Only Commander Ryan seemed sane to Brandon, and he seemed to have a fixed, unchangeable mission: to put in as many miles on the road as possible.

Everybody was hoarse, everybody's eyes were red and itching.

The rockhopper was showing wear; on the second day out of the canyon, red warning lights flashed in the cockpit of the rockhopper. The front left wheel had seized up.

Ryan examined it. The wheel was frozen, and he pulled it off to examine it. He traced the problem to abrasion due to grit leaking through the seal and into the bearing. It was far beyond any possible repair—the friction of the wheel seizing up had melted parts of the bearing, and then when it froze, twisted it into scrap. Feedback circuitry on the drive motor should have shut it off when the motor current increased; instead, it had burned out the motor as well.

There was nothing Ryan could do about it, and there no spare. He picked up the useless wheel, and hurled it as far away from the rockhopper as he could. It careened off of a rock and spun to a stop in a sand drift.

"Shouldn't we save it?" Brandon asked. "What if we need it later?"

"For what?" Ryan said. "Nothing here can fix it, that's for sure. It's just dead weight."

He cannibalized the motor and the wheel from the middle left side and moved it to the front to replace the one that had frozen. "This one isn't in mint condition either, but it should do," he said. It was fortunate that the six-wheeled rockhopper had a lot of redundancy; the wheels were designed to be independent and interchangeable precisely so that the loss of any one of them would not cripple the rover.

"Can you fix the seals?"

Ryan shook his head. "They just weren't made for this much constant use. Okay, we're ready to roll. Let's go."

They switched drivers. Tana, who'd had the last shift running scout on the dirt-rover, dismounted to take over driving the rockhopper.

As Tana walked toward him, Brandon noticed something odd. Through the dusty faceplate of the helmet, it was hard to tell, but he inspected her again, carefully; it wasn't an illusion. "You're blond," he said.

"What?" Tana laughed. "Not by a long shot, boy."

He peered through the faceplate of her helmet. She looked funny; the light hair stood out in stark contrast to her dark skin. "That's what's different. You're a blond."

"No way, guy."

"Yes! Really." Brandon looked around. There was nothing like a mirror anywhere around. Finally he went to the rockhopper. He scrubbed the dust off of one of the windows until he could see his own reflection, and invited Tana over to look. "Look."

Tana looked at her reflection for a long time. Her hair, although not exactly golden, had turned to a light shade of brown, like wheat. "You're right. There aren't any mirrors around, or I would have noticed it." She turned and looked at Brandon. "You're blond, too. Take a look at yourself. And, come to think of it, so is Estrela. I've been thinking that she was doing something to her hair—it was just so gradual that I couldn't quite put my finger on it. She used to have dark black hair."

"What is it?" Brandon whispered.

"Peroxides in the soil," she said. "It's a natural bleach. No matter how we try to keep the dust out, we can't help getting a little exposure to the soil every time we put on and take off our suits. We're all getting a peroxide job."

Suddenly Brandon put it together. "That's why our eyes are so itchy all the time."

"Yours too? I thought it was just me. Yeah, that's probably it."

"What do we do about it?"

"Aren't blonds supposed to have more fun? So, let's have some fun." She laughed. "The dust sure isn't going to go away, I can tell you that. So we'd better learn to adapt." Tana looked at Brandon. "Say, are you all right? You look a little run-down."

"I'm fine," Brandon said. I'm stuck on Mars with psychotics, he thought. Half of us aren't going to make it back. And there's nothing to do, nothing to distract us. I'm going to go nuts. "Fine, fine, fine, fine."

7

BROTHERS' PACT

At first meeting, Brandon hated his newfound brother Trevor. They fought like cats, backs arched, hissing at each other and threatening to scratch. "No use bitching about it, Branny," his mother told him. "Like it or no, he's going to stay your brother." And so every vacation, every summer, every holiday they were together.

But it was eerie how similar they were. Trevor liked the same virtual reality world that Brandon did, Dirt City Blue. He loved history and hated algebra, like Brandon did, and had a crush on the same virtual actor, Tiffany Li, the one that all the other kids thought was flat-chested and ugly. Brandon could quote a single word from the lyrics of a stomp song, and Trevor would know what song it was. He would complete the quote and toss a single word back, and just like he could read Trevor's mind, Brandon always knew which song Trevor was thinking of, even if it was a stupid dumb word like "love" or "night" or even, once, "the."

Despite the difference in their ages, they looked so much alike that sometimes when Trevor was visiting Colorado, people would think he was Brandon, and when Brandon went down to Arizona, people would talk to him as though he were Trevor, especially when he wore some of Trevor's outgrown clothes.

Trevor was a shade more obedient, Brandon just a little more rebellious toward authority, and Brandon's mother considered Trevor a good influence on him. Trevor was a Scout, and knew about rock climbing, something Brandon had always wanted to do. So Trevor taught him, and after that every summer they would go out rock climbing.

And when the announcement came out about the expedition to Mars, they both looked at each other. Trevor was twenty now, a junior at Arizona State. They didn't see each other as often—Brandon was just applying to colleges—but when they did, they still instantly clicked together, as if they'd never been separated.

"You're thinking what I'm thinking," Trevor said. It was a statement, not a question.

"Yeah."

"Too young."

"Yeah."

Trevor thought about it for a moment, and then nodded. "Okay," he said.

"Great!" Brandon broke into an enormous grin. He didn't need to ask what Trevor was talking about; as always, they were thinking the same way. "Thanks a lot!"

Tickets to the Mars lottery were a thousand dollars. They bought thirty tickets each.

Brandon reached his hand over his head, and Trevor clasped it. "Brothers forever!" Their words were spoken so nearly simultaneously that, had there been anybody else there, they would have thought it was a single voice.

It hadn't occurred to Brandon to doubt Trevor for even a moment; his single word—okay—was as good as a vow. The problem had been simple: Brandon was too young for the Mars lottery. Trevor would be twenty-one by the time the tickets were drawn, but Brandon would barely be turning eighteen. The rules were clear: If your ticket won the lottery, if you were over twenty-one and could pass the health screening, you got a slot on the Mars crew. If you were too young, or too old, or couldn't pass the health exam, you had to take an alternative prize.

Brandon was too young to go to Mars

But Brandon could pass for Trevor; he'd done it dozens of times.

What Trevor had agreed to, with barely a moment's contemplation, was a substitution. If Brandon won the lottery, he could take Trevor's identification. They were genetically identical; the identity tests would show a perfect five-sigma identity match to Trevor Whitman.

Brandon Weber could become Trevor Whitman, and take the trip to Mars.

8

OVER THE LINE

The next day was no better. The horizon dropped away on their right, and they found themselves paralleling the rim of another enormous chasm. "Gangis Chasma," Ryan announced. "The orbital views show some large landslides from the rim. They're over on the north side, but I don't know if we can trust how stable the rim is." He was beginning to lose his voice and continued in almost a whisper. "We'd best not venture too close."

Brandon wanted to ask how serious the danger really was—Mars had been around for billions of years, was it really likely that there would be a landslide at the exact moment they were passing by? But by now all of their throats hurt, and nobody talked more than necessary. They kept moving.

And the following day a second wheel of the rockhopper jammed and had to be pulled off and junked.

The part that Brandon liked most was when he had a shift driving the dirt-rover. They all traded off on the dirt-rover, except for Estrela, who still had one arm in a sling. It allowed him to be alone, to play his music in his head and remind himself of what it would be like when he got back home. Home seemed farther and farther away, though, and it was hard for him to remember what it had been like. It seemed as though he'd been here, driving across Mars, for forever, and the idea that he would return home seemed like something far away and unobtainable.

Driving as the trailbreaker, it was his task to find the easiest route, and it was quite a while before he realized that, for several hours now, the gentle valley that they had been following was the path of a long dried-up riverbed. Once he realized it, it was easy enough to spot. The ancient river had cut into the rock on either side, exposing the strata in parallel stripes of the darker rock. When they stopped for a break, and to trade off drivers, Brandon walked to the embankment to examine the rock in more detail.

To his disappointment, it was not the sandstone or shale they had seen in the canyon, but apparently some volcanic rock.

No place to look for more fossils.

The closer they got to the equator, the stronger the wind blew. The rockhopper had been designed for a scientific exploration and had a science instrumentation panel set in a position in front of the copilot's seat. Brandon happened to glance at the science panel, and saw that the record of wind gusts was hitting a hundred kilometers per hour. He mentally converted—

"That's over sixty miles an hour," he said out loud.

Ryan glanced over at the panel. "Yep," he said. He didn't seem surprised.

"But that's, like, almost hurricane speed."

Ryan shook his head. "Not on Mars."

It was true. The next time they stopped, he stood out in the wind with his arms outstretched. He could feel the breeze, but barely. The sand didn't move.

In another day they approached the equator itself.

"Shouldn't there be some sort of ceremony?" Brandon asked.

"Like what, exactly?" Ryan said.

"I don't know. Champagne?"

"Yeah, you wish."

"Well, something, then. At least we could stop and look at it," Brandon said.

"Why? How's it going to look any different than any other spot? It's just an imaginary line—there's nothing to see."

"I don't know. Just because."

Ryan checked the time, and the readout from the laser-gyro navigation system. "We should reach the equator in about twenty minutes, if we keep up our average rate. Well, it's nearly time to stop somewhere for the change of shift anyway. If you really insist, then we'll stop at the equator." He radioed ahead with instructions to Tana, who was piloting the dirt-rover, to stop and meet them for the change of shift.

The land was rough where they stopped, low broken hills and loose rock. At Brandon's insistence, Ryan found a spot where sand had accumulated in a small hollow, checked the navigation, and drew a line in the dirt. "Okay," he said. "There it is."

"Are you sure?" Brandon asked.

"As best I can figure it."

Brandon stood just south of the line, and with great ceremony stepped over it. Then he stepped back. "One," he said.

"In olden times, sailors used to pierce their ears the first time they crossed the equator," Tana said. "You want we should pierce yours?"

"Already pierced," he said. He stepped over the line again, and back, and then did it again. "Two. Three."

"We could do it again," Tana said.

"Already pierced again," he said, stepping across the line again. "And again. Five. Six."

"What the heck are you doing?"

"Nine. Ten." Brandon kept on stepping back and forth over the line. He looked up at Tana. "Setting a record, what do you think? Most equator crossings on Mars." He gave up on stepping, and started to hop from one foot to the other, each foot coming down on the opposite side of the line. "Fourteen fifteen sixteen seventeen eighteen nineteen twenty."

"Shit," Tana said. "I don't believe it."

Ryan shook his head. "Well, at least he's getting rid of his excess energy," he said.

After a few minutes, Brandon stopped.

"That's it?" Ryan asked.

"I think so. A hundred and twenty. You think that record will last?"

Ryan nodded. To every direction, the landscape was barren, sterile rock. Nobody was here. Nobody had ever been here before, and if the expedition failed to reach the return rocket, probably no humans would ever return. "Yes," he said. "I expect it will last quite a while."

9

B R E A K D O W N

The riverbed they had been following had merged into another, larger riverbed, and other riverbeds had joined it, until it was the dry course of some enormous river, a Mississippi of Mars. Under the ubiquitous dust, the riverbed seemed to be made of some form of dried mud, smoother than the surrounding terrain. It flowed in approximately the right direction, and so they drove along it, grateful for the highway.

Until four days later, without warning, the rockhopper broke down.

This time there was nothing they could fix. The entire right side had completely frozen, and there were simply no longer enough parts to cannibalize to repair it.

"We're dead," Brandon said. "We're dead."

Ryan was working on the dirt-rover. He had taken off one of the rockhopper wheels and was disassembling two aluminum beams from the wheel-frame truss of the rockhopper to use for a makeshift trailer that could be pulled by the dirt-rover. "No."

The riverbed they were following had widened out until it was a broad, flat plain. There was nothing to see from horizon to horizon in either direction except pale yellow-orange dust. The rockhopper lay on its side, where it had tipped and skidded to a halt, the pressurized cabin crumpled in on one side. The unbreakable carbide window hadn't shattered, but it had buckled free of its frame and was half-embedded in the sand where it had hit. They were all clustered around Ryan, working on the dirt-rover as if there were some way that, by continuing to work, he could put off the inevitable.

"Don't lie, I can read a map," Brandon said. "It's over three thousand miles to the pole."

"It is too far," Estrela added. "Even if we were athletes."

Ryan pressed down on the wheel, looked at the amount of flex in the joint, and lashed three more wraps of superfiber around it. "So we go to plan B." He looked up at Brandon. "It's been obvious that we were going to have to make a change in plans for days. This just makes it official."

"What?" said Brandon.

"What is this plan B?" Estrela said.

"You never talked about any plan B," Tana said.

"Six hundred kilometers," Ryan said. "Six hundred kilometers to go."

"You are crazy," Estrela said.

"I can't do kilometers in my head," Brandon said. "How far in miles?"

"About four hundred," Ryan said. "A little less."

"You're completely crazy," Estrela said. "We can't get to the pole in six hundred kilometers."

"We're not going for the pole," Ryan said. "Acidalia. What we have to do now is get to Acidalia."

"Acidalia?" Estrela asked.

Tana replied for him. It was obvious to her now. "Acidalia Planitia. Of course, the Acidalia rim. Where else could we go?"

"I don't know what you're talking about," Estrela said. "Where?"

"The landing site of the *Agamemnon*."

10

T R E V O R ' S   W I N N I N G
T I C K E T

All that summer before the Mars lottery, Brandon and Trevor spent together in Arizona. A ten-million-dollar consolation prize might have been a big temptation to some other boy, but for Brandon and his brother, there was only one prize: the trip to Mars.

They both knew that, even if they won, they would still have to make the final crew selection cut. It would mean nothing if they won the lottery, and then at the final cut, the mission commander—

Brandon and Trevor studied the fine print of the lottery like they had studied for no other exam in their lives. And there was a lot of fine print. The mission commander, as they discovered, had the final decision in the choice of crew. Trevor could win the lottery, and pass all the health screenings, and go through all the training—and if the mission commander said out, he would be out. There would be no appeal.

The expedition had already named the mission commander, some old-fart war hero, name of Radkowski. It was the mission commander that they would have to impress, and it looked from the dossier that this would be difficult. He was a hardnose, or so it seemed, one of those types who did everything by the book and expected everybody else to do likewise. Lots of flights to the space station, including one that they couldn't get any information on. Apparently he had done something, broken some rule or other, something to do with the leak on the failed Russian *Mirusha* space station. It had apparently earned him some sort of reprimand. But they couldn't find any details.

They spent the summer working to make sure that their credentials were so solid that he would say yes. Brandon finished his Eagle scout work, the sort of thing that would impress an Air Force guy. They worked out in the gym together and practiced rock climbing, and survival skills, backpacking for days in the desert.

They followed the first lottery drawing on an ancient television; the cabin in Arizona was too primitive to have the bandwidth for a good VR connection. They knew the odds, but still, with the number of tickets that they had bought between them, it just felt impossible that they could fail to be chosen. At first with hope, and then with disappointment, and then with rising glee, they watched the winner be drawn, and then accept the second place prize instead.

"This is it, Brandon," Trevor said. "This one is us. For certain."

They both concentrated. It was going to be one them. It *had* to be one of them. But which one?

They called out the winning ticket number, and then an instant later, checked the name against the data bank. It was some lawyer in Cincinnati.

"Oh, man, Brandon," Trevor said, when his description and picture were flashed across the world. "Look at that fat slob! Just look at him! How could he win, and we don't?"

"It sure doesn't seem fair," Brandon said. "Don't seem fair."

"All that money," Trevor said. "And what did we get? Nothing. Not a damn thing."

That night they got drunk on beer stolen from Brandon's mother's refrigerator.

"No sense staying inside and moping, boys," Brandon's mother said the next day. "Moping isn't going to do you any good. You boys get outside, go play. Climb your rocks or something."

She had no idea how they felt, Brandon thought. No possible idea.

Trevor looked at him. "You want to go climb?"

Brandon shrugged. "Might as well."

Trevor went out to get the gear and bring the car around, so Brandon took the time to log in to the outside world and check the news.

The lawyer had washed out, for undisclosed reasons. Because he's a fat slob, Brandon thought. He'd never make it to Mars. The news was just breaking on the television and VR channels. They had made a third drawing. The ticket number was posted on the net: 11A26B7.

The insides suddenly dissolved away from Brandon. They hadn't yet checked the database and announced the winner's name, but they didn't have to. He felt numb, like he wasn't really present in his body, as if there were a sudden void where his body should have been, or as if he had been suddenly glued in place. He sat down.

He knew that number. All the tickets they had bought had been 11A series. That tagged the sale to eastern Arizona.

And 26B7 was his brother, Trevor Whitman.

11

THE LONG WALK

Ryan told them to leave everything that they didn't absolutely need behind with the rockhopper. Even so, the pile of stuff to be taken with them was enormous. The trailer towed behind the dirt-rover bulged out, three times the size of the dirt-rover itself. The vehicle looked like an ant attempting to pull an enormous beetle behind it.

And so they began to walk. On foot, the land seemed a lot less flat. In a few minutes the rockhopper was hidden behind the folds of the terrain. When they crested a small ridge, a mile farther along, Brandon looked back and saw it. It was almost on the horizon. It looked like a toy, abandoned in the sand, the only patch of a color anything other than red in the entire landscape. He knew that they would never see it again and wanted to say something, but couldn't think of anything worth saying.

Ryan looked back at him. "Come on, Trevor," he said. "We've got to keep the pace up."

He looked back at it one more time, then turned forward to the long road ahead.

A day later, the dirt-rover failed. They were on foot.

They went through the pile again and cut it down by ten percent. It was still too much to carry. There were too many things that they needed: The inertial navigation system, for one. Repair parts for the suits. Vacuum-sealed ration bricks. Electrolyte-balance liquid for the suits' drinking bottles. The habitat bubble. They went through the list again.

"What if we backpack some of the load?" Tana said.

Ryan thought about it. "We might be able to carry thirty, maybe forty kilograms," he said. "The life-support packs are already twenty kilograms, so that's not much extra."

"We could carry more than that," Tana said. "I've backpacked more than that on Earth."

"Maybe. But we don't dare let the load slow us down. Better to travel light and travel fast."

"The gravity is lower than Earth."

Ryan nodded. "Low, but not that low. But it will help some."

"It will help a lot," Tana said.

"I figure we should target fifty kilometers per day," Ryan said. "I'm counting on the low gravity helping a lot."

"Thirty miles a day," Tana said. "Should be doable."

"If we're not overloaded, yes. Barring another accident, it will be twelve days to reach the *Agamemnon*."

12

THE FALL

Brandon didn't tell Trevor. Nor his mother, nor anybody else, but especially not Trevor.

Later, he couldn't precisely articulate why he didn't tell. Perhaps he wanted one more day together with Trevor, climbing rocks with his twin brother, before Trevor suddenly became the most famous boy in the world and they were ripped apart by the pressure of training for the mission. Brandon knew that, no matter how Trevor said that they would always be brothers, things would be different, and Trevor would never have time for him again.

It wasn't much of a rock, really; just a small sandstone wall five miles outside of town that they sometimes liked to go practice on. It was barely thirty feet at the highest pinnacle.

It wasn't technical climbing at all, just something for them to do to keep their bodies active, while Trevor tried to forget that they had not been selected to go to Mars, and Brandon tried to think of what he should say to his brother. You're going to Mars, asshole, he thought. You don't even know it.

You're going to Mars, and I'm not.

Maybe it was the hangover. Maybe they were lax. Maybe Trevor didn't inspect the equipment well enough. They had been using the same rope for two years and had had more than a few falls; it was due for replacement.

In any case, Trevor shouldn't have slipped in the first place.

Brandon was on belay, and when Trevor suddenly called out "falling," he knew what to do. He braced himself, firmed his grip on the rope, got ready for the sudden tension as the rope hissed through the anchor nuts.

The rope caught Trevor in mid-fall, and stretched. Trevor jerked to a stop in midair, windmilling with his arms to stop his tumble. He looks like an idiot, Brandon thought. The rope slacked, bounced, stretched, and suddenly snapped.

The free end whipped upward like an angry snake. Trevor screamed as he fell.

The scream stopped with a sudden thud when he hit the rocky ground below.

For a moment Brandon was paralyzed. "Oh, shit. Oh shit. Hang on, Trevor, I'm coming." He scrambled down the cliff as fast as he could. He was hyper-aware of his every movement, suddenly afraid of falling. "Hang on, hang on."

His brother's crumpled body lay on the ground below, one leg twisted impossibly around, a coil of climbing rope spilled over him like a scribble. Brandon saw one arm move. He was alive.

"Hang on, you'll be all right. I'm calling an ambulance. Hang on, damn it, hang on!"

It took ten minutes for the ambulance to arrive. On the emergency ride into town, the news of the Mars selection had played. The back of the ambulance was cramped and filled with equipment, but Brandon insisted on riding with Trevor. The paramedic had made only cursory objections.

"Wow," the paramedic said. He was watching the news with half of his attention, while immobilizing Trevor's leg with the other. "I don't know who that Trevor Whitman is, but"—he deftly set an intravenous drip of some clear fluid—"I tell you, he sure is one lucky son of a bitch. Wish I could change places with *him*." He looked down at Trevor critically. "Hell, bet you wish you could trade places right now, too."

Trevor's leg was broken in five places. Brandon could still see the jagged ends of white bone sticking through the skin. Trevor wasn't going to Mars. Trevor wasn't going anywhere but to a hospital bed, and to a long, painful recuperation.

Brandon leaned over and whispered into Trevor's ear. "You're Brandon Weber," he said. "Brandon."

Trevor's face was white and covered with sweat. His teeth were clenched tightly together. Brandon couldn't tell if he had heard him.

"Brandon." Trevor's free hand reached out and grabbed him by the shirt. Brandon's heart jumped. "You're going to Mars. Make me proud, little brother. Make me proud."

A broken rope had given Brandon the chance to go to Mars. So, a year later and a hundred million miles away, when Commander Radkowski's rope broke, Brandon Weber knew what it was like to be the one who watches. Trevor had given his slot to Brandon.

It was cruel to think of it, but Radkowski had been the commander. Trevor knew that when the final moment came, Radkowski would want to go himself. Putting aside sentimentality (and Brandon had never really liked Radkowski), thinking with nothing but cold calculation, Radkowski's death had opened the door for one of the crew to go back.

13

SURVIVAL

Estrela was in a bleak foul depression—a depression that had followed her around for days, like sandpaper rubbing against her brain.

Knives tore at her throat with every breath she took. She sucked down the water bottle in her suit within a few minutes of when she put it on, sometimes before she'd even made it outside of the bubble, and it didn't help. She couldn't speak, could barely croak sometimes.

But the others didn't seem to notice.

She plodded methodically across the surface, not looking at the land-scape, trying not to even think. Oh, that would be the best, if only she did not have to think! If only she didn't know what was happening and could just be mindless, a piece of wood that walked on legs of wood and didn't have a past or a future.

Sometimes she pretended to herself that she was already dead. But somewhere inside her was a terrified animal, an animal all teeth and claws, a vicious biting thing with beady red eyes that said no, I'm not going to die. Whatever it takes to do it, I am going to survive. Other people die, but not me, never me, never never never me. She wondered that the others didn't see it, that they didn't flee in terror, that they somehow continued thinking her a civilized human being, and not a cornered rat-thing.

She was going to survive.

Estrela plodded across the Martian land, not thinking, not feeling, clenching her teeth to keep from paying attention to the pain in her throat and the claws ripping into her heart. All she knew was one thing. She was going to survive.

14

THE BROKEN LANDS

The territory became increasingly rough and broken.

As they traveled, the wind began to increase. It was very odd. Brandon could hear the wind, could hear a high-pitched whistling, almost (but not quite) too high to hear, but he could feel nothing. There was a gale blowing outside, and there was no force to it. He spread out his arms, and felt . . . nothing.

"The subsolar point is moving north," Ryan said. The northern hemisphere was turning from winter to spring. They were still deep in the Martian tropics, not that far from the equator. On Mars, the tropics still meant weather barely above freezing at noon, and well into the negative numbers during the middle of the night.

At noon the sun was directly overhead. This made him feel completely disoriented. His sense of direction had gone bonzo, and with no shadows he had no clue which way was which.

They were walking across sand today. The terrain was flat enough that, had they still been in the rockhopper, Brandon would have thought that it was perfectly level. On foot, he found how deceptive that was. The land had minute slopes to it, up and slowly down. The rims of craters, Ryan explained. The craters had formed, and eroded, and been buried by sand, and all that was left was the faint change in slope at the buried rim.

It was in the afternoon that Brandon first noticed something moving. At first he caught a glimpse of motion out of the corner of his eye, but when he turned to look, there was nothing there. Your eyes are playing tricks on you, he thought. There's nothing there. Then, later, he saw it again. This time he refused to turn to look. If I'm going crazy, he said, I don't want to know.

The third one was too close to ignore. At first he saw the movement, and he looked involuntarily. There was nothing to see. But then he noticed that, even with nothing there, there was a shadow moving across the land.

And then he looked above it, looked at the sky, and saw the twisted rope of sky, a rotating column of a darker shade of yellow curling upward, writhing into the sky. It was—

"Tornado," he shouted. "Look out!"

It turned and suddenly darted away across the land. Brandon craned his neck back. There was no top to it, not that he could see. It was hard to tell how far away it was, whether it was right next to them or a mile away.

It turned again, and darted right toward them. He threw himself on the ground, spreading himself flat. "It's coming!" he shouted. "Look out!"

Nobody else moved.

There was no place to take cover. He hugged the ground. A few inches in front of his helmet, two grains of sand started to move. They quivered, danced a few steps to the left, made a tiny circle, and then settled down.

Brandon looked up. The rest of the group was looking at him. The tornado was retreating, staggering like a drunkard off toward the horizon.

"It's a dust devil," Ryan said gently. "We've been seeing them for an hour or so."

"That one came right over us," Tana said. "I could feel it when it passed."

"They're not dangerous?" Brandon felt incredibly stupid. Dust devils. He had been afraid of a dust devil.

"Don't think so. Must be a wind of a couple of hundred kilometers an hour, maybe." Ryan shrugged. "But with the thin atmosphere, it's no big deal."

"They're pretty, though," Tana said. "Break the monotony."

What had made it hard to see was the fact that the dust devils were precisely the same shade as the sky, only a tiny bit darker. Now that he knew how to look, they were easy to spot. By the afternoon there were two, sometimes even three dust devils visible at any one time. Brandon wondered if this was natural, or if something was wrong. He could remember that the briefings had talked about dust devils, but were there supposed to be this many? But after his embarrassing dive to cover, he didn't want to ask.

15

THE LUCKIEST BOY IN THE WORLD

The radio and the television and the VR stations had all converged at the front of the house. Brandon slipped into the back and quickly changed into Trevor's favorite orange silk shirt, then put on the turquoise bolo that Trevor had gotten as a gift. Checking in the mirror, he was surprised at how much like Trevor he looked.

"I'm Trevor Whitman," he said, testing it out. "I'm Trevor Whitman. I *am* Trevor Whitman."

It was surprisingly easy to step into Trevor's place. The instant that the announcement had been made public, Trevor's life had changed completely, even before he went off to Houston to train. It was a surprise, really, how few people really had to know.

Brandon had been a virgin when the lottery had selected Trevor Whitman as the boy who won the trip to Mars. Not that he would ever possibly have admitted to it. But being the most famous boy in the world has its advantages, and Brandon took them. He could walk into a coffeehouse or a cabaret and say, "I'm Trevor Whitman, I'm going to Mars," and half a dozen girls would tell him that they found him "fascinating" and wanted to know him better. He figured that if a girl wanted to know him for no other reason than the fact that he was famous, well, that meant that he had every right to take advantage. And he did. The first one, he was nervous, certain that she was going to tell him, hey, you're too young, you can't be Trevor Whitman. But after the first few, it was easy.

It was fun to be famous.

GEOLOGY LESSONS

Her mind would wander. Sometimes Estrela imagined that her brother was with her. It had been decades since Gilberto had left her. She had not thought about him for years, nor about the streets of Rio. And yet she could bring him forth perfectly in her mind, just as he had been, wiry and street smart and still larger than her. "Hey, *moça*," he might say. "These North Americans, you're in some rich company, aren't you?" He would give her a sly look, and she knew that he would be thinking, What did they have that he could grab? Yeah, that would be just like Gilberto, always on the lookout. "Better stay alert, moça, they don't care about you. You're fat, you lost your reflexes, haven't you? Don't think you're like them. They look at us, they don't even see us, they just see filth in the street. They'll kill you and not even laugh when you're gone."

That's not true, she wanted to tell him.

And sometimes she would imagine João walking beside her. She would call him up in her mind, and she would think of how he might comment on the rocks as they passed.

"Hold up a moment, look at that one. Look, that's a layer of limestone. See how it weathers differently? There were ocean deposits here, I'm sure of it."

"I don't care about limestone," she would tell him, but not aloud. Her throat hurt too much for her to say anything aloud. "Go away." It felt bitter and yet also sweet for her to see him again, even if he was dead. Even when she ignored him.

But for a moment she would be happy, showing off for João, identifying rocks and landforms for him. "That's gabbro," she might say, trying to sound completely confident.

"Close. Andesite, I'd say. What's that outcrop there?"

She looked at it. A rounded ridge, with an abrupt scarp at one end. "Anticline?" she imagined saying. "Dip and scarp."

João shook his head, almost in pity at her ignorance. "Sheepback rock, I'd say," he said. "There was a glacier here once, I'd bet on it."

But João was gone.

They stopped for a break, and to Estrela's complete surprise, Tana pulled her over and wanted to talk. They had been walking in silence for so long that it came as a surprise.

"Say, Estrela, you want to know something?"

Tana didn't wait for Estrela to answer.

"Even with the chance that we won't make it home," Tana said, "you know, I'm still glad I came. This is the adventure that most people will never make in a lifetime; if it means my life, this is the price that we always knew we might have to pay. Sometimes I still can't believe how lucky we are. Even with everything that's happened—we're on Mars. Nobody else can say that."

Tana fell silent, staring off into the distance.

She is crazy, Estrela thought. She is completely crazy.

17

DEVILS IN THE SAND

The next day they saw the first dust devil at ten in the morning. Brandon watched two of them dance together like mating birds, circling each other, approaching in toward each other warily and then suddenly darting away, finally twisting around each other and then merging together into a single column that marched off over the horizon and vanished.

More followed. By noon there were a dozen at once.

When one passed directly over him, Brandon closed his eyes, but nothing happened. He could feel the wind as it passed, but it was a feeble push, barely enough to be noticeable by Earth standards. He was afraid that the scouring sand would sandblast his helmet, but when he mentioned that, Ryan quickly put him straight.

"What's getting picked up is dust, not sand," he said. "It's fine particles. More like talcum powder than grit. It's harmless. If you want to worry about grit, worry about the stuff we kick up walking, not about the stuff in the air."

"It's gotten noticeably dimmer," Tana said.

Ryan looked up. The sky was a deep pale yellow. The sun was, in fact, dimmer. He could almost look directly at it without blinking. "Yeah."

"Think it's a dust storm?"

"Wrong season." Ryan thought about it. "Not the season for a planetary dust storm, anyway. Maybe a local storm." He thought about it some more. "That makes sense. We're right about at the subsolar point; we're getting maximum solar heating right about now. The heat is making a lot of thermals. I guess it's not surprising it might pick up some dust. In fact, I bet this is how the dust gets into the atmosphere in the first place."

"Is it dangerous?"

"Not that I can see." Ryan pointed forward. "Let's keep moving."

They had made fifty kilometers the first day of walking; fifty-five the second. Over sixty miles, Brandon calculated. No wonder his legs were aching. But that was sixty miles closer to the abandoned base at Acidalia, where Ryan hoped they could find supplies.

And then what, Brandon wondered? What if they did find supplies? Would there be enough to get them to the pole?

As the sun set and their eyes adjusted to the dusk, they noticed an odd phenomenon. The bases of the dust devils were surrounded by pale sheets of blue flame.

"I don't believe it," Brandon said. "They're on fire."

All of them stared. The pale fire brightened and flickered. Sometimes it wrapped around and then in a flash coiled all the way up the dust devil, a column of light disappearing into the heavens. For a moment it would vanish, and then flicker back to life, a blue glow dancing at the base of the column of dust.

"Plasma discharge," Ryan said.

"What?"

"Static electricity," he said. "The wind blowing over the dust must generate an electric potential. Like, like rubbing over a carpet on a dry day. Something like lightning, but the pressure is too low for an arc. They're natural fluorescent lights."

"Is it dangerous?"

"I don't know." Ryan pointed ahead. "But I think we're about to find out."

Brandon stepped back involuntarily as the dust devil raced forward. It seemed fixated on Ryan, and enveloped him. For a moment it hovered over him, dust swirling all around. Ryan began to glow, first with blue light from his fingertips, then the blue glow jumping to his helmet, his backpack, and then for a moment he was entirely outlined in blue fire.

"Ryan!" came Tana's voice over the radio. "Are you okay?"

For an answer there was only a burst of static. And then, almost reluctantly, the dust devil peeled away. The sheet of pale fire clung to Ryan for an instant and then faded.

Ryan looked down, then up, and then his voice came across the radio. "Testing, one, two. You hear me?"

"Coming through fine," Tana said.

Ryan flexed his fingers, and then laughed. "Well. I guess that answers your question."

Ryan's suit, a moment ago covered with a film of brick-colored dust, was as clean as if it had been through the laundry.

"Still," he said. "I think that maybe it's time we should get inside."

18

THE STORM

The next day they were in the middle of a fully developed dust storm. There were no more dust devils; now the dust was all around them.

The landscape was odd. It was dimmer than before, lit by a soft, indirect light that was easy on the eyes. The sun was a fuzzy bright patch in the yellow sky. It was the exact color of the gravy on the creamed chicken that the high school cafeteria served, Brandon thought. Babyshit yellow, that was what the kids called it.

Brandon wondered what the kids back at his school were doing right now. He looked at the clock, but then realized that it wouldn't help him; it was set for Martian time, for a twenty-four-hour-and-thirty-nine-minute Martian sol, not for an Earth day. He could ask Ryan—Ryan always seemed to be able to calculate that kind of stuff in his head—but what would be the point?

The training they had done on Earth before the flight had told him all about Martian dust storms. Mostly they talked about the global dust storms, storms that covered the entire planet for months at a time. But now that he thought about it, he remembered that they had told him about smaller dust storms too. How long did they last, a week?

"How bad is it going to get?" he asked Ryan.

Ryan lifted his wrist and made a measurement of the sun. His wrist carried a tiny sensor designed for a spot check of the illumination for virtual reality photography. He looked at the reading and then did some calculation in his head. "I'd say that this is about the peak of it," he said. "Optical depth right now is about as high as it's ever measured."

"This is it?" Brandon was incredulous. "This is a great Martian sandstorm?"

"Sand? No." Ryan shook his head. "It's not a sand storm. I don't even know if Mars has sandstorms. I doubt it. It's just dust. And, yes, this is as bad as it gets."

This wasn't bad. Above him, he could see the occasional flicker of blue light across the sky. It flashed in sheets, like an aurora, darting in silent splendor from horizon to horizon. It was like walking on a slightly hazy day, like a Los Angeles smog. The air seemed clear around them, but their shadows were blurred. Rocks far away in the distance were a little less sharp, and the horizon was blurred. Mountains in the distance were indistinct, blending smoothly into the yellow of the sky.

"This is a dust storm?" he said. "Heck, I've been through worse than this on Earth."

Ryan shrugged. "Guess they're a bit overrated," he said.

19

W A L K A B O U T

The morning was Brandon's time alone, the only time, really, that he could be by himself. He had never needed much sleep, and the adults just took too long to get moving in the morning.

The others had at last come to accept the fact that he wanted to go out exploring first thing in the morning, and let him. Mostly he didn't even really explore, just found a rock to sit behind, where he was out of sight of the others, where he could look out in the distance, pretend he wasn't locked up inside a tiny awful suit, pretend that his friends and his music and his virtual reality were just around the corner, and that in just a few moments he would go inside, and everything would be there.

But mostly he just wanted some time to be by himself. When he had wanted to join the Mars expedition, nobody had ever warned him that going to Mars would take away his privacy. On the whole expedition, he was never far away from the others. Even when he jerked off, it had to be in a hurry, something quick and furtive in the tiny bathroom cubicle, and he was sure that half of the others were talking behind his back while he was in there, asking just exactly what he was doing that was taking so long.

Being out on Mars in the morning was simply a chance to be alone.

The dust storm was still going, but he was used to it now and hardly noticed. One side of the habitat was covered with a fine layer of dust; it was peculiar how it had deposited on just one side. The downwind side.

The terrain he walked over still looked like sand, but the sand was cemented together, firm as concrete. *Indurated soil*. The phrase came back to him from the hours of geology briefings. *Martian duricrust*.

He didn't feel like sitting, so he picked the most interesting landmark, a miniature butte perhaps half a mile away, and climbed up to the top. It was smaller than it looked, only about twenty feet high.

From the flat top, he could see other buttes, all seeming to be the same height, twenty feet or so above the ground. It was just like the southwest, he thought. He knew this territory. The original surface had been higher, where he was standing, and over the millennia, the winds had eroded down the surface, leaving slightly harder rock, like what he was standing on, behind to stand up above.

It must have been dust storms just like the one that was happening now that did it. So much for Ryan's confident prediction that the dust was too fine a powder to erode anything. But then, he thought, it may have taken millions of years to erode. Billions, even. Even pretty fine dust might be able to carve down rock over a billion years.

Still, the dust storm was somewhat of a disappointment. He had pictured a storm like something from one of the songs, howling winds and sand: "the naked whip of a vengeful god / that cleanses flesh to alabaster bone." He had pictured coming out of a tent and finding themselves buried. Something a little more than a smoggy day with heat lightning.

Looking back the way he had come, he could see the habitat. They had picked the bottom of a gentle dip in the ground to put up the bubble, and inside it he could see the shadows of the other three Mars-nauts just beginning to stir about. They weren't even breakfasting yet, he thought. Slowpokes.

He thought about giving them a call on the radio, just to check in, but decided they just might ask him to come back in and help deflate the habitat. It would be ages before they would be ready to move on, and he didn't feel like coming back yet.

He scrambled down the edge of the miniature butte and walked over to climb the next one.

There was still plenty of time to explore.

MORNING CALL

The habitat was deflated and packed away. Tana and Estrela were suited up, as was Ryan, and they were ready to go.

"Ryan Martin to Brandon," Ryan broadcast, once again. "Calling Brandon. Calling Brandon. Come in."

Where the hell was Brandon?

"Possibly his suit radio is malfunctioning," Tana said. "Maybe he hears you, but can't respond."

If his radio had failed, it didn't seem likely that he wouldn't return immediately, but maybe he had found something interesting. "Brandon, we're not receiving you. If you're hearing this, return immediately. Brandon, return immediately."

In the worst case, even if his radio had completely failed, he would trigger his emergency beacon, which ran from a separate thermal battery, completely separated from the rest of the systems. The suit could fail completely and the emergency beacon would work.

But where was he?

The wind and the settling dust had thoroughly erased his footprints. Ryan had no guess even which direction to look. He had vanished without a trace.

"Brandon, come home," Ryan broadcast. "Brandon, we're here. Brandon, come home."

There was no answer.

COMING HOME LATE

Brandon Weber wasn't worried, not yet. He had been waiting for the call for him to return to the campsite, and enjoying the chance to walk during their delay. He mildly wondered what the others were doing that was taking them so long to get moving, and wandered a little farther than he had planned.

He checked the time, and with a shock realized that it was after nine. Where the heck were they doing? Where was that radio call, anyway?

He toggled his radio. "Brandon, ah, Whitman, checking in. What's up, guys?"

No answer. He toggled his radio again, and then with a sinking feeling noticed that the red light didn't come on.

Uh-oh. The suit radio wasn't working. No wonder they hadn't called; they'd probably been calling for an hour and were going to be as mad as hell.

He toggled it a couple more times. Was it was possible that it was the light that had failed, not the radio? "Hello, camp. Brandon here? Are you there?"

Nothing.

"Uh, I'm coming back. Wait for me, okay?"

They were going to be pissed.

A radio check was part of the space-suit checkout, but nobody else had been around when he went through the check list. He couldn't recall if the red light had come on or not.

It didn't matter now. He had better get back to camp, pronto.

They were going to be mad as hell.

22

MISSING

Ryan started the search by climbing to the top of one of the mesa formations nearby. From that height, he could see much farther, but no Brandon.

The dust storm was continuing at full vigor, but the suspended dust barely impeded his visibility. The wind had completely vanished, and there was no trace of motion anywhere to be seen. The sky was flat, as uniform as if it had been spray-painted onto smooth plaster no more than an arm's length away.

From up here the horizon must be four or five kilometers away, but it was only slightly blurred from the dust. Brandon was nowhere in sight. The countryside was like a maze, Ryan thought. There were almost a hundred of the little mesas in view, and lots of places he couldn't see. Brandon could be behind any one of them.

He tried the radio again. "Brandon! Come in, Brandon!"

It was impossible that he could be lost. He had an inertial compass. And, if he got completely lost, why didn't he trigger his emergency beacon?

"Brandon! Report immediately! Brandon!"

23

WALK

For the last hour, Brandon had been thinking, with rising uneasiness, the habitat must be just behind that next butte. No, it's the next one. The next one.

At last he stopped. It couldn't be this far. He must have, somehow, walked past it.

Okay, don't panic.

For the tenth time since realizing that he was due back at the habitat, he scrambled up one of the little buttes and looked around. For miles around, nothing.

Don't panic, don't panic.

The dust was like a smooth brick dome over his head, circumscribing the world.

He must have gone too far. It was easy to get confused here. All of the little buttes looked so much alike. He should have paid more attention to the landscape. Don't panic, it will be okay.

He must have gone right past, somehow missed seeing it. Okay, he wasn't lost. He'd have to backtrack. He still had his sense of direction. He looked up at the sun, but it was little help, just a slightly brighter patch of sunlight almost directly overhead.

Maybe he should to trigger his emergency beacon, he thought. It wasn't an emergency, not really, but the others would be worried. If he triggered his beacon it would show them that he was all right.

And it would give them a radio signal to locate him.

No, it wasn't really an emergency, but it would be prudent to be safe, he thought. They wouldn't blame him for being cautious, would they? The emergency beacon was mounted at the back of his suit, where his hip pocket would be, if it had a pocket. The thermal battery required that you break a seal, then pull a trigger tab that mixed the chemicals that reacted to power the signal.

He could feel the emergency beacon, right where it was supposed to be, but he couldn't find the trigger tab. He twisted around to look.

The socket that should have held the battery was empty.

Don't panic, don't panic.

Brandon Weber began to run.

24

They searched all day, fanning out in widening spirals away from the base. Over and over Tana or Estrela saw what they thought were footprints, that on close examination turned out to be just weathered depressions in the rock. The hardpan soil did not take tracks, or if it had, the wind and the gently settling dust had erased them. And dust had settled over everything, erasing contrast, making the rocks almost indistinguishable from the soil or the sky.

After they had searched for a kilometer in every direction from the dome, they searched again, this time more meticulously, checking each notch between rocks, every narrow cleft, every crack, fracture, or ravine where Brandon might be lying injured or unconscious.

He was nowhere to be found.

By nightfall they realized that Brandon was not coming back.

25

A SENSE OF WHERE YOU ARE

By nightfall Brandon realized he was not going to find his way back.

He had been walking for hours. He remembered running blindly and screaming, only coming to his senses when he tripped over a fracture in the sandstone. His sense of direction, always infallible on Earth, had betrayed him. He had no idea where the others were, one mile away or a hundred, or even whether they had decided he was gone and left without him.

At last, too tired to go on, he climbed to the top of one of the endless maze of buttes. In every direction, nothing but empty Mars. Even the sunset was a disappointment, a slow dimming of the light into brick red haze.

There was a fracture line running down the middle of the butte; one half of it was two feet higher than the other. It made a natural seat. Without any sense of wonder, without even a sense of irony, he reached out and touched it. Embedded in the layered sandstone exposed by the crack, it held a perfectly preserved fossil. It looked like a cluster of shiny black hoses, clumped together at the bottom, branching out into a dozen tentacles at the top. In the same section of rock, he could see others, of every size from tiny ones to one three feet long. There were other fossils too, smaller ones in different shapes, a bewildering variety.

"I name you Mars Life Brandonii," he said.

There was not much he could do. The suits needed service, he knew. Every night Ryan changed out the oxygen generators. He wasn't sure quite what was done to make them keep on working, but he knew that the oxygen supply wouldn't run overnight. He could even remember, with a near-hallucinogenic clarity, the lessons that they had been given about the suit's life-support systems. The briefing technician had told them that twenty hours was an absolute, complete, do-not-exceed design limit for the suit's oxygen generation capacity. The technician had chuckled. "Of course, you won't ever have any reason to put in more than a quarter of that."

The water recycler had already quit on him, and his throat was dry and hurt like hell.

He was going to die on Mars.

With the geologic hammer that Estrela had given him, he scratched into the stone beside the fossils. It was soft, as easy to carve as soap. BRANDON WEBER WAS HERE, he wrote, and then tried to think of a witty line. He couldn't. At last he added I DID IT.

It would be his tombstone, he thought. The idea seemed vaguely funny, nothing to be taken seriously. But tombstones need dates, so he added: 2010–2028.

And then, he wrote: SO LONG, STOMPERS.

Brandon Weber sat down, rested against the sandstone ledge, and stared into the dark toward the sunrise he would never live to see.

26

E strela had been silent for almost a week. Her throat hurt too much for her to talk. She wanted to say, stop searching, it's too late, he's dead. We need go get moving. But she had no voice.

But Ryan was adamant; they wouldn't abandon one of the crew.

They continued the search the next day.

It was afternoon when Ryan thought he saw something on top of a mesa. It was the same color as the rocks, but the shape was different, and something seemed to be reflecting skylight. One side of the mesa had crumbled away to form an easy ramp to the top. He climbed up to look.

It was Brandon.

"I've got him," he said. "Tana, Estrela, I found him." They were about five kilometers away from where they had camped. Over the horizon; it was hard to believe that he would have wandered this far. What could he have been thinking?

Tana's voice over the radio. "Where are you?"

Ryan walked over to the edge and looked around. Estrela and Tana were visible below, only a hundred meters away. "Up above you," he said. "Look up."

In a few moments they had climbed up to reach him.

Brandon was sitting on the top of the fractured mesa, his back against a low wall. His body was covered with a fine layer of dust, and at first it looked like just a different shape of stone.

"You found him!" Tana came up beside him. "Is he okay?" She reached out and shook his shoulder. "Trevor! Trevor, are you okay?"

Brandon leaned over, and slowly toppled onto his side.

"I think we're too late," Ryan said. He knelt down, brushed the dust away from Brandon's faceplate, and peered inside, trying to see. Brandon's eyes were open, looking at nothing.

Tana was trying to take a pulse, a nearly hopeless task through the stiff suit fabric. Ryan checked Brandon's suit pack. The life-support system said it all. The oxygen fraction was too low to breathe; the carbon dioxide level up to nearly twenty percent, well above the poison level. He checked the electronic readout. Brandon had not drawn a breath for seventeen hours.

Estrela had reached them now. "How is he?" she whispered.

Tana shook her head.

Estrela knelt down across from Ryan and reached down to the body. She unclipped something from the suit, looked at it, handed it to Ryan.

It was Brandon's emergency beacon. Ryan examined it, turned it over. Nothing visible seemed to be wrong with it. The thermal battery was unused. It was disconnected from the beacon. Had Brandon taken it apart, trying to fix it? The beacon was supposed to be unbreakable. He replaced the battery connections, broke the arming seal, and pulled the activation tab. The thermal battery grew warm in his hands, and a red light started flashing in his suit indicator panel, showing the direction and strength of the emergency signal.

The beacon was working perfectly. So why hadn't Brandon used it?

Ryan looked up, and for the first time focused on the wall behind Brandon. There was writing there, crudely incised into the soft sandstone. BRANDON WEBER WAS HERE. I DID IT. 2010–2028. Underneath, in smaller letters, it said, SO LONG, STOMPERS. He knew he was going to die, Ryan thought.

But that didn't explain it, he realized. The inscription didn't make any sense. Why would Trevor Whitman sign the name Brandon Weber? Why had he demanded to be called Brandon at all? Why were the dates 2010–2028? The last date was correct, but Trevor had been born in 2007. What did he mean, he did it?

He looked at it. There was only one answer. Ryan Martin didn't like it, but it seemed to stare him in the face. Trevor Whitman was not, had never been, the person he said he was.

27

HARD QUESTIONS

Once back in the hobbit habitat, they went through Brandon's things.

Brandon Weber, Tana thought. Not Trevor Whitman. All this time he had deceived them.

It had taken only a few minutes to find where Brandon had written down the password to unlock his communications. Brandon had saved just a tiny clip of his incoming mail, but it was enough. The boy who stared out of the picture looked just like Brandon.

Ho, Brand. Man, I hope you're having a ball up here. I can walk on the leg now, but it still hurts some, mostly when it rains. I wish I stayed back in Arizona. Oh, man, I wish I could have made it. I just hate you, you know that? Nah, don't worry, I'm not going to tell our secret. Hey, I hope you've got into the pants of that Brazilian babe by now, she's hot. Do good stuff out there, okay? Kill 'em for me. Trevor signing off.

The picture of the two of them together, geared up in climbing harness, was uncanny, a mirror of the same person twice, one slightly older, one slightly younger.

It took an hour of sleuthing through Brandon's effects to piece together the story. When she found out about Trevor's climbing accident, Tana gave out a long, low whistle. Wow.

She called to Estrela. Estrela looked up at her, questioning.

"Climbing accident," Tana said. "Broken rope. And Brandon Weber gets what he wanted. Sound familiar?"

Estrela nodded.

Tana was remembering something now. She was remembering how many times she had seen Brandon alone with Commander Radkowski. He was begging, she realized, pleading with Radkowski to pick him when it came time to choose who would go home on the Brazilian ship.

Radkowski hadn't made a choice. It wouldn't be like him to choose before he had to. But Tana wondered if maybe he'd said something that Brandon had interpreted to mean that he had made the selection, and Brandon wasn't it.

When a ship sinks, sometimes people would kill to get on the lifeboat.

A climbing accident. A broken rope.

And once again, Brandon got what he wanted.

It was all clear to her now. She'd thought that the broken rope was suspicious. It had been Brandon.

And now Brandon was dead.

SCOTT'S FOSSILS

The fossils that Brandon had found on his last night were magnificent. Tana stood in front of them and marveled. How had he managed to find it? Was this what he was looking for? Was this what he had died to find?

The fossil his body had been found next to looked as if it were the complete organism, or possibly a casting of the complete organism, permineralized by a more durable material. It looked as though it were carved from onyx.

The organism itself looked something like a medusa, or perhaps some branching plant, with sinuous branches or tentacles radiating out from a cylindrical body. Was it an animal or a plant, Tana wondered? Or, on Mars, was there even a difference?

She took out the rock hammer and began, carefully, to chip around the edges. "You want to give me some help in excising this specimen?" she said.

Ryan, standing behind her, said nothing.

She looked up, slightly annoyed. "Come on! It'll go faster if you give me a hand here."

"There's no point in it, Tana," he said softly. "We can't take them with us. I'm sorry."

"Ryan, you don't understand." She put down the hammer and looked directly at him. "This is the greatest discovery of the twenty-first century. Life existed on Mars. This proves it. Even if we don't return ourselves, we have to preserve these. We have to! This is why we're here." She picked up the hammer again and began to chip at the stone, using sharp, clean blows now that she had defined the edges. "This is more important than any of us."

"Like the Scott expedition," Ryan said.

Tana put down the hammer and looked up. "What?"

"Antarctica," Ryan said. "They were the second to reach the south pole. When they got there, they found Amundsen's abandoned camps, and discovered that they had missed being first by thirty-four days. It must have been a crushing disappointment. But it was a scientific expedition. On the way, they found fossils in the mountains near the south pole. Fossils, almost at the south pole! At the time, it must have been quite an important scientific find. They were perilously low on supplies, fighting frostbite and blizzards and ferocious winds. They were dying slowly of vitamin deficiency, but they collected fifty pounds of rocks from those mountains and dragged the samples behind them for over a thousand kilometers on foot, because they thought that the scientific samples would make their expedition a success, even though they failed to reach the pole first."

"And?" Tana asked.

"And they died," Ryan said. "Every one of them."

Tana was silent for a moment. "It was the fossils?" she said.

Ryan shrugged. "If they hadn't tried to carry rocks with them, useless dead weight, would they have made it? Who can say? But I can tell this: It didn't help."

Tana dropped the rock hammer and sighed.

"Okay," she said, and stood up. "We leave the fossils."

Ryan had brought one rock with him, the small fossil that Brandon had found that day at the wall of the Valles Marineris. The fist-shaped rock seemed small and tawdry next to the large fossils of the fault wall, but it was the one Brandon had found.

They had left Brandon's body propped up where he had died, leaning against the wall and sightlessly staring toward the eastern horizon. Ryan leaned down, placed the little fossil in Brandon's right hand, and closed his left hand over it. "Trevor—Brandon—whoever you are," he said. "I guess it's too late now to really even know. Goodbye, Brandon."

He paused. "Wherever you are—good luck."

When they returned to the habitat for the night, Ryan gathered them together to talk about their plans. It was frightening to see how few the expedition had become. We knew people were going to die, he thought. We knew it, and yet, when it happens, we still can't quite get a grip on it. Chamlong, and then John, and now Trevor, gone. He knew that Trevor—Brandon, he should think of him as Brandon now—had deceived all of them, that he must have killed Radkowski, but somehow he still couldn't quite believe it. He lied right from the beginning, he thought. He deceived all of us.

What secrets did the others have?

Ryan had liked him. The betrayal was somehow worse for that. And now he's dead, too.

"We can't afford any more accidents," he said. "The expedition is already dangerously small. We can't lose anybody else; we can't make any mistakes. From here, we travel light and fast, no sidetracks, no exploration, no sight-seeing, just speed. No more wandering. We make a straight-line dash for the *Agamemnon* site.

"We leave behind everything that we don't absolutely need. *Agamemnon* was the Cadillac of expeditions. They had everything, and they abandoned it at the site, for the most part completely unused. We'll resupply there."

"Showers," Tana said.

"Decent food," Estrela whispered.

"All that," Ryan said. "All that, and one thing, the most important thing of all.

"*Agamemnon* brought an airplane."

PART SIX

R Y A N   M A R T I N

Above, the cold sun hovers half the year,
And half the year, the dark night covers all.
A place more barren than the very pole
No green, no brooks, no trace of life appears.

The worst of all the horrors of this world
The cold cruelty of this sun of ice,
The night, immense, resembling ancient Chaos.

—Charles Baudelaire, "De Profundis Clamavi,"
Les Fleurs du Mal

There are no eyes here
In this valley of dying stars
In this hollow valley
This broken jaw of our lost kingdoms
In this last of meeting places

—T. S. Eliot, "The Hollow Men"

1

It gave him a sense of déjà vu.

Ryan had been here before. When could he have been here? Never; it was impossible. But yet he felt that the territory was familiar.

They had crossed an area of low hills, and then for two days they had walked through a region of immense buttes, imposing flat-topped mesas that loomed hundreds of meters above them. Ryan felt the pressure of the landscape, felt that they were as small as ants moving across an inhumanly large landscape.

Now they had left the mesa territory behind. The land was furrowed. Low, rolling ridges ran parallel to their direction of travel, with half-buried boulders tumbled in clusters around. It was a flood plain, Ryan realized. An ancient deluge had carved these grooves and moved these boulders. In his memory this rang a distant bell, but he couldn't quite bring it to mind.

A low, lone mountain—a volcano, perhaps—rose up out of the plain, and it too looked weirdly familiar. As they moved across the land, and moved into a new perspective, he saw that it was doubled, like the twin humps of a Bactrian camel, and that didn't surprise him. Of course it was a double peak.

Because now he remembered where they were. He'd been here hundreds of times in virtual reality, learning about Mars geology. Suddenly it all came back to him in vivid detail: the Twin Peaks, the oddly named rocks: Yogi, Flat-top, Barnacle Bill, Moe. As a kid, he'd spent whole days downloading the pictures of this place from the Internet; it was when he'd first become interested in Mars. More than anything else, this place was the whole reason he was here. It was the landscape of his dreams.

It was the Pathfinder site.

They were crossing Ares Vallis. Yes, of course, to get from Coprates Chasma to Acidalia they had to cross Ares Vallis, they had no choice. But of all the spots to cross it, right here! "But this is history," he whispered. "We're walking on history."

"Say again?" Tana's voice said.

Instead of answering, Ryan started to walk faster. It had to be right here, just ahead of them. He started to jog, barely even noticing the boulders he had to detour around. Right, exactly here. They couldn't be far away from the actual landing site; it couldn't be more than a hundred meters.

Right here!

He stopped abruptly.

Where?

The ridged terrain spread out in all directions. He could tell from the perspective of the mountain that they had to be at the right place. All the rocks looked familiar, but every time he looked closer at any one of them, it turned to be not quite right. It couldn't be far away, but where, exactly, was it?

"Ryan!" It was Tana, coming up behind him, panting. "Are you all right?"

His legs ached. They had been walking for days, and even the brief exertion of breaking into a jog made him suddenly aware of the ache in his muscles. "This is the Pathfinder site," he gasped. "Look!"

Tana looked around. "Say, you could be right. It does kind of look like it, doesn't it? Is that why you were running?"

"It is! Take a look!" He pointed. "There are the Twin Peaks." He swung around. "That big one over there? That rock is named Couch. Or maybe that one." He stopped, momentarily unsure. It was easy to get confused. Was either of them really the boulder named Couch? Or was it another one that looked similar?

Tana looked around. "Wow," she said. "Pretty neat. So, where's the *Pathfinder* itself? It wouldn't have moved, would it? So it must be here."

"Let's find it!" Ryan said.

"Wait a second," Tana said. "You said that we weren't going to make any stops, we weren't going to go exploring."

"It won't take long," Ryan said. "We must be standing practically right on top of it. It's gotta be right around here. It's got to stick out like a sore thumb in this."

But it didn't. After an hour of searching, Ryan finally had to admit that the Pathfinder was invisible. Even the inertial navigation system he had scavenged from the dirt-rover was no help; it told them exactly where on the planet they were, but the navigation system of the ancient spacecraft had only given its position on the planet to within a few kilometers. But they should be able to see it. "We know it's here," Ryan said. "So why can't we find it?"

"Dust," Tana said. "Think about it. How long ago did that land? Thirty years ago? How many dust storms have there been since then?" She thought for a second. "It'll be so covered with dust that it will blend right in. Just a funny, lumpy patch of the soil."

"Dust," Ryan said, dejected. "You're right. I didn't think of that. Shit. We probably walked right past it and couldn't see it. What now?"

"Onward," Tana said. She quoted his own words back to him. "No sidetracks, no exploration, no sight-seeing, just speed. *Agamemnon*, or bust."

"*Agamemnon* or bust," Ryan echoed. "Okay. Let's get a move on!"

2

T H E   A R R O W

Ryan Martin could not even remember a time when he had not wanted to be an astronaut. He could remember being six, and riding on his father's shoulders. The Canadian night had been cool and clear, and he had leaned back and just gazed at the stars blazing above him, tiny lighthouses on the road to infinity. He could imagine that he was falling upward, endlessly falling among the stars, and thought, there. I'm going out there. He had leaned back, farther and farther on his father's shoulders, and then let go, to feel himself falling upward.

His father had caught him by the legs before he hit the ground—his father had always had incredible reflexes—and all that he had felt was disappointment.

In the Scouts, he had been on the archery range. He hadn't cared much about target shooting, and unlike the other boys, he had no secret longing to hunt and kill. But the bow itself seemed to him a thing of perfect beauty, an object that could not have been more elegantly designed. He marveled over its clean and simple design. One day he took his bow, drew it back as far as he could, and aimed it directly upward into the sky.

The arrow flew up, straight and true, and vanished with a whisper into the aching blue above, and he stared after it, his bow arm still extended in the air, mesmerized by the beauty of the flight.

"Martin!" the scoutmaster shouted. "What the hell are you—"

The arrow came down, so fast it was only a streak, and with a soft whickersnack buried itself to the feathers in the Earth.

The scoutmaster turned pale, his eyes bulging, and then he exploded. "Martin! Get over here!" He grabbed him, his fingers digging painfully into his shoulder, and ripped the bow out of his hands.

Ryan had almost forgotten he still held it.

None of the other boys had been watching when Ryan had launched his arrow skyward, and they all turned to stare, baffled at the sudden in-explicable fury of the scoutmaster.

"You—you—" The scoutmaster was completely incoherent, and slowly, almost as if from a dream, Ryan came to his senses and realized, yes, it might have killed someone. It might have killed him. It had been a dangerous thing to do.

But in his mind's eye he could still see it, that one perfect moment when the arrow hangs in the air, quivering, straining, longing to go higher, and then falls, defeated.

And he realized, that is me, the arrow is me. That is where I want to go.

To go upward, forever upward, and to never come down.

3

CAMP AGAMEMNON

They were tired, and then more than tired, a complete weariness that transcended all consciousness. The world compressed down to one step, then another, then another. The landscape had changed color, darkening from the light, almost orange color of their original landing site to a dark burned-brick color. They were walking on bare bedrock. But none of them looked at the landscape, none of them focused any farther ahead than the next step.

Ryan kept a readout of their position using the inertial navigation system from the dirt-rover. Occasionally he would read out their progress—"Three hundred kilometers to go"—until at last Tana told him to stop; it was too depressing. None of them dared to think of what would happen if the inertial navigation failed, if they were unable to find the *Agamemnon* site as they had been earlier unable to find the Pathfinder.

Two hundred kilometers to go.

One hundred kilometers.

When they came to the edges of the *Agamemnon* camp, it took them several minutes before they even recognized it. A discarded drilling-lubricant cylinder. Not far past that, a seismic recording station. They were beyond curiosity now, and the technological detritus went unremarked.

They crested a dune, and started down the far side, and none of them looked up until they almost stumbled over the camp.

Agamemnon lay before them.

"We're here," Tana said, almost in a whisper.

Ryan looked up. "We're here. It's here!"

Estrela, trailing behind, echoed in a whisper, "Here. Here!"

The *Agamemnon* camp was spread out. The *Agamemnon* lander itself sat a kilometer off to the east, a squashed hemispherical shell sitting on its heat shield and surrounded by the shreds of its airbag cushion like a half-melted mushroom. Spread all around were the remains of the encampment: the abandoned fuel-manufacturing plant and its electrical generator plant; two bubble habitats, long deflated; a toolshed; a domed greenhouse module; a half dozen scientific stations; communications antennae; a sheet metal quonset hut; piles of trash and discarded equipment; electrical and data cables spread spaghetti-style across the ground. No one from the doomed *Agamemnon* had bothered to be neat; they were too worried about survival.

Every horizontal surface was covered with a layer of dust.

There was no hope that Agamemnon's electrical generating plant would still work, but the bubble habitats both seemed intact. Over the six years they had been on Mars the gas that had originally inflated them had slowly leaked away, but when Ryan checked, they were still intact.

Using the *Agamemnon* camp was a risk. If any of the original fungus had survived the six years on Mars and was still viable, and still virulent, they could face a repeat of the runaway infection that had ultimately led to the *Agamemnon* disaster. In theory it would not survive the six years without a host. In theory, even if it survived, it would not colonize healthy humans. In theory, even if it did, they had the pharmaceuticals to be prepared for it this time. In theory.

But they had little choice.

Ryan salvaged several solar array panels from the lander, and after cleaning away the dust layers, found them still functioning. It would be enough power to provide heat and light for the habitat.

And, if the transmitters still functioned, enough to communicate with Earth.

"We've got a new camp, crew," Ryan announced. He should have felt triumph. Instead, all he felt was weary. "And it looks like everything still works."

4

THE MINIONS

Through grade school Ryan had built model rockets, taught himself calculus and aerodynamics, built his own telescope and a special tracking platform for it so he could watch the Russian space station *Mir* when it passed overhead and plan for the day when he, too, would be up there, looking down on Canada from above. In high school his science fair project, a gyroscopic stability system for a model rocket, had won a prize and a scholarship, enough that, along with earnings from an outside job programming computers to recognize speech, he could afford to go to MIT.

To Ryan, being an undergraduate at MIT had been like being at a banquet with each course more appetizing than the last. Finally he was stimulated to stretch his limits, and sometimes to exceed them.

At the end of his freshman year, Ryan got involved with a project to fly a student-designed satellite. He volunteered for the task of building the control system. It was a small but intensely dedicated team.

They had two unofficial mottoes. The first was, "It doesn't have to be good—it *does* have to be done." The second was, "We don't need no stinkin' sleep!" Everybody else called them the satellite gang, but to one another, they were the Minions of the Satellite God. They made a pact with each other: The satellite came first. Everything else—their sleep, their health, their grades, their lives—came second.

Their satellite flew as a secondary payload on a Delta rocket, hitchhiking its way into space with a free ride on the third stage of a rocket whose main mission was to put a communications satellite into geosynchronous orbit. The entire gang went to Florida for the launch, crammed into a battered Volvo station wagon. They stayed, eight of them in one room, at a cheap hotel on Cocoa Beach. It was the first time Ryan had ever been so far south.

The launch was on a cold and cloudy day. The wind was so high that they had been certain that the launch would be canceled, but they went out to the public beach with their binoculars, their cameras, and a small battery-powdered radio. The tide line was covered with seaweed and the drying corpses of Portuguese men-of-war, improbably bright blue balloons slowly deflating in the air.

The Delta had launched on the exact second the launch window opened. It climbed silently into the air, the light of the solid rocket boosters sparkling a trail across the choppy water, almost too bright to look directly at, and then vanished into the clouds. For a few seconds the cloud glowed with the light of the booster, and then it faded, and there was nothing left but the empty pad and the white smoke.

Only then did the sound come rolling across the water, a roar so intense that you could feel it as well as hear it. And then that, too, faded into the distance, and there was only the surf and the seagulls.

Not one of the Minions was old enough to drink, so when the announcement came that the launch had been a success, they celebrated by pouring grape juice over each other.

The satellite—and more particularly Ryan's control systems—worked perfectly, taking photographs of the polar aurorae for over a year.

Ryan spent that year going to classes when he had to, but never far enough away from the satellite control center that he could not be paged to return at an instant's notice.

The control center consisted of a few computers and a fast Internet connection hooked up in a windowless room in the basement of the wind tunnel building. With the launch, the tight group of the Minions began to drift away to other projects and other concerns. Dave left for a year in Israel, Darlene got involved in a new project in the physics department, Anu quit to start up a software firm and become a millionaire, Steve got married and stopped coming around, and Ted simply declared that he needed to spend time on coursework, and wasn't about to let the satellite run his life.

There were new undergraduates to help out, bright-eyed and eager, but of the original Minions, only Ryan stayed with the project to the end. Whenever anything went wrong, Ryan was there to debug the problem and design a work-around for it. They found that he had a talent for visualizing orbital mechanics, and an almost mystical understanding of the secret world of torque wheels and magnetic dampers and predictive control systems. He could figure out, from the slightest bump in a chart, which part was failing, how the underperformance was affecting the satellite, and what was needed to write a software patch to keep the satellite running.

For Ryan, it was not just a student project. It was his life.

5

CALLING HOME

It was a task that Ryan dreaded, but there was no help for it. *Agamemnon* expedition had left behind a complete set of high-bandwidth communications gear and a gimbaled high-gain antenna. He had to call Earth.

After inflating the *Agamemnon*'s main operations habitat, it took him an hour to get the communications gear powered up and to reset the computer to calculate the position of the Earth and adjust the antenna to track it. He almost hoped that the antenna would fail to lock on to the Earth; fixing that would give him another few hours to avoid making the connection. But no such luck.

At least he didn't have to do it alone. He called in Estrela and Tana. "We're all in this together," he said. "Ready?"

Estrela nodded, tossed her hair, and attempted a wan smile. Tana said, "Ready."

He flicked on the camera and began transmitting.

"Earth, *Don Ouijote*. This is Ryan Martin, Tanisha Jackson, and Estrela Conselheiro, calling in. We've reached the *Agamemnon* site at Acidalia Planitia." He paused. That was the easy part. "It is with great regret," he said, and then stopped. He didn't even know what to *say*. He looked over at Tana, but she shook her head infinitesimally and mouthed silently, "you." He turned back to the camera. "I regret to inform you that, uh, we've killed off—I mean, we've had some casualties here. Uh, that is, we. Shit. I hate doing this. Look, it's like this." He took a deep breath, and then said quickly, "We've had a bit of a hard time here, and Captain Radkowski and Bran—Trevor Whitman are dead. Got that?"

He turned off the camera, and slumped down. "Okay, it's done."

"We're not done with the broadcast, are we?" Tana said. "We have to tell them more than that. And I thought we were going to ask for advice."

Ryan shook his head. "No. I mean, yes, no we're not done."

"Then—"

"It will be half an hour before we get a reply from Earth," he said. "It'll probably be a while after that before we get anybody who can give us anything we need. Don't worry. We have time." He composed himself, turned the transmitter back on, and then gave them a brief synopsis of how Captain Radkowski and Trevor Whitman had died. He kept it strictly to the facts, with nothing about Trevor Whitman actually being Brandon Weber, nor about their conjecture that Radkowski had been murdered.

The person who appeared on the monitor looked startled. He looked like he'd just woken up. "Uh, *Don Quijote*, Houston. We got you." Ryan didn't recognize him; he wasn't one of the regular communicators. "Uh, this is great. Wow, it's really great to hear from you. We were worried—" Just at the moment the news about Radkowski and Trevor must have arrived; the technician looked startled. "Wait one," he said.

Ryan calculated the time on Earth. 05:45 Greenwich; that would make it 12:45 at night in Toronto, 11:45 at the space center in Houston. Late; they were transmitting to the second shift. No wonder they had to wait, probably had to go wake somebody up.

It was a slow conversation. Ryan and Tana talked for a while, answering some of the questions from Earth and ignoring others. Then they would break and listen to the feed from Earth, replies to their queries of half an hour ago.

First, they learned there was still no hope of a rescue mission. Ryan had never expected one; he'd asked just out of a perverse sense that he had to check the obvious. Second, they were told that the engineers on Earth had not come up with any unexpected new ideas, although not for lack of trying. Their only chance was still the Brazilian *Jesus do Sul* return rocket, at the pole. There were now hundreds of news reporters asking for interviews; Houston was holding them off, but did they want to talk to reporters? When their "no" answer came through, nobody seemed surprised.

"Copy that," was the reply. "One more thing for you. Hold on a moment. I think you may want to hear this directly from our orbital mechanics guy."

The orbital mechanics guy, as it turned out, was a middle-aged woman. Ryan recognized her; what was her name, Lorentz? She had a reputation for being both hard-working and smart. She spoke in a Texas accent, launching in without bothering to say hello first. "We tracked down the complete specs on that Brazilian rocket, checked it out against a matrix of trajectories available for your launch window. Here's the lowdown. Stripped to the bone, no rock samples, dump all the spare supplies, no margin for underperformance: You'll have fuel for one hundred and forty kilograms of human payload. That's top; you'd be wise to leave a little margin."

"Copy," Ryan said. "What if we—" Then he stopped. If they what?

What could they think of that the ground engineers hadn't already thought of? If she said one hundred and forty kilograms, that was the end of it.

One hundred and forty kilograms.

Now they knew.

Only two of them were going back.

6

RYAN IN LOVE

In his own little social world, Ryan was boisterous, talkative, and outgoing. Outside of the nearly vanished circle of the Minions, though, the guidance counselors labeled him withdrawn and introverted. He hadn't paid any attention to the tall, talkative girl who chanced to sit near him in the cafeteria whenever he came down for a meal, not even when she began to talk to him, and slowly but patiently drew him out. It didn't occur to him that she might be interested in more than a lunchtime companionship until she invited him to her dorm room, closed the door, put a Nirvana CD to play on her stereo, and started to take off his clothes. "It was the only way I could get your attention," she told him.

Kaitlyn was, he discovered, the smartest person he had ever met, and he was eternally baffled by what it was she saw in him. Sex, to her, was playful. They would take her Toyota Corolla on long weekends up to Maine, and they would take an old logging road far into the woods and camp, making love far into the night. "Let's try something new," was her catch-all phrase. Or they would tryst on one of the rooftops of the Institute, the altitude and the fear of somebody coming across them adding to the thrill of sex.

One summer they spent in urban spelunking. She showed up in his dorm room one day with two flashlights and a crowbar. The game was, find a manhole and see what was underneath it. Sometimes it was nothing. Sometimes it led to tunnels and pipes that seemed to go everywhere in Cambridge. "Hmm, guess you're not claustrophobic," Kaitlyn had said the first time he got stuck and had to wait in the dark while she went to fetch a block and tackle to pull him out. "You should be an astronaut."

She was the first girl he ever fell in love with. A week after they both graduated—he in computer science, she in mathematics—Kaitlyn asked him to marry her. He hadn't even told his parents yet—he was going to spring it on them when he went back home for the American Thanksgiving holiday—when a pickup truck sideswiped her going around a curve, and her Corolla fishtailed and hit a lamppost.

It was hard for him to believe that she was really dead. For years afterward he would wake up with some thought in his head, and think, I'll have to remember that to tell Kaitlyn.

It took him a long time to get over her. He moved back to Toronto and got a job working on software for an aerospace company. Eventually a quiet, patient girl named Sarah, who he kept running into at work, broke through his reserve and attracted his attention. She worked as a temp, adept at filling in at secretarial jobs when the company was shorthanded, but her real avocation was viola, which she played in a chamber orchestra in Toronto.

He had never heard a chamber music concert, he finally had to admit to her. He wasn't really quite sure what kind of music it was. "Well, I guess I'll just have to show you," she told him.

And from then, his weekends were filled with music. Sarah was both patient and had a sense of humor; her musical tastes ran from Beethoven to Weird Al, and she was fond of pointing out little things to him. "Listen there. That's a cowbell," she might say, or, "See what you think of this, it's written for glass harmonica. You play it by rubbing your finger on wine glasses."

He got accustomed to her company, and when she went out of town for a performance, he missed her, and hung around his apartment, not knowing what to do with himself.

They were tentatively beginning to talk about making a commitment for life. The only thing was that Sarah was always so tired. She barely had the energy to go to her concerts. She looked pale.

She hadn't always been so tired. When she first started to chat to Ryan over lunchtime, over breaks at work, she had been full of energy. "She's a real 240-volt live wire," was how the other engineer in his office described her. Now she could barely make it from breakfast to lunch.

Ryan took her to a doctor.

The doctor ordered tests. When the tests came back, he wouldn't talk about them, but ordered more tests, and a CAT scan. When the new tests were completed, a new doctor came to talk about them, a specialist.

It was cancer: in her liver and her pancreas, and beginning to spread. The cancer was aggressive and inoperable. The day before Easter, he brought a minister and a wedding license to the hospital, and they were married. Three days later she was dead.

Twice was enough. He went back to school for three more degrees, one in astronautical engineering and two in computer science, and decided that from then on he would stick to his studies, and would never curse another woman by becoming too close to her.

7

BUTTERFLY

Butterfly didn't look like anything, least of all like an airplane. It was a pile of thin, transparent foil.

The Martian atmosphere is more than a hundred times thinner than the Earth's atmosphere. Even with the low gravity of Mars, flying in the thin air of Mars is a challenge. To fly, an airplane has to have forty times more wing area than an airplane on Earth, or else fly six times faster. Or else weigh forty times less.

Butterfly did a little of each. Its wing area was absurdly high, by the standards of Earthly airplanes, and it flew at nearly sonic speed; yet despite its high speed and large wing area, it weighed almost nothing. It was constructed out of a monomolecular membrane, a tough plastic sheet so thin as to be almost invisible. The main spars of the wings were pressurized bags, balloon-stiffness providing the rigidity. The fuselage likewise was stiffened by inflation. Ultralight foam ribs formed the wings into a high-lift airfoil.

"Do you know why they named it Butterfly?" Ryan asked.

"Because it's so light and fragile," Tana said. "Like a butterfly."

Ryan smiled. "Nope. Got named when the lead engineer took one look at it, shook his head, and said, 'Well, it butter fly.' "

The only item of any real weight was the engine.

A propeller was almost useless; the tenuous air of Mars is too thin to give a propeller much to grab. A jet engine is pointless; how can you burn carbon dioxide? Instead, *Butterfly* used a ram-augmented hybrid rocket engine. A feed stream of liquid oxygen was injected into a cylinder of dense rubber and ignited; the burning rubber forms a rocket engine. Rather than just shooting the exhaust product out through a conventional rocket nozzle, additional atmospheric carbon dioxide is collected—the ram part of "ram augmentation"—and mixed into the exhaust stream to augment the thrust.

The result was a high-power engine that used the thin atmosphere of Mars to increase its thrust.

This was the vehicle that Ryan Martin examined. His first task was to inflate its wing spars and fuselage with compressed gas; after that he had to fill the engine's tanks with liquid oxygen. This second task was a tricky problem. The *Butterfly* had been designed to use oxygen produced from the Mars atmosphere by the same chemical plant that manufactured rocket fuel for the return vehicle. But the fuel manufacturing plant for the *Agamemnon* expedition was identical to the one that had failed *Dulcinea*.

But *Butterfly* was an airplane, not a rocket. It required less than a tenth of a percent as much liquid oxygen as was needed to launch the return rocket. Consultation with the experts on Earth concurred on the opinion that, for the tiny amount of liquid oxygen needed, Ryan could bypass the main atmosphere compression and Sabatier reactor and just use the electrolysis system and the Stirling liquefier. Taking precautions to avoid stressing the seals that has failed so catastrophically on *Dulcinea*, he should be able to fill the tanks in a few weeks of operation using only solar power. No more than a few months even under worst-case conditions.

And so, drop by drop, Ryan fueled his airplane.

8

ON ANCIENT SHORES

They were camped at the shore of what had, long ago, been an ocean. How many fossils were there in that ancient dry ocean bed, Estrela wondered? How far had life come? Had life on Mars emerged from its oceans, only to become extinct as the rivers dried and the planet froze? And what, exactly, had caused the oceans to evaporate and the atmosphere to leak away?

Estrela was beginning, slowly, to come out of the deep depression that had enveloped her over the last weeks. Eight days at the *Agamemnon* campsite had revived her. For the first three days she had stayed inside the habitat dome, and then she took to leaving the habitat dome for just one hour each day.

First she would walk over to the greenhouse module. She was amazed that it had survived, untended, for years on the Martian surface, and even had plants inside, some sort of tough yucca and several evergreen shrubs. She rubbed her hand over them, feeling the prickly points. You are like me, she told them silently. We are survivors.

Then she would go to walk along the deserted beach just before sunset.

The water of the ancient ocean was long gone; the sands of the beach had long ago cemented into a rocklike caliche. She could read the ebb and flow of the waves in the ripples frozen into the sandstone. She would find a shallow basin and brush away the covering dust, and find below the white layer of evaporite, salt crystals.

One time, walking a little inland, she found yet another fossil, embedded in the wall of a limestone cliff. It was exactly the same shape as the others, but this one was immense, as large as a whale, ten meters from end to end. Estrela wondered that these were the only type of fossils that they saw. Had there been only one form of life on Mars? Or perhaps only one type had fossilized.

And the sun would set, and she would return into the habitat.

Inside the dome was paradise, with plentiful liquids and warmth, with enough water to heat an entire liter of bathwater at once and let it dribble, sensuously, over her body. It felt like a decadent luxury.

Her throat no longer hurt so much. She could even speak, in a voice louder than a whisper.

She carefully plaited her now-blond hair, and barely wore clothing. Ryan was the one who would make the decision now, she knew. Two women, and he would be able to take only one home.

But Ryan barely looked at her, although she tried in a dozen subtle ways to contrive to be there, nearly naked, when he was in the habitat, and he would hardly have been able to miss her. But he never made a move.

Ryan was good-looking. Oh, not as good as João—Santa Luzia, who could possibly be as gorgeous as her beautiful João had been?—but he was fine. But he seemed to pay no attention to her.

Two women, and only one would get to go with him back home. Well, the odds were much better than they had been. She knew men, and knew that if there had been two men, somehow the men would have contrived a way to show that it was logical for the two men to go home to Earth and the women stay behind to die. It was just the way of the world.

She wondered if Tana knew how much she hated her.

9

THE CANADIAN
ASTRONAUT

At SPAR Aerospace, Ryan Martin worked on designing tether deployment systems for space; much later, his expertise on the use of tether systems played a major part in his role in the failed *Mirusha* rescue attempt. He spent a year in France, to earn a degree in space studies at the International Space University in Strasbourg, and the day he came back to Canada he put in his application to join the small Canadian astronaut corps.

His application went in just in time to apply to join the first Canadian cadre selected specifically for duty to the space station. His low amount of piloting time counted against him. He had taken flying lessons and spent as much time as he could afford practicing, but he certainly had far fewer hours in the air than the RCAF pilots that applied for the same few slots. But no one had a more thorough grasp of every aspect of astronautics and microgravity science than he, and in the end that counted more than his relative lack of flight hours. He wasn't being trained to be a pilot anyway; the Americans would never select a Canadian to fly their shuttle. For the tasks Canada wanted astronauts for, they needed expertise in all areas, and no one scored higher than Ryan.

He graduated at the top of his astronaut training class.

His appointment to the astronaut corps elicited mixed feelings for him; during those years the fate of the space station was uncertain, and whether the space station had any role at all in the future exploration of space, or if instead it was an expensive orbiting dinosaur, was quite unclear. He wondered if the real future might instead lie in commercial space, where new, small launch vehicles were beginning to make enormous profits from launching tiny, cheap satellites.

But he wanted to do more than just send up other people's satellites.

Ryan Martin wanted to go to Mars.

Mars was his obsession. He thought about Mars, made calculations, read every book, science or science fiction, that had ever been written about

Mars, published papers suggesting possible solutions to the finicky engineering details of a Mars mission. After a while he started to be invited to give lectures about Mars missions, and he found that he was good at it. He would rent an airplane and fly to some distant city and talk. Schoolchildren, Masonic temples, library groups—he loved the moment when a group of strangers suddenly warmed up, and his contagious enthusiasm spread.

He didn't chase women—to tell the truth, he had never learned how to approach a woman—it seemed to be an arcane trick that other men learned in some class he had failed to attend—and so he treated all the women he met exactly the same way he treated the men: as coworkers or as friends. But occasionally women would ask him out, and he wasn't against going out to a restaurant, or to a concert, or for a walk on the beaches of Lake Ontario. And afterward, if sometimes a female friend asked him back to her apartment, or his, well, he had taken no vow of chastity.

He had only two rules to his relationships, rules that he never broke. Never promise anything.

And never fall in love.

10

RIDING THE
SLINGSHOT

B*utterfly* had been designed for short hops and aerial reconnaissance, not for a two-thousand-mile flight, and it had not been designed to carry three people. Over the months that they spent at Acidalia, Ryan ripped out every part that was not critical to flight: all the redundant control systems, the scientific instrumentation. He cut off the landing gear; when she landed, the *Butterfly* would land on snow. And she would never take off again.

They would have no margin, but at last he had an airplane that would make it to the pole.

For the take-off, Ryan laid down two strands of the superfiber cable for three kilometers along the desert sand. At the far end he staked it down to bolts drilled into bedrock, and then went back and used the motorized winch to stretch it. The elastic energy that can be stored in superfiber is enormous: If it were to suddenly break, the release would snap the cable back at almost hypersonic velocity, setting free enough energy to vaporize much of the cable, as well as anybody who stood nearby.

Once he had it stretched, he held it stretched with a second anchor bolt. It formed a two-mile-long rubber band. Ryan would use the world's largest slingshot to launch the airplane.

The airplane had only two seats, so Estrela and Tana both were crammed into the rear copilot's seat of the airplane, Estrela perched on Tana's lap. In their bulky Mars suits, they fit into the space with barely millimeters to spare.

Ryan closed and sealed the cockpit around them and took the pilot's seat.

"Ready?" Ryan asked.

"As ready as we're going to be," Tana's muffled voice said.

"Get on with it!" Estrela said.

"Armed," Ryan said. He pulled out an arming switch on the remote control, and said, "Launch!"

The explosives fired in silence, but Ryan could see the flash behind him, severing the strap that held the stretched superfiber down. Instantly he was pressed back into his seat as the superfiber slingshot, attached to the airplane at the motor mount, grabbed the airplane and shot it forward. Behind him he heard Tana say "Yikes!" and Estrela let out a sudden grunt as the sudden weight pressed into her.

The ground rushed past them with terrifying speed. Ryan concentrated his attention on keeping the wings level; with even a slight brush of a wingtip against the sand the fragile airplane would disintegrate around them. He couldn't spare any attention for the airspeed indicator, but he could feel the wings beginning to pull against the air. He held forward pressure on the stick to keep the nose down; they needed to reach flying airspeed as quickly as they could. He shot a glance down at the airspeed; not yet, not yet. Now.

He eased back on the stick—not too much, or the wings would be ripped off—and the ground dropped away under them. Now *Butterfly* was lofted like a kite being towed behind a running boy. The pressure from the slingshot eased off; they were running out of stretch. It had been only a few seconds. He concentrated on keeping his airspeed up while milking the last little bit of altitude out of the quickly relaxing slingshot.

The slingshot slackened and fell away. For a moment *Butterfly* was soaring. He commanded the valves on the liquid oxygen tanks open, armed the ignition switch, and watched for the green light. After a terrifying pause, it flickered on.

They were ready.

Ryan hit the ignition button, and with a shudder, the ram-rocket chuffed to life.

For the first time in weeks, Ryan felt a surge of hope. Maybe they would make it after all. They were flying. *Flying!*

11

MOMENTUM
MANAGEMENT

Other astronauts who flew up on the shuttle with him felt sick. Ryan felt exhilarated. Every part of it was exciting, the training, the launch, and now the free-fall. This was what he'd always wanted. He tried a slow flip, then a fast one. "This is great," he said.

But he was here to work, not to play. He had the map of the space station memorized. The others went quickly to find the station physician, or at least to find vomit bags. "They'll get over it in a day or so," the station physician said. "How about you? You okay? Need a patch?"

"No. I'm fine."

The doctor nodded. Ryan was fascinated to see how his body moved infinitesimally in the opposite direction as he did. "Some people aren't affected. Guess you're lucky."

He went to work.

After a while, when he was alone in a module, one of the female astronauts floated over. She casually snagged a handrail next to him, and looked at him, floating upside down.

He looked up.

"Are you gay?" she said.

"Huh? No." He tried to remember her name. He was supposed to know the names of all the people on the station, but he'd never been good with names. Britta, he recalled, Britta Silverthorne. That was it.

"Nothing wrong if you are," she said.

"Nope, nothing wrong if I were," he agreed. "Happens I'm not."

"Oh. That's okay; I just wanted to know."

He waited, saying nothing.

She rotated herself over until she reoriented so that her head pointed the same way he did. "That's better. Now I can look at you," she said. "Say, you're better in microgravity than any other newbie I've seen. You must have been upside before?"

"Nope," he said, "first time." And then, "I think I like it."

"I'm impressed. You're a natural."

There was a pause.

"You did get the orientation, didn't you?" Britta asked. "You know about our first-night custom here? The welcome-aboard ritual?"

Ryan considered her. She was cute, in her way. She had a round face, with short dark hair and deep brown eyes; her rather baggy coveralls failed to conceal a body that was compact and fit. He knew about the space station's rite of *jus primae noctis*, of course; there was no way to avoid it. The other astronauts—the male ones, anyway—had made sure about that, with a lot of ribald comments and pointed innuendo. But it was not his way of dealing with the people. "Sure."

She paused, licked her lips nervously, and looked at him sidelong. She was blushing. "You want to?"

He looked at her calmly. "Are you asking?"

She looked away. "I'm not supposed to ask."

"Are you?"

"Well, damn it, yes. Yes."

"Well, then," he said, "sure."

It was sweet and complicated, almost like an exercise in momentum management. And it was slow, so slow. Whenever he tried to be hasty, he pushed her away from him, and she would say, "Slow, keep it slow and easy." Afterward, she clung to him, and in a few moments he realized, somewhat to his amazement, that he wanted to do it again.

And sometime after that, she kissed him on the nose. As she drew her coveralls back on, she said, "I'm pleased to be able to say that you are now a member of the microgravity society." Then she smiled, and said, "Very definitely pleased."

For the first few weeks Ryan was assigned to momentum management. This meant two things: garbage dump detail, and processing wastewater into fuel for the resistojet thrusters. He used the garbage dump as a chance to experiment with the tether, trying swinging deploys, crack-the-whip deploys, getting a feel for the tether system.

"You actually *like* garbage detail, don't you?" one of the astronauts said, incredulous. "You spend more time working on the garbage drop calculations—everybody else just reads out the computer and plops the answer into the drop parameters."

"One day we're going to use a tether on the way to Mars," Ryan said. "I'm getting ready."

The other astronaut shook his head. "You sure are," he said. "You sure are."

12

BUTTERFLY IN A
HURRICANE

Mars looked different from above.

Ryan flew fast and low. He had to stay low, with the *Butterfly* so over-loaded, he had to stay in the densest part of the tenuous atmosphere to fly at all. Still, the view was remarkable. From above, it was clear that they were following the coastline of an ancient sea. To the east, a jumble of mountains and chaos interrupted by ancient riverbeds flowing down to a beach. To the west, a flat and smooth basin, broken by craters.

Tana pressed against the cockpit window, enrapt. She turned forward to point out something to Estrela, to ask about a massif that loomed on the horizon, and with astonishment saw that Estrela had her eyes closed. She was asleep.

Asleep, through this greatest airplane trip ever taken!

As the liquid oxygen burned off, the airplane gradually lightened, and Ryan slowly gained attitude. "No such thing as an airplane that flies itself," Ryan's flight instructor had told him, long ago, and on another planet. "You have to be alert every second. The moment you think that the computer is going to do the flying, the moment you think you can relax and stop paying attention, that's when you're going to screw up. That's when pilots die."

Butterfly came as close to flying itself as any airplane ever did. Once the take-off had been completed, Ryan could have taken his hands off the controls and let the autopilot take over. They were heading due north.

The land below had been shaped and reshaped by enormous impact craters and by vast lava flows. As they continued northward, Ryan noticed odd craters with a peculiar, melted look, as if the impacting meteoroid had splashed into thick ice cream.

The first of the three liquid oxygen tanks was sputtering, nearly empty. Ryan opened the valve to start feeding from the second tank, and felt the engine surge with the increased fuel flow. He diverted boil-off gas through the first tank to blow the last of the oxygen out, and then, satisfied that it was completely dry, jettisoned it. Freed of the weight and drag of the extra tank, *Butterfly* jumped upward.

Two tanks left.

Farther north he started to see white, at first just a narrow rim of shiny frost on the north-facing side of the crater rings, and then more and more frost, patterns of white in spiderweb traceries across the hills, limning the slightest changes in topography.

He was approaching the polar circle.

Ryan looked up. Ahead of him, the sky had lost its pale ochre color. It was an ominous deep brick red, with knots and swirls of darker color. He cursed under his breath and checked the altimeter. Eleven hundred meters above ground level. He pulled back slightly, trading speed for rate of climb, but it looked like there was no way he could gain enough altitude to climb over the storm.

He could see something moving below. Snakes.

He looked again. Under him, ribbons of white slithered snakelike across the landscape. It was rivers of blowing snow, he realized, following the sinuous path of least resistance across the lowest passes between the hills. The wind velocity at the surface must be horrendous, he thought; it would take fifty meters per second, or even more, for air as thin as the Martian atmosphere to pick up and carry snow.

Spring was coming to the Martian pole. The winter snows, a mixture of carbon dioxide and water ice, were evaporating away with the return of the sun. The sheer mass of vaporizing atmosphere was blasting off the part of the snow that was made from water ice and blowing it south, creating little storms at the edge of the polar cap.

He wouldn't be able to fight those storms, not directly, but they would be local, not global. He banked to the west, turning parallel to the looming banks of cloud, hoping to circle the storm, looking for a gap between the storm cells.

The land below was tundra now. He was at the arctic circle, and below the fluid rivers of airborne snow, the ground was patchy with ice. The ground was ridged in a network of enormous hexagons and triangles and squares all jumbled and fit together like a crazy jigsaw puzzle, the lunatic work of some mad geometer.

He checked the level of liquid oxygen in the fuel tanks. The second tank was almost dry. There was no reserve set aside for detours; if he didn't head back north quickly, they would not have enough range to make the pole.

He switched the fuel feed to the third and final tank, purged out the last little bit of fluid from the second tank, and jettisoned it. At least the *Butterfly* would be more responsive.

There. A pale color of sky, a wide canyon of clear air between the polar storms.

"Hold on," he said. "The ride is going to get bumpy." He banked to the right, following the edge of the storm north.

The polar cap revealed itself as a series of ice cliffs, each one rising above the last, the ice glistening blue. Past the ice cliffs, the polar cap itself was smoking, the ice boiling away in the summer sun.

And then, suddenly, the ice below him dropped away. He was above an immense ice canyon. A hurricane wind drove down the canyon, a torrent of wind sweeping the airplane helplessly to the west. The wind from the entire evaporating polar cap was funneled into this channel, etching away the ice.

This was the immense Chasma Borealis. Over the eons, the swirling wind had carved away a kilometer's thickness of ice, making a channel for the outflow of the evaporating atmosphere. The bottom of the chasm below him was jumble of dark rock, glacial moraine. He crabbed crosswind across the canyon, onward. To the left, an immense wall of blue ice rose a kilometer up from the jumbled rock of the base to the top.

He barely cleared the top, and abruptly it was calm.

At the top of the cliff was a rippled plain of snow-covered ice, stretching to the horizon. The pole, according to the inertial navigation system, was three hundred kilometers away.

It might have been a thousand.

Butterfly was out of fuel.

Ryan made another fifty kilometers before the rocket died completely. Engine out, in the thin atmosphere *Butterfly* could glide about as well as a brick. He stretched the glide as far as he could, eking out a few precious kilometers, and then flared it in to the lightest touchdown he could. It skidded across the snow like a sled, and Ryan struggled to hold the wings level as it fishtailed down the snow. It sledded, bumping against the irregular ice, and sledded—Ryan was beginning to wonder if it was ever going to stop. Until suddenly there was a boulder in the middle of the ice field.

There was no way to steer the aircraft. Ryan pulled back hard, but the airspeed was too low to hop the boulder. The rock ripped across the bottom of the fuselage. He did his best to keep the wings level, but the airplane slewed around and the right wing scraped on the ground. With a spray of snow, the wing buckled, and the ripped wing spar suddenly lost pressure. The wing bent back and tore off. The airplane rolled up, cartwheeled, and came apart.

T ana's seat had come to rest upside down, completely detached from the fuselage, but remarkably intact otherwise. She unbuckled her harness and pushed the seat away. Debris from the airplane was scattered for a hundred meters down the ice. Estrela had been thrown clear and landed spreadeagled in a drift of snow a few feet away. Ryan, and the front half of the fuselage, protruded from a snowbank.

She could see Estrela moving, and then standing up. Her body was smoking. She brushed the smoke away, and with relief, Tana realized that it was just dry ice vaporizing away from the heat of her body.

In another moment, Ryan unfastened his harness and took a few steps onto the ice.

They were alive.

Ryan looked across at her. He seemed unhurt. The snow had apparently cushioned the landing.

She toggled her radio on to the common band. "Ryan, Estrela, are you okay? Any injuries to report?"

"Think I'm okay," Ryan said. "Nothing broken, anyway."

"*Foda-se!*" Estrela said. "Yes, I'm okay. I think."

Tana wasn't sure what she could have done if they had reported injuries anyway. The nearest emergency room was over a hundred million miles away. She looked across the ice. Liquid oxygen tanks, supplies, shards of aluminum-lithium alloy, the burned-out rocket engine, shreds of wing fabric; pieces of the *Butterfly* were spread on both sides of the skid mark the plane had made sliding along the snow. There was no way it was ever going to fly again. Jesus, that had been the most frightening moment of her life. She was amazed that Ryan had managed to hold it together for so long. "And what now?" she asked.

The question hung in the air for a moment, and then Ryan answered. "What choices do we have?"

A tremor shook the ice, and a moment later a sharp report. "What in the world—"

Tana pointed wordlessly.

A few hundred meters to the east, a geyser had sprung up from the snow, a brilliant white plume shooting a hundred meters into the air. Fragments of ice pattered down on the snow all around them. The ground below the geyser split open, and the glittering plume spread out, at first slowly, and then with increasing speed along the crack in both directions until it was a wall of glistening spray that raced toward the horizon in both directions.

Ryan reached down and touched the ground tentatively. The polar cap surface was dust mixed with ice, a rough, crusty surface. He tapped it gingerly. It seemed solid. "Ice," he said. He rapped on it solidly and looked up at them. "The crust is ordinary water ice. But below the crust, it must be carbon dioxide—dry ice. It's slowly sublimating away in the heat. When it gets trapped—wham. It all blows out at once."

Already the sudden geyser was beginning to die away. In a few minutes, all that was left of it was a patch of broken snow.

"For certain we can't stay here," Ryan said. "We head north."

"On foot?" Tana asked. Nobody said anything; the answer was obvious. "How far?"

"About two hundred and fifty kilometers," Ryan said.

"You've got to be kidding."

It took Tana ten minutes of searching to find the inertial navigation system. The laser gyros had no moving parts; it was a design that had been built to locate airplane crash sites on Earth. She checked it. "Still working. We ought to write the manufacturer." It had been designed to be tough.

Ryan was ripping parts of skin off the *Butterfly* and examining their flexibility, but they didn't seem to meet his needs. He moved over to salvage struts out of the wreckage of the seats, apparently a bit more to his liking. He looked up. "Do you know how to ski?"

"Now you really *have* to be kidding," Tana said.

He held up one of the struts. It was a piece of aluminum-lithium alloy, strong and light. He had been able to flatten it down, and bent a crude curve at one end. He examined it critically, and then started to work on another. "Do you have another idea?"

Tana shook her head.

"North," Ryan said.

14

TO THE FARTHEST
NORTH

The sun was circled by a luminous double halo, with mock suns on either side. It never set, but only circled constantly around them, dipping down almost to the horizon in front of them and then rising up at their backs.

The ground was a jumbled chaos of pressure ridges and fragmented ice-blocks half buried in snow. In regions the ground was solid ice, criss-crossed with cracks that hissed out jets of snow-laden vapor, and in other regions gleaming new snow lay flat and smooth and inviting. Ryan cheerfully steered into the middle of one of these, and as his makeshift skis touched the snow, it hissed and foamed around him. All friction vanished, and he skidded helplessly away on a cushion of foaming carbon dioxide vapor.

It took him an hour to painstakingly make his way out of the trap, warming each step down until he reached solid footing. After that, they learned to avoid the areas of new snow.

After six hours of skiing, Ryan called for a halt. They pulled off their skis and inflated the emergency habitat.

The emergency habitat was a cylinder, two meters long and a meter and a half in diameter, with translucent walls made of polyimide impregnated with netting of ripstop superfiber. An even, pinkish-orange light filtered through the habitat walls, making the inside look like the interior of a furnace. But the inside was cold. The only heat came from the radiators of the isotope power units on the Mars suits. It was so tightly crowded inside that it was hard for them to take their suits off; it had been designed to keep one person alive while waiting for rescue. But nobody was coming to rescue them. They silently stripped down to just the suit liners and piled together in the middle for warmth.

It was nearly impossible to sleep, and they huddled together, too tired to move, too tired to complain. With the continuous sunlight, there was no sense of time. After six hours, without any discussion, they put their suits on.

When they got outside, they saw that the waste heat from the sausage habitat had sublimed the ice away from under it, and the sausage had settled into a hollow half a meter deep.

They continued north.

For the first three days, snow geysers burst forth unexpectedly all around them, and they constantly worried that at any moment one might open beneath them. As they worked farther north, the snow geysers got smaller and less frequent, until they stopped being a threat.

In some places, the ice was just a thin crust suspended above a layer of gas below. The first footstep to touch it would trigger a collapse, and with a rattling crunch, an area as large as a soccer field would suddenly fragment and fall a distance of two or three centimeters.

They would walk on the rough ice, and ski across the snow, until Ryan called a break. He inflated the sausage, and they crawled into the cold, stinking interior. It was a relief to take the suits off, even briefly. After a month of nearly continuous wear, every wrinkle and irregularity of the suits was rubbing their skin raw.

But in the constant light, none of them could really sleep. They took to resting only for three-hour naps, huddling in a semiconscious stupor that was neither sleep nor wakefulness, until Ryan told them it was time for them to put on their suits and push onward.

They came to cliffs of ice and laboriously hacked steps into the ice to climb. The route was upward, ever upward. Twice they came to immense crevasses, hundreds of meters wide, crossing their path. The depths were misty with a white fog, fading into darkness as far down as they could look. It was impossible to cross them, and so they detoured around, cursing at the delay.

They continued north.

15

A C R O S S   T H E   I C E

Estrela Conselheiro had experienced snow, but never so much of it. In the years she had lived in Cleveland, the winters had been mild, and snow was a rare thing, something that came once or twice a winter, melting in a day or so. Some of the older people in the city told stories of how in the last century it had been different, how the winters had been cold, and snow a meter deep, but no one really remembered.

Now she was surrounded by it.

In places the wind had sculpted the snow up in ridges like frozen waves. Other places the ice was swept clear of snow and glowed almost blue in the pale sunlight.

In all directions, as far as it was possible to see, there was only ice. Estrela had to confront the secret that she had never shared with any of the crew: The immensity of Mars terrified her.

They moved in silence. Estrela felt as if she were alone on the face of an uncaring planet. She seemed to be walking in a narrow cavern, a knife-thin slot between the blue-white ice below and the dirty yellow sky above. She felt that she was small, an insignificant speck crawling across the wrinkled ice.

But, to her surprise, she realized on the second day that it no longer terrified her. The ice was just ice, the sky just sky. Neither ice nor sky cared who she was or what she had done. She didn't have to explain herself to them, didn't have to pretend to be anybody. She could forget the others, forget even João, in the presence of uncaring immensity. It was as if she weren't even there at all.

Estrela walked as if hypnotized, half-numbed from cold, numbed from lack of sleep, ignoring the others, alone inside her suit.

Alone between the ice and the sky, Estrela Conselheiro felt free to be nobody at all.

16

THE BURIED
SPACESHIP

I t took them eight days to reach the pole.

They came over the ice ridge, and *Jesus do Sul* was visible. Or the top half of the spacecraft was visible.

Jesus do Sul had sunk into the ice.

Estrela stopped abruptly, as if suddenly waking from a long trance. "*Jesus do Sul*," she said softly, as if it were some puzzling words she were trying to understand, and then, more firmly, "*Jesus do Sul*." Then suddenly she screamed and ran toward the ship. "João! João!"

Around the spacecraft, the snow was clean and undisturbed. Not even a ripple marked the locations where the two Brazilian explorers had fallen.

Ryan started to go to her, and Tana held him back. She switched over to the private channel. "Leave her be," she said. "I think she needs to be alone for a while. Let's go check out the spacecraft."

They were desperately in need of the supplies. They had eaten the last of their ration bricks two days ago and were living on nothing but one liter of recycled water per day. It wasn't enough, and they were all suffering from the effects of dehydration.

There was a habitat module at the base of the *Jesus do Sul*. Ryan knew where it had to be—he had watched the tapes of the Brazilian exploration hundreds of times and had memorized all the details of the base—but nothing was visible. It was buried beneath the snow.

Estrela was looking around frantically. "João!"

Tana ignored her own advice and went toward Estrela. "Estrela?" she said. "Are you all right?"

Ryan turned to the rocket. They had to get into the habitat, and they didn't have any extra time.

The Brazilians had taken a much more streamlined approach to the design, and the part of the rocket that protruded from the snow looked like the spire of an onion-domed cathedral, with two smaller domes, the tops of the two first-stage boosters, to either side.

The dome at the top of the spire of *Jesus do Sul* contained the Earth Return Module, the uppermost stage of the Brazilian rocket. Ryan climbed the ladder to reach it. The hatch was over his head at an awkward angle. He pulled at the latch.

It didn't move.

It's locked, Ryan thought, and then immediately, no, that's ridiculous. Nobody would put a lock on a spaceship hatch. It's just stuck. He put his full strength against the latch and pulled. Nothing.

He paused to think. Cold. Cold, and dry, sitting in the cold and dry for eight years. The hatch had sealed solid against the rim. He went down the ladder back to the snow where he had left his skis, picked up one of the makeshift metal skis, and returned to the hatch. Using the end of the ski as a hammer, he methodically pounded, working around the edge of the sealed hatch. The metal of the ski twisted; he ignored it and kept working, moving clockwise around the seal once, twice.

He used the ski as a lever to pry against the hatch handle and tried it again. No success. He put both hands on the lever and pulled with his full strength against it, and felt something, a slight, almost infinitesimal give. He jerked it again, and then began to rhythmically pull with a succession of quick jerks. With an abrupt sucking, the bottom of the hatch pulled open, and then the top. He nearly fell backward as it opened.

The interior had two couches and a control panel. It was completely dark.

If even the emergency batteries were dead, they were in trouble. But no, when he switched over to emergency power, a feeble cockpit light came on, enough for him to see the controls.

Good enough. He looked around. The advice from the ground had mentioned that there was an EVA maneuvering gun, a small rocket engine mounted on a pistol-grip that could be used if ever there had been a reason to go outside the spacecraft. The ground crew had listed it as a possible item to discard to decrease the launch mass, but Ryan had a different use for it now.

Buried below the snow there was a habitat module, stocked with food and water and an electrical generator, all the necessities for the three hundred and fifty days the Brazilians had planned to stay on the surface.

Ryan intended to melt his way down to it.

17

"He's buried, Estrela," Tana said. She tried to be as gentle as she could. "He's at peace."

Estrela's only reply was an inarticulate moan. She had been on her knees on the ice, at the spot where João had lain, for an hour.

The ice was empty. Over the eight years since João had fallen, his body had slowly sunk into the ice, and new snow had fallen on top, until now only the barest shadow under the ice marked where he had died.

Estrela had been crying continuously. Tana had never before seen her cry; she'd always seen Estrela as being cold and unemotional, sensuous, yes, in her negligent way, but not affected by anything. Tana tried to remember what it felt like to love a man like that. Had she ever loved Derrick so much? She couldn't remember.

Ryan had melted a tunnel down through the ice to the habitat. Or sublimed a tunnel, rather; at this pressure ice vaporized rather than melted. He was beginning to get the solar arrays cleared and the habitat systems powered up. Good old Ryan, she thought; if there's any possible technical solution to a problem, Ryan will find it.

The heat of Estrela's suit had vaporized down six inches of ice around her. The heaters on the suit were good, but at sixty degrees below zero, being pressed right against the snow was pushing them beyond their limits. Why, she must be freezing, Tana thought.

She reached out for Estrela's arm and pulled her up. "Come on. Aren't you cold? We have to get you inside."

Estrela twisted her arm free and shoved Tana away. Wordlessly, she turned back to the little hollow she had melted into the ice and went back down to her knees.

Ryan came up. "I've got the habitat powered up." He looked down at Estrela. "Has she been here this whole time? Is she okay?"

Tana shook her head. "I think she's going hypothermic."

Between the two of them, they managed to pull her to her feet. She struggled fiercely for a moment, and then allowed them to guide her without resisting.

After eight days sleeping inside the sausage, the tiny fiberglass habitat of *Jesus do Sul* seemed like a cathedral. Inside, Tana pulled Estrela out of her suit, and then released her own. "Yikes!" she said. "Sweet Christ, it's cold in here."

"Sorry," Ryan said. "The power system is underperforming. It should warm up in a bit. Coveralls in the storage locker over here."

Tana, starting to shiver, went to the locker. Ryan had already pulled on a coverall. The air in the little dome was frigid. Their breaths came out in white puffs, and the walls around them grew a coating of frost from the exhaled vapor in their breath.

Estrela, stripped down to only her suit lining, had not moved. She was completely still, not even shivering. The tears on her face had frozen into tiny glistening icicles down her cheeks and chin. Tana reached out and touched her on the side of the neck. Her skin was icy to the touch. Tana swore briefly under her breath.

"She's hypothermic, all right," she said. "She's not shivering; that's a bad sign. A real bad sign."

She looked around. "We've got to warm her up. Can you heat up some water?"

"Water supply is still frozen." Ryan shook his head. "It'll be an hour before we get enough power to heat up anything."

"That's too long," said Tana. "Wrapping her in a blanket won't do, she's so cold that there's no heat to conserve. Her skin is too cold."

Tana stripped Estrela down to bare skin. Estrela made no objection; she didn't seem to even notice them. Then Tana peeled away her own clothes; first the coveralls and then her suit liner. The air of the habitat was frigid winter against her bare skin. She wrapped her arms around Estrela, hugging her as close to her as she could, trying to maximize skin contact. It was like hugging ice cubes.

"Can you find a blanket?" Tana asked.

Ryan went to their suits and detached the thermophotovoltaic isotope power supplies. He arranged these around Tana and Estrela. The waste heat from the radiators felt good. It helped. Not enough.

"You, too," Tana said.

Ryan fetched a blanket, and then stripped. He hesitated for a moment at his underwear, and then turned his back and stripped them off. He quickly stepped behind Estrela and pulled her close, and then wrapped the blanket around the three of them.

But Tana had seen.

Christ almighty, how could he have a hard-on in a place like this? Tana thought. This is not an erotic situation. Just as quickly, she thought, I shouldn't judge, it's not as if he could help it. And at the same time, she thought, he got that from looking at Estrela, not me. I wish my body had an effect like that.

And then: It must be difficult for him, I guess.

"Come on, Estrela," she said under her breath. "Warm up. Start to shiver. Come on, you idiot, you fool, you mad goose. Don't die on us. Come on!"

She was still muttering it when she fell asleep.

18

DEATH AT THE POLE

After a full day powered up, the habitat was slightly warmer, but their breath still was visible in the air. Tana had spent the entire day inside, tending to Estrela. Ryan had spent it melting ice away from the rocket. *Jesus do Sul* now protruded vertically upward through the center of a deep shaft through the ice.

"I checked the rocket the best I can," he said. "It's in pretty remarkable shape for something that's been sitting on the surface for so long. If there's something wrong with it, it's beyond my ability to diagnose."

"Don't tell me about the rocket," Estrela said. She had mostly recovered from her episode of hypothermia, but she still looked pale. Spent. "I don't care about the rocket. I want to know about João. What happened to João?"

Ryan shrugged. "Does it really matter?"

"It does matter!" she shouted. Her voice was hoarse, and it came out as a harsh whisper. "Tell me how João died!"

Ryan looked away. "They were poisoned."

"What?" Estrela whispered hoarsely. "Tell me."

Ryan sighed. "It was a simple mistake. Their fuel manufacturing plant made methane out of hydrogen, and it released carbon monoxide. No big deal; carbon monoxide is a natural component of the Martian atmosphere anyway. Do you remember that I had an episode of anoxia? The same thing happened to them. The sensors on their breathing electrolyzers were poisoned with sulfur contamination. But they were making fuel on the spot, so there was an excess of carbon monoxide. When their oxygen sensors failed, what got through was carbon monoxide. It poisoned them."

"How do you know this?" Tana asked.

"Whose fault was it?" Estrela asked.

Ryan shrugged. "Once I knew what to look for, it wasn't hard to see the evidence."

"But whose fault was it?" Estrela insisted.

Ryan shrugged. "Nobody's fault, really. It was an oversight."

"An accident? It was just an accident?" She sat down and looked away. "That's all?"

"It was an accident. The same thing almost happened to us." He looked up at her and saw that she was crying. "I'm sorry."

Tana patted her on the back and echoed what Ryan said. "I'm sorry."

19

"It's time," Ryan said. "We have to choose."

Everyone was silent.

Ryan held out his fist. The ends of three strips of paper protruded. "Pick a strip. One of the strips is shorter than the rest. The two long ones go home."

Estrela shook her head. "It doesn't matter," she said said. "I've made my decision already. It doesn't matter who draws which slip of paper. I'm staying."

"What?" Ryan and Tana said, at almost exactly the same time.

Estrela smiled, a wan smile. "I surprised you, didn't I?"

Ryan was gripped by a contradiction of emotions. His heart was telling him, let her stay here, let her stay, I'm going home. But his conscience told him that they couldn't let her kill herself, not after all this; they were in here together. He said cautiously, "It's a surprise, yes." Then added, "But it wouldn't be fair to have you make the sacrifice. We'll all take the same chance."

Estrela shook her head. "It doesn't matter whether you go back or not. I'm staying here."

"How would you survive?" Tana said.

Estrela tossed her hair, and for a moment a spark of her stubborn vitality showed through. "I can survive. I'll go back to the American base; plenty of food and water there, plenty of supplies for the expedition that did not stay. Even a greenhouse."

Ryan was startled. Yes, he thought, it might be possible. Maybe. "You can't count on a rescue," he said.

"In two more years they will send a ship," she said. "Or maybe four. They will send the fourth expedition, and it will rescue me."

She sounded so perfectly confident that for a moment Ryan believed it. Of course they would rescue her. Why had he ever thought they wouldn't? And then common sense took over. "You can't count on that," he repeated.

Estrela shrugged. "Or six years. Or, maybe I won't even wait for a ship. I'll live here."

"But, why?"

"I like it here," Estrela said. "I've decided to stay." She looked at them, looked at their surprised expressions, and laughed. "I know. You thought that I was a survivor, that I would do anything to get on the return trip. I thought that too. That's why I killed Trevor, to take his spot."

Tana looked up in surprise. "You—"

Estrela had a distant smile. She nodded. "Yes. That's right. I killed him."

Ah, Ryan thought. That should have been obvious. His death was too convenient. "Why?" he asked.

"Why do you think?" she snapped back. "Because only two of us could return. Because he was one more person who might make it back in what should have been my place. And because he was a liability to the expedition. That's why."

"What did you do?" Ryan asked.

Estrela looked him right in the eyes. "I stole the battery out of his emergency beacon," she said, "and then I made sure his gyro compass was miscalibrated. And a couple of other little things like that. I wanted to make sure that if he got lost, he would stay lost. He was always sloppy in checking his equipment; I figured it would only be a matter of time before he got lost."

"But why?" Tana said. "Are you sorry?"

"I told you. Somebody had to die. I decided it would be him."

"I thought it was an accident," Ryan said.

"Call it an accident, then," she said. She shrugged. "I didn't force him to wander around and get lost, I guess. You can call it an accident, if it makes you feel better."

"And Commander Radkowski, too," Ryan said, suddenly realizing. "You thought he wouldn't pick you. So you killed him. It wasn't Brandon at all; it was you!"

Estrela shook her head. "That was an accident. Sure, of course I wanted to kill Radkowski, didn't you? But I'm not stupid. I was frantic when he died; I didn't think we could make the pole without a leader."

"An accident," Ryan said slowly.

Estrela nodded. "He switched ropes at the last moment. He took the rope Trevor was supposed to use, and rappelled off the cliff before I could think of an excuse to stop him."

"Shit," Ryan said. "So what the hell are we supposed to do now?" He paused for a moment, and then asked, "and why are you telling us this? You were home free now. Why didn't you just kill one of us? We never would have known."

Estrela smiled. "I changed my mind."

20

THE LAST CHANCE

ana used the day to continue her inventory of the supplies left at the Brazilian base, and Ryan checked out the snow rovers left behind by the Brazilian expedition. Regardless of what had happened on the long road since they had left Felis Dorsa, or who would stay behind on Mars, Estrela's idea to return to the American base at *Agamemnon* was clearly a sound plan. And the one who stayed behind, whoever it would be, would need supplies and a working snow rover.

Since that night they had not talked about Estrela's confession. Ryan was working alone in the tiny hangar that held the snow rovers when Tana came to him. She stood there, silent, watching him work. At last she called his name, and he looked up.

"Do you believe her?" Tana said. "I need to know." She bit her lower lip. "Do you think she really did—?"

Ryan had the fuel cell of a snow rover taken apart. He was carefully checking the seals, making sure that the sulfur poisoning had not penetrated and embrittled the power system. It was his way of avoiding thinking about it. He put the fuel cell down and looked at Tana, thinking. "Yes," he said.

"But are you sure, really sure?" Tana asked, and when Ryan nodded, she said, "So what should we do?"

Ryan considered for a moment. "What do you suggest? The death penalty?"

"No, no," Tana said. "But we could—" she stopped. "I don't know."

"What more do you want from her? We can't take her home and put her on trial. And even if we could, we don't have any actual evidence of a crime, do we?"

"But, we have to tell *somebody*."

Ryan shook his head. "Who would we tell? What would we say?" He waved his hand to indicate the planet around them. "She says she's going to stay behind on Mars. Think of it this way. Mars is a prison more secure than Alcatraz could ever be, a prison with walls that cannot be climbed. Are you really worried that this isn't penance enough?"

"But what do we *do*!? How can we just leave her here?"

"Ah." Ryan sighed. Yes, that was it. Despite what Estrela had told them, leaving her behind still seemed a betrayal. After all the distance they had traveled together, how could they just leave her behind? But was there an alternative? "I don't know," he said. "I don't know."

He bent back to his inspection. After a while Tana was gone.

At last the night came, and the three of them ate in silence. After eating, they gathered in the pressurized module. The habitat was still cold, but not as cold as it had been. Ryan sat down and looked at Estrela with a long, steady gaze.

She looked back. "Well?" she said.

"No more holding back," Ryan said. "I need to know. Tell me, why do you want to stay behind?"

"Do you really care?" she said. "I'm telling you that you get to go home. Take it, it's your life, and I'm giving it to you free. Do you care why?"

"Ah, but I do care," Ryan said. "We have been together too long for me to just leave you behind without ever knowing why. It's too late for deception now. Tell me."

"I did tell you. I changed my mind."

Ryan shook his head. "That's not enough. You said that you killed two people to get back home . . . and now that you're here, you decided you don't want to go. I'm not going to judge you, but I need to understand. Why?"

Estrela leaned back and closed her eyes. "All my life," she said, "all my life I've been surrounded by people. In the city where I grew up. In the school. When they sent me north. Always, people all around me. Boys wanting to be with me to pull down my pants, reporters interviewing, even João, wanting to sit with me and drink coffee and talk, and talk.

"Even on Mars, we were never alone—here on Mars, we were more crowded than anywhere. Crowded in the habitats, crowded in the rovers. Always together. Even when I thought I was going off by myself, there were the voices in my earphones, telling me that I would never be alone.

"Did you know that this place terrified me at first? These huge, empty distances. But then, when we kept on walking, when the airplane crashed and you told us that we had to keep on walking, something changed. In that long walk, we were each of us alone, truly alone, and I found, yes, I can be alone. I can be just me. The snow doesn't care who I am. The rocks don't care who I am. The sky doesn't care who I am.

"I tell you this. Always, all my life, I have been pretending to be somebody I'm not. For so long that I don't think I even know who I really am.

"I'm done with that.

"I decided, I don't care if I go back. I don't need it. There's nothing for me back there. I changed my mind. I like it here.

"I want to be alone."

21

L E A V I N G   M A R S

The sun on the horizon was almost blue, surrounded by a luminous golden orb of light and a double halo. The day was still; the snow reflected only the pale yellow sky.

And then the snow began to glow.

The snow erupted, cascading outward in a tidal wave of sudden incandescence, raising a billowing cloud that was lit brilliant red by a light from inside. The glow, a flame almost too bright to look at, rose slowly and silently, shrouded in the roiling cloud.

Jesus do Sul broke out of the cloud, and the light of its exhaust, a second and brighter dawn, set the icescape aglow. Gathering speed, it headed skyward. It was almost out of sight when the booster stage fell away. The Earth-return stage, only a tiny pinprick of light, sped off, like a fallen star rising again to return to its home, into space.

Below, an insignificant figure sat on a small ridge of ice. She continued to stare into the sky for long after the tiny speck of light had vanished.

And then she turned back to return to the habitat. There was no use continuing to watch; it would be nine months before their journey would finish. There was a lot for her to do before then.

Estrela Carolina Conselheiro was, at last, home.